The Play Out of Context

This is a volume of essays which examines the relationship between the play and its historical and cultural contexts. Transferring plays from one period or one culture to another is so much more than translating the words from one language into another. The contributors vary their approaches to this problem from the theoretical to the practical, from the literary to the theatrical, with plays examined both historically and synchronically. The articles interact with each other, presenting a diversity of views of the central theme and establishing a dialogue between scholars of different cultures. With play texts quoted in English, the range of themes stretches from a Japanese interpretation of Chekhov to Shakespeare in Nazi Germany, and Racine borrowing from Sophocles.

Most of the essays are based on papers presented at the Jerusalem Theatre Conference in 1986. The book will be of interest to students and scholars of the theatre and of literature and literary theory as well as to theatregoers.

£30-00

The Play Out of Context

Transferring Plays from Culture to Culture

edited by
HANNA SCOLNICOV *and* PETER HOLLAND

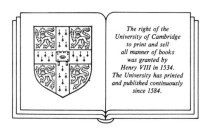

The right of the
University of Cambridge
to print and sell
all manner of books
was granted by
Henry VIII in 1534.
The University has printed
and published continuously
since 1584.

CAMBRIDGE UNIVERSITY PRESS

Cambridge

New York   New Rochelle   Melbourne   Sydney

Published by the Press Syndicate of the University of Cambridge
The Pitt Building, Trumpington Street, Cambridge CB2 1RP
32 East 57th Street, New York, NY 10022, USA
10 Stamford Road, Oakleigh, Melbourne 3166, Australia

First published 1989

Printed in Great Britain at the University Press, Cambridge

British Library cataloguing in publication data

The play out of context: transferring plays from culture
to culture.
1. Drama. Sociocultural aspects
I. Scolnicov, Hanna
II. Holland, Peter
306'.484

Library of Congress cataloguing in publication data

The play out of context: transferring plays from culture
to culture/edited by Hanna Scolnicov and Peter Holland.
    p.   cm.
"Most of the essays are based on papers presented at the
Jerusalem Theatre Conference in 1986" – P.
ISBN 0 521 34433 6
1. Drama – Translating – Congresses.
2. Stage adaptations – Congresses.
3. Theater and society – Congresses.
4. Intercultural communication – Congresses.
I. Scolnicov, Hanna.
II. Holland, Peter.
III. Jerusalem Theatre Conference (1986)
PN1621.P58 1989
418'.02 – dc19   86–23434

ISBN 0 521 34433 6

CE

CONTENTS

Contents

ILLUSTRATIONS

CONTRIBUTORS

Carol Bardenstein, *Dartmouth College, New Hampshire*
Erika Fischer-Lichte, *Literaturwissenschaft, Universität Bayreuth*
Dwora Gilula, *Departments of Classics and Theatre Studies, The Hebrew University of Jerusalem*
Albert-Reiner Glaap, *Anglistisches Institut, Universität Düsseldorf*
Vera Gottlieb, *Drama Department, Goldsmiths College, University of London*
Werner Habicht, *Institut für Englische Philologie, Universität Würzburg*
Peter Holland, *Trinity Hall, University of Cambridge*
Ruth von Ledebur, *Fachbereich 3: Sprach-und Literatur-Wissenschaften, Anglistik, University of Siegen*
Yehouda Moraly, *Department of Theatre Studies, The Hebrew University of Jerusalem*
Patrice Pavis, *Institut d'Etudes Théâtrales, Université Sorbonne Nouvelle*
James Redmond, *Department of Drama, Westfield College, University of London*
Eli Rozik, *Theatre Department, Tel-Aviv University*
Hanna Scolnicov, *Department of Theatre Studies, The Hebrew University of Jerusalem*
Gershon Shaked, *Department of Hebrew Literature, The Hebrew University of Jerusalem*
Shoshana Weitz, *Theatre Department, Tel-Aviv University*

Introduction

HANNA SCOLNICOV

Chekhov did not believe that non-Russian audiences could possibly understand the full meaning of the selling of the estate in *The Cherry Orchard*. So worried was he about his plays being misunderstood in foreign tongues, that he regretted not being able to prevent their translation and production abroad. Chekhov's repudiation of translation represents an extreme position: a total denial of the possibility of transferring a play from one culture to another.

This volume is a collection of essays which examine the relationship between the play and its historical and cultural contexts. The problem of the transference of plays from culture to culture is seen not just as a question of translating the text, but of conveying its meaning and adapting it to its new cultural environment so as to create new meanings. The approaches presented by the different contributors vary from the theoretical to the practical, from the literary to the theatrical. Plays and productions are examined both historically and synchronically. The papers tackle the same problems from different national and theoretical perspectives.

The articles interact with each other, presenting a diversity of views of the central theme, and establishing a dialogue between scholars of different cultures. One discussion surveys the general problem, tracing its complexities. Another provides a theoretical scaffolding, an abstract, *a priori* structure into which yet another builds his pragmatics. Other papers analyse particular issues as instances of the theoretical and methodological questions involved.

The various articles show how critical the question of cultural difference is to the theatre, but also point to the theatre itself as a unique machinery for overcoming these differences and reaching out towards other cultures, other peoples and even other people. With the exception of some contemporary and local stagings, each production can be seen as a dialogue between the non-shared values, emotions, conceptions and beliefs of two, or more, cultures.

The volume opens with an essay by Gershon Shaked, which maps the ground, indicating the many cultural and linguistic gaps that must be crossed or translated if an audience is to be able to comprehend an essentially alien performance. His central example is that of the gap between Christian and Jewish perceptions and feelings, and the difficulty of overcoming them in the theatre. He speaks of cultural worlds that are 'light-years away' from each other. Shaked sees the theatre as a means of translating, of changing an alien, incomprehensible, and therefore frightening experience into an understandable one.

Patrice Pavis redefines the theme as translation in the widest possible sense: not just the finding of linguistic equivalence, but also of appropriate cultural and gestural parallels. Every translation is an appropriation of one text by another, by way of the concrete reception of a particular audience. Instead of speaking about the translation of a 'dramatic text', Pavis chooses to discuss 'translation for the stage'. He tries to formulate new standards for translation based on the present day perception of the indissolubility of theatrical word and gesture. The task of the translator concerned with performance is to preserve and transfer the 'language body' of one language to another. Pavis concedes that in the case of classical texts such a technique often involves a simplification and modernization which 'may shock philologists', but it alone can recover the 'language body' of the original and restore to the text its lost playability and vitality.

Peter Holland focuses on the transformations of the theatrical space by different playwrights. He sees stage-space and movement as constituting their own system of theatre language. Three representative plays, *Oedipus Rex*, *Bérénice* and *Waiting for Godot*, are analysed as culturally determined transpositions of the same basic perception of movement in the given space of the theatre. The fluidity and flexibility of the English Renaissance stage is contrasted with the intensity of meaning generated by the constricted and unified space defined by the Greek, French neo-classic, and Beckettian theatres. This analysis offers a novel way of approaching the multiplicity of adaptations and variations of classical plays, through their articulation of space rather than their handling of language or theme.

The eclecticism of today's stage repertoire points to the theatre having become, among other things, a museum of plays. Revivals necessarily mean that plays are staged out of their original contexts. James Redmond shows how, paradoxically, it is the irrelevant plays that do not lose their savour with the years. Plays which are immediately relevant are, using Shaw's terminology, 'useful plays' and therefore date quickly when the social and cultural environment changes, but they may become relevant once again through adaptation. Among other examples, Redmond follows the fortunes of Dumas's *La Dame aux camélias*. Its theme of illicit love threatening bourgeois morality is completely dependent on the nineteenth-century social context. Modern productions have either sentimentalized the love story or emphasized purely aesthetic qualities. But the play has been made 'useful' again in a recent feminist adaptation. The relevancy issue has been superseded only in Verdi's *La Traviata*, a work 'not of an age but for all time'.

Periodical reinterpretations of the classics have always inspired new artistic movements. Having shown how *mimesis* came to mean the imitation of a classic, Hanna Scolnicov goes on to discuss Shakespeare's formulation of the Renaissance concept of art as a mirror of life. This is a three-way mirror reflecting its source, Elizabethan society and the actual audience. Shakespeare is seen to have almost anticipated being performed 'out of context' and to have accommodated for it through his complex mirror image. The primacy of reality over its stage image was challenged by Antonin Artaud who saw reality as the theatre's double. But the very persistence of avant-garde theatre is a living proof that it in no way comes close to replacing the classical tradition.

Dwora Gilula addresses herself to what is commonly accepted as the first historical instance of transferring plays from culture to culture: the Roman adaptations of Greek drama. All the extant Roman comedies are of Greek origin, with Greek settings, names, clothing, currency, etc. The playwrights adhered to the Greek milieu self-consciously, as witnessed by Plautus's words: 'Now writers of comedy have this habit: they always allege that the scene of action is Athens, their object being to give the play a more Grecian air.' The paper comments on the difference in the cultural and social contexts of the theatre in Greece and in Rome, and on the impact of the performances on the respective audiences.

The political implications of cultural transference are investigated by Werner Habicht, who writes on Shakespearean productions and scholarship under the Nazi regime. Surprisingly, these activities continued during the Third Reich despite the ideological requirements imposed on the theatre. Ideologically acceptable principles of interpretation had to be devised. Shakespeare's plays were seen as political drama in which private values and experiences are subordinated to public ones – to the State in the histories and tragedies, and to social structures in the comedies. These public values were then identified with the Nazi concept of the *Volk*. Shakespeare was appropriated as a 'Germanic' writer, but also purged of those elements which were ideologically unacceptable. The production of Shakespeare's plays was encouraged by Goebbels because they were seen as embodying Germanic ideas of leadership and allegiance. Habicht provides wide-ranging examples that show how plays were manipulated and distorted to suit the perverse political propaganda.

Eli Rozik approaches the question of transferring plays from culture to culture from quite a different angle, assuming an a-historical, structuralist point of view. He is interested not in a proven instance of adaptation, but in the transformational rules of adaptation. Rozik compares Calderón's *Life Is a Dream* with Sophocles' *Oedipus the King*, showing how the different poetic conventions, religious beliefs and moral sensitivities generate the different articulations of the same basic myth.

The question of how to produce a classic is tackled by Yehouda Moraly in his comparison of two modern approaches to the production of Molière. Both Claudel and Vitez wished to free Molière's texts from the stultifying influence of their traditional interpretations and productions. One way of doing this is by dissociating the theatrical sign from what it signifies. Thus Moraly shows how both Claudel and Vitez employed the same stratagem of mismatching roles and actors in order to estrange the text and liberate it from its conventional staging.

A wider gulf has to be breached when translating Molière into a totally alien target-system. Carol Bardenstein discusses the Egyptian poet Jalāl's adaptation of *Tartuffe* into colloquial Arabic. Her investigation focuses on the new version, *al-Shaykh Matlūf*, and its relation to nineteenth-century Egyptian culture and literary norms. Jalāl's work is analysed in the context of the growing interest in Western culture and the wish to appropriate sections of it and 'Egyptianize' them.

Vera Gottlieb analyses the British productions of Chekhov's plays. These seem to suffer more than most when transplanted from one culture to another. Although performed as period pieces, British productions have tended to ignore the social and historical context of the works, assuming an 'apolitical' stance. The plays were seen as mournful evocations of a valuable life gone for ever, and it is only in the last few years that Chekhov's ideas and his use of irony have been explored in productions.

An instance of even greater cultural incompatibility is presented by Erika Fischer-Lichte. She considers a contemporary Japanese production of Chekhov which self-consciously manipulates the discrepancy between the theatrical traditions of East and West. Fischer-Lichte describes how, after an initial rejection of traditional Japanese theatre in favour of Westernized theatre, a new theatrical movement arose, which searched for some kind of synthesis between the traditional and the Western. Suzuki's production of *Three Sisters* is seen as an example of such a synthesis.

Shoshana Weitz deals with the pragmatics of performances. Assuming a statistical approach to spectator response, she analyses the different responses among Hebrew speaking and Arab speaking audiences in Israel to a bilingual production of *Waiting for Godot*. The different responses clearly show the extent of the influence of political and ideological positions on the spectators' perceptions of a given production.

Edward Bond's *Saved* would seem to be a play too dependent on local milieu and language to be translated into another language and another culture. Ruth von Ledebur discusses the different productions of *Gerettet* in Germany and shows that despite the formidable obstacles confronting both translator and director, the play proved to be a great success in Germany, arousing reactions not very different from those in England. This is attributed to the regular cultural interchange between the two countries, particularly to the Brechtian influence evident in Bond's work, facilitating his acceptance in Germany.

Albert-Reiner Glaap presents an interesting test case: a play rewritten by its English author for the American production. Here the cultural transfer is effected by the playwright himself, and within the space of a few years. This is almost a laboratory case, which is analysed meticulously to show which of the changes introduced is 'merely' linguistic (underlining the difference between American and English), and which is a question of the different cultural context. What complicates the issue is the change in the sex of the main role undergone in this transference.

Most of the essays are based on papers presented at the Jerusalem Theatre Conference 1986, which was devoted to the same topic as the present volume, 'The play out of context: transferring plays from culture to culture'. The Conference was organized by the Department of Theatre Studies in the Hebrew University of Jerusalem in association with the Israel Festival. I am indebted to the many friends and colleagues, both in Israel and abroad, who have helped in various ways to bring about this book, and to Sarah Stanton of Cambridge University Press for her

Hanna Scolnicov

unfailing good judgement and advice. Special thanks are due to Peter Holland, with whom it has been a pleasure to work on this volume, and to James Redmond, without whose encouragement and support there would have been no book.

The play: gateway to cultural dialogue

GERSHON SHAKED

Translated by Jeffrey Green

I

A far-reaching assumption could be made, that we are generally unable to understand plays foreign to our own culture. One might go even further and posit that the understanding of any play or other literary work is necessarily limited. That is because reading or viewing is the constant process of translating an alien experience, with its own memories and associations, to our own realm of experience, with its memories and associations. That process of translation leaves gaps and interstices between our own world and the image of the world created within us by what is read or viewed.

We have already learned from Ingarden and others that authors attempt to restrict our possibilities for understanding by building various limitations into the text, but we break through them, translating unfamiliar relations to ones familiar to us. When we attempt to fill the gaps deriving from our misunderstanding of a text or spectacle, we try to translate an alien subjective experience (which, on the theatrical level, takes on a quasi-objective dimension, appearing as reality in its own right) to a close subjective experience. That process creates a gap between the original and the translation, and moreover, within the process of translation, various intermediaries stand between us and absolute misunderstanding or partial understanding, seeking to bring the distant closer and put the near at a distance.

The more our reading or viewing is public, the more it is imposed upon us. When seeing a play, an entire group is programmed in advance to respond to a phenomenon according to collective, extra-theatrical experiences which it brings to the ceremonial setting known as the theatre. There it must react to a new and unknown world in accordance with laws legislated from the stage.

The theatrical effects used by the director, from the sets and costumes, through the music and the lighting, to the establishment of a semiotics and stage behaviour for the actors, are all intermediaries between the different worlds which meet during the play. The director seeks to formulate that dialogue between reception and translation which takes place between the stage and the audience, so as to convey the message adequately.

Paradoxically, we are arguing that the process of reading a text or viewing a play is, to some degree, one of misunderstanding, *misunderstanding which is the only way one can understand*, because it implies transmission from someone else's realm of experience to our own. In any attempt at reconstruction, the reconstructor is always present, and he cannot, at least emotionally, reconstruct except within the realm of his own understanding.

When staging a classical play, the director stands as an intermediary between the spectator and the play, as a kind of translator, trying to bring an experience from the tradition closer to that of the audience, even though that tradition might be extinct. The Rabbis did something quite similar in the Midrash: they interpreted the Biblical text to give it universal appeal in the generation of their readers, who were unable to fathom the inner life of the original writers. After the Temple was destroyed, the Jews no longer witnessed daily sacrifices, and therefore the Rabbis substituted prayer for sacrifice: rather than atone for sinful speech by sacrificing bullocks, speech took the place of the bullocks. That is what is done by most directors who try to bring traditional texts back to life. They attempt to translate the tradition and the language of the past into the language of culture close to that of the audience attending a play here and now.

II

As we distance ourselves further in time and mentality, the process of translation becomes more complex. Take, for example, two common words in Hebrew: *yeshiva* and *heder*. They have entirely different meanings in different contexts. A *yeshiva* can be either a meeting or an institution of higher Jewish religious learning, and a *heder* can be simply a room, or a Jewish religious primary school. For an addressee unfamiliar with traditional eastern European Jewish education, no brief explanation can convey the world of experience embodied by those words, and if that is true of Jews from various Jewish cultures, it is doubly true of non-Jews. Or, to take another example, how is one to translate traditional Jewish dress such as the caftan, the fur hat (*shtraimel*), and the rest, to people in the hot Middle East unfamiliar with such garb or to Europeans dressed in jeans or black tie?

Obviously we refer to the difficulty of presenting a work such as *The Dybbuk*, with the semiotics of the *shtetl* and the norms and values of Hassidic society, ruled over by a strange charismatic leadership in the persons of the *tsaddik* and his secular assistants, the wardens. In that world marvellous events take place, possession by a spirit and its exorcism. How do we transfer it to the secular, modern Jewish world? Or, further, how can the strange semiotics of that play be grasped, depending, as it does, upon folkloric elements expressed in costume, symbols, customs, and a complex structure of cultural signs, in a non-Jewish world which does not even have symbolic memories of that sort.

Productions of *The Dybbuk*, particularly the classic production by Vakhtangov, are probably among the most successful examples of trans-cultural transmission, and we shall discuss them below at greater length. Similar problems are posed in translating the ceremony of the Mass into Hebrew for an audience unfamiliar with it, one for whom the notion that bread and wine are transubstantiated into the flesh and blood of the Son of God is rather strange. How can they understand who priests and nuns are? Permit me to cite a personal example. When my daughter was seven, we took her to the Vatican museum in Rome. As we passed from painting to painting, she kept asking, 'Why did they draw so many pictures of that poor man nailed to two pieces of wood?'

An adult might perhaps be able to understand such things intellectually, but does such understanding penetrate to the place which literature and plays wish to reach, the audience's feelings? I have in mind a long series of Christian plays, from the medieval morality and mystery plays through those of Lope da Vega to T. S. Eliot's *Murder in the Cathedral* (1935), and even some of Beckett's recent plays, which the reader unfamiliar with the symbolic world and customs of Christianity must translate from one cultural system to another one, closer and more understandable to him. What significance can one find in the experiences latent in Christian morality plays or, for that matter, in Japanese No theatre? How can that significance be conveyed to an audience whose universe of discourse is light-years away from those cultural worlds?

The task of the theatre can be illustrated by contrast to raw, documentary spectacle. What, for example, does it mean to non-Moslems when they see a man remove his shoes and turn to face Mecca when he prays, or how can we interpret self-flagellation, which seems sadomasochistic to us, meant to imitate the tortures inflicted upon Ali, the central figure in Shiite Islam? We view these ceremonies on television as a sort of documentary theatre before they are made into artistic theatre or cinema. We are all exposed to the ceremonies of foreign cultures and societies, although those

9

ceremonies have little meaning for us. They merely arouse the fear and dread one feels before what is strange and alien. That televised world remains foreign and threatening because the viewers are unable to translate it into their own concepts, terms, and symbols. Art takes over where documentary can no longer assist us, for only the art of the theatre, through its experience in translation on the stage, can bring the distant near and reduce the dread.

The foregoing remarks do not apply only to purely religious or social problems, but also have a deep effect on what might seem to be private matters: how does a matriarchal society relate to the father? How can people unfamiliar with the concept of human sacrifice understand the full depth of meaning of Euripides' *Iphigenia in Aulis* (407 BC)? We have many theatrical versions of that myth: Racine's French play of 1674 and Gerhard Hauptmann's German version of 1943. There is also *Iphigenia in Delphi* (Goethe wrote an outline for such a play, and Hauptmann wrote one as part of his trilogy about the House of Atreus in 1940–3, a tragic, sombre interpretation of the Nazi period in Germany) and Goethe's version of Euripides' *Iphigenia in Tauris* (1786). Each one brings out another aspect of that dreadful structure of relations in which a father sacrifices his daughter, a son and daughter murder their mother and her lover, and a brother and sister meet again after many years in order to renew the dynasty, which, as it were, had been doomed to extinction. Each play attempts in its own way to convey the theme to the psychologies and mentalities of different cultures in different ages. They are all apparently close to the subject of Jephthah's daughter and the Binding of Isaac, but also distant from it. They are not easily grasped and must be reinterpreted to bring them closer to their audience.

From these efforts and from various productions of these plays we see the path to be taken by a playwright who wishes to establish a bond with a motif tradition containing, according to his understanding, eternal truth, but which must be explained and interpreted in different ways on different stages. A fresh confrontation with a subject may take various forms. At times it can be quite primitive, as with an attempt to adapt and remodel a subject to make it fit new artistic and social norms in a new context. For example, the Yiddish playwright, Yakov Gordin, wrote *Mirele Ephros* (1898) as a kind of adaptation of *King Lear*, placing it in the context of the Jewish bourgeoisie of the late nineteenth century. The royal father's place was taken by the Yiddishe *mamme*, Mirele Ephros and, instead of Lear's three daughters she has, of course, three sons. As in Shakespeare's play, two of them wish to usurp their mother's fortune while she is still living, and the third is loyal and decent. Of course, that modification of the basic elements created a new play, which, though similar to Shakespeare's in its basic structure and main theme, conveys an entirely different message because of its new raiment, the Jewish cultural and social context, and the semiotics, which were changed from top to bottom.

A more sophisticated alternative available to the director is to present a traditional play in modern dress without changing the text itself, transposing the materials without changing their basic norms. The director thus takes the play as a given, but attempts to shed new light upon it.

A more extreme solution would be to write a new play based on an ancient myth. It goes without saying that in that case the playwright intentionally modifies and adapts the materials to fit the needs of his own time, accounting for the theme in a new way and giving it a new form, to bring it home to an audience whose world of experience is unable to accept the causality of the classical theatre. Moreover, when modern playwrights rewrite a traditional play, they frequently produce a parody of the original work, creating new interactions among the ideas and symbols remembered by readers and viewers familiar with the tradition. The playwrights create an anti-message, conveying to the audience their opposition to the tradition, demanding resistance to values which have lost their vitality. An excellent example of that approach, related to plays I have already mentioned, is Sartre's *Les Mouches* (1943), a parody of the House of Atreus, the central character of which is Oreste, who has murdered his mother and her lover, Egiste. Even in the latter version, the play remains open to reinterpretations by directors who serve as intermediaries and transmit it from generation to generation, from city to city, and from society to society.

Another issue raised by the theatre is the conflict between romantic love and arranged marriages. In *Romeo and Juliet* the couple wish to marry against their families' wishes, and the same happens even in modern adaptations of that play such as *West Side Story*; but in modern Western society marriages are not normally arranged by the couples' parents. What then can be the meaning of a play like *The Dybbuk*, where a troth plighted by the parents is broken, against the wishes of the young couple, who were mystically bound to each other?

That play is based on the bizarre poetical hypothesis that the troth plighted between the parents is what joined the souls of the young couple miraculously united by it. A modern audience cannot accept those hypotheses literally and so must translate them into terms such as fate, necessity, and love at first sight, rather than the irrational, magical bond upon which the play is based. The play claims that a betrothal arranged before birth is more powerful than a marriage arranged between two grown people, asserting the priority of the original bond: every lawful, human effort to circumvent that irrational connection fails. The assumption is that the world of oaths and dreams is far more powerful than the waking world of bourgeois life. Here the director must translate a belief into spectacle and overcome the audience's basic scepticism by dramatic means, both linguistic and non-linguistic. That world of primordial bonds, of connections made by magic rather than through the development of actual relations, is foreign to the audience. The director must struggle with a justified and rational prejudice and convince the audience that the irrational is more logical than the rational. The dance of the beggars, for example, is one of the ways of actualizing that powerful force, which is beyond rational logic.

The problem is not merely to translate various elements of a semiotic system (a positive view of marriages decreed in advance, the woman in a society with many women, etc.). The problem is to translate the place of each element in the entire structure. The woman has a different meaning in traditional Jewish society from American society, beyond the specific norms of social and sexual behaviour applying in the two societies. The man too has a different meaning, the extended family has a different function, and, above all, the economic and social structure of the society affects every component of the structure. Every element has a different function and meaning in the two systems. How then can we translate the relations between the ensemble and the various details? How can one translate the place of the *tsaddik*? Someone who took him merely as a rabbi, or as a parallel to a rabbi in Western religious institutions, a minister, priest, or preacher, could not understand the play. The effort to view him as a sorcerer, saint, or the like must be given a highly convincing theatrical translation so that the audience unfamiliar with that figure and his place in the society will understand the character's function.

III

The differences in semiotic systems exist in life before they reach the theatre, and those who encounter them often stand helpless and uncomprehending in the face of a sealed, impenetrable world. In life, however, one might be able to ask questions to help create a full or partial model of the alien reality. With a play one has only the text or the performance. Through them one must decipher an alien world which one is sometimes encountering for the first time. In some sense it is easier in the theatre: the distant and closed world has been placed in a framework which can be viewed as a closed paradigm, the principles of which may be deduced; one understands the opposing forces through their dramatic clashes; one learns at least what transpires without reference to the outer world. Nevertheless, the audience is not prepared to view the play as a closed paradigm to be understood by its inner structural relations. The audience wants to know what the play refers to, what is the extra-theatrical world which the stage, as world, symbolizes in the world which is a stage?

I can picture to myself a Chinese audience at a performance of *Fiddler on the Roof* – and I have heard that for some reason Sholem Aleichem is rather popular among intellectuals in China, and his books are widely circulated; or I can imagine an audience of Japanese seeing Hochhuth's *Der Stellvertreter*, which is far removed from their own religious and other problems. Similarly, Israeli audiences at performances of Osborne's *Look Back in Anger* (1956) or Lorca's *La Casa de Bernarda Alba* (1936), are seeing plays quite distant from them culturally, plays with deep roots in the semiotics, folklore, and culture which produced them. A theatrical translation of those works cannot be merely a literal translation, but must find an appropriate objective correlative in cultural complexes which cannot be transferred as written from one vessel to another if one does not wish to bring about total misunderstanding of the original culture by the target culture.

The foregoing remarks about cultural distance apply also to works separated from the audience by time. The distance is not merely linguistic, but it involves a structure of referents whose signs are no longer decipherable by present day audiences.

The past is a closed world unless we translate it into the present. The political regimes, ways of behaviour, transportation, communication, and architecture of the past are all insufficiently understood in the present. Therefore they are reinterpreted: candles become electric lights, swords and bows become rifles and mortars, human labour becomes machines, slave society becomes capitalism.

Understanding of the past, as of another culture, is a constant process of translation permitting communication, on the one hand, but also creating an area of misunderstanding, on the other. That misunderstanding is productive, in that it underscores the fact that one's fellow man and the past are different, giving one the good feeling of being different.

Understanding another culture means constantly grasping the differentness of one's fellow man, and it is bound up in a constant effort to translate differences to our own world of experience, to bring the distant near, make the past present, and the incomprehensible understood. Yet we realize that, although we can approach the other, some distance must remain, and just as the different is strange to us, we too are strange to what is different. Cultural awareness therefore implies a dialogue in which one acknowledges what is different and struggles over what is similar. This is the principal process of grappling with any strange text, and in this lies the enormous power of the theatre, which possesses extra-textual resources permitting it to emphasize the similarity of what is different without forgoing the differentness.

Anyone pretending to have completely deciphered the alien simply does not acknowledge its strangeness and differentness. On the other hand, anyone closing himself off from the possibility of approaching what is alien remains shut up within his own four walls. He is unable to compare his world with others, enriching it by a constant process of analogy and metaphorization between himself and his fellow man outside himself. The function of every theatre, and of the director as an intermediary, is to preserve that balance between bringing foreign cultures closer and preserving their identity.

IV

Our approach to foreign culture is generally accompanied by prejudices deriving from a limited knowledge of the facts and a hidden expectation that the foreign culture will be like ours. We tend to be suspicious of foreigners, and we are not open to accepting their differentness. Our propensity for translating alien worlds and cultures into the language of our own world derives from our fear of what is impenetrable and strange. We do not understand things as they are, but either distort them for our own purposes or reject them entirely as incomprehensible or unacceptable.

Prejudice, therefore, further limits knowledge because it precedes close familiarity. We first try to fill in the gaps and read the foreign culture in accordance with our prejudices: a Jew who appears on stage in Shakespeare's world is ridiculous, cruel, and avaricious even before he opens his mouth. When the code-word 'Jew' appears in an English, American, or German play, it conjures up the image of a person endowed with certain traits even before the character appears. Sometimes the character is portrayed in contrast to that image, and then a kind of de-automatization of the stereotype takes place, an innovation permitting us to see it with new eyes. That, for example, is what Lessing did with *Nathan der Weise* (1799), which frustrated the expectations of the presumably anti-Semitic German audience, in contrast to the Jew in Fassbinder's *Garbage, The City, and Death* (1985), which tries to smash the philo-Semitism of modern Germany and restore the faded glory of the old stereotype.

Similarly, a Cossack in a Jewish play arouses atavistic fears before he actually does anything (take, for example, Y. D. Berkowitz's play, *He and His Son*). A German appearing in a Hebrew or Yiddish work, or even a French one, evokes a certain image based on a model to which the audience is accustomed. Any opinion one brings to a performance or reading is a prejudice created by previous readings or by pre-existing knowledge of various sorts. Further, even more limited character traits associated with some nation or ethnic group can conjure up prejudices in us, e.g. a girl with black hair in an English play or novel in contrast to a redhead in a Hebrew play or novel. For reasons related to climate and culture, the colour of characters' hair indicates their strangeness, arousing fears and presumptions regarding their characters which can be either confirmed or refuted.

We are equipped with prejudices regarding every landscape, figure, and human behaviour. In certain cultures, for example, there are prejudices regarding men with moustaches or beards. Or, it is clear to everyone, as it were, what it means when a woman wears a low cut dress or what lies beneath the outward appearance of an orthodox Jewish woman who covers her hair with a scarf.

The need to translate derives primarily from the contradictions between prejudices belonging to the semiotic system of the audience and the customs and patterns of behaviour implied by the text which do not fit that system. One could view the process of putting on a play as an attempt by the director to force the members of the audience, with the prejudices they bring to the theatre, to revise their opinions in response to the surprises offered by the play. The director translates the play from a language which the viewers do not understand, one which alarms them because it is different from their expectations, to a language they do understand, one which permits them to see that the different is different but not in an essential way; or, if it is essentially different, that the peculiarity of the alien is justified in the overall context, where principles of behaviour apply which differ from those they are used to.

On the one hand, the audience will find that a small change in the cultural context is likely to cause the stereotypes which are always with us to make way for a structure in which those stereotypes no longer work, because the new structure is informed by other stereotypes. In a culture different from our own, redheads might be considered quiet and obedient, and brunettes stormy and demonic. In some places, moustachioed gents do not indicate the degree of their masculinity by the bushiness of their moustache. In other cultures, a moustache could be an obligatory and therefore insignificant facial ornament. Israelis could learn from Arab

Gershon Shaked

plays that Arabs are not like some of us imagine *all* Arabs to be, just as the Hebrew theatre could teach them that we are not the way they picture *all* Jews. When a director depicts each nation and ethnic group in its own setting and time and with its own code of behaviour, indeed different from those of the audience in the 'opposing' nation, both parties realize that they are different from each other, but that the difference is far from their prior opinions, which were based on stereotypes of one sort or another.

Anti-humanistic plays are those which reinforce the stereotypes we bring to the theatre. Incitement is the reinforcement of a stereotype, to the joy of those who are filled with hatred. Humanistic, artistic education entails the breaking down of stereotypes, to the dissatisfaction of the prejudiced, but to the joy of those who seek to break out of vicious circles in which pseudo-art and life create stereotypes and the audience expects them in order to reapply them in life and reinforce their warped values.

V

Moreover, every great playwright is capable of violating the stereotypical expectations common in his society. He can understand the differentness of his own culture from the point of view of greater proximity. He does not depict his characters according to the pre-existing expectations of his audience, but in line with human similarities that transcend differences. Shakespeare did not grasp his Shylock only as a ridiculous, miserly Jew in accordance with the stereotype of his age, but as a person with his own pride, who has something to say for himself and about the relations between himself and his environment. A great creator interprets the differences within his society in a new and unexpected way in his works, forcing his audience to change their attitude towards their stereotypes. That is not to say, of course, that the audience will immediately abandon their prejudices because of a given literary work, but it does mean that when a work confronts prejudices, there is some hope that the new outlook might bring about a change in social values.

Even when a playwright or filmmaker does not attempt to present a cultural encounter in his work, but rather tries to understand a given culture in its own right, he causes a certain modification in prejudices. Stereotypes derive from distance and ignorance, and a unique character originates in knowledge which produces a modification of the stereotype existing in the viewer's world. Moreover, a different understanding of the stereotype, revealing that it is not peculiar to the culture of any one nation, but rather susceptible to translation from culture to culture, removes its sting.

One should perhaps emphasize that the less a work is stereotypical and the more it presents figures with independent status and detailed characterization, the more it is the task of the intermediary (the director or critic) to prevent extra-theatrical prejudices from usurping the theatrical interpretation. That is to say, he must prevent the spectator from seeing his own prejudices instead of the play. He must see to it that the non-fictional world brought with him by the spectator does not frustrate the playwright's efforts to struggle against the audience's prejudices and modify them. The director and his staff, the set designer, the composer, etc., here act as interpreters who seek to bring out all the subtleties of the text, for by means of the subtleties and their appropriate translation into theatrical terms, the spectator learns that the world of the text is different from that of his expectations, and that the latter must be modified.

The play forces the spectator to look at its referents in a new fashion. For example, the Swiss audience of Max Frisch's *Andorra* had a favourable opinion of themselves as citizens of a neutral country, who do not submit to pressure and are not easily swayed by prejudice. While they did have certain prejudices about Jews, they believed they would not act on them if driven into a situation permitting or forcing them to do so.

Frisch destroyed the worldview of his intended Swiss audience. He showed that it could happen there too, and now, proving they were chock-full of prejudices. Even while standing trial for their opinions, he argues, they are not prepared to admit they are motivated by them. The only thing they are prepared to admit is that they erred in identifying the object of their prejudices.

This play is directly tied to a certain time and place, and it aroused much opposition there. In other contexts (the United States, for example), directors were unsuccessful in presenting the functions and meanings of the prejudice implied by this play (though prejudices in the United States are commonly directed both against other objects and the same ones, no less than elsewhere).

Some attention should be given here to a form of thought very characteristic of the audience of works in which a cultural confrontation is presented. Part of A. B. Yehoshua's novel, *The Lover*, was adapted for the theatre in a play called *Naim* (which is the name of the young Arab protagonist). That play was quite successful in Israel. It is centred upon a cultural and social confrontation between Jews and Arabs, through which Yehoshua sought to create an anti-stereotype in contrast to the common stereotypes about Arabs. Prejudiced people would be likely to be astonished by the relations between Jews and Arabs as presented by both the play and the original book. Before seeing the play, most Israeli Jews would be rather unlikely to approve of a love affair between a young Arab and a Jewish girl. The play shows persuasively that such a love affair is possible, almost necessary, in that the figure of Naim is so attractive that it breaks down possible stereotypes, including that of the Arab as a threatening and negative erotic figure. Since then, many similar attempts have been made in the theatre and cinema, some of them so simplistic and run-of-the-mill that they themselves have become stereotypes.

Most audiences therefore bring prejudices with them which are derived from pre-artistic sources. The play shows how things which, according to the audience's prejudice should be impossible, actually are possible, giving human justification to what might have seemed unacceptable because of the basic prejudiced assumptions.

It is *The Lover*'s function to change the prejudices of the average Israeli and open him to the possibilities of another existence which does not appear to exist in actual life, so long as it is not undergone at least in the imaginary realm.

VI

We become familiar with foreign cultures through plays because in the process of viewing or reading them, we must interpret and translate materials, patterns of behaviour, and images of the world which are alien and incomprehensible in order to expand our world and familiarize ourselves with the unknown.

I shall now consider several examples of struggles with foreign theatre in order to define a possible extra-literary world through them. First I wish to return to the classic Jewish play mentioned previously, *The Dybbuk*, widely acknowledged to be a classic of the early twentieth century. Major text-books of the modern theatre refer to the play in Vakhtangov's production at the Moscow Art Theatre in the USSR. Thus, for example, John Gassner says: 'Vakhtangov took charge of the training of the company's actors and staged *The Dybbuk* in Hebrew with memorable stylization.'[1] Similarly, Sheldon Cheney writes 'The Habima Jewish Theatre which had been encouraged under the more liberal cultural policies of Lenin's time, and which gained international fame with its rich production of *The Dybbuk* under Vakhtangoff's direction, settled eventually in Israel.'[2]

The Dybbuk had a cultural influence far beyond the borders of the Jewish or Israeli cultural sphere. Moreover, because the play was on the road in Europe, where few of the Jews or non-Jews in the audience knew Hebrew, it demanded many non-linguistic forms of communication (dance, music, movement). The dress of the characters was also different from that of the audience. The people who actually wore *shtraimels*, caftans, and ritual fringes did not attend the play.

Anyone attending the play left the theatre having been exposed to an extremely religious Hassidic milieu, which the play presented as background. Yet the ceremony of the theatre and the religious ceremonies presented in this play cannot dwell beneath the same roof, for anyone who believes in the ceremonies presented on the stage does not believe in the theatre, and a believer in the theatre must be convinced by it of the power of faith in which he (as opposed to the true believer) does not at first believe. That which seems natural and self-explanatory for a believer, arousing no argument or doubt, is something of which the theatrical sceptic must be convinced by his own powers of self-persuasion and those which he has absorbed from the depicted world. The play is an effort to revive the religious force of a structure of customs and beliefs for an audience of non-believers, to present it so that the incredible becomes consistent with the rational values of the audience and earns their belief.

Paradoxically, we expect that the religious structure, which has become an empty symbolic structure in the theatre, will be filled anew with the audience's power of faith and will be accepted by them in its transformed guise. Vakhtangov, therefore, had to translate faith for the unbelievers. The story of two young people who were not sworn to each other except by the obligations assumed by their parents, which magically obligate them as well, is not exactly suited to Western logic. Here we find no romantic rebellion against a bourgeois marriage agreement, but rather a bourgeois arrangement standing in opposition to a romantic marriage agreement, which creates a bizarre identification between bride and groom. The groom cannot live without the bride, nor can she live without him. He breaks metaphysical boundaries. The director must show that the romantic marriage agreement is the true one. It determines the identity of the two participants and its violation means the loss of identity, and no tribunal, either heavenly or earthly, may deprive a person of his identity. The violation of the agreement is a misdeed expressed in the dance of the beggars and the grotesqueness of the bourgeois marriage, which is a violation of the marriage from on high. Vakhtangov made a folktale, in which both sides believe in the power of a handshake, into a play showing the infinite opposition between fidelity to identity and bonds which are significant beyond life and death, and a falsified, man-made identity which does not derive from the depths of the cosmic soul or personality. The Jewish audience felt a new kind of religious truth. For them, the play was strangely bound up in the national revival movement and the movement for a national theatre. It became a ritual and a ceremony in its own right. The meaning of that ritual was that neither society nor even religion could sever a person from his soul or detach him from his longings, and that if anyone tried to deprive a person of those attachments, he would be possessed by a dybbuk until condemned to death.

Vakhtangov succeeded in giving the play an allegorical message similar to the allegorical interpretation given by the Rabbis to the Song of Songs. He linked the existential significance of the fateful erotic bond to a more general form of significance, hinting at the connection between a person and his yearnings. The audience's ability to relate to that bond also as a romantic–national link remained an open possibility. It was a many-levelled experience which emphasized that interhuman relations on all levels have irrational depths which are more profound than the command-ments of religion and beyond the power of the *tsaddik* who represents them, and certainly deeper than the possibilities offered by bourgeois life.

The religious materials received an almost anti-religious significance (if one takes religion as religious law). Vakhtangov might not have understood the meanings of the religious experiences being depicted, but he did feel the existential and national romantic longings of the young actors, who were bringing out a new form of religious desire in the play, one which had not yet succeeded in speaking rationally, but which already possessed spiritual depths.

This play is a prime example of reinterpretation, of misunderstanding which became deeper understanding. The metaphorical transformation of ritual and other materials succeeded in attaining a new meaning which was most relevant to the immediate audience (secular Jews in Western Europe) as well as to the more distant one, for whom the staging of the production gave out the strange call of romantic nationalism struggling for its identity.

The religious structure was distant and alien, void of contents for the audience. It underwent a complex and interesting metamorphosis, becom-ing a new irrational system, with very intense religious depths which were not susceptible to an interpretation that also fitted the original structure. It might be better to say that, from a certain point of view, the new structure appeared to combine messages and meanings connected to the traditional structure (the Song of Songs, the national allegory, opposition to secular, bourgeois existence, spirit and matter), and the changes which took place in the theatre not only interpreted the old by means of the new but also renewed the old and gave it a strange, new power.

No play presents more difficulties to a Jew of every generation and class than Shakespeare's *The Merchant of Venice*. This is a classic example of art which created a stereotype in life: Shylock's pound of flesh, on the one hand, and the thirty pieces of silver received by Judas Iscariot, on the other, became fixed images in anti-Semitic stereotypes of Jews. One might almost judge the character of a society's culture by the interpretation given to *The Merchant of Venice* in productions for the stage. For example, the Nazi film, *Jew Süss*, is a kind of facile mixture of traditional German stereotypes and those borrowed from other anti-Semitic literary traditions, i.e., Shylock.

In the Shakespeare critical tradition one can find various and diverse interpretations given to Shylock's figure over the generations. J. M. Murry says he was 'both the embodiment of an irrational hatred, and a credible human being'.[3] C. L. Barber writes that Shylock was 'made a scapegoat in the cruelest, most dishonest way'.[4] In summary, as has often been said, critics and actors have identified Shylock as a hard-hearted opponent, an unfeeling wretch, a perfect villain, a clown or as a genuinely sympathetic figure.

I do not intend to present a lengthy discussion of the theatrical interpretations given to *The Merchant of Venice* in various countries and periods. I shall make do with several general remarks and then discuss the interpretations given to Shylock here in Israel during the 1970s.

It is not surprising that after World War II there was a tendency to make a hero of Shylock, an effort to misunderstand Shakespeare and emphasize a secondary aspect of the character in order to make up for the crimes of history in art. This interpretation takes the ridiculous anti-hero and makes him into the hero of the play. In England Sir Laurence Olivier played Shylock as a tragic hero, and in Israel the part was given to the most heroic looking of local actors, Aharon Meskin. The young men who wished to fleece the old man were humbled, the old man's heroic revenge was shown to be justified, and Portia turned justice to injustice (though traditionally she is seen as doing the reverse). Everyone identified with the hero who was brought low after his daughter was taken from him, whose money was confiscated, and who was left miserable and penniless on the stage while his victors celebrated unjustifiably.

That interpretation is of course the opposite of the original one, which justifies the comic celebration and holds that Shylock deserved to be sacrificed because he tried to keep his daughter Jessica from marrying Lorenzo and because he insisted upon carrying out his cruel contract with Antonio, the merchant of Venice, to the letter.

These changes in interpretation derived from social circumstances which no longer permitted the presentation of Shylock as a buffoon and a victim whom everyone is glad to see sacrificed. He became the international symbol of a social group which had become the collective victim of

Western culture. He who had been offered up on the altar of history could no longer be sacrificed on the stage.

The theatre paled before the power of history. It lost its effect because the audience identified the victim on the stage with the victim of history, and the collective punishment seemed disproportionate even to the sins of an individual who increasingly appeared as an accuser on the stage rather than as the accused. Modern history continues to add its weight and connotations to the accusing words of the literary hero.

However, in 1970, a young Israeli director, Yosef Yezraeli, dared to stage a production of the play in which Shylock was not a historical hero but rather a poor little anti-hero, a usurious money-lender trying to get his money back. As an unfortunate little father whose life was destroyed because his daughter had preferred a non-Jewish suitor, leaving him and his world, the role of Shylock was given to a short, rather homely actor who speaks too quickly (Avner Hizkiyahu). Shylock was thus made completely unheroic.

Yezraeli showed theatrical originality in other respects as well. The Jews were dressed in black, and non-Jews in white. The characters wore masks which they lowered only while talking within their own ethnic group, but when conversations between ethnic groups took place, the masks were raised. First of all, Yezraeli showed an understanding of the significance of prejudice, which divides the world into black and white, not relating to the individual but rather to his social mask. He tried to show that even a little Jewish usurer, an ugly person who did not resemble Sir Laurence Olivier or some other heroic actor, had certain rights. He deserved rights because he was a defenceless anti-hero, not because he was a tragic hero for whom deprivation of rights was a form of grace, giving him poetic justification and providing tragic catharsis both for himself and the audience. Here the interpretation was reversed, I might almost say secularized. Neither side is absolutely good or absolutely evil, but even the side which is slightly evil and slightly ridiculous deserves its rights. One may be a little Jewish sinner and also be partially in the right.

That the Jewish protagonist erred or sinned or was cruel does not give his enemies the right to persecute him. That was more or less the purport of Yezraeli's reinterpretation: it was a translation of Shakespeare's world, with its prejudices and conventional meanings (along with the interpretative tradition imposed on the play in particular after World War II) to the conditions and needs of the independent Jewish state, which was capable of saying to itself that Jews need not be perfect in order not to be persecuted. Moreover, this was also a correct presentation of human relations based on prejudice, in which both sides play their parts according to the identity of their partners. In the tension between the traditional text, the director as an intermediary, and the audience, a new reality was created by the way patterns were transposed to new contexts, emphases were shifted (which is also a form of translation), and the characters were cast (another way of bringing out gaps and adapting to the new expectations of the audience or working against those expectations). The theatre became the arena for the confrontation between that new reality and the culture of the past, for the struggle of a culture with the stigmas which had embittered its life and history.

VII

The play, like all literature, is a gateway for culture because it allows one to receive a more or less familiar foreign culture within a single, complete framework. In reality, we receive foreign cultures piecemeal, without clear contexts, and we are limited to those cultures which we can actually reach. Objective research presents facts and numbers outside their living contexts. Only a play can bring a past or distant culture to its audience in its authentic fullness. Moreover, although that culture is illuminated from the limited point of view of a single observer, the play is always grasped as paradigmatic, no matter how much it also represents a world beyond the stage. Now, because it is always presented to a group of spectators who regard themselves as, or appear to be, representative of a larger target audience, responding to the play as a group and not a congery of individuals, the confrontation of the theatrical process is always between two social paradigms. The transmitting paradigm sends its message to the paradigm of the addressee, which accepts or rejects it. The director constantly struggles to transmit one alien world to another and to create bonds of similarity between them which emphasize the affinities between the world on the stage and that of the spectators in the audience, but without forgoing the essential, mutual differences.

In the eternal gap between any two social, cultural, and normative worlds, the audience confronted with a strange world is expected to make a constant effort at confrontation, translation, and cognisance both of what is similar and of what is different. That process is one of cultural awareness and understanding. It brings the distant and strange closer. It is the primary acknowledgement that one's fellow man has a right to exist although he is different, and that the stranger's world is similar to ours if we translate it from his language to our own. That process also means that one of the best ways to understand ourselves is to understand our fellow man.

Gershon Shaked

It is no coincidence that totalitarian societies and religious sects (and even entire religions in their totalitarian manifestation) fear the power of the free theatre. The theatre presents a pluralistic option and creates interhuman relations of understanding the other which are perhaps no less dangerous to those societies than direct encounters with other cultures or societies, encounters generally limited in time and place. What is dangerous to totalitarian societies is a source of hope to free and open societies. Thus the gateway of the theatre must be thrown open, for it is the gateway to social understanding, through which true lovers of mankind shall enter.

Notes

1 John Gassner, *Masters of the Drama* (New York, 1940), p. 758.
2 Sheldon Cheney, *The Theatre* (New York and London, 1952), p. 531.
3 J. M. Murry, quoted in J. Wilders, ed., *Shakespeare: The Merchant of Venice. A Casebook* (London, 1969), p. 242.
4 *Ibid.*, p. 178.

Problems of translation for the stage: interculturalism and post-modern theatre

PATRICE PAVIS

Translated by Loren Kruger

Towards specifying theatre translation

Although the problems of translation, and of literary translation in particular, have gained some recognition, the same cannot be said of theatre translation, specifically translation for the stage, completed with a *mise en scène* in view. The situation of enunciation specific to theatre has been hardly taken into consideration: that is, the situation of enunciation of a text presented by the actor in a specific time and place, to an audience receiving both text and *mise en scène*. In order to conceptualize the act of theatre translation, we must consult the literary translator *and* the director and actor; we must incorporate their contribution and integrate the act of translation into the much broader translation (that is the *mise en scène*) of a dramatic text. The phenomenon of translation for the stage (my chief concern here) goes beyond the rather limited phenomenon of the *inter-lingual* translation of the dramatic text. In order to outline some problems peculiar to translation for the stage and the *mise en scène*, we need to take account of two factors:

1. In the theatre, the translation reaches the audience by way of the actors' bodies.
2. We cannot simply translate a text linguistically; rather we confront and communicate heterogenous cultures and situations of enunciation that are separated in space and time.[1]

Problems peculiar to translation for the stage

The intersection of situations of enunciation

The translator and the text of his/her translation are situated at the intersection of two sets to which they belong in differing degrees. The translated text forms part of both source and target text and culture, assuming that the transfer simultaneously involves the source text's semantic, rhythmic, aural, connotative and other dimensions, necessarily adapted to target language and culture. In the theatre, the relationship between situations of enunciation must be added to this phenomenon 'normally' common to all linguistic translation: in other words, the text. The text makes sense only in its situation of enunciation, which is usually virtual, since the translator usually takes a written text as the point of departure. It can (rarely) happen that this text-to-be-translated is contained in a concrete *mise en scène* and is thus 'surrounded' by a realized situation of enunciation. But even in this case, as opposed to that of film dubbing, the translator knows that the translation cannot preserve the original situation of enunciation, but is intended rather for a future situation of enunciation with which the translator is barely if at all familiar – hence the difficulty and relativity of his/her work.

We can represent the source text's situation of enunciation as a part of the source culture. Once this text (in its translated form) is staged for the target audience and culture, it is itself surrounded by a situation of enunciation belonging to the target culture. The result is the real or virtual intersection of these situations of enunciation in differing degrees in the text. We must take into account this concatenation of situations of enunciation while privileging the target situation of enunciation, distinguishing between (1) the part of the situation of enunciation that belongs exclusively to the source or target, and (2) the mixture of the two. In the case of a concrete *mise en scène* of the translated text, we arrive at the situation of enunciation in the target language and culture. Going 'upstream', the translator would find the situation more difficult, because in translating, s/he must adapt a virtual situation of enunciation that s/he does not yet know to a situation of enunciation which will be actual only later. Before even broaching the question of the dramatic text and its translation, we must realize, therefore, that the real situation of enunciation (that of the translated text in its situation of reception) is a transaction between the source and target situations of enunciation that may glance at the source, but that has its eye chiefly on the target. The theatre translation is a hermeneutic act – in order to find out what the source text means, I have to bombard it with questions from the target language's point of view: positioned here where I am, in the final situation of reception, and within the bounds of this other language, the target language, what do you mean to me or to us? This hermeneutic act – *interpreting* the source text – consists of delineating several main lines translated into another language, in order to pull the foreign text towards the target culture and language, so as to separate it from its source and origin. As Loren Kruger has shown, translation does not entail the search for the equivalence of two texts, but rather the appropriation of a source by a target text:

> The reception of a particular translation as appropriate depends on the extent to which the situation of enunciation of the source text, the translator, and the target discourse can be said to correspond: this appropriateness is thus reflected in the apparent invisibility of the appropriation. The meaning of the translated text arises not so much out of what one can take over from it, as what one does to it.[2]

The series of concretizations

In order to understand the transformations of the dramatic text, written, then translated, analysed dramaturgically, staged and received by the audience, we have to reconstruct its journey and its transformation in the course of these successive concretizations.

The original text $[T_o]$ is the result of the author's choices and formulations. As Jiři Levý notes, 'it is not objective reality that penetrates the work of art, but the author's interpretation of reality'.[3] We shall leave aside the question of the work's textualization, pointing out only that the text $[T_o]$ is written and can be described in accordance with its auto-, inter-, and ideotextual dimensions.[4] The text itself is readable only in the context of its situation of enunciation, especially in its inter- and ideotextual dimensions, that is, in relation to the surrounding culture.

The text of the written translation $[T]$ depends, as we have seen, on the initial, virtual situation of enunciation of T_o, as well as on the future audience who will receive the text in T_3 and T_4. This text T_1 of the translation constitutes an initial concretization in the sense I have given elsewhere, following Ingarden and Vodička.[5] The translator is in the position of a reader and a dramaturg (in the technical sense): s/he makes choices from among the potential and possible indications in the text-to-be-translated. The translator is a dramaturg who must first of all effect a *macrotextual* translation, that is, a dramaturgical analysis of the fiction conveyed by the text. S/he must reconstitute the plot according to the logic that appears to suit the action, and so reconstitute the artistic totality,[6] the system of characters, the time and space in which the agents develop the ideological point of view of author and period that show through in the text, the individual traits of each character and the suprasegmental traits of the author, who tends to homogenize their discourse, the system of echoes, repetition, responses, and correspondences that maintain the cohesion of the source text. The macrotextual translation – possible only in a reading of the text – of textual and linguistic microstructures involves in return the translation of these very microstructures. In this sense, theatre translation (like any translation of literature) is not a simple linguistic question; it has too much to do with stylistics, culture, and fiction, to avoid these macrostructures. As George Mounin rightly notes: 'A playable theatre translation is the product, not of linguistic, but rather of a dramaturgical act – if not, as Mérimée said of the translation of *Révizor*, "one would translate the language well enough, without translating the play".'[7] This initial translation or dramaturgical concretization is fundamental, because it 'moulds', in Lotman's sense, and constitutes the text. Far from being an external 'expressive' formulation of an already known meaning, the translation breathes life into the text, constituting it as text and as fiction, by outlining its dramaturgy.

The dramaturgical analysis and stage T_2 of the translation process must incorporate a coherent reading of the plot as well as the spatio-temporal indications contained in the text, the transfer of stage directions, whether by way of linguistic translation or by representing them through the *mise en scène*'s extralinguistic elements. The dramaturgical analysis and the concretization which follows are all the more necessary when the source text is archaic or classical. In such cases, the translation will be more readable for a target audience than the source text (in the original language) would be for the same audience. Hence a paradox: Shakespeare is easier to understand in French or German translation than in the original, because the work of adapting the text to the current situation of enunciation will necessarily be accomplished by the translation. Shakespeare thus lives on in French and German, while being long since dead in English. The dramaturgical analysis consists of concretizing the text in order to make it readable for a reader/ spectator. Making the text readable involves making it visible – in other words, available for concretization on stage and by the audience.

The dramaturgical text can thus be read in the translation of T_0. A dramaturg can also act as interpreter for translator and director (of T_2) and can thus prepare the ground for a future *mise en scène*, by systemizing dramaturgical choices, both by reading the translation T_1 – which, as we have seen, is infiltrated by dramaturgical analysis, and possibly by referring to the original. From a theoretical point of view, it is not important whether this dramaturgical function is verbalized or not, separated from the work of T_1; what matters is the process of concretization (fictionalization and ideologization) that the dramaturg effects on the text.[8]

The following step – T_3 – is testing the text on stage, which was translated initially in T_1 and T_2: concretization by stage enunciation. This time the situation of enunciation is finally realized; it is formed by the audience in the target culture, who confirms immediately whether the text is acceptable or not. The *mise en scène* – the confrontation of situations of enunciation – whether virtual [T_0] or actual [T_1], proposes a *performance text*, by suggesting the examination of all possible relationships between textual and theatrical signs.

The series is not yet complete, however, since the spectator has yet to receive this stage concretization T_3. We could call this last stage the *recipient concretization* or the *recipient enunciation*. This is the point at which the source text finally arrives at its endpoint: the spectator. The spectator thus appropriates the text only at the end of a torrent of concretizations, of intermediate translations that reduce or enlarge the source text at every step of the way; this source has always to be rediscovered and reconstituted anew. It would not be an exaggeration to say that the translation is simultaneously a dramaturgical analysis [T_1 and T_2], a *mise en scène*, and a message to the audience, each unaware of the others. We shall attempt in due course to demonstrate the connection between the various situations of enunciation, the individual body of the actor, and the social body of a culture. It is already clear that the enunciation (and thus also the meaning of the utterance) depends on the way in which the surrounding culture focuses attention and makes the characters (as carriers of the fiction) and the actors (who belong to a theatrical tradition) express themselves. Several factors thus organize and facilitate the reception of a theatre translation. We shall review them quickly, focusing on the spectator's hermeneutic competence and command of rhythm.

The conditions of theatre translation reception

The hermeneutic competence of the future audience   As we have seen, the act of translation concludes with the recipient concretization, which in the final analysis depends upon the use and meaning of the source text T_0. This stresses the importance of the target conditions of the translated utterance, which are specific in the case of the theatre audience who must hear the text and understand what has led the translator to make certain choices, to imagine a particular horizon of expectations on the audience's part, while counting on their hermeneutic and narrative competence. According to René Poupart, the translator represents him/herself and his/her discursive partners in a way that can correspond to the response that s/he gives to various questions s/he is supposed to ask: 'Where do I stand with respect to this translation procedure? For whom should I follow this procedure?'[9] In this evaluation of self and other, the translator establishes a more or less appropriate idea of his/her translation. This idea depends none the less on other factors.

Patrice Pavis

The future audience's competence in the rhythmic, psychological or aural spheres   The rhythmic and prosodic equivalence or at least transposition of the source text [T_o] and the text of the stage concretization [T_3] is often treated as dispensable for a 'good' translation.[10] In effect, we need to take account of the form of the translated message, in particular of its rhythm and duration, since 'the duration *per se* of a stage utterance is part of its meaning'.[11] The criterion of the playable or speakable text is valid on the one hand as a means of measuring the way a particular text is received, but it is none the less problematic once it degenerates into a norm of 'playing well' or of verisimilitude. Certainly the actor has to be physically capable of pronouncing and performing his/her text, which entails avoiding euphonics, gratuitous play of the signifier, or multiplying details at the expense of a rapid grasp of the whole. This demand for a playable or speakable text can, however, lead to a norm of the well-spoken, or to a facile simplification of the rhetoric or phrasing or of a 'properly' articulated performance by an actor (cf. French translations of Shakespeare). The danger of banality lurking under cover of the text that 'speaks well' lies in wait for the *mise en scène*. Furthermore, the works of directors such as Vitez, Régy, or Mesguish, no longer acknowledge this criterion and instead consider every text playable, even those texts – and types of translation – that tend more towards the condition of babble, a dramatic poem or an *exercice de style*, than towards the rapid, 'lively' dialogue of light comedy. What is much more important than the simple criterion of the 'well-spoken' is the convincing adequation of speech and gesture, which we shall call later the *language-body*.

The corresponding notion of an audible or easily received text also depends on the audience and the faculty of measuring the emotional impact of a text and a fiction on the spectator. We shall see that contemporary *mise en scène* no longer recognizes these norms of phonic correction, discursive clarity, pleasing rhythm, 'speakable' language or 'playable' text. Other criteria replace these excessively normative notions of a well-spoken text that is pleasing to the ear.

In examining the theatre translation's conditions of reception, we have already broached the question of the *mise en scène*, in particular the way in which the stage takes over from the linguistic text.

Translation and its mise en scène

Taking over the situation of enunciation   The translation [T_3] (already inserted in a concrete *mise en scène*) is linked to the theatrical situation of enunciation by way of an entire deictic system. Once it is thus linked, the dramatic text can relieve itself of terms which are comprehensible only in the context of its enunciation. This is accomplished by considerable use of deictics – personal pronouns or omissions – or by relocating descriptions of people and things in the stage directions – waiting patiently for the *mise en scène* to complete the text. The translation that is intended for the stage makes this economy even clearer, by trimming the source text even more: one might for example translate: 'I want you to put the hat on the table' by 'Put it there' accompanied by a look or gesture, thus reducing the sentence to its deictic elements.

This economy of the dramatic text and *a fortiori* of its translation for the stage, allows the actor to supplement the texts with all sorts of aural, gestural, mimic and postural means. Thus, at this point, the rhythmic invention of the actor comes into play; his/her intonation can say more than a long speech, his/her phrasing can shorten or lengthen tirades according to taste, structuring and deconstructing the text. All these gestural procedures ensure exchange between word and body (to which we shall return). What remains is the delineation of a debate, more normative than theoretical, on the inscription – or its absence – of the *mise en scène* in the translation.

Translation as mise en scène   Two schools of thought on the subject of the relationship between translation and *mise en scène* confront each other in the work of recent translators and directors; the polemic expressed in this debate may not make for an easy solution, but can be clarified within a theory of concretization in series.

1. For the translators who jealously guard their autonomy and who often think of their work as publishable as it stands, unattached to any particular *mise en scène*, translation does not necessarily or completely determine the *mise en scène*; it leaves the field open for future directors. For Danièle Sallenave, 'neither translation nor direction comment on the text; one can comment only with words in the same language. Translation and direction rather involve transposition into another language or system of expression.'[12] There is therefore no interpretation *stricto sensu* of the text; 'one of the rules for theatre translation and for translation in general is never to appear as an interpreter of the text, but to keep oneself in check, so as to maintain its mystery'.[13] It is true that it is criminal to remove an ambiguity or resolve any enigma that the text has especially inscribed in it. Can any reading, any translation, avoid interpreting the text? This would be a difficult position to maintain. Sallenave herself does not maintain it for long, as she suggests that hearing voices or seeing bodies still does not entail thinking about *mise en scène*: 'Translating for the stage does not mean

jumping the gun by predicting or proposing *mise en scène*; it is rather to make the *mise en scène* possible, to hear speaking voices, to anticipate acting bodies.'[14] Perhaps it is just a false conception of *mise en scène* that leads Sallenave to deny any organic link between it and translation. One would not want to hold against her the wish to preserve the text's enigma if it is indeed a constitutive part of the source text. Other translators, such as Jean-Marie Deprats, qualify positions like this one by making the translation not so much the *mise en scène à l'avance*, but a preparation for this *mise en scène*: 'the translation must remain open, allow for play without dictating its terms; it must be animated by a specific rhythm without imposing it. Translating for the stage does not mean twisting the text to suit what one has to show, or how or who will perform. It does not mean jumping the gun, predicting or proposing a *mise en scène*: it means making it possible.'[15]

Sallenave and Deprats thus both reveal their concern not to encroach on the work of the director, and to allow him/her the freedom to produce his/her own concretization, the theatrical enunciation [T_3], which does indeed rewrite and go beyond T_0, T_1, and T_2. On the other hand, it would be difficult to make a move without T_1 and T_2, for the reasons already indicated. The very fact of leaving aside certain zones of indeterminacy or of not solving the mystery involves taking up a position with respect to the text, and leads to a certain kind of dramaturgical, theatrical, and recipient concretizations. Once uttered on stage, the text cannot avoid taking sides about its meaning possibilities. That does not necessarily mean, however, that the *mise en scène* is predetermined by the text.

2. For this reason, we shall give more credit to the opposing thesis, proposed by Vitez, Lassalle, and Regnault, for example, who tend towards cancelling the translation against the *mise en scène*. According to Vitez, 'because it is a work in itself, a great translation already contains its *mise en scène*. Ideally the translation should be able to command the *mise en scène* and not the reverse . . . Translation or *mise en scène* – the activity is the same; it is the art of selection among the hierarchy of signs.'[16] François Regnault, dramaturg and translator, has chosen as far as possible to subordinate the *mise en scène* to the text: 'The translation is destined to be performed in a particular *mise en scène* and is linked to a particular stage production . . . The translation presupposes first of all the subordination of the *mise en scène* to the text, so that – at the moment of the *mise en scène* – the text is in its turn subordinated to theatre.'[17] For Jacques Lassalle, theatre translation, and the theatrical enunciation in particular, fill the gaps in the source text: 'in every text of the past there are points of obscurity that refer to a lost reality. Sometimes only the activity of theatre can help to fill

the gaps.'[18] A translation theoretician like Hans Sahl in fact uses a theatrical metaphor to define translation: 'Translating is staging a play in another language.'[19]

It would be easy to show how, in Claude Porcell's translation of *Der Park* by Botho Strauß for the *mise en scène* by Claude Régy (1986), a term as 'simple' as 'tüchtig', as in 'tüchtige Gesellschaft', translated as 'société efficace' (efficient society), where one might have expected, given French stereotypical notions about Germany, something like 'société travailleuse' (industrious society), leads in the French version to a *mise en scène* of a hyper- or postmodern society, dedicated to electronics, to bureaucratic chilly efficiency. In Peter Stein's *mise en scène* at the Schaubühne, the focus was rather on the Germany of petit bourgeois and working class myth. The translation of 'tüchtig' by 'efficace' sets the French translation on a track that orients the *mise en scène* in a one-way direction. In the same way, the fact of translating the semantic isotope *Streit, streiten* (quarrel, to quarrel) by varying the terms (problèmes, éternelles disputes, se disputer) involves the French version in quite another isotope and loses the thematic coherence which 'Germanness' might offer, if not impose. In this sense too, the translation predetermines dramaturgical and theatrical concretization. How could it be otherwise once the translation, as a reading interprets the source text T_o and as a translation, cannot but pronounce judgement on this source?

These then are some of the problems facing theatre translation for the stage. What remains to be seen is how this hypothesis of the series of concretizations – weighing more and more heavily on the meaning of the actually received text T_4, is established in relation to an exchange between spoken *text* and speaking *body*, and with respect to the interaction of cultures juxtaposed in the hermeneutic act of intercultural exchange.

From text to body, from body to text

We have described the successive phases of concrctizations from T_o to T_4, highlighting the series of enunciations. This done, we have barely outlined the way in which these enunciations confront the actor with the text, word with gesture. In order to grasp this confrontation, we need to reconstitute the passage from source text to target text, while examining the process of intersemiotic translation between the preverbal [1] and verbal systems of the source [2], and target [5] texts.

33

Patrice Pavis

Translation as mise en jeu

[1] represents the little known situation – before the dramatic text is written. This global situation is not yet semiotically structured; reality has not yet been appropriated in a cultural and semiotic system. We can speak of a hypothesis of a general picture, within which a situation and the fragments of a text are not yet clearly articulated. In this ante-textual magma, gesture and text coexist in an as yet undifferentiated way.

This preverbal element does not therefore exclude speech; rather it contains it, but as *speech* uttered within a situation of enunciation, and as one of many elements in this global situation preceding the written text. Thus the preverbal is not limited to gesture, but encompasses all the elements of a situation of enunciation preceding the writing of the text: apart from gesture, this includes costume, the actor's manner, imagined speech, in short, all the sign systems that make up the theatrical situation of enunciation.

In the dramatic source text [2], we are left with only the linguistic trace of the preceding gestural and preverbal processes. Speaking hypothetically – in order to get from source text [2] to target text [5], we must pass through the *mise en jeu* of the source text [3] and the *mise en jeu* of the target text [4]. We have to return to a preverbal (oral and gestural) situation, in the imaginary *mise en jeu* of the source text in a situation of enunciation within which the text would be confronted with the bodily gesture of the actor. Source [2] and target [5] texts are thus captured in this verbalization which takes the form of a written trace.

The *mise en jeu* of the source seeks an equivalence or a match for the gestural situation of enunciation and the linguistic utterance. We shall see in a moment that the exchange between [3] and [4] is effected by comparing and trying out word and object presentations in the two languages and cultures and in adjusting the *language-body* of the two systems accordingly. Once the *mise en jeu* of the target text [4] has been accomplished, it is transcribed in terms of a purely verbal system, that of the target text [5], moving away from word and object presentation in an attempt to reduce the *mise en jeu* [4] to a purely linguistic system. When this text thus translated is staged – placed within a theatrical and recipient situation of enunciation [T_3 and T_4] – it will return to a global situation of enunciation and will have actually arrived at its destination.

What remains is to refine the terms of this scheme: *word-presentation* (*Wortvorstellung*) and *object-presentation* (*Objektvorstellung*) refer in Freud's work to two dimensions of the linguistic sign: word-presentation or sound picture (*Klangbild*) is the aural representation of the word, its auditive dimension, form of expression of the aural signifier. The object-presen-tation (*Objekt-* or *Sachvorstellung*) is the visual presentation ensuing from the object (we might call it the referent) which we associate with the object-presentation. According to Freud, 'the object-presentation is a combination of associations arising from the most varied representations: visual, aural, tactile, kinesthetic and others'.[20] These two kinds of presentation play a crucial and complementary role in the perception of an orally delivered linguistic text, particularly in the perception of its substantives. What is at issue here is the signified of the word's reference, on the one hand, and its aural signifying dimension, on the other. Starting with the word, we can thus invoke the visual presentations that are associated with it and its aural, rhythmic, prosodic make-up.

Applying Freud to translation theory

In the exchange and the 'trial and error' in the *mise en jeu* between [3] and [4], we should take account of the word and object presentations in the two linguistic and cultural systems. We must transfer from the source to the target text both rhythmic and phonic signifier and some of the associations that are signified and conveyed by the source text. This double transfer is accomplished under varying conditions and according to varying propor-tions, since as Freud remarks, 'object presentation does not seem to be a complete representation and is unlikely to be completed, whereas word presentation is apparently something complete, even if it can be expanded upon'.[21] Applied to theatre translation, this would mean that the transfer between [3] and [4] takes place unevenly: the word-presentations in the target language are not infinite in number and have a limited number of correspondences in [4] and [5]. As a result, the phonetic and rhythmic dimension of the text can be relatively well established and transferred. On the other hand, object-presentation in the same text – its semantic dimension (concerning signified and referent) – is much more difficult to predict: the translation of signifieds and their linguistic signifiers in the two languages is very uncertain and difficult to predict or describe. We should remember that the Freudian distinction between word and object or thing allows us to conceive of the process of verbalization as conscious per-ception and its repression as a presentation that cannot be expressed in words. It is by recourse to the verbal image that the memory trace comes into consciousness: as Freud states, 'Conscious presentation encompasses thing presentation, followed by the corresponding word presentation, while unconscious presentation involves only thing presentation. The system of the unconscious contains the investment of objects (*Sachbeset-*

zung der Objekte), the initial and real investment; the preconscious comes into play when this object presentation is completed by way of a link to corresponding word presentations.'[22]

What becomes of Freud's theory when applied to translation, in particular to this relationship between verbalization at the source [2] and at the target [5], via the double *mise en jeu* at the level of [3] and [4]?

Let the Freudian analogy prompt us to differentiate between the verbal and the preverbal, the conscious from the preconscious and the unconscious. [1], [3], [4], and [6] are situated at the level of the preverbal object presentation, where gesture and language are still undifferentiated. This is the exclusive province of the unconscious. Metaphorically speaking, one might say that the gestural/preverbal [1] element, the *mises en jeu* of source and target [2] and [4], and the future *mise en scène* [6] represent the unknown repressed part of the source and target texts [3] and [5], or the gestural and theatrical unconscious of the dramatic source and target texts. This provides a more or less precise picture of the situation of enunciation within which the linguistic text might be placed, having been enunciated in a way that (necessarily) limits its potential and adapts it to a concrete situation.

[2] and [5] are situated at the verbal level, that of word presentation and the preconscious. The relationship between these two levels, between [2] and [3] on the one hand, and between [4] and [5] on the other, is that of conscious presentation: the attempt to render conscious and known, both text and performance, both word and gesture, to attach linguistic utterance to gestural and situational enunciation, to delineate the union of word and gesture, which we shall call the *language-body*. What we call the language-body, the union of thing-presentation and word-presentation, would in the context of theatrical enunciation be the union of spoken text and the gestures accompanying its enunciation, in other words, the specific link that text establishes with gesture. Each *mise en jeu* and later *mise en scène* would be characterized by a specific enunciation that links text and gesture. Translating source *mise en jeu* into target *mise en jeu* calls above all for the transfer of the language-body of one system into another: we need to find equivalent word-presentations (at the level of the verbal signifier) and object-presentations that 'adequately' match the source text (level of signified and referent). The language-body is the orchestration, peculiar to a language and culture, of gesture, vocal rhythm and the text. It is simultaneously *spoken action* and *speech-in-action*. This resembles the notion of a 'dramatic unity between action and language'[23] that replaces the notion of 'equivalence'. We must grasp the way in which the source text, followed by the *mise en jeu* of the source, associates a particular

gestural and rhythmic enunciation with a text; then we would look for the language-body that fits the target language. In order to effect the translation of the dramatic text, we must have a visual and gestural picture of the language-body of the source language and culture. This economy of the *language-body* cannot work in such frameworks as Freud's word-movement, Barthes's empire of signs, Brecht's gestus, Dalcroze's eurhythmics or Stanislavsky's tempo-rhythm.

Intercultural translation

A semiotic definition of culture

Without entering into the debate on the definition of culture in various humanistic disciplines, we shall take as a point of departure a semiotic concept of culture, that of Uspensky and Lotman, who define culture as the 'non-hereditary memory of community'[24] and insist on the phenomenon of translation of text or reality in semiotic terms as 'the mechanism of cultural appropriation of reality'. If culture is thus defined as the semiotic appropriation of social reality, its translation into another semiotic system poses no problem, once we set up an interpretative relation.[25] The difficulty in establishing this interpretative relation lies in evaluating the distance between source and target cultures, and in choosing the attitude to adopt towards the source culture. This choice is not simply technical; it involves a socio-political image of culture.

Attitudes towards culture

We could choose to keep allusions to the source culture in the translation as far as possible, by not adapting its ideologemes and philosophical concepts to the target culture, in other words, by accentuating the difference between them. We would run the risk of incomprehension or rejection on the part of the target culture: by trying too hard to maintain the source culture, we would end up by making it unreadable.

On the other hand, we could try to adapt the source culture to the target culture, by smoothing out differences, by 'normalizing' the cultural situation to the point at which we no longer comprehend the origin of this all-too-familiar text.

By choosing the first solution – maintaining the source culture by refusing to translate its terminology for example – we could isolate the text from the public and address only specialists, without passing from one side to the other. Such is the danger confronting Jean-Claude Carrière in

37

his adaptation of the *Mahabharata*, which he describes in the following way:

> In refusing to translate certain Indian words like *dharma* or *kshartrva*, I want to point out that the French language and way of thinking cannot cover everything. On the other hand, however, this refusal runs the risk of producing an esoteric language for the initiated; how many times do we hear of oriental theatre specialists who use only Japanese words and so keep the theatrical object at too great a distance from us.[26]

The second solution – total adaptation to the target culture – can betray a condescending attitude to the source text and culture:

> In the *Mahabharata*, there is the possibility of unconscious colonization by way of vocabulary, since the action of translating Indian words translates our relationship to an entire civilization. To say that we could find equivalents for every Indian word implies that French culture can in a word appropriate the most profoundly reflected notions of Indian thought.[27]

A third solution, the middle road most often used, consists of effecting a compromise between two cultures, of producing a translation that would be a 'conductor' between the two cultures and which would cope with proximity as well as distance. This third solution deserves a closer look; we should observe the ways in which the two cultures can be made to connect in the sense of 'connecting vessels' (*vases communicants*). In the *mise en scène* of the *Mahabharata*, Peter Brook and Jean-Claude Carrière had to take account of the difficulty that the French audience had in penetrating a totally foreign world: 'In order simultaneously to bring the *Mahabharata* close to our audience *and* keep it at a certain distance, we had to direct from below rather than from above.'[28] The translation and the *mise en scène* were used to introduce what we might call a 'reception adaptor', in this case a narrator in the French performance tradition, who ensured the link between the Indian story and the audience – what Brook called 'a story-teller who would be from our side, that is, a French-speaker close to the French'.[29] Making the source and target cultures connect with each other in this way ensures that contact is established between them, that phatic communication is maintained. In the same way, the child to whom the narrator tells the story reproduces the listening auditor, by obliging the narrator to translate the story for the child within him or her. The 'reception adaptor' connects the two cultures, always from the final perspective, that of the target audience.

Cultural reinterpretation and cross-coding

The translator's difficulty is thus not to establish the cultural identity of the source text, nor to find a 'reception adaptor' that is appropriate, but to analyse the cultural reinterpretation and the cross-coding among sub-groups within a culture that is no longer homogenous, since an infinity of languages, borrowings, and reinterpretations rework it continually. Take the example of *The Park* by Botho Strauß, translated into French by Claude Porcell (1986). The difficulty of this kind of translation lies in rendering, on the one hand, the cultural and linguistic standardization of the society presented in the play, and, on the other, the proliferation of allusions to microculture, such as the jargon of Berlin intellectuals, punks or petit bourgeois and workers. Cultural standardization invites us to read and translate this text as archetypical of Western, liberal, data-based (*informatisée*), and standardized culture, and thus not to anchor it specifically in Berlin or West Germany. On the other hand, it is rather difficult to find either direct transliterations or equivalents for allusions to historical or socio-cultural details, which fit the French context. What is almost impossible to transfer, however, is the infinite mixing of microculture in Strauß's text. The translation of languages and microculture seems to take place within the source text itself, as if it were thematized as the very subject of the play. So the French translation of this cultural mixing is problematic, because we must first understand the intertextual system in the source text and separate the threads of cultures, discourses, and ideologies. The internal cross-coding of various subgroups in the play (as regards age, sex, socio-professional milieu, kind of desire, etc.) is ramified to such an extent that the text seems to be a bunch of heterogenous cultural elements, an ethnographic, ideological, and discursive *bricolage* of Western society. What the translator needs is not so much the illusory faculty of detecting and transplanting this *bricolage*, as the courage to choose a translation strategy, a vision of this cultural discursive mix, which is perhaps schematic but at least systematic. The translator will succeed in this endeavour only if s/he is supported by the director, who will make these voices recognizable through selection for performance, which are likewise clear and systematic.

Intergestural translation: the example of the Mahabharata

The difficulty of translating the mythic aspect of the dramatic text may discourage the theoretician of translation, but it may also stimulate the inventiveness of the director and push him/her to find other means beyond the purely linguistic or philological to convey the myth. This is characteristic of directors like Wilson or Brook; their shows – sequences of images – constitute a visual narrative that exceeds the textual narrative, and which we can treat only as myth. Once again, let us consider the example of the

Mahabharata: Brook and Carrière tell a story that exceeds text and anecdote, and constitutes itself as myth, by way of gestural discourse – a language of the body, in Brook's words – and a language of the stage: the event of this body, in action and speech. The myth is thus completed and translated by this theatrical discourse:

Something that is quickly forgotten is that a story, even history itself, is a language. I mean that we have a tendency to treat history as an end in itself. We tell a story, believing that we do it simply to hear the story, without realizing that the very principle of myth is that of listening to a story, submitting to its charm at the first degree: simply following a story, while asking ourselves: who are these people, what are they doing, what is going to happen? ... At the same time, we receive impressions of something that cannot be expressed in spoken or written language.[30]

The myth thus created on stage no longer passes by way of the text (in that case, it would be translatable) but by way of the stage action constituted as language. This would mean considering the real translation of the *Mahabharata* as the intergestural dynamic, which alone is capable of conveying theatrically the myth contained in the Indian text.

This intergestural dynamic is accomplished only if the actors show – in their gesture and action – a real harmonization of gestural moments (*gestualités*), despite the diversity of their ethnic and national origins. The paradox of this harmony goes as follows: the actors are chosen for their differences, but each actor must deepen his/her difference, while at the same time stripping him/herself of superficial traits cultivated as 'national' in each country, since as Brook says, 'in indissolubly linking the act of theatre with the need to establish new relationships with different beings, the necessity of forging new cultural links becomes clear'.[31] Culture here is more anthropological and ethnological than historical and ideological. It is what brings together people and traditions, tends to ward universality: civilization, in Lévi-Strauss's sense.[32]

Culture is no longer social *Gestus*, limited to a social function, to what Barthes called 'body, which has been grasped and fashioned by history, societies, regimes, ideologies'. In Brook's case, we can no longer say, as Vitez does, that 'it is in the selection of one gesture rather than another that politics, history, and ideology can be absorbed'. Gesture for Brook is not the pivot of ideology, but the terrain of a universal encounter among actors of different cultures.

Carrière's properly linguistic translation/adaptation moves in the direction of this gestural universality. He tries to avoid the cultural echoes of Christianity and the Middle Ages (as regards religious and social concepts) and the classical or neoclassical tradition, as regards descriptions of 'a soul in torment', or the Parnassian tradition, as regards cheap effects of local colour. Having dispatched these cultural allusions, we are faced with a very simple vocabulary. We rediscover words that have not completely lost their power: 'heart', 'blood', and 'death': three very simple words form the basis of the play. Hence the actors' training and the relative harmonization of gestural moments and performance styles (despite the diversity of the actors' psychic and corporeal investment) coincide with the universalization of myth and language that expresses it. The text of the translation has the effect, because of its simplification and universalization, of an enigma that has been preserved, of a musical refrain that is engraved in the memory, while the details of the plot are impossible to memorize. The *mise en scène* plays on the spectator at a level that can no longer be controlled by the conscious mind and its immediate decoding, but is rather governed by a rhythm that is ceremonial, and which extends the effect of the *mise en scène* far beyond the performance. The awareness of the myth's untranslatability – as elsewhere in the text of *The Park* and its *mise en scène* by Régy – does not preclude a kind of fascination and almost childlike understanding of the story; it seems as though the translation has passed through every sign beyond the word, as if, following the culture of each successive concretization, it has burnt its traces: in particular at the stage of dramaturgical analysis, as if it cast doubt on a linear and philosophical scheme of dramaturgical, theatrical, and recipient concretization.

Conclusion

The examples of Brook and Régy prove that translation for the stage borrows means other than those of a purely linguistic translation and that a real *translation* takes place on the level of the *mise en scène* as a whole. It is not necessary to insist once again on the complexity of the hermeneutic operations involved in this process. We may say that translation in general and theatre translation in particular has changed paradigms: it can no longer be assimilated to a mechanism of *production* of semantic equivalence copied mechanically from the source text. It is rather to be conceived of as an *appropriation*[33] of one text by another. Translation theory thus follows the general trend of theatre semiotics, reorienting its objectives in the light of a theory of reception.

Reflection on translation confirms a fact well known to theatre semioticians: the text is only one of the elements of performance and, in the context of the activity of *translating*, the text is much more than a series of words: grafted on to it are ideological, ethnological, and cultural dimensions. Culture is so omnipresent that we no longer know where to start investigating it. We are limited here to teasing it out into a series of concretizations, which varies according to the social context of the observer, and which is complete only when a given audience appropriates the source text. The set of gestural moments and variations in the *language-body* show how the translation involves the transfer of a culture, which is inscribed as much in words as in gestures. We would have to broach the question of the actor shaping and finally interpreting his/her text and body; the actor can salvage the most ridiculous translation, but can also wreck the most sublime. The phenomenon of intergestural and intercultural translation brings to mind the fact that culture intervenes at every level of social life, and in all the nooks and crannies of the text. Once again, we must comprehend the double movement activating cultural theory. On the one hand, we are witnessing – as the case of the *Mahabharata* clearly reveals – a universalization of a notion of culture, a search for the common essence of humanity, which suggests a return to the religious and to the mystical, and to ritual and ceremony in the theatre. On the other hand, it is time for acknowledging cultures, individualities, minorities, sub-cultures, pressure groups, and thus for refining socio-cultural methods of measuring the extent and effects of culture, which sometimes leads us away from a global conception of society and towards solutions that are partial and technocratic. Even if this very contradiction within the notion of culture – which is not recent – exacerbates the problem of translation, it leads none the less to a mythic conception of culture and translation. Culture thus becomes this vague notion whose identity, determination, and precise place within infra- and superstructure we no longer know. Translation is this undiscoverable mythic text attempting to take account of the source text – all the while with the awareness that such a text exists only with reference to a source-text-to-be-translated. Added to this disturbing circularity is the fact that theatre translation is never where one expects it to be: not in words, but in gesture, not in the letter, but in the spirit of a culture, ineffable but omnipresent.

Notes

1 I will not be discussing here the notion of translation as equivalence which has been refuted by Loren Kruger in 'Translating (for) the Theatre: the Appropriation, *Mise en Scène* and Reception of Theatre Texts', Ph. D thesis, Cornell University, 1986, and Mary Snell-Hornby in 'Sprechbare Sprache – Spielbarer Text. Zur Problematik der Bühnenübersetzung', in *Modes of Interpretation*, ed. R. Watts and U. Weidmann (Tübingen, 1984). Snell-Hornby has written, 'the concept of equivalence, whatever the way in which it has been structured and interpreted, is essentially abstract, static and unidimensional; it ignores the

changing dynamic of language and remains illusory. Its validity is limited to a few areas of technical translation, which depend on a conceptual identity independent of context, and employ a terminology linked to the establishment of objective norms' (p. 113). I will replace the concept of equivalence with that of *language-body*.

2 Kruger, 'Translating for the Theatre', vol. 1, p. 54.
3 Jiři Levý, *Die Literarische Übersetzung* (Frankfurt, 1969), p. 35.
4 Cf. P. Pavis, 'Production et reception au théâtre', in *Voix et images de la scène* (Lille, 1985), pp. 228–93.
5 *Ibid.*
6 See Levý, *Die Literarische Übersetzung*, p. 44.
7 G. Mounin, *Problèmes théoriques de la traduction* (Paris, 1963), p. 14.
8 Pavis, 'Production et réception au théâtre', pp. 268–94.
9 Réné Poupart, 'Traduire le théâtre', unpublished MS thesis, p. 5.
10 The translation should restore the aural and rhythmic quality of the source text. It is none the less self-evident that each culture appreciates and evaluates rhythmic and tonal qualities, and syntactic construction in a different way and thus that the transfer of the aural and rhythmic qualities is not mechanically applied to that of the source text and culture. See Zlatko Gorjan, 'Über das akutische Element beim Übersetzen von Bühnenwerken', in *Italiaander* (1965); Marta Frajnd, 'The Translation of Dramatic Works as a Means of Cultural Communication', in *Proceedings of the International Comparative Literature Association* (Innsbruck, 1980).
11 R. Corrigan, 'Translating for Actors', in *The Craft and Context of Translation*, ed. W. Arrowsmith and R. Shattuck (Austin, 1961), p. 106.
12 D. Sallenave, 'Traduire et mettre en scène', *Acteurs*, no. 1 (1982), p. 20.
13 *Ibid.*
14 *Ibid.*
15 Jean-Marie Deprats, 'Le verbe, instrument du jeu shakespearean', *Théâtre en Europe*, no. 7 (1985), p. 72.
16 Antoine Vitez, 'Le Devoir du traduire', *Théâtre/public*, no. 44 (1982), p. 9.
17 François Regnault, 'Postface à *Peer Gynt*' (ed. Théâtre National Populaire, 1981), p. 184.
18 J. Lassalle, 'Du bon usage de la perte', *Théâtre/public*, no 44 (1982), p. 13.
19 Hans Sahl, 'Zur Übersetzung von Theaterstücken', in *Italiaander* (1965), p. 105.
20 S. Freud, 'On Aphasia' (1891) Standard Edition, vol. 4 (1953), p. 296.
21 *Ibid.*, p. 170.
22 S. Freud, 'The Unconscious' (1915) Standard Edition, vol. 14 (1953), p. 201.
23 Snell-Hornby, 'Sprechbare Sprache – Spielbare Text', pp. 113–14.
24 B. Uspensky and J. Lotman, 'On the Semiotic Mechanisms of Culture', *New Literary History*, vol. 9, no. 2 (1978), p. 213.
25 See E. Benveniste, *Problèmes de la linguistique générale* (Paris, 1974), vol. 2, p. 61.
26 J.-C. Carrière, 'Chercher le coeur profond', *Alternatives théâtrales*, no. 24 (1985), p. 14.

27 *Ibid.*
28 *Ibid.*, p. 8.
29 *Ibid.*
30 *Ibid.*, p. 5.
31 Brook, *The Empty Space*, 1976.
32 See *Anthropologie structurale* (Paris, 1973) vol. 2, p. 417.
33 See M. Vinaver, 'De l'adaptation', in *Ecrits sur le théâtre* (Lausanne, 1982).

Space: the final frontier

PETER HOLLAND

Towards the end of Sophocles' *Oedipus the King*, Oedipus pleads with the Chorus: 'Quickly, / for the love of god, hide me somewhere, / kill me, hurl me into the sea / where you can never look on me again.'[1] That desperate demand to go away, out of Thebes by leaving it or by dying, becomes, with Creon's entrance a few lines later, the final battleground between Oedipus and Creon in this play. Creon, disgusted by the public vaunting of the pollution, demands that Oedipus be hustled indoors: 'Get him into the halls – quickly as you can. / Piety demands no less. Kindred alone / should see a kinsman's shame. This is obscene' (lines 1564–6). Oedipus would rather be driven out than in: 'Drive me out of the land at once, far from sight, / where I can never hear a human voice' (lines 1571–2). Creon, as usual, hesitates and Oedipus reiterates his plea, envisioning a moment of cyclical completion, a satisfying return, through exile, to Cithaeron: 'let me live on the mountains, on Cithaeron, / my favourite haunt, I have made it famous. / Mother and father marked out that rock / to be my everlasting tomb – buried alive. / Let me die there, where they tried to kill me' (lines 1589–93). Yet he realizes that that may not be the answer: 'Well, let my destiny come and take me on its way' (line 1598). It is some time before the topic returns in the play. Only at the very end, before the final and probably spurious chorus, does Creon demand again that Oedipus go in. Oedipus still wants exile but Creon leaves that to the gods' decision and, in the meantime, forces him to go through the palace doors, announcing cruelly and sneeringly, 'Still the king, the master of all things? / No more: here your power ends. / None of your power follows you through life' (lines 1675–7).

Most of us, asked to describe the end of the *Oedipus*, misremember that moment. Conditioned by post-Senecan texts we remember Oedipus leaving Thebes, preparing the way for the long journey to Colonus. Cocteau's libretto for Stravinsky's *Oedipus Rex*, for instance, ends with a drawn-out slow exit for Oedipus as the chorus sing a sad farewell. But that was not Sophocles' intention. Instead the movement of the drama at the end depends on an intense consideration of the two possible movements for the character Oedipus. The resolution of the scene, and hence of the play, or perhaps its lack of resolution, is defined in the choice of ways in which Oedipus can leave the stage. The change in Oedipus's fortune is emblematized or rather, since that may suggest a non-literal representation, is actually present in the choice between the long exit across the expanse of the orchestra and down the *eisodos*, the entrance-road, that leads away from the city and the exit back through the palace doors, the only entrance he has been able to use throughout the performance of the play. Oedipus desperately wants to leave Thebes and may indeed foresee his use of the *eisodos* for that journey. The drama forces him to exit back into the place of pollution, the place of his mother–wife's death, of his beginning, his incest and his blinding.[2]

Throughout the play Oedipus had assumed that he had entered the palace doors for the first time from outside, from the road that leads away from Thebes, as the outsider who had answered the riddle of the Sphinx. He discovers that he was born in the palace. He comes from it and must at the end of the play return to it, to the place where he belongs, his *oikos*, his family-home. The space of the play, the space in front of the palace-doors at Thebes, is a point of decision between, on one side, the *eisodos* that leads to the city, from which the suppliants come to their king and, on the other, the world outside Thebes, the world falsely assumed by Oedipus as his true world but in fact the world from which the news of the circle will come, the circle from Thebes to Cithaeron to Corinth to the crossroads and back to Thebes, the circle of his journey that is slowly reconnected in the course of the play. We are told of the two journeys Oedipus made along this *eisodos*, out as a baby and back to marry Jocasta; we see the geography of the drama completed and his final return into the palace from which the mapping of the journey had begun. Oedipus hoped the journey could end on Cithaeron, but it must end in the polluted house – not that way, but this.

From the perspective of this final movement much recent criticism of the play seems at best misguided. The play cannot be the drama of the *pharmakos*, the scapegoat, since Oedipus is not driven out but in.[3] Power has left Oedipus and he is compelled by Creon to go in, against his will. It would be better for him – and crucially for us in the audience too – if he could leave. It would be a release, if I dare use the word, a cathartic liberation from the confines of the play. But there is no way out that way, along that *eisodos*, only this way, inwards, away from us and back into the claustrophobic confines of the palace of Jocasta's death. His acquiescence in the power of Creon is the final humiliation.[4] Oedipus, forced by Creon to wait on the decision of the gods, is witnessing the extension into the personal and political of the divine humiliation that it has been the trajectory of the play to demonstrate. The distance from the play's beginning, from that powerful and arrogant entry from those same palace doors, is marked by the need meekly to accommodate his will to the demands of Creon, to move under compulsion and not by an assumed freedom to choose.

Now I obviously cannot explore this extraordinary moment fully. But the space of the tragedy is in a remarkable way here constituted as co-extensive with the space of the stage. However far the action of the play may conjure up the places beyond, the play's form of metaphysical determinism holds the individual in place, in the fictive and theatrical spaces, on stage and in front of the palace of King Oedipus. The meaning of the play is closely defined by the possibility of Oedipus's movement on, off and across the stage. This form of tragic determinism in the actor's movement is peculiar to the most formal and formalized modes of tragedy. Those qualities that we recognize as fundamental to English Renaissance drama are qualities of fluidity and changeableness, of infinite possibility in space and instant alteration, qualities of location and dislocation, qualities of flux. The theatre's flexibility is bound up with the drama's. Flexibility of place is inimical to the intensity of meaning generated by entrance and exit in the Greek theatre and in French neo-classic theatre and, the third area for this discussion, Beckett's theatre. There is nothing in the whole of Shakespeare like the treatment of stage-space in the *Oedipus* or Racine's transposition of the Greek sense of space in *Bérénice* or Beckett's transposition of that in turn in *Godot*. Each and every one of the fictive spaces in Shakespeare may be examined momentarily by him. There is the tension in *Macbeth*, for instance, between the door that leads to Duncan's chamber and the door at which the morning's visitors knock at the castle for admission. But such effects are no sooner created than dispelled. They never have the dominant, pervasive and sustained significance of the palace doors and the two *eisodoi* in the *Oedipus*. They never constitute the locus for demonstration of the play's meaning that they are for Sophocles, Racine and Beckett. The nearest Shakespeare comes to this is in his most classically-defined play, *Comedy of Errors*, with its two houses and two exits, especially the tantalizing one that leads to the harbour and escape from Ephesus. Equally it is Ben Jonson, as arch-classicist, who so brilliantly explored the claustrophobia and magic of the single house in *The Alchemist*, a house that seems created before us with a greater solidity than any other on the English Renaissance stage.[5]

Even within a neo-classic tradition the creative reinterpretation of the meaning of movement on stage is very rare indeed. Space is a constitutive part of the play that playwrights rarely contemplate in their trans-cultural appropriation of other forms of dramaturgy, other means of representing meaning. My title, then, which comes from *Star Trek*, is not just a hope that I, like the Starship Enterprise, will 'boldly go where no man has gone before'. But rather that space *is* the final frontier, not only because in the three plays I am using it is that which cannot be crossed by the characters but, much more importantly, because it is that which the playwrights have crossed in their creative transposition of stage-movement out of one theatrical context and into their own, a dramatic form that for both Racine and Beckett was remarkably unlike any contemporary context within which the frontiers of theatrical space had yet been understood. In the work of three great writers, the context of the predecessor, displaced, is repossessed in a way as pregnant with possibility as any analysis of purely verbal borrowing might suggest.

At some point in the 1660s Racine annotated his Aldine edition of Sophocles.[6] It was not the *Oedipus* but the *Electra* which most interested him and which he annotated most extensively at this stage. Many of his notes are convenient summaries of speeches but the cumulative effect of the annotation is to show a remarkable attempt to *see* the play. He notes, quite carefully, the movement of characters on and off the stage. He identifies sometimes the placing of the actors on stage so that, at one moment, he records, 'it appears that Electra is in a corner of the stage, taking no part in that which the Chorus says'.[7] His greatest admiration is reserved for a moment of staging, a moment of use of stage-space: 'there is nothing more beautiful on stage [sur le théâtre] than to see Electra weep for her dead brother in his presence' (II 851). At all times the action of his reading is an intense transposition into theatrical visualization, a maintaining of a dramatic perception through reading in a way that is, to say the least, rare in the period. There is no mention of the reader, only of the member of the audience, 'le spectateur'. The old man who guards the gate is there so that 'le spectateur' finds nothing strange in Oreste's not being heard in the house (II 853); the characterization of Egisthe prepares for the audience, 'aux spectateurs', the pleasure of his surprise in finding the corpse of Clytemnestre rather than Oreste (II 854). Perhaps we should find nothing surprising in the fact that a dramatist reads dramatically, but the attention to entrance and exit is so strong here and elsewhere that it warrants underlining.

When, probably a few years later, Racine annotated a different edition of Sophocles he made only one comment on the *Electra*, though a remarkable one. Opposite the first speech, the pedagogue's speech, Racine noted 'Sophocles takes marvellous care to establish straightaway the place of the scene. He makes use here for this of a very pleasant device in introducing an old man who shows Oreste the surroundings of the palace of Argos since he had been taken away from there very young' (II 865), and he goes on to compare this opening strategy with the identical device in the *Philoctetes* and the *Oedipus at Colonus*. The note is much more than a passing admiration for Sophocles' art of exposition,[8] for all that the problems of exposition so obsessed Racine and his contemporaries. Instead it is a remarkable combination of place and movement, the identification and significance of the locus of the action marked out in the definition of imagined place as the necessary locus *for* the action. This *is* where the play takes place; this *must* be where the play takes place. It represents part of an attempt to see what place, that fictive space deictically indicated, since for Sophocles not in any way visible in a stage set, means theatrically.

Racine learnt Sophocles' lesson well. In *Bérénice*, the play with which I am going to be centrally concerned, the combination of space and movement is critical. The exceptional choice of space and the remarkable concentration on a single form of movement identifies the core of the play, constitutes the play's meaning in a way that is for me exactly analogous with the final movement of the *Oedipus*, a transposition of a Greek technique into France to an extent that an English dramatist could not have done. Every risk that the definition of space created for French drama, every threat that the trap of unity posed, widely perceived and anxiously analysed, is for Racine in *Bérénice* a delight, a resource, an aim. The singleness of place in Greek drama, the elaboration of meaning through that single space becomes, transposed, the function of *Bérénice*. The technique of Greek drama is not just taken out of its own theatrical context, a context that could only have been very dimly perceived, given how little was known of Greek stagecraft, but it is enabled to flourish in a fundamentally alien theatre, a theatre where its techniques had been usually rendered anaemic – for all the apparent French allegiance to Greek practice.

In the published text Racine noted the location of the play with extraordinary precision: 'La scène est à Rome, dans un cabinet qui est entre l'appartement de Titus et celui de Bérénice.' No one had been so specific before. In the major change of French set-design in the seventeenth century, the transition from the *décor multiple* to the single set, the new design of space had become generalized. It was the 'palais à volonté', a composite space which could appear to respect the demands of the unities while compromising its link to a concretely defined place. The perceptual unity disguised in its apparent reality the unreality of the demands it placed on the action, vraisemblance marginally giving way to the tyranny of unity. As Jacques Truchet has stimulatingly suggested, 'il ne s'agissait plus d'imiter ce que pouvait faire un personnage se déplaçant dans un temps limité, mais ce que pouvait voir un spectateur qui ne se déplaçait pas'.[9] For d'Aubignac, publishing *La Pratique du théâtre* in 1657, there was a practicable difference between the unity of place of the stage-floor and the flexibility of the walls – I quote from the accurate English translation of 1684 – 'But we must remember, that this Place, which cannot be suppos'd to change, is the *Area* or floor of the Stage, upon which the Actors walk . . . 'Tis not the same with the sides and end of the Theatre, for as they do but represent those things which did actually environ the Persons acting, and which might receive some change, they may likewise receive some in the Representation.'[10] This delightful solution which ensures that the audience get that 'ravishing' pleasure of scene changes was not acceptable to Corneille, for whom the stage could represent two or three particular places defined within the town where the play is set.[11] This flexibility in the 'décor unique' is extended in a remarkable passage in Corneille's *Discours* to define a space like that of Racine's *Bérénice*, 'une salle sur laquelle ouvrent ces divers appartements', a place private enough for people to speak as if in private and public enough for people to be found there.[12]

When Corneille wrote his play on the subject of Bérénice, premiered a week after Racine's, although probably written first, he left the space general, a classic example of 'le palais à volonté'. Racine's space, by contrast, was defined to an extent that was, to say the least, 'unaccustomed'.[13] When Michel Laurent, the scene designer at the theatre, noted down the requirements of the play in his book, he needed 'un petit cabinet roiallle', the only time his notes call for that particular set amongst the dozens of plays needing 'un palais à volonté'.[14] For Laurent what was most striking was its size. This 'petit cabinet' is compact, a reduced space for a tragedy, analogous of course to the reduced extent of action, the reduced scope that is part of Racine's purpose, a purpose explicitly linked to a desire to transpose classical forms into a context more used to grand and heroic subjects: 'For a long time I have wanted to see if I could make a tragedy with that simplicity of action which had been so much to the taste of the Ancients' (I 466).

The first speech of *Bérénice* is as precise a reformulation of the opening of the *Electra* as one could hope to find. Racine has put his perception of Sophocles' skill into practice. Antiochus and his confidant Arsace enter:

Arrêtons un moment. La pompe de ces lieux,
Je le vois bien, Arsace, est nouvelle à tes yeux.
Souvent ce cabinet superbe et solitaire
Des secrets de Titus est dépositaire.
C'est ici quelquefois qu'il se cache à son cour,
Lorsqu'il vient à la Reine expliquer son amour.
De son appartement cette porte est prochaine,
Et cette autre conduit dans celui de la Reine. (1 469)

When Racine's play is in its turn taken out of context and translated into English, the failure to perceive and carry across this especial quality of deictically defined place is immediately striking. Thomas Otway produced his version of the play as *Titus and Berenice* in 1677, only the second adaptation of Racine to be performed in England. Its cut-down state, about 300 lines shorter than Racine but with an extra 160 lines of Otway's in that figure,[15] allowed it to be played in three acts as the first half of a double-bill with Otway's adaptation of Molière's *The Cheats of Scapin*. In itself Otway's definition of the set, 'A Palace', massively generalized though it is from Racine's precise demand, is a striking change from English neo-classical practice, where for all the notional obeisance to the principles of the unities, space changes far more frequently than d'Aubignac or Corneille would have accepted. Any Racine play transferred to an English context necessitates that the translator–playwright confronts the demands of the single set. Otway was perceptive enough to know that nothing is to be gained by 'opening out', that creation of adjacent spaces that is now so familiar in the filming of stage-plays. But the recognition of the fact of a unitary space is by no means the same as the recognition of the specific meanings Racine's text creates. Even though the English set of 'A Palace' may have shown an equivalent of Racine's 'cabinet', Otway's version of Antiochus's opening speech demonstrates his limited comprehension and his failure to find a new context for the scene, displaced from French drama to English. Otway simply does not understand what space means for Racine. His translation of the opening in his delightful lurching couplets transposes the space glaringly:

Thou my *Arsaces* art a Stranger here,
This is th'Apartment of the Charming Fair,
That *Berenice*, whom *Titus* so adores,
The Universe is his, and he is hers:
Here from the Court himself he oft conceals,
And in her Ears his charming story tells,
Whilst I a Vassal for admittance wait,
And am at best but thought importunate.[16]

51

Peter Holland

For Otway, the space belongs only to Berenice; we are in her apartment. For Racine its decisive characteristic is that it is *between*, 'un cabinet qui est *entre* l'appartement de Titus et celui de Bérénice'. It is that quality of being between that is crucial. The play sustainedly questions whether there is or can continue to be such a state of being between at all. The stage's two directions, serving as bipolar oppositions, define themselves as a need to choose: either/or but not both/and. As the play develops it makes more and more complex and subtle its rejection of a middle way, a way in which, for instance, Titus could marry Bérénice and remain Emperor. The necessitous structure of the drama demands that this state of being between cannot be sustained and that the individual must accede to the need to choose between the two ways out, and the need to recognize that he or she cannot choose to remain between. The possibility that the space itself represents has to be dismantled and rendered temporary, evanescent, as impermanent as the duration of the play itself.

Initially the space is defined by Antiochus as one that excludes himself. The play is fascinated by Antiochus's extraneousness to the action, the embarrassment foisted on him by his being extra. He wishes to place himself between but he is displaced. As Woody Allen commented, sex between a man and a woman can be a wonderful thing, provided you get between the right man and the right woman. Poor Antiochus defines the space of the stage as one that does not allow him space at all. It is the space of Titus's love for Bérénice ('C'est ici quelquefois qu'il se cache à son cour / Lorsqu'il vient à la Reine expliquer son amour'); Antiochus wants it to be the space in which he can declare his love for her. The space defines that substitution as impossible. Only at the end of the play does Antiochus reveal to Titus that he is his rival: 'Mais le pourriez-vous croire en ce moment fatal, / Qu'un ami si fidèle était votre rival' (1 518). But the space is by then exclusively Titus's. Even Bérénice has to leave it. This room onto which apartments open as Corneille suggested does not lead to Antiochus's rooms at all apparently. He has no space and hence no status. The space squeezes Antiochus out. It makes plain the threat to him present in the choice between the two suites of rooms it separates. He begins the play as he ends it, leaving: 'il faut partir' (1 471).

But as a space between, the space of the stage is also a space of transition, of movement from one place to another. The drive of the play is the desire to achieve the state of being permanently with the person you love. To resolve that the lovers would have to exit together. The eventual solution, the permanence of solitude is to leave through separate doors. Except for one remarkable moment in Act 5, Titus and Bérénice do not enter or exit together through the same door. In every other case, Titus

52

comes in through his door and Bérénice through hers. The play focuses on the impossibility of making an exit across the stage. As if tied to their entrance-ways, like Oedipus made to enter and exit through the palace-doors, the two cannot cross. It is so absolute that it is as if an imaginary barrier interdicts the movement. The action of the play, its extent, can be seen as the elucidation of the multiple circumstances which constitute that interdiction. The tragedy's structure of determinism is the characters' inability to cross the stage to exit; the audience's protest at that determinism is our desire that the move should be accomplished.

Crucially for the play the meaning of the impossible move changes. Initially it seems simply to be predicated on Roman law. Emperors cannot marry queens; status determines fate. Social rank is here far more important than Raymond Williams thought when he commented that in neo-classical drama, rank signifies only its 'accompanying style'.[17] Titus and Bérénice can exit together through Titus's door if he is prepared to overturn the people's will, the will of the Rome that lies beyond that door.

At this point the action of the play appears to involve an abdication of individual will, a subservience to an externally defined necessity, Roman law. But as the play continues, determinism is not externalized at all; it is not defined by the power of law which Titus could so easily overthrow. Instead it is revealed as an internalized notion of the selfhood achieved through individual responsibility and obligation. What stops the lovers making an exit together proves to be the lovers themselves. They must acquiesce in the interdiction on movement as completely as Oedipus acquiesced in the interdictions on his movement. The grandeur of the play, its accomplishment of the creation of that extraordinary emotion that is for Racine 'all the pleasure of tragedy', 'cette tristesse majestueuse' (I 465), is dependent on this transition from the forces beyond to the forces within. Will is realized as the opposition to desire, and out of that conflict the tragedy is accomplished.

In that dazzling display, *Sur Racine*, Roland Barthes argues that there are three spaces in Racinian tragedy: the chamber, the ante-chamber and the outside. For Barthes's argument it is necessary that the outside is always seen as a denial of tragedy: 'L'Extérieur est en effet l'étendue de la non-tragédie.'[18] To escape the stage is to avoid tragedy. 'L'Orient bérénicien', Barthes's term for the East to which Bérénice will eventually depart, is 'un *éloignement* de la tragédie', a space in which life submits to the forces of anti-tragedy comprised under the heading 'permanence', 'solitude, ennui, soupir, errance, exil, éternité, servitude ou domination sans joie'.[19] But for all its brilliance Barthes's model is too simple, too linear to account for this play. His sequence of spaces, while entirely appropriate for *Phèdre*, say, or *Athalie*, where we can read them off as chamber, ante-chamber, outside, has to be read in both directions in *Bérénice*. The choice between the two apartments is between two chambers, two interiors, and at the same time between two outsides, Rome and the East. Each inside leads to an outside; each outside is equally problematical.

Barthes's definition of the outside as non-tragic means that the stage itself marks out the limits of the tragedy. Tragedy is an action onstage; to leave the stage is to leave the arena for tragedy. There has been a recurrent desire in the history of the response to the play to find it fundamentally and irredeemably non-tragic: Voltaire called it an 'eclogue in dialogue', Gautier 'une élégie dramatique'. The two responses are close to Barthes's: he finds in permanence the elements of non-tragedy brought to their highest pitch; they object to the play's immobility, its stasis. But the development towards that stasis is in itself a discovery of the tragic meaning of permanence. The impossibility of the move across the stage defines the possible meaning of that stasis. To enter 'l'Orient bérénicien' by exiting alone is to render the state of tragedy as permanent as it was for Oedipus.

As Bérénice makes clear early on in the play, her love for Titus is for himself, him as a self: 'l'ardeur extrême, / Je vous l'ai dit cent fois, n'aime en lui que lui-même' (1 475). If Titus is not himself, then she cannot love him. It is from that perspective that the strange moment in Act 5, when Titus does rush into Bérénice's rooms, makes sense. There is in the Titus of this scene something more than a little hysterical, and when Bérénice, coming back on stage with him, speaks to him in tones that are annoyed and almost contemptuous, the attitude is not effaced by our subsequent discovery of her plan of suicide. Titus's precipitate action has been an unwelcome disturbance of the precarious balances he has achieved. Balance allowed for tragedy. His action, breaking the interdiction on crossing the stage, shows him diminished by virtue of his wildness. The Titus who could do this is not the Titus with whom Bérénice was in love. A stage such as this, like Othello in the middle of his epileptic fit, marks out the demeaning and belittling of the dignity of the self, the dignity that is for Racine so necessary for the existence of the self in the public world. Titus undignified is Titus no longer. Like Hamlet's apology to Laertes, but with all *its* complex layers of irony and difficulty stripped away, that Titus was not Titus at all:

> Was't Hamlet wrong'd Laertes? Never Hamlet.
> If Hamlet from himself be ta'en away,
> And when he's not himself does wrong Laertes,
> Then Hamlet does it not, Hamlet denies it. (v.ii.225–8)

Racine's characters have the advantage of short memories. This wimpish Titus becomes so quickly the dignified figure who can make the enormous speech of self-explanation: 'Madame, il faut vous faire un aveu véritable' (I 516). Here he explores what it would mean to give up the empire and leave through her door. It would be, for both of them, a humiliating and embarrassing possibility: 'Vous-même rougiriez de ma lâche conduite: / Vous verriez à regret marcher à votre suite / Un indigne empereur, sans empire, sans cour' (I 517). Even suicide would resolve nothing. Instead, the acceptance of a permanence of separation is the only resolution, an acquiescence in the pain of fulfilling one's self.

For many writers, tragedy is not tragedy unless there is blood. Some strange blood-lust takes over when tragedy is being discussed. Dryden could not understand Shakespeare's *Troilus and Cressida*: 'The chief persons, who give name to this tragedy, are left alive; Cressida is false, and is not punished'.[20] Gautier announced quite simply that *Bérénice* was not a tragedy because it is only running with tears, not blood. But blood could not end this play. The realization of the self that would fulfil the tragedy is not in giving up resisting, as Titus toys with, but in continuing to resist. It is perhaps a lesson that Racine found at the end of Euripides' extraordinary and under-valued play, *Heracles*, when the hero, discovering what he has done, consents to follow Theseus rather than die and leaves the stage towards Athens and the world of the audience, as the text says, 'In Theseus' wake like some little boat'.[21] Heracles' tragedy is brought to its climax by his acceptance of the need and responsibility to survive, his suffering magnified by its endless continuance. Racine's play does not end with its last word, Antiochus's moving sigh of despair 'Hélas' (I 520), but with the action that fulfils Bérénice's last words 'Pour la dernière fois, adieu, seigneur' (I 520). The lovers must separate to leave the stage, their last exit defining their permanent separation, the pain of agreeing to be apart. Like that glacial moment at the end of Harold Pinter's *No Man's Land* when the subject has changed for the last time, Titus and Bérénice must learn the lesson proclaimed by Spooner: 'You are in no man's land. Which never moves, which never changes, which never grows older, but which remains forever, icy and silent.'[22] The characters have accepted that they can move only into the two exteriors of the play, moving out but also moving inwards, withdrawing, by their adoption of their public function, into permanent incompleteness. Like the opening of the play, it was a moment that Otway misunderstood completely. Racine's care in making Antiochus's word complete the final couplet and in not allowing Titus a final word was too much for Otway:

> *Berenice.* Thus, Sir, your Peace and Empire I restore.
> Farewell and reign, I'le never see you more.

On which line she exits, leaving Antiochus and Titus to complete the play:

> Antiochus. Oh Heaven!
> Titus.   She's gone and all I valu'd lost:
> Now Friend, let *Rome* of her great Emp'ror boast.
> Since they themselves first taught me cruelty,
> I'le try how much a Tyrant I can be.
> Henceforth all thoughts of pitty I'le disown,
> And with my arms the Universe ore-run;
> Rob'd of my Love, through ruins purchase fame,
> And make the world's as wretched as I am.[23]

Otway's wretched end, if truer to Suetonius than Racine had been, can make no sense of Racine's grief, his discovery of the tragedy of tranquillity. In that final movement in *Bérénice*, leaving together but in opposite directions, the tranquil close asserts the fullest sense of the meaning of the movement the stage-space has allowed and the one it has forbidden. The space of the stage becomes the yawning gulf separating the two lovers.

In 1956 Beckett, trying to find a way of putting off translating *L'Innomable*, re-read Racine for the first time in years. He wrote to a friend about *Bérénice*, 'That's another one where nothing happens.'[24] Coming from the author of *Godot* that might be thought to be praise. But Beckett's attitude towards the play was always wry and enigmatic. In 1930 he gave lectures on Racine at Trinity College, Dublin and treated *Bérénice* as a comedy. Bérénice goes away at the end, according to Beckett, because she is a tolerant sophisticated woman. For Beckett the play is a comedy because of its establishment of equilibrium. The equation is simple: tragedy abolishes any need for equilibrium; the finality of divine justice removes plurality and without plurality there is no need for equilibrium. He did at least accept that there is some plurality at the end of *Bérénice*, but her tolerance balances it out completely. As far as Beckett was concerned, the final gesture of the play was simply expedient, not heroic, and, since Racine could not take heroics seriously enough to make tragedy from it, the play is a comedy of the wasted grand gesture.[25]

Beckett is obviously enjoying the paradox he created in the lecture. In an odd way, Beckett's argument here is exactly analogous to the traditional distinction between comedy and tragedy offered by Donatus in a famous passage of his commentary on Terence: 'In comedy all is disturbed at the beginning and tranquil at the close; in tragedy the order of progression is exactly reversed.'[26] Donatus's structural model is based on the assumption that 'the moral of tragedy is that life should be rejected; of comedy, that it should be embraced';[27] Beckett's, like Dryden's or Gautier's, though for different moral reasons, is essentially the same. Racine and Euripides – and indeed Sophocles in the *Oedipus* – see tragedy embracing life and being forced to do so in the action of the characters. The move towards accepting life becomes at the same time the fullest possible acceptance of the movement of tragedy. *Waiting for Godot*, one might want to argue, moves in the same direction.

But my purpose in moving from Racine to Beckett, from *Bérénice* to *Godot* is not that glib. Rather, I want to suggest that Beckett has consistently chosen to investigate the meaning of stage-space in a context derived directly from a Racinian model, that his plays have in this developed from a sustained exploration of the renewed possibilities of a neo-classical model for space, transposed out of its own context into one which reveals it anew. The meanings of those spaces explore similar consequences of constriction, the constriction of space for action constricting the character. Titus and Bérénice desire to be together but will themselves to separate. Vladimir and Estragon desire to leave permanently but cannot resolve their desire into their will. The removal of an ability to will, to translate desire into willed action is again predicated on the possibility of exit: '"Let's go" *They do not move.*'[28]

Increasingly in the plays since *Godot*, Beckett has explored the limits of this removal of will as a *physical* impossibility. Movement is either impossible or so completely controlled as to be outside the will, outside the sense of self and desire. In *Act Without Words 1*, for instance, the figure is exhausted and discouraged by the failure of each attempt to defeat the mockery of the unseen forces. In the end he lies on his side, facing the audience. The temptations are repeated but as the stage direction says, four times, 'he does not move'.[29] *Happy Days* recontextualizes Aeschylus's *Prometheus Bound* in transforming Prometheus's immobility into Winnie's. In *Play* the inertia has become the compulsion to act under duress. The characters must speak when the light is on them, cannot speak unless the light is on them. The light is as Beckett states 'a unique inquisitor';[30] it enforces the endless repetition of response, the repetition of the play in that unique stage direction '*Repeat play*'.[31] That same inability to control speech but instead being aware of having it controlled, compelled out of the self, reaches its climax in *Not I*, where the self, Mouth, in its logorrhoea, is able only to refuse to assert the sense of self, though the language pours out willy-nilly, the woman finding herself speaking. The movement of speech is substituted for physical movement on stage, defined as increasingly unimaginable or as painful as May's in *Footfalls*. Such examples in Beckett's work are familiar.

Less well known and much more provocative in this context is the draft for an uncompleted play written in 1967–8. The play, a two-hander, is first sketched as a series of movements: 'Arrivée femme . . . [de même] homme . . . Elle l'expédie . . . Femme seule. Elle le ramène. Il l'expédie. Homme seul. Il la ramène. Ils l'expédient.'[32] Once Beckett has defined and numbered these four stages (woman and man, woman alone, man alone, woman and man), he offers timings for each one, 10 minutes, 20 minutes, 5 minutes, 10 minutes. This shape once defined, with equal outside sections but with the woman's monologue timed at four times the length of the man's, Beckett then poses himself a series of questions further down the sheet: '1. Quel dialogue? 3. Que fait l'homme seul? 4. Quel dialogue? Et pourquoi décision l'en finir?' He notes down some possible subjects for the dialogue and for the woman's monologue and then, triumphantly, at the bottom of the sheet he notes for section 4: 'Base de la décision. Lui: "On a ri. On rit ici."'

It is a remarkable document. Beckett gives priority to the shape and timing of the drama, defining the units as the movement on and off stage, defining the timing apparently irrespective of any notion of what might fill the time other than the fact that the character or characters on stage will have to speak about something. Though there are hints in the notes that he has thought about these characters as having histories that will provide material for dialogue, it is the abstract shape of movement that counts. Like a comedian preparing a solo spot, he is most concerned about how to get them off-stage, how to give them a reason for an exit and he finds it in laughter: 'Peut-être rire inévitable'. The play, in this case, quite simply *is* the sum of the movements; entrance and exit define the reason for dialogue and dialogue is itself only that which fills the gap before the next movement. In many respects the text anticipates such a wordless and movement-filled play as *Quad* with its demented monks scurrying around their cloister without ever meeting, or the shapeliness of *Come and Go*, with its assumption that if three women sit on a park-bench and one leaves the other two will gossip about her, a pattern repeated through its three possible permutations.

But this shapeliness, this classicism of awareness of the formality of form is as present in *Godot* as in the later plays. It is clear from Beckett's work for a German production that he relishes the intensification of the shapeliness of the play. His approval of the costumes for that production was for the joyous pattern he created through them. In Act 1, Vladimir wore a black jacket and pinstripe trousers while Estragon wore pinstripe jacket and black trousers. In Act 2, Estragon wore the black jacket and pinstripe trousers, Vladimir the pinstripe jacket and black trousers. The two suits were chasing their other halves across the actors' costume changes without ever meeting up, like the lost human halves of Aristophanes' speech in Plato's *Symposium*. The form, in this excited costume chase, becomes a game, mocking and taking delight in its own state of being form.

Space, I want to suggest, is similarly self-consciously and playfully formal. The example of *Bérénice* is a difficult model and Beckett takes a clearer line on the definition of the spaces of the stage and its adjacent areas from a work such as *Athalie*. Racine's sequence there runs, the outside, dominated by Athalie, the antechamber which is the set of the play, the inside of the temple, which is obviously dominated by God. By comparison Vladimir and Estragon find themselves at an arbitrary point along a country road, with a mound and a tree, but a place that emphatically marks out the space between (that quintessentially Racinian characteristic): on the one side is the outside where Estragon sleeps in a ditch and is beaten and, on the other is the inside, the wished-for place, the inner world which is Godot's. Didi and Gogo are in that permanent state of the ante-chamber, kept outside the inner sanctum, the domain of Godot, but also, while they are in this lobby-limbo, inside, safe from the outer world. Onstage the two cannot be hurt but also cannot be safe. The outer comes in as Pozzo and Lucky, disturbing, threatening, unappeasable. The inner appears as Godot's messengers, the boy and his brother who force the tramps to stay where they are, commit them to the necessity of not leaving, of staying in the arena of dramatic action, denied the supposed comfort of Godot's arrival. In one sense very much like Racine's *Athalie*, it is the inner world, the world of 'Dieu des Juifs', God of the Jews, or of Godot, that triumphs, enforcing its control.

By the end of *Bérénice* the space of the play's action has its function as a place of meeting finally removed. It is no longer a place of passage, a place of possibility. It is instead a vast gulf of being between, the marked-out space of separation. It is a space with a meaning only of what has passed, what is now the past, a memory of what once might have been. The space has been given a permanence. In *Waiting for Godot* the function of the space is continuous but also drained of meaning; the country road is now fully revealed as going nowhere, a space of arrested motion, like the *eisodoi* in *Oedipus* that for Oedipus can lead nowhere, are not ways he can travel in this play. Space marks out the permanence of stasis; endless repetition shows the obverse face of our traditional notion of tragedy as a drama denoting an irreversible movement. Unlike the incapacity to move across, that Titus and Bérénice must learn, the movements of *Godot* are endlessly re-run. If *Bérénice* is finally centrifugal, *Godot* is as strongly centripetal. The displacement of the Racinian model of space has redefined it as a space where change has no meaning. It does not matter on this country road whether the tree has leaves, the boots fit, Pozzo can see or Lucky can talk. Pozzo's blinding, a deliberate displaced echo of Oedipus, only enables him to enunciate his perception of the unchangeability of event, the days merging into one. If *Godot* appears to stretch its use of the classical unity of time by taking place on two separate days, it mockingly chooses to proclaim that the days are the same and its subservience to the unities is complete.

There is one further, familiar twist in Beckett's re-accommodation of a Racinian model of space to a displaced context of twentieth-century drama. The constrictions of Racinian space, the fitting of the drama to the single space it is permitted, were for Racine and his contemporaries a terrible risk. It is the subservience to orthodoxy that enforces on space a propriety which makes the stage in Truchet's words 'un lieu terrible, piège et prison pour les héros'[33] and also, I would add, a snare for the dramatist in his subservience to his audience. Beckett of course freely acknowledges the audience and the reality of performance as a trap in Vladimir's advice to Estragon, for instance:

We're surrounded! (*Estragon makes a rush towards back.*) Imbecile! There's no way out there. (*He takes Estragon by the arm and drags him towards front. Gesture towards front.*) There! Not a soul in sight! Off you go. Quick! (*He pushes Estragon towards auditorium. Estragon recoils in horror.*) You won't? (*He contemplates auditorium.*) Well, I can understand that.[34]

The impossible fracture of the fourth wall is the play's metatheatrical awareness of its own mimetic status, the status of the space it occupies as a drama in performance. Space, one might rather easily say, finds its final frontier in the barrier that, for all its acknowledged existence, still separates play from the audience. As Shakespeare's Don Armado says, at the end of *Love's Labour's Lost*: 'You, that way; we, this way.'

Much as we would wish otherwise, our study of theatre is too often an unacknowledged combination of language-based and quasi-thematic criticism. Even the development of theatre semiotics has rarely meant sustained attention to the abstract, open space on which the play is performed.[35] Yet even a theatre like the English stages of Shakespeare has found its practice fundamentally controlled by the problem of entrance and exit, as in the lists of entrances that make up the *platts* which hung beside the stage for the book-holder's and actors' use. Stage-space and movement constitute their own tight system of theatre language, a codifying that can be understood and recreated in its new context as in Racine perceived by Beckett, or misconceived and bastardized even in more direct translation as in Otway's *Titus and Berenice*. The responsibility on us is to learn the meanings given to the terms of that language, of that system of relationships. Then we will, I believe, discover a new way of perceiving what happens when the system is taken from its own context and re-created in another. Then space will no longer be the final frontier.

Notes

1 Sophocles, *The Three Theban Plays*, trans. Robert Fagles (Harmondsworth: Penguin Books, 1984) lines 1543–6.
2 Much of my analysis here has been deepened by the attention drawn to this problem so brilliantly by Oliver Taplin in *Greek Tragedy in Action* (London: Methuen, 1978), pp. 45–6, and, at greater length, in 'Sophocles in his Theatre', *Entretiens sur l'antiquité classique (Fondation Hardt)*, vol. 29 (1982), pp. 155–74.
3 See Taplin, 'Sophocles in his Theatre', pp. 170–2.
4 For a different interpretation of this final movement see M. Davies, 'The End of Sophocles' *O.T.*', *Hermes*, vol. 110 (1982), pp. 268–77.
5 See Ian Donaldson, 'Jonson's Magic Houses', *Essays and Studies* new series, vol. 39 (1986), pp. 39–61.
6 For the date of these annotations see R. C. Knight *Racine et la Grèce* (Paris: Editions Contemporaines, 1950), pp. 152–3.
7 All quotations from Racine are taken from *Œuvres complètes*, ed. R. Picard (Paris: Gallimard, 1950), 2 vols., here II 851.
8 See Knight, *Racine et la Grèce*, p. 218.
9 'It was not a matter of imitating what a character could do, moving around in a limited period of time, but of what a member of the audience could see without moving at all.' J. Truchet, *La Tragédie classique en France* (Paris: Presses Universitaires de France, 1975), p. 30.
10 F. Hédelin, Abbé d'Aubignac, *The Whole Art of the Stage* (1684) Book 2, pp. 100–1 or *La Pratique du théâtre*, ed. P. Martino (Algiers: Jules Carbonnet, 1927), pp. 101–2.
11 P. Corneille, *Writings on the Theatre*, ed. H. T. Barnwell (Oxford: Basil Blackwell, 1965), p. 77.
12 *Ibid.*, pp. 78–9.
13 As Jacques Scherer calls it in *La Dramaturgie classique en France* (Paris: Librairie Nizet, 1950), p. 195.
14 *Le Mémoire de Mahelot, Laurent et d'autres décorateurs*, ed. H. C. Lancaster (Paris: Edouard Champion, 1920), p. 113.
15 For precise statistics see A. Lefevre, 'Racine en Angleterre au XVIIᵉ siècle: *Titus and Berenice* de Thomas Otway', *Revue de littérature comparée*, 34 (1960), pp. 251–7.
16 T. Otway, *The Works*, ed. J. C. Ghosh (Oxford: Clarendon Press, 1932), 2 vols., here I 258.
17 R. Williams, *Modern Tragedy* (London: Chatto and Windus, 1966), p. 25.
18 R. Barthes, *Sur Racine* (Paris: Editions du Seuil, 1963), p. 11.

19 *Ibid.*, p. 93.
20 John Dryden, *Of Dramatic Poesy and other Critical Essays*, ed. G. Watson (London: Dent, 1962), 2 vols., 1 240.
21 Euripides' *Heracles*, trans. W. Arrowsmith, line 1424, in D. Greene and R. Lattimore, eds., *Euripides II* (London: University of Chicago Press, 1956).
22 H. Pinter, *Plays: Four* (London: Eyre Methuen, 1981), p. 153.
23 Otway, *The Works*, 1 297.
24 D. Bair, *Samuel Beckett: A Biography* (London: Jonathan Cape, 1978), p. 475.
25 These comments are taken from a summary of Rachel Burrows's notes on Beckett's lectures prepared for Daithi MacLiath, 'To the Core of the Eddy', *Granta* December 1976, pp. 21–3. A slightly different account of the lectures and of Beckett's whole relationship to Racine is rather chaotically presented in V. Mercier, *Beckett/Beckett* (Oxford: Oxford University Press, 1977), chapter 4.
26 See J. V. Cunningham, *Tradition and Poetic Structure* (Denver: Alan Swallow, 1960), p. 164.
27 *Ibid.*
28 S. Beckett, *Waiting for Godot* (London: Faber and Faber, 2nd edn, 1965), pp. 54 and 94.
29 S. Beckett, *Collected Shorter Plays* (London: Faber and Faber, 1984), p. 46.
30 *Ibid.*, p. 158.
31 *Ibid.*, p. 157.
32 The manuscript was item 376 in J. Knowlson, *Samuel Beckett: An Exhibition* (London: Turret Books, 1971), p. 118 and is illustrated in the catalogue.
33 Truchet, *La Tragédie classique*, p. 30.
34 *Godot*, p. 74.
35 See, however, Anne Ubersfeld, 'The Space of *Phèdre*', *Poetics Today*, vol. 2, no. 3 (1981), pp. 201–10 and M. Issacharoff, 'Space and Reference in Drama', *Poetics Today*, vol. 2, no. 3 (1981), pp. 211–24.

'If the salt have lost his savour': some 'useful' plays in and out of context on the London stage

JAMES REDMOND

Par la comédie, par la tragédie, par le drame, par la bouffonerie, dans la forme qui nous conviendra le mieux, inaugurons donc le théâtre utile ...

Dumas fils, *Le fils naturel*, Préface, 1868

The highest [theatrical] genius ... is always intensely *utilitarian*

Shaw, 'Should social problems be freely dealt with in the Drama?', 1895

Was für ein erlauchter, *nützlicher* und gefeierter Platz wird mein Theater sein!

Brecht, *Der Messingkauf*

In 1895 in his contribution to a symposium on the Problem Play, George Bernard Shaw made a distinction that is very important for our theme:

A Doll's House will be as flat as ditchwater when *A Midsummer Night's Dream* will still be as fresh as paint; but it will have done more work in the world; and that is enough for the highest genius ...[1]

This distinction has been important since the emergence of a theatre with a widely eclectic disposition, eager not only to perform plays written specifically for its own audience, but also to search other periods and other cultures for dramatic material.

Non-comic drama has always been committed to elements of tribal history, of the sermon, of metaphysical speculation, of religious ceremony and ritual. In our culture it also has a very strong interest in the material of the local gossip, of the daily newspaper, of the political hustings, of the intellectual journal, of the confessional memoir and, most importantly in this context, in the contents of the museum of world drama. Shaw's

63

distinction applies to the modern period but would not have been understood by a citizen of Periclean Athens, since it was unthinkable that plays from ancient periods or foreign cultures could be performed in the theatres of Dionysus. Nor would our theme have been of interest to an Elizabethan since, except for students who might perform them in the process of their education, Roman plays in England had the two functions that Greek plays had had in Rome: they were read by scholars in the library and they were used as raw material to be transformed into contemporary drama for performance in the playhouse. No one thought that an old or foreign play could be theatrical fare to attract a paying audience. In those days they consumed their drama fresh, like bread and milk.

But Shaw is also making another distinction. *A Doll's House*, or the aspect that held Shaw's attention, was concerned with themes defined by particular social circumstances: it was aimed at a very specific audience – contemporary middle-class people who had developed a sharp awareness of the roles a citizen might play in modern society.

This paper will consider some related examples of the genre of the non-comic play intended to be 'useful' – and this is the recurring, defining term – in the sense that each play was meant to be of immediate didactic value within the very specific context for which it was written. *A Midsummer Night's Dream*, Shaw might have sparkled, is indeed not of an age but for all time, because it was as socially irrelevant in 1595 as in 1895: and the demand for immediate relevance is central to the genre of the useful play. 'Staging *Don Juan* or Racine is fine', Sartre said in criticizing the Théâtre National Populaire in 1955, '. . . but it is *irrelevant*. For a people's audience the first thing you have to do is to produce its own plays – plays written for it and speaking to it.'[2] Der Philosoph in Brecht's *Der Messingkauf* defines his dream of useful theatre (*Thaeter* as distinct from *Theater*) as being 'nicht für ewige Zeiten' but as offering to serve 'Nur der Not des Tages, gerade unseres Tages'.[3]

The history of *A Midsummer Night's Dream* has confirmed what its first audience might have supposed: it has spoken magically to many generations in many climes. But what of the play meant to be of immediate usefulness to its first audience with no promises made to posterity: how has the useful play fared out of context?

In dedicating *The London Merchant* to an alderman of the City of London in 1731, George Lillo put in very direct terms the argument common to the playwrights who will hold our attention: 'the more extensively useful the moral of any tragedy is, the more excellent that piece must be of its kind'. The value of this new type of serious play, like the claimed value of some kinds of classical and Renaissance comedy, is to be identified with its direct utilitarian function:

... it is more truly august in proportion to the extent of its influence and ... more truly great to be the instrument of good to many who stand in need of our assistance ...[1]

Lillo established the central content of the useful play as the critical analysis of contemporary society, and he developed some crucial metaphors that were taken over by later playwrights in the tradition. I shall look at a handful of plays which have employed similar techniques for similar purposes, and consider some of the effects of their being performed in and out of context.

From the first lines of the play, Lillo makes it clear that the plot will be a mere framework to support his analysis of English society and the lessons to be derived from the analysis. Thorowgood is the representative London merchant, and he spends the first scene expounding the economic philosophy of his class. Money, as controlled by the merchants in the City, is the underlying force beneath all aspects of English life. In the face of threatened invasion, the monarch and her parliament turned to the financiers who had recently come to dominate the country's economy: they have used their international business connections to neutralize England's enemy and at the same time to further trade. In this way, we are told, capital is the guarantor of the royal throne, of pure religion, of liberty and of the law. Whereas in the bad old days kings were led to raise revenue by force to pay for foreign wars, in this new age of reason, instead of 'taxes great and grievous to be borne' (p. 12) there is an opportunity for the City to save the country through financial manipulations and to make an appropriate percentage in the process. The only thing to fear is that Spain might acquire enough gold and silver in the New World to achieve financial and therefore political dominance. International commerce is war conducted by other means, and the message is offered proudly to the audience, for victory seems secure: 'Der Krieg ist nix als die Geschäfte', Mother Courage was to sing at the high point of her trading career (Scene 7).

Thorowgood's daughter Maria is a key figure. She is his only child, will inherit his fortune, and is in the extraordinary position of not having to marry for money. Her father, nevertheless, is eager for her to choose a husband, and the reason is made explicit: 'the fruits of many years' successful industry must all be thine', he tells her, 'Now it would give me pleasure great as my love to see on whom you would bestow it' (pp. 13, 14). There is no sentimental gesture about acquiring the son he never had, or of grandfatherly longings: he wants to know who will get his daughter and his ducats. And the positive message for the middle-class audience is that upward social mobility is possible for them. By marriage Maria may rise into the aristocracy, or she may choose to elevate some lucky young man into the rich financier class. The system demands loyalty and dedication to its rules, but in return it offers rich opportunities.

In the third scene we are introduced to Millwood, a great dramatic creation to be imitated by several later playwrights. She is a prostitute who puts herself forward as representative of those without capital in the capitalist system. Lillo is pioneering the dramatic use of the prostitute to stand for those in modern society who, having no estate, do not have freehold of their own bodies; 'Slaves have no property – no, not even in themselves' (p. 15). And the revenge she longs for is the attainment of the financial dominance Thorowgood and Maria have been rejoicing in:

> *Millwood:* I would have my conquests complete, like those of the Spaniards in the New World, who first plundered the natives of all the wealth they had and then condemned the wretches to the mines for life to work for more. (p. 16)

There is an element of sex-war in Millwood's position, because the established system is so male dominated and the immediate agents of her exploitation are men. But the war is most importantly about money, and internally as well as internationally commerce is the means of waging the war. Millwood's interest is at one with her male associate Blunt, who is afraid that Millwood's plans may fail and that all in her household will starve. She is no more an enemy of Thorowgood than of Maria, for in their dealings with men Maria may buy while Millwood must sell.

Millwood's chosen victim is George Barnwell. She will seduce him and use him as a means to attack his class financially. Like everyone else in the play, Barnwell sees all important aspects of life in terms of money – not good husbandry, not productive industry, not professional competence, all of which receive lip service – but money, however gained. At the moment of his seduction, he is emotionally torn and reaches for the revealing metaphor:

> Reluctant thus, the merchant quits his ease
> And trusts to rocks and sands and stormy seas;
> In hopes some unknown golden coast to find,
> Commits himself, though doubtful, to the wind. (p. 24)

In the second scene of the second act there is an injection of high-flying rhetoric, with biblical reference and some deeply pondered phrases about Time: this is where the metaphysical speculation might be in an Elizabethan tragedy, but Barnwell's best friend Trueman offers the cure for Barnwell's potentially suicidal despondency: 'business requires our attendance – business, the youth's best preservative from ill, as idleness his worst of snares' (p. 29). And this is followed by a scene in which Thorowgood and Trueman sing hymns of praise to the ideal of commerce, which is associated with science, reason, nature, humanity, the arts, peace, plenty, and mutual love. Trueman, at the age of eighteen, has observed that

those countries where trade is promoted and encouraged do not make discoveries to destroy but to improve mankind – by love and friendship to tame the fierce and polish the most savage; to teach them the advantages of honest traffic by taking from them, with their own consent, their useless superfluities. (p. 40)

And his mentor Thorowgood fills in the important details: the useless superfluities to be extracted from foreigners in the process of improving mankind are 'glittering gems, bright pearls, aromatic spices, and health-restoring drugs . . . unnumbered veins of gold and silver ore' (p. 40). The general principle behind international trade is that

It is the industrious merchant's business to collect the various blessings of each soil and climate . . . to enrich his native country. (p. 40)

The usefulness of Lillo's play in its first context was that beneath the surface pieties it gave expression to thrillingly harsh truths about bourgeois capitalism: the play invites pride in the system without denying its true nature. The appeal to the audience's moral sensibility is matched by the appeal to its thirst for money. Bourgeois cupidity is identified with bourgeois business morality, which is offered as the only morality. The great power of the play comes from the directness with which it addresses its audience, the force with which it tells them what they want to hear.

In the last scene of the third act Barnwell kills his uncle. Lillo borrows a lot from *Macbeth*, but he greatly simplifies the issues. Barnwell kills for money alone, and the relationship is more explicit than Macbeth's with Duncan. His father's brother, Barnwell tells us, '. . . has been to me a father' (p. 49), and 'Murder [is] the worst of all crimes, and parricide the worst of murders, and this the worst of parricides' (p. 52). We shall see that, like prostitution, murderous conflict between child and parent was taken over into the modern useful play as a metaphor for violent social strife.

Millwood's function is central. When she is apprehended, her speeches of defiance are worthy prose equivalents of Vittoria Corombona's great verse arias in the third act of *The White Devil*; their purpose is to elaborate the central idea that as a prostitute she represents London social life – she sees herself not as a pariah, but as the paradigm of the individual striving for self-sufficiency through self-help.

My soul disdained, and yet disdains, dependence and contempt. Riches, no matter by what means obtained, I saw secured the worst of men from both. I found it, therefore, necessary to be rich. (p. 64)

And from her customers, who are members of all the professions, she has learned the skills necessary for survival in London society – wickedness, pride, contention, avarice, cruelty, and revenge: she especially mentions priests and magistrates as having taught her the central truth that

All actions are alike natural and indifferent to man and beast who devour or are devoured as they meet with others weaker or stronger than themselves. (p. 65)

This use of the dangerous jungle as a metaphor for society was to be taken up regularly in the twentieth century, but Wedekind, O'Neill and Brecht at their most scathing are not more violent than Millwood.

The fifth act is given over to general moralizing. Barnwell in scenes with Thorowgood, Trueman, Maria, and Millwood emphasizes the message and moral of the play. The message is that English law, English commerce, the English class structure, and English religion are great God-given benefits that must be held in reverence. The moral is that young people in the audience must learn from the fate of Barnwell and Millwood: they must respect their elders and work patiently within the present structure of society, where obedience and diligence will be rewarded.

The play was a great critical and box-office success, and at this distance in time we can only trust the reports of those who tasted the pudding when it was fresh and hot: they found it extremely palatable and very nutritious. The reviews in the middle-class journals hailed the play as a major pioneer work in a crucially important genre. For example, we are told of the audience reaction that 'a most profound Silence argued the deepest Attention, and the sincerest Pleasure imaginable . . . '[5]

The London Merchant had an immediate and enduring success in print, in both of the patent theatres, with touring and provincial companies. For the best part of a century it was performed every year on public holidays, so that apprentices and servants could see it. It offered them a penetrating analysis of contemporary mercantile mores, together with an emotionally convincing defence of the system. Underneath the conventional piety and self-righteousness, we are allowed to see the ruthless acquisitive urge in Thorowgood as well as in Millwood. Lillo was very far from satirizing the business ethic; he was, rather, packaging its rapacity in an elaborate sermon which gave the philosophy of bourgeois capitalism a surface respectability that was to prove attractive for several generations: and when the package lost its capacity to convince, when the play had lost its context, it stopped being useful.

To say that *The London Merchant* expounds not only the surface defence but also the harsh underlying philosophy of business is not to argue that this was at the front of George Lillo's mind, or that it was a preoccupation of those who recommended the play as moral instruction for the young. It is probable that to them the philosophy was transparent. In a lecture delivered in 1960, Sartre has a shrewd paragraph on the legitimate heirs of *The London Merchant*, plays committed to supporting contemporary established middle-class values.

All these bourgeois plays have always seemed to me to be chock full of philosophy; only the bourgeois don't recognize it because it's their own . . . They only see it when the philosophy is someone else's; if it's their own, well, they believe it's the truth, and they say, 'How well that is put.'

. . . The unfortunate people who by their passions have set fire to some bourgeois institution or other are blasted and disappear, or else the best of them have yielded to something that was an aberration and returns to the fold.[6]

Sartre describes how deviations from established order are explained in such plays in terms of some personal psychological weakness; like Barnwell, the criminal will be in love, or he will be mad,

and therefore, of course, such people only have to be reasoned with, or if the case proves hopeless you cut off their heads . . . the purpose of this theatre is to deprive acts . . . of their significance.[7]

This analysis of pro-bourgeois drama in the middle of the twentieth century in Paris fits *The London Merchant* very closely and explains why the play was such a success. Barnwell's theft and his act of murder are presented as being empty of significance: he rejects both crimes as soon as they are committed and he acts out all of the possibilities mentioned by Sartre. He repents his deeds, he returns to the fold, and he embraces his execution as due punishment. Millwood is likewise a very talented individual who is tragically flawed: her gifts are perverted by some devilish force. As Sartre sums up the general argument, 'No one who wants to get out of the bourgeois order for moral or political reasons has the slightest chance.'[8]

The message of the play is that any opposition to the established system will be self-destructive, being hateful to man and God. *The London Merchant* is an excellent example of the kind of useful play which was to hold its popularity for two centuries in the West. Its function was to support the received ideological basis of its own society and, of course, in the Eastern bloc its equivalent was to be developed in the concept of Socialist Realism.

The most sustained discussion of *The London Merchant* by major twentieth-century critics has come from Cleanth Brooks and Robert B. Heilman. They compare the play to *Doctor Faustus* and *Macbeth* and they argue that Barnwell should be, but is not, the centre of the drama: they see Barnwell's struggle with temptation as the crucial issue,

and therefore his role should have received the emphasis which would be conferred by fuller development. Instead, Lillo makes Barnwell share our attention with too many other people, none of them essential to our understanding of Barnwell. That is, he uses a form more suitable to depicting the *state of society* than the *struggles of an individual*. Why does he fall into this error?[9]

They complain that the didactic passages take the play away from tragedy and instead 'into the realm of the problem play, which is concerned with the issues faced by a given society at a given time'. Lillo is accused of allowing his interest in 'sociology' to destroy the tragic tone: he is 'scientist rather than artist when he describes the impact of society on Millwood', and when he allows the play to 'get involved in "propaganda" for the commercial classes'.[10]

Now here we have the clearest example of one way in which a play can lose its context. Brooks and Heilman were intelligent, well-read and perceptive critics, but their discussion of the play is vitiated by their inability to believe what Lillo says about his dramatic purpose. They find the terms of his preaching hateful and alien, and they wish he had written a different kind of play. Whereas generations of Londoners in the eighteenth century could sit through performances absorbing the philosophy and propaganda without consciously knowing that they were doing so, the ideological content of the play is now cripplingly obtrusive. Brooks and Heilman argue against the play in false terms: the fault is not that Lillo was tendentious; it is simply that his argument is now long out of date. *The London Merchant* offers the clearest example of the useful play whose temporal content has been lost for ever. The content and much of the style are as flat as ditchwater, and it could not now be performed without being a travesty of its original self. Early in the nineteenth century it already irritated Charles Lamb as being no more than a 'nauseous sermon'[11] and indeed sermons that do not confirm our own prejudices are sure to be offensive. But for several decades the play did the work it was designed for, and that fact cannot be annulled retrospectively. Sartre ends his essay 'Writing for One's Age' with a brief allegory:

It was said that the courier of Marathon had died an hour before reaching Athens. He had died and was still running; he was running dead, announced the Greek victory dead. This is a fine myth; it shows that the dead still act for a little while as if they were living. For a little while, a year, ten years, perhaps fifty years; at any rate a *finite* period; and then they are buried.[12]

The fault of *The London Merchant* is the reverse side of the central positive quality of the useful play. Being very specifically designed for a precise time and place its relevance, though extremely potent, was finite: for several decades it had an extraordinarily active life, but then it died and it was buried.

I want now to consider some modern plays of a similar kind which have had interesting experiences in and out of their contexts. For the sake of coherence I have chosen plays which take up Lillo's choice of metaphors for bourgeois capitalism. The plays have been selected for their intrinsic interest and also to achieve variety within the coherence: and because they were in performance on the London stage when this paper was written.

The younger Dumas was one of the most committed advocates of the useful play, and the great box-office success of his first attempt at the genre made it certain that the image of the prostitute would recur very frequently in nineteenth-century drama. His materials are the same as Lillo's, and his disposition is in important ways similar. He too is in support of established bourgeois morality, and his raisonneur, the elder Duval, gives a calm, forcefully argued defence of the structure of contemporary respectable society: the play as well as the character argues that Marguerite's happiness must be sacrificed for the sake of Armand and his sister; and, in more general terms, that Marguerite – sad victim of circumstance though she is – represents a pernicious force which threatens to destroy the fabric of bourgeois society. In the famous confrontation in Act 3 Scene 4 it is crucial in performance that there should be agreement rather than conflict between Georges Duval and Marguerite Gautier, for she functions as George Barnwell did and is not at all like Millwood. Duval's solid reasonableness very easily wins over Marguerite's emotional vulnerability. The process is the one described by Sartre: by becoming a lover rather than a whore she has threatened the bourgeois system and 'such people only have to be reasoned with, or if the case proves hopeless you cut off their heads'. Marguerite's tender, emotional, lyrical response to Duval's paternally wise argument is not one of opposition. Beneath all her personal pain, she knows that he is right. Like Barnwell, Marguerite repents her threat to the system and like him she embraces her own destruction as an expression of her sense of social crime. The play's main message is that marriage and the stable family unit are the crucial elements in bourgeois life. The playwright's lifetime preoccupation with this theme obviously derived from the great suffering caused him by his being illegitimate, and that powerful emotional involvement is clear in the play, as is the extent to which he is wreaking personal revenge on Marie Duplessis. The nature of the audience response invited by Dumas is determined by the complexity of Marguerite's position: she is beautiful, she is in love, she has been wronged, she is physically and emotionally vulnerable, she is warm and generous; but she represents a force that must be destroyed. *La Dame aux camélias* began life as a play about the pernicious threat of prostitution to decent bourgeois family life in Paris in the middle of the nineteenth century. Out of that context, what has it become?

In the playhouse it is a vehicle for the star actress, with the attention entirely upon her wide range of stage emotion. We admire her display of frivolous gaiety, ecstatic true love, heartbreaking pain, modest self-effacement, deep physical suffering, and loving generosity to the last. The Duvals, *père et fils*, have become mere satellites. Above all, the emotional involvement with the heroine's plight has smothered any interest in Georges Duval's social reasoning. Dumas in the retrospective preface of 1867 felt obliged to re-emphasize the play's social arguments very explicitly; but the case has proved hopeless. What has happened to Dumas's play out of context is nicely represented by the Hollywood film of 1936. In the central scene, Garbo might as well be alone in front of the cameras. She lives through all the appropriate emotions while a very frail Lionel Barrymore, apologetic and obsequious, feeds her with her cue lines. The whole social argument is lost: what was of immediate and crucial importance for Dumas and his first audience in 1852 has retained no interest at all; nothing is left but a love story in fancy costume. Garbo's performance, of course, is in the mode of Bernhardt and Duse, and Shaw sums up a tradition of acting that is irreconcilable with the useful play:

she is beautiful with the beauty of her school, and entirely . . . incredible. But the incredibility is pardonable, because, though it is all the greatest nonsense, nobody believing in it, the actress herself least of all, it is so artful, so clever, so well recognized a part of the business . . . that it is impossible not to accept it . . . [it] is not the art of making you think more highly or feel more deeply, but the art of making you admire her . . . She does not enter into the leading character, she substitutes herself for it.[13]

The irresistible glamour of this kind of theatre persuaded Meyerhold to mount his major production of Dumas's play in the late 1930s as a vehicle for Zinaide Raikh. Of course the emphasis was entirely on production values: Meyerhold shifted the play from the 1840s to the 1870s because he wanted to see Paris through the eyes of Manet, and he introduced an extremely elaborate use of music to help create the various emotional atmospheres.[14] The play was used as a framework on which to display the extraordinary theatrical imagination of the director and the irresistibly vulnerable beauty of the star. This production was being performed when the Meyerhold Theatre was closed in January 1938 following an attack in *Pravda* under the title 'An Alien Theatre', in which the president of the Supreme Committee for the Control of the Arts poured hatred and contempt on Meyerhold's work. A useful theatre of Socialist Realism was required by the Party and the nation, but a decadent aesthetic theatre was being flaunted at them.[15] The persecution and murder of Meyerhold were heinous crimes, but unlike many such crimes in Stalin's USSR they were not mindless. That committee knew what it was doing.

In November 1985 the Royal Shakespeare Company transferred its production of Pam Gems's *Camille* to the West End. It is interesting that Ms Gems should have adopted the title of the film rather than the title of Dumas's play, for she has reversed the common pattern by taking the scenario of a non-useful work and creating her own decidedly useful play. In the programme notes she tells us that she began to write for the stage in the early 1970s when she 'realized that there was no authentic work about women: they were occasionally celebrated but never convincingly explored.' Marguerite and the other women in this play give voice to their creator's 'sense of outrage' in her attempt to reclaim the truth about women's lives from 'the dustbins of male historians'. Just as Dumas's intention was to offer a moral defence of male-dominated marriage and society, and to support the male side in the conflict between the sexes, Ms Gems offers a feminist account of the sex-war that has violent intensity. Her Armand is coldly cruel in his physical abuse of all the women: he buys their bodies and mistreats them loutishly; and his capacity for affection seems to be restricted to a homosexual attachment to Prince Bela, one of his gambling and whoring companions. Similarly, among the adults in the play Marguerite's tenderness is reserved for Sophie, who has just had a knitting-needle abortion of Armand's child. He has discarded her and Prince Bela guffaws at her misery and pain. 'I've stopped bleeding', Sophie tells Marguerite, 'She only left an arm in me. I was all festered!'[16]

The frequent references to abortion (a subject avoided by Dumas, but a constant necessity for the women concerned) serve to create an atmosphere of Zolaesque naturalism, as does the rotting corpse of Marguerite dug up from the grave for identification: but they also serve as significant metaphors for the play's central themes. As is common in militant feminist drama, the most bitter indictment of men is that they deprive women of their babies. Marguerite agrees with Strindberg's Captain Adolf that the ability to bear children separates women from men as a different species of animal: it is their unique advantage and the source of men's murderous envy. Marguerite is preoccupied with the issue:

You have no idea what difference a child makes. Your life is quite changed. For ever. Of course, with a man, this can never happen . . . You're no longer alone. You're connected . . . with someone who is, and isn't you. Your own flesh. . . . you're on your own. Until, if you're a woman, you have a child. Then you're never alone again . . . Part of you. Of your body. You have a reason . . . purpose – oh, no destiny too fine, for the child!
[*Pause*]
[*Light*]: I hardly ever see him. He thinks I'm his aunt.[17]

Marguerite's history with regard to men has been uniform. From before the age of five she has been sexually violated, and her son Jean-Paul was the result of rape when she was fifteen by the sadistic marquis in whose house she was a servant. She was dismissed and had no choice but to go to Paris as a whore. As a result of her life-long victimization at their hands, she reacts with derision to the question of whether she could ever feel love for a man.

At this stage two problems arise for a spectator who knows the story-line, as they must have arisen for the playwright. How is Marguerite to feel love for Armand, since he is a man and a typical man; and what reasoning from his father could persuade her to give him up, since she has only hatred and contempt for the established society that Dumas's heroine yielded to?

The scene of confrontation with the elder Duval answers both questions. It emerges that he is the marquis who raped her; he is the father of her beloved son, who is therefore Armand's half-brother. She can love Armand because he is the nearest thing to her baby. And she can, in turn, be persuaded to reject Armand for the sake of Jean-Paul, because the lover must be sacrificed to the claim of the blood-child. The deadly irony is that to save Jean-Paul from starvation, ignorance, and a life of servitude she must give him to the brutal, loathsome elder Duval for adoption.

Marguerite: Shall I . . . shall I see him again?
Father: Perhaps . . . when he is a man. Let time create him for us. Then we'll see. A fine child. I congratulate you.[18]

Time and the father's influence will create the man Jean-Paul will turn out to be – he will be like the other two Duvals, who violently abuse women and, one way or another, deprive them of their children as an act of cruel revenge. All of this material, of course, was familiar in the theatre of fifth-century Athens, and in the work of Strindberg – the fact that the elder Duval is referred to always as the Father is a clear indication that Ms Gems has been retrieving truths from Strindberg's dustbin as well as Dumas's. But in late 1985 the very powerful effect of Ms Gems's play depended upon the fact that it was not at all a nineteenth-century play out of context. It was a fresh and startling piece doing useful work as an allegorical account of the sex-war as seen from one of the feminist points of view. In London, in November 1985, it was forcefully eloquent in its own proper context, whatever strange adventures it may have in other times and other places.

The London Merchant disappeared from the stage when its temporal context was lost. *La Dame aux camélias* has died as a useful play, but it has survived as a permanent success in very different genres in the playhouse. And this is more intensely the case in the opera-house: music can give wonderful expression to the tender lyrical suffering of Violetta Valery, but Verdi could not possibly find an effective musical equivalent for Giorgio Germont's solid bourgeois ethic. *La Traviata* is not of an age but for all time: it was never designed to do a day's work in the world.

Bernard Shaw took to writing plays with the sole purpose of reintroducing the useful play to the London stage. The theatre must be changed from a palace of second-rate pleasures into 'a factory of thought, a prompter of conscience, an elucidator of social conduct, an armory against despair and dullness, and a temple of the Ascent of Man'.[19] He shared this view of the theatre with Lillo and Dumas, but he had a very different view of society. Shaw speaks of the tradition of bourgeois literature as having passed from the whole-hearted celebration of middle-class mores initiated in the eighteenth century, through a period of criticism, but essentially positive criticism, in the middle of the nineteenth century, and then into a very aggressively negative period.

In this new phase we see the bourgeoisie, after a century and a half of complacent vaunting of its own probity . . . suddenly turning bitterly on itself with accusations of hideous sexual and commercial corruption.[20]

His choice of examples is pertinent. Speaking of Zola as a representative of the third phase, he tells us that when Zola 'found a generation whose literary notions of Parisian cocotterie were founded on Marguerite Gauthier [*sic*], he felt it to be a duty to shew them Nana. And it was a very necessary thing to do.'[21] *The London Merchant* is the play which best exemplifies that phase when useful literature set out to extol the values of bourgeois society, and *La Dame aux camélias* the second phase of positive criticism. I shall now look briefly at a handful of plays which changed the nature of the genre. The useful play, from being bourgeois propaganda, became in its most interesting examples virulently anti-bourgeois, attempting to undermine rather than bolster the ethos dominant in its society. For good ideological reasons, Lillo and Dumas found a congenial context that was subsequently lost: for good ideological reasons the plays we now turn to were contextually problematic from the beginning.

In *Mrs Warren's Profession* Shaw's main intention was to revolutionize the useful play. Lillo's purpose had been to condemn Millwood's diabolical viciousness. Dumas's purpose, and the purpose of his British followers – Boucicault, Wilkie Collins, Pinero[22] – was to blame the social evil of prostitution. Shaw's purpose is to impeach the audience:

Nothing would please our sanctimonious British public more than to throw the whole guilt of Mrs Warren's profession on Mrs Warren herself. Now the whole aim of my play is to throw that guilt on the public itself.[23]

And Shaw made it clear that he was blaming all aspects of British society. Millwood emphasized the priests and magistrates among the professional men who had shaped her life. Shaw adds the police, all property owners, the universities, newspapers (proprietors and journalists), restaurateurs, lawyers, public officials, landlords, the Church of England, shareholders, and everyone who plays a part in society, by as little as buying a box of matches, while complacently ignoring Mrs Warren's existence.

To the third, bitterly negative phase of bourgeois literature, no one contributed with such violent passion as Marx and Engels. They recurringly refer to the thousands of prostitutes who swarmed the city streets as 'the most degraded victims of the bourgeois regime',[24] and they offer ample documentation for their argument that the metaphorical alignment of prostitution with a system where everyone must buy or sell corresponds to a literal alignment in everyday life. It was a matter of course, we are told, for factory masters to exert their accepted right to treat the girls in their factories as their harems, and that being without 'consideration for the hypocrisy of society, they let nothing interfere with the exercise of their vested rights',[25] so that, for example, most of the prostitutes in Leicester 'had their employment in the mills to thank for their present situation'.[26] Commerce is war and prostitution, as a form of slavery, is the most representative mode of commerce. The spirit of Millwood informs all forty volumes of Marx and Engels's *Collected Works*. Shaw argued that

Marx's *Capital* is not a treatise on Socialism; it is a jeremiad against the *bourgeoisie*, supported by . . . such a relentless genius for denunciation as had never been brought to bear before.[27]

And the same may be said of Shaw's play.

The most devastating attack on a play meant to be useful is to deny it performance. The published text of *Mrs Warren's Profession* was rightly seen to be harmless, for a play in print is out of its only important context, and its possible dangers are neutralized. Shaw screamed for years that the stage censorship that stifled his play was misguidedly recruiting women into the trade by making certain that prostitutes were shown only when beautiful, exquisitely dressed, sumptuously accommodated, and on the added condition that they died romantically. Naturally, Shaw argues, the poor girls in the gallery will believe in the elegance and see that the untimely death is mere stage convention. This is all true, but the Lord Chamberlain's Examiner of Plays was fulfilling his function admirably for, although the play is not in the least salacious, it is single-mindedly subversive. Kitty Warren has some key speeches that exactly parallel those of Millwood. The difference is that Shaw's play reverses the effects intended. In *The London Merchant* they could be dismissed as the foul rantings of a vice-ridden social outcast. In *Mrs Warren's Profession* they are offered as simple truths:

You think people are what they pretend to be: that the way you were taught at school and college to think right and proper is the way things really are. But it's not: it's all only a pretence, to keep the cowardly slavish common run of people quiet ... Vivie: the big people, the clever people, the managing people, all know it. They do as I do, and think what I think.[28]

Kitty Warren, like Millwood and her Satanic precursor, has adopted the motto 'Evil be thou my good':[29] and the play attributes the same motto to the entire establishment.

The licence for *Mrs Warren's Profession* was withheld for more than thirty years, and when the play was at last performed in public in London it was received as a quaintly interesting period piece. Shaw's response characteristically veiled his bitter exasperation with good-natured exuberance:

the Press assured us all that we might now enjoy the play as a striking early specimen of my well-known artistic virtuosity, as of course the state of things it dramatizes has long since passed away. I was irresistibly reminded of the cheerful village boy who, when they told him the tragedy of the Gospels, said 'Oh well, since it happened so long ago and it's all so dreadful, let's hope it aint true.'[30]

The play had received its first public performance 3,000 miles from its intended context, but it still earned much of its invited response. In 1905 the New York police arrested the cast and they were tried on a charge of indecency. Reviewers used that same word and added 'morally rotten', 'immoral and degenerate', the play was a 'pig stye' which glorified

debauchery.[31] At the end of the one New York performance there were
cheers of rabid support and outraged catcalls of abuse. At that one
performance the play was useful: it touched exposed nerves and prompted
violent public debate.

In 1985 the play came into the repertory of the National Theatre. It
was performed in the Olivier, with its enormous stage and 1,200 seats.
The costumes and set designs were very attractive – Victorian clothes and
furniture look glamorous on stage, and in such costumes the actors move
with elegance and panache. The play calls for four very small acting
spaces – a cottage garden, part of the cottage interior, a vicarage garden,
and an office in the City of London, where Vivie retires to do the work
that Barnwell was once engaged in. The small acting spaces were
surrounded by huge black and white projected scenes that successfully
suggested late Victorian photographs. Clearly the director and designer
(despairing of making the play speak directly to a 1985 audience) resolved
to put the whole action into a frame that would emphasize the temporal
and temperamental distance of the piece. Every seat was sold and the
audience had a very pleasant evening. I made a point of seeing the
production with forty undergraduates who did not know the play. In the
following seminars they expressed only warm enthusiasm: they admired
the zest, the linguistic and visual stylishness, the aura of intelligent
vivacity, the ability of the actors to follow Shaw in taking Kitty and Vivie,
Crofts and Praed, Gardner and Frank in and out of caricature, mixing
moments of sharp insight into social pressures with moments of senti-
ment, all within a general medium of good-natured comedy. No one felt
personally accused or that the play had anything to say about contemporary England with its mass unemployment where there is talk, started
sanguinely by the Prime Minister and taken up with bitter irony in
socialist circles, of a return to Victorian values. What the audience saw
and enjoyed was a comedy of manners.

Shaw explains his purpose in writing the three *Plays Unpleasant*: 'I have
shewn middle-class respectability . . . fattening on the poverty of the slum
as flies fatten on filth.'[32] In 1943 Sartre used the same Old Testament
image to metaphor the lives of collaborators during the Nazi occupation of
France. Orestes, like George Barnwell, murders the figures representing
parental authority, Aegisthus and Clytemnestra, standing for German
oppressors and Frenchmen in the puppet government. Unlike Barnwell,
Orestes rejoices in his murders and in his rebellion against authority.

In 1943 the Pétain regime and its supporters in the Church were telling
the French people that the Nazi dominance of their country had moral as

well as military might. There were national sins to be atoned for and Frenchmen must do penance by accepting the inevitability of German rule: newspapers, radio broadcasts, and posters conducted a war of black propaganda with the purpose of spreading a sense of national worthlessness and guilt, which in turn would lead to passive acquiescence, and obeisance. Sartre's play spoke in unmistakable terms to its first audience. The nation must reject the anti-French propaganda. Orestes' determination to commit the murders and to glory in them was an allegorical incitement for the audience to reject all thought of national guilt.

George Barnwell has a crucial line:

I now am – what I've made myself. (p. 74)

Lillo is thinking of Macbeth, who destroyed his existence as a person and opened before him a desert of despair. Orestes uses a similar formula to the opposite purpose:

My crime is wholly mine; I claim it as my own . . . it is my glory, my life's work . . .
As for your sins and your remorse . . . I take them all upon me . . . your faithful flies have left you, and come to me. Farewell, my people. Try to reshape your lives. All here is new, all must begin anew.[33]

Again the crimes cause despair; but whereas that was the despondent end for Macbeth and Barnwell, for Orestes and his audience it is a necessary phase on an optimistic journey, since human life and freedom begin on the far side of despair.[34]

Electra represents the broad mass of Frenchmen who disliked the occupation but were passive: Orestes comes to represent the active resistance fighter, and his great rhetorical speeches celebrating personal freedom and pride in national identity must have wonderfully thrilled the play's first audience. Here was theatre at its most immediately useful. Sartre summed up his central argument:

Anyone who wished to work for the future should act in the Resistance, without repentance, without any feeling of remorse.[35]

A minor irony was that the play was first performed in the theatre named as a memorial to the art of Sarah Bernhardt. A major irony arose soon after the war when *The Flies* was performed in the zone of Germany under French occupation, and then in Berlin. The play enjoyed a great success, but there were serious doubts about the reasons for its warm reception by German audiences. One critic put it bluntly:

Do not deceive yourself Monsieur Sartre; your play's success is largely due . . . to the fact that it bestows a gigantic pardon, a summary general absolution . . . Are you conscious of assuming . . . the responsibility for preventing, by your opposition to repentance, the German people from . . . renewing its moral existence?

. . . the Nazis wanted to instill remorse into your country. In our country . . . they would like to inhibit it, and they are now forging explanations which, beyond good or evil, are preparing the next massacre.[36]

This is another way for a useful play to be out of context. *The London Merchant* became ridiculous and unactable. *La Dame aux camélias* dwindled into a costume romance, *Mrs Warren's Profession* became an ideologically empty vehicle for elegant design and stylish acting. *The Flies* was actually made to stand on its head, when it was received as an incitement for Germans to forget or even deny the crimes of the Third Reich.

In November 1985 one of the major drama schools in London used *The Flies* for a diploma performance. Since as a teacher and examiner I see more than fifty such performances each year, I am familiar with the circumstances. Partly because I was for once a visiting stranger, but mainly because the present subject was on my mind, I was shocked to realize for the first time how utterly irrelevant the play's meaning is on such occasions. The audience comprises relatives and friends of the cast, teachers concerned about the development of their students' skills, theatrical agents looking for new blood to inject into their lists of clients, and examiners who are grading performances, for there are gold medals to be won and careers to be launched. To ask the question 'What did you make of the play?' would be as bizarre as it would have been if put to Mrs Abraham Lincoln after that interrupted performance at Ford's Theatre on 14 April 1865.

Sartre was always very conscious of the danger of a play being performed out of context. In retrospect he spoke very warmly about his first experience as a playwright. In 1940 he was a prisoner in Germany and at his first attempt, in *Bariona*, he achieved a paradigmatically useful play. It was written, directed and acted by prisoners, with scenery painted by prisoners: it successfully deceived their enemy gaolers and addressed the audience on the subject of their concerns as French political prisoners. Sartre uses phrases that remind us of the first audience of *The London Merchant*: 'as I addressed my comrades across the footlights . . . when I suddenly saw them so remarkably silent and attentive, I realized what theatre ought to be'. And yet he makes the point that the play was entirely for that unique occasion: 'so much so that I have never since then permitted it to be staged'.[37]

In 1945 Sartre visited the United States. His main response to the bastion of capitalism was to write *The Respectful Prostitute*, in which a white woman is the key witness in the approaching trial of a black man falsely accused of having raped her. In the first version of the play she is persuaded by the son of the Southern Senator to testify against the black man. Sartre wrote the piece as a didactic farce, with the prostitute as an anti-hero who chooses lies rather than truth. But for its long, successful run in New York it was presented as a melodrama (thus reversing the sea change suffered by *The London Merchant* out of context: for Pip in *Great Expectations*[38] as for many in the nineteenth century, the melodrama had become a farce). Sartre therefore rewrote his play when a production was planned for Moscow in the early 1960s. 'I knew too many young working-class people who had seen the play and had been disheartened because it ended sadly.'[39] So Moscow audiences were presented with a heroine who refuses to give false testimony, refuses to yield to the oppressing capitalists, to betray class solidarity, to work against the coming revolution. What in New York succeeded as a sentimental prostitute-melodrama had as great a success in Moscow as a didactic Communist Party sermon. Two such contrasting contexts demanded two very different versions of the play. Sartre attended the 400th performance in Moscow, by special invitation.

Sartre tells us that for almost thirty years he had had a very false impression of Brecht's first great international success, because he had seen the play in a misleading context:

... look at the difference between the Brecht of today [1959] and the Brecht of the time when *The Threepenny Opera* was being performed in Paris. Nowadays we know what Brecht is. But when we saw *The Threepenny Opera* with Simone de Beauvoir before the war, we only saw what is usually called a social satire. It was very amusing. It was delightful. But Brecht's real intention was entirely lost on us. More than twenty years ago [1930] after I'd seen the play – and here's a prime example of a play being changed by its audience – I thought it was purely anarchist, for the bourgeois are all corrupt, the chief of police is a crook; but on the other hand, the play shows us the masses as beggars and their leaders as thieves who deceive them. I entirely missed the positive aspect of this two edged criticism, as indeed the whole audience did at the time.[40]

The Threepenny Opera, however, is deeply problematic. It has always been extremely popular, but there is a question mark over the issue of whether it ever has functioned as a useful play. The first audiences at the Theater am Schiffbauerdamm in 1928 seem to have enjoyed the piece as Sartre and de Beauvoir did – as a delightful, amusing, and politically weightless romp. In the 1985 season of Promenade Concerts in the Albert Hall it was received with great enthusiasm in the form of the *Kleine Dreigroschenmusik*. The exuberance in the audience was unmistakable. After Janáček and Bartók, they delighted in being offered something so gorgeously culinary, such irresistible melodies to whistle on the way home. I've seen the Berliner Ensemble rendition and perhaps a dozen other productions of the opera before the 1986 National Theatre version, and the effect has always been the same. The play, to the extent that there *is* a useful play, is fixed permanently out of context by being immersed in that paralysingly charming and witty music. Brecht's life-long fear of the effect of music on his plays was well founded. But rather than consider *The Threepenny Opera* in production, I want finally to look at the fate of an American piece entirely inspired by it.

In December 1935, in New York, Brecht spent a productive evening with Marc Blitzstein and his wife Eva Goldbeck. They had both translated some of Brecht's work and Blitzstein was later to make the version of *The Threepenny Opera* that ran in New York for seven years. On the evening in question Blitzstein performed a song inspired by *Die Dreigroschenoper*. Called 'The Nickel Under Your Foot', it portrayed the song's persona, a young street-walker, as the epitome of American capitalist society: for her as for everyone else the difference between eating and starving depends upon having, rather than not having, a nickel. Survival, as in Lillo's London, depends upon money, however gained.

Brecht listened to the song and was encouraging:

Very good so far, but why not a whole play about all sorts of prostitution – the press, the clergy, and so on.[41] To literal prostitution you must add figurative prostitution – the sell-out of one's talent and dignity to the powers that be.

Blitzstein was inspired by this enthusiasm, and the resultant opera, *The Cradle Will Rock*, was dedicated to Brecht. On paper, the piece was much admired by progressive theatre practitioners in New York, in particular by Orson Welles, who was then just twenty-two years old and at the height of his career as a stage director. The trouble was that it seemed to demand an extremely expensive production. John Houseman and Hallie Flanagan, however, were won over and they made the extravagantly provocative decision to mount the opera with government dollars, under the aegis of the Work Progress Administration. The WPA was the national scheme set up to preserve American democracy by getting potentially revolutionary people into government-sponsored jobs, so that they would support the system rather than threaten to overthrow it.[42]

Orson Welles's production concepts were extremely grandiose: to portray the wide range of locations he 'devised an extravagant scenic scheme that called for a triple row of three-dimensional velour portals between which narrow, glass-bottomed, fluorescent platforms, loaded with scenery and props, slid smoothly past each other'.[43] There was to be a cast of sixty, a twenty-eight piece orchestra and elaborate choreography: star performers were especially bought in to lead the resident company. Welles was determined to make a Broadway Musical that would cap his wildly successful 'Voodoo' *Macbeth*.

In 1937, during the months of rehearsal, industrial strife increased throughout the country, especially in the steel industry. As its opening approached, *The Cradle Will Rock*, set in a representative American city called Steeltown, increasingly became a violent expression of the extreme left-wing case in the midst of a national labour crisis. The steel lobbyists went to work and word came from Washington that the production must not open. The doors of Maxine Elliott's Theatre were closed and WPA guards occupied the building: no scenery, props or costumes must be used or removed. Eighteen thousand tickets had been sold in advance, mainly to government-sponsored organizations. Washington informed the groups that their bookings must be cancelled.

Orson Welles and John Houseman decided to take over as independent producers, resigning as agents of the WPA, and to persevere against all the pressures. The musicians' and actors' unions then forbade their members to take part in any performance under the change of management, since they were federal employees.

An hour before the arranged time of curtain-up, there was no theatre, there were no sets, props, costumes, actors or musicians. There were hundreds of potential audience members and dozens of newspaper reporters in the street. And then there was a miracle of improvisation. A neglected empty theatre was found, and a tinny upright piano was hired. The crowd made its way from 39th Street to the Venice Theatre on 59th and Seventh Avenue, growing in numbers to 2,000 as it went.

Orson Welles addressed the over-filled auditorium, outlining the production as planned and rehearsed, and also explaining that Marc Blitzstein would play all of the music on the bare stage on the old piano, and perform the whole play by himself. The first number, 'I'm checkin' home now', belongs to the young street-walker: she has a factory job for two days a week, but has turned to prostitution because it's also nice to eat on the other five days. A few lines into the song, Olive Stanton, 'a thin girl in a green dress with dyed red hair', began to sing her part as Moll: 'stiff with fear, only half audible at first in the huge theatre but gathering strength with every note'. John Houseman remembers 'the throat-catching, sickenly exciting quality of that moment'.[44] Other performers followed her lead, and the performance was acted throughout the auditorium wherever the individual members of the cast happened to be sitting. Archibald Macleish later recalled the event with amazed pride:

> There was no audience. There was instead a room full of men and women as eager in the play as any actor. As actors rose in one part and another of the auditorium the faces of these men and women made new and changing circles around them. They were well-wishing faces: human faces such as man may sometimes see among partisans of the same cause or friends who hope for good things for one another.[45]

The response was one of ecstatic jubilation that spilled out onto the street. The performance was not reviewed in the entertainment sections of the New York newspapers. Instead, it filled the headlines of the front pages, and made history as the greatest success of any American exercise in useful theatre: 'WPA Actors Take Over Play, Act from Seats', 'Strike Play Opens Despite WPA Ban', 'WPA Opera Put on as Private Show'.[46]

Here is a very different effect of a play losing its intended context. If the production had gone forward as planned, the glamorous Maxine Elliott's Theatre with its stunning stage designs and rich Broadway production values would have provided a paragraph in the history of the American Musical. Instead it found an audience as involved, as committed, as those prisoners who helped to create Sartre's first play: and apart from mere theatrical lore, it found a place in American political history, being remembered by non-theatre people almost fifty years later as a great moment of social defiance. By accident and by desperate improvisation, a useful play discovered its most effective context.

In 1985 it had another interesting shift in context when John Houseman, the original producer, brought it to London with the New York Acting Company. It took its place in the season of plays at the Old Vic, or rather at the very new and different Old Vic as it has been restored at the cost of £2 million by 'Honest' Ed Mirvish, a Canadian supermarket tycoon who says he is in the theatre business to make money. The Old Vic is now the most sumptuously glamorous playhouse in London, and the seats are appropriately expensive. The customers are very different from those of the nearby National Theatre, in that they buy tickets on subscription for each production in the season, and are lured by the prospect of seeing stars of film and television on stage – Deborah Kerr, Peter Ustinov, or in this case John Houseman, whose career as an actor began when he was seventy-one years old but has led him to the main role in a very popular, long running television series. The production, with a bare stage and one upright piano, was an attempt to recreate the poor-theatre success of the first improvised performance. The prosperous middle-aged audience looked very fine in their Liberty blouses and Jaeger skirts. They applauded politely, but they were very puzzled. If the piece had been tried at the Roundhouse or even at the Royal Court during the miners' strike, it might have been more than a song-and-dance show with what for that audience was perversely eccentric subject matter. It proved to be a good example of what one of our most thoughtful actors has pinpointed as the perennial blight in modern theatre:

Too often plays have been brought forward like corpses, rouged and bewigged, their dead limbs manipulated from behind to give the illusion of life.[47]

The Cradle Will Rock did its work in Manhattan in 1937; at the Old Vic in 1985 its limbs were dead and, unlike the man from Marathon in Sartre's allegory, it had no useful news to bring.

In the twentieth century our theatre is extremely eclectic; we are as a matter of principle interested in the plays of all lands and all periods, so that it was natural in 1909 for the committee advising on the establishment of a British National Theatre to put more emphasis on the need to revive international plays of the near and distant past than on the production of new work written for contemporary London.[48]

This busy eclecticism has of course raised some difficulties. In 1948, when he was at last working in a German language theatre after fifteen years of exile, Brecht was daunted by the difficulty of establishing a coherent style of production, of creating a normal 'context' in the sense we are considering. In the *Antigonemodell* he laments the confusion of theatrical procedures in this age 'which exhibits plays of every period and every country and invents the most disparate styles for them, without having any style of its own'.[49]

It is easy for us to overlook the fact that our extreme catholicity means that our theatre cannot have a context in the way that contexts have existed in periods in which there was long continuity of dramatic genres, where the content and style were fairly well defined, and where only plays written for the present were performed.

In London in the 1980s it is of course very interesting each week to see three or four plays from the world repertory in competent productions. But for almost all of the time our major playhouses are like museums, and sometimes like mausoleums. There are occasional opportunities for intense immediacy in our theatre – the first nights of *Bariona* and *The Cradle Will Rock* were astonishing examples – but for most of the time plays for us, our own as well as all the others, are out of context.

Notes

1 'Should social problems be freely dealt with in the Drama?' *The Humanitarian*, VI, May 1895.

2 *Sartre on Theater*, ed. Michel Contat and Michel Rybalka (London: Quartet Books, 1976), p. 45. *Un théâtre de situations*, Jean-Paul Sartre, textes rassemblés, établis, présentés et annotés par Michel Contat et Michel Rybalka (Paris: Gallimard, 1973), p. 69. In future notes references will be to the English translation, with the original French volume page numbers in parentheses: the model for this reference being *Sartre on Theater*, p. 45 (p. 69).

3 *Schriften zum Theatre 5* (Frankfurt am Main: Suhrkamp Verlag, 1963), p. 241.

4 George Lillo, *The London Merchant*, ed. William H. McBurney (London: Edward Arnold, 1965), p. 3. Page numbers for future references to this volume are given in parentheses in the text, following quotations.

5 *The Weekly Register*, Saturday, August 21, 1731.

6 *Sartre on Theater*, p. 96 (p. 124).

7 *Sartre on Theater*, p. 96 (p. 125).

8 *Sartre on Theater*, p. 96 (pp. 124–5).

9 Cleanth Brooks and Robert Bechtold Heilman, *Understanding Drama* (New York: Holt, Rinehart and Winston, 1948), p. 181.

10 *Ibid.*, p. 183.

11 'If this note could hope to meet the eye of any of the Managers, I would entreat and beg of them, in the name of both the galleries, that this insult upon the morality of the common people of London should cease to be eternally repeated in the holiday weeks. Why are the 'Prentices of this famous and well-governed city, instead of an amusement, to be treated over and over again with the nauseous sermon of George Barnwell? . . . Were I an uncle, I should not much like a nephew of mine to have such an example placed before his eyes. It is really making uncle-murder too trivial to exhibit as done upon such slight motives; – it is attributing too much to such characters as Millwood; – it is putting things into the heads of good young men, which they would never otherwise have dreamed of. Uncles that think any thing of their lives, should fairly petition the Chamberlain against it.' Charles and Mary Lamb, *Miscellaneous Prose*, ed. E. V. Lucas (London: Methuen, 1912), p. 118.

12 Jean-Paul Sartre, *What is Literature?* trans. Bernard Frechtman (London: Methuen, 1967), p. 238.

13 George Bernard Shaw, *Plays and Players: Essays on the Theatre*, selected by A. C. Ward (London: Oxford University Press, 1952), pp. 34–5.

14 Vsevolod Meyerhold, *Meyerhold on Theatre*, trans. Edward Braun (London: Eyre Methuen, 1978), pp. 274–8.

15 *Meyerhold on Theatre*, p. 250.

16 Pam Gems, *Three Plays: Piaf, Camille, Loving Women* (Harmondsworth: Penguin Books, 1985), p. 86.

17 *Ibid.*, p. 107.
18 *Ibid.*, p. 136.
19 'Our Theatres in the Nineties', *The Complete Prefaces of Bernard Shaw* (London: Paul Hamlyn, 1965), p. 779.
20 'Three Plays by Brieux', *The Complete Prefaces of Bernard Shaw*, p. 196.
21 *Ibid.*, p. 198.
22 Dion Boucicault, *Formosa*; Wilkie Collins, *New Magdalen*; Arthur Wing Pinero, *The Second Mrs Tanqueray.*
23 *The Bodley Head Bernard Shaw: Collected Plays with their Prefaces*, ed. Dan H. Laurence, 7 vols. (London: Max Reinhardt, 1970–4), vol. 1, p. 254.
24 Karl Marx and Friedrich Engels, *Colleted Works*, 40 vols. (London: Lawrence and Wishart, 1975–83), vol. 4, p. 422.
25 *Ibid.*, p. 422.
26 *Ibid.*, p. 441.
27 Archibald Henderson, *George Bernard Shaw: Man of the Century* (New York: Appleton-Century-Crofts, 1956), p. 219.
28 *The Bodley Head Bernard Shaw*, vol. 1, p. 351.
29 *Paradise Lost*, IV, 110.
30 *The Bodley Head Bernard Shaw*, vol. 1, p. 366.
31 *Shaw: The Critical Heritage*, ed. T. F. Evans (London: Routledge and Kegan Paul, 1976), pp. 139–40.
32 *The Bodley Head Bernard Shaw*, vol. 1, p. 33.
33 Jean-Paul Sartre, *Altona, Men Without Shadows, The Flies*, trans. Sylvia Leeson, George Leeson, Kitty Black and Stuart Gilbert (Harmondsworth: Penguin Books, 1962), pp. 315–6.
34 *Ibid.*, p. 311.
35 *Sartre on Theater*, p. 195 (pp. 232–3).
36 *Ibid.*, pp. 193, 195 (pp. 230, 232).
37 *Ibid.*, p. 39 (pp. 62, 61).
38 Chapter 15.
39 *Sartre on Theater*, p. 134 (p. 165).
40 *Ibid.*, p. 72 (p. 99).
41 James K. Lyon, *Bertolt Brecht in America* (London: Methuen, 1982), p. 16.
42 John Houseman, *Run-Through: A Memoir* (London: John Lane, 1972), pp. 245–6. The factual information about the 1937 production of *The Cradle Will Rock* is derived from this volume, from David Ewen, *Complete Book of the American Musical Theater* (London: Museum Press, 1959), and from Hallie Flanagan, *Arena: The Story of the Federal Theater* (New York: Limelight Editions, 1985).
43 *Run-Through*, p. 248.
44 *Ibid.*, p. 268.
45 *Ibid.*, p. 273.
46 Barbara Leaming, *Orson Welles: A Biography* (London: Weidenfeld and Nicolson, 1985), p. 138.
47 Simon Callow, *Being an Actor* (London: Methuen, 1984), p. 220.

48 See Bernard Crick, 'The Political in Britain's Two National Theatres', in *Drama and Society*, Themes in Drama, vol. 1, ed. James Redmond (Cambridge: Cambridge University Press, 1979), p. 169.

49 *Brecht on Theatre*, trans. John Willett (London: Methuen, 1974), p. 214.

Mimesis, mirror, double

HANNA SCOLNICOV

In today's pluralistic theatre, so-called classical plays continue to be performed side by side with avant-garde pieces. Clearly, the old plays do not spring from present day issues and are not concerned with contemporary social, political or scientific problems. Yet, we often find them strangely relevant. Despite their outdated mores and beliefs, they seem to carry on a dialogue with us, reaching over the gap of centuries to confront us with the different dramatic positions taken up by their protagonists.

The idea of reproducing old plays and regarding them either as *exempla* of what a play ought to be, or as repositories of human experience which is pertinent to our own time, lies at the heart of classicism. One may retrace this theoretical attitude to Horace, who recommended 'the study of Greek models',[1] the 'treating of well-worn subjects',[2] and 'imitating another writer' without falling into the trap of 'a slavish translation'.[3] Horace's concept of *imitatio* is in itself an imitation of the Aristotelian *mimesis*. Horace advocated the imitation of literary Greek models, whereas for Aristotle *mimesis* was 'the imitation of an action', i.e., the imitation of the significant structure of human action itself.

The notion of artistic *mimesis* as an imitation of a classical writer was taken up from Horace by the Renaissance thinkers. Roger Ascham distinguished between imitation as a 'faire livelie painted picture of the life of everie degree of man' and imitation of the choice authors who wrote in Greek and Latin.[4] It is to the second sense of imitation that he turned his attention, citing, among others, the example of the relationship between the plays of Terence and Menander. According to Ascham and many others, the Latin imitations of Greek models set a classical precedent for the procedure of imitation itself.

In England, the neo-classical view of translation was largely shaped by Chapman's translations of Homer and Hesiod, and by Ben Jonson's theorizing. For Jonson, poesy is

The Queen of Arts: which had her Originall from heaven, received thence from the *'Ebrews*, and had in prime estimation with the *Greeks*, transmitted to the *Latines*, and all Nations, that profess'd civility.   (*Timber* 2382 ff.)

In a poem which pays tribute to Chapman's translation of Hesiod, Jonson praises the translator for having found the way to bring the treasure from the Greek coast to the shores of England. In his view, Chapman has not stolen or plagiarized the classics but has enriched English literature by grafting it onto Greek literature.

One of Jonson's comical satires, *Poetaster*, is devoted to the question of where translation ends and imitation begins, where imitation ends and plagiarism begins. For Jonson, 'imitation' is not a derogatory term, but refers to a consciously creative effort – an effort to re-create in a modern language a classical literary work. He himself practises imitation in those scenes in the play which are avowed transpositions of Horace's Satires into the dramatic mode. Imitation is thus shown to be a legitimate literary procedure. Plagiarism, on the other hand, is an unacknowledged misappropriation of another poet's work, a literary theft.

Jonson's poetic disciples, Alexander Pope and John Dryden, developed imitation into an accepted literary mode, standing between original invention on the one hand and translation on the other. Dryden, himself an important translator and adapter, distinguished between three modes of translation:

metaphrase, or literal translation; paraphrase, in which the sense rather than the words of the original is followed; and imitation, in which both the sense and the words are altered at will.[5]

Western art has periodically rejuvenated itself by going back to classical culture as to the source and reinterpreting it. Periodical reinterpretations of the ancients have inspired new artistic movements. But in our century there has grown a general uneasiness with the old forms, a feeling that they have worn out and are no longer adequate for the expression of our experiences and perceptions. Playwrights and theorists have felt that one must look to a 'naive' art in order to find alternative forms. In their search for alternative forms of theatre, some of them discovered the folk theatre and the theatre of far-off, exotic lands. Likewise, in their flight from classicism, twentieth-century painters and sculptors have turned for inspiration to the naiveté of children's works and to the primitivism of African masques. In fact, naive art can be defined as art that has no knowledge of a classical heritage.

Early medieval drama wears just such a look of innocence about it. Twelfth- and thirteenth-century plays like *Le jeu d'Adam* or *Le jeu de la feuillée* possess a youthful exuberance which is no doubt due to their artless simplicity and directness. Of course, it cannot be said that medieval theatre had no conventions, but these were independent of the conventions of the classical tradition.

With its variety of forms and genres, the medieval theatre can serve as a reservoir of possible alternatives to the classical theatre. It is unique in Western civilization in its development *ex nihilo* of dramatic forms irreconcilable with the classical tradition, in complete oblivion of the theatrical culture of the past. With a blissful lack of awareness of the existence of an institutionalized 'viewing-place' in antiquity, the Middle Ages developed a diversity of physical acting spaces. Like the variety of dramatic forms, the different acting places provide us today with suggestions for other environments for performances. The possibility of performing in a diversity of existing architectural spaces, such as churches, hangars, ruined castles, or simply in the street, radically alters the very concept of theatre, shaking up our basic assumptions about its artistic nature and social function.

But the classical tradition still holds its ground, tempting us with its supportive structure while threatening our creative freedom with its stifling conventions. It is conservative to its roots, conservative in its backward-looking perspective. Even Aristotle spoke of the old proven myths as providing the best plots for tragedy. The number of plays on Oedipus, Antigone or Medea, both ancient and modern, can bear out the acuteness of his observation. Aristotelian *mimesis* continues to haunt the critical scene, demanding to be reckoned with, refusing to be disregarded.

Aristotle thought that tragedy imitates life, 'and life consists in action . . . for it is by their actions that [men] are happy or the reverse'.[6] Plato's criticism of tragedy, and of art in general, is directed precisely at its superficial realism, at its imitating external appearances instead of representing the true nature of things.[7] Plato's descending scale of truth, as imitation is piled on imitation, has left the rational Westerner gaping at the man-made artifact, wondering what it is that it represents and wherein lies its truth.

The bold attempt of the late Middle Ages and early Renaissance to tackle truth frontally, through allegory, through direct impersonation of ideas, is of a Platonic rather than Aristotelian nature. It is an attempt at cutting through the mimetic regression, to confront the Ideas directly. Allegorical plays, like the Dutch *Elckerlyk* or *Man's Desire and Fleeting Beauty* or the English *Wit and Wisdom*, depict abstractions instead of characters, and substitute scholastic debate for dramatic action. The unending quirks of human nature are replaced by religious and ethical absolutes. But this approach to drama is too artificial and dogmatic for contemporary taste and cannot serve as a modern solution to the Platonic quandary.

For Aristotle, tragedy was a particular kind of *mimesis*, distinguished by its medium, manner of representation and object of imitation from other art forms. What he failed to note was that, according to his own conception, theatre is the most mimetic of arts. This aspect was plainly revealed by the realistic theatre of the nineteenth century, which made the stage mimic life: the actor's movements and expressions became the direct representations of living gestures and speech. The imitation of appearances, the giving up of the struggle for the inner truth, was an instance of the belief that man's true nature could be completely expressed by externals, that there was in fact nothing beyond them, that the 'inner life' of a character, his thoughts and his secrets were reducible to observable, objective reality. Classicism had thus developed from humanism to scientific rationalism which had no use for the mysterious, the mystical or the metaphysical.

In realistic theatre, imitation had come to mean the imitation of externals or of texture. It could no longer mean the imitation of significant inner structure simply because nothing remained hidden 'inside' – science had externalized, objectified and quantified what had once been considered qualitative and inherent. Although dealing with individuals, realistic theatre also laid a claim to universality, showing how individual behaviour can be understood in terms of general economic, sociological, psychological and even biological laws. No less than Renaissance theatre, realistic theatre too is a direct descendant of the classical tradition.

It is this quality of universality, transcending the particular and individual, which makes the plays written in the classical and humanist tradition transferrable from culture to culture. On the other hand, the medieval mystery cycle which deals with the most comprehensive of subjects, the history of the world and of mankind from Creation to Doomsday, is dependent for its full effect on local presentation in York or in Chester and on an audience which shares its religious outlook.

In his dramatization of the murder of Julius Caesar, a particular historical event, Shakespeare underlines the power of drama to transcend geographical and cultural boundaries. In a passage for which there is no precedent in Plutarch, but which seems to be pure Shakespearean invention,[8] Cassius smears his hands with dead Caesar's blood and declares:

> . . . How many ages hence
> Shall this our lofty scene be acted over,
> In states unborn, and accents yet unknown!
>
> *Julius Caesar*, III.i. 111–13

Here the playwright manipulates the audience's response. By insisting that the murder we have just witnessed was the real thing and an object of future *mimesis*, the actor playing Cassius reminds us that this is all play and not in earnest. The effect is one of alienating the spectators from the immediacy of the shocking experience they have just undergone, and reminding them that they are in fact watching an English 'imitation' of the Roman assassination. This effect is further heightened when the play is performed in translation.

Cassius's words point to the sacrificial nature of the killing of Caesar, the climactic scene of the play. Behind the juggling with illusion and reality lies Shakespeare's serious claim for the primacy of his *mimesis*: whatever the precise historical facts, it is Shakespeare's reconstruction which remains as a sort of collective memory of the event, re-enacting time and again the drama of the killing of the would-be emperor. It is immaterial that the dipping of hands in Caesar's blood is unhistorical. Here, poetic truth gains the upper hand over historical fact. The event gains its meaning and implications through the particular artistic shaping. The theatrical image has come to stand for the actual murder, long since lost from sight and accessible only as historical narrative.

Shakespeare's awareness of the power of the visual and symbolic image he created is expressed in the game of mirrors played by him with his own imitation of the event:

> How many times shall Caesar bleed in sport,
> That now on Pompey's basis lies along,
> No worthier than the dust!
>
> *Julius Caesar*, III.i. 114–16

In this speech, Brutus too is suggesting that what we are viewing is the real assassination of which there will be mock theatrical representations in the future, which is our present. Beyond the artistic playfulness, there is the sense of the importance of repeated performance, of the ritualization of the murder of Caesar, of the codification of this single moment in history as a symbolic gesture.

The same idea of the play as the preservation of a collective memory is expressed in the totality of *Hamlet*, the play that Shakespeare wrote in the wake of *Julius Caesar*. Here, a perfect murder has been committed, one that has left no trace. Except for the murderer, Claudius, no one has witnessed the event, and Claudius naturally wishes to forget; except for Hamlet, the son and heir, no one suspects that the death was anything but natural. The Ghost appears in order to convey the memory of the murder to his son, who now becomes the repository of that memory. This is why he is constantly admonished to 'Remember'.

Hamlet's dramatization of his father's murder is based on the story as narrated by the Ghost. Similarly, Shakespeare's reconstruction of Caesar's murder is based on Plutarch's historical account. Hamlet makes use of an old play, *The Murder of Gonzago*, into which he inserts a few lines of his own. The stylized manner of the inner play estranges and distances it, an effect similar to that produced by the reference to future performances of Caesar's assassination. Hamlet achieves his desired effect when Claudius recognizes the relationship between the imitation and his own criminal act. Shakespeare achieves *his* desired effect too, forcing the audience to accept the murder of Gonzago as the representation of Hamlet Senior's murder. The Ghost's expository narrative is dramatized only in the middle of the play, belatedly materializing in front of our eyes. Jostled out of its natural time and place, formalized, framed and alienated, the scene succeeds in codifying the essential experience of the heinous murder and collaboration.

Here too, as in *Julius Caesar*, Shakespeare establishes the supremacy of theatrical expression. Although it is clear that *The Murder of Gonzago* is a different, supposedly existing play, which is not based on what has taken place in Elsinore, yet it is its depiction of the murder which becomes stamped in our imaginations as the true representation. It is the imaginary, artistic concretization of the event rather than its historical documentation that has the power to stir and influence not only contemporary but also future audiences.

In a unique passage, Shakespeare provides us with his protagonist's ideas on theatrical theory. Being a dramatic utterance, the views should be examined within their dramatic context. Known as 'Hamlet's advice to the Players', this monologue serves as a short defence of poesy, explaining its special function:

> to hold as 'twere the mirror up to nature; to show virtue her own feature, scorn her own image, and the very age and body of the time his form and pressure.
>
> *Hamlet*, III.ii, 18–20

Art as a mirror of life was a familiar metaphor in the Renaissance, and Hamlet's view is derived from Cicero's oft quoted definition of comedy as *imitatio vitae, speculum consuetudinis, imago veritatis*.[9] *Speculum* and *imitatio* are used here synonymously, indicating that imitation is to be understood as a reflection of human life. What we can see in this mirror, however, is not a simple image but one that accentuates ethical and social aspects.

Hamlet's phrasing sounds misleadingly smooth and unproblematic, but it is in fact full of critical cruxes: Which 'nature' does the mirror reflect? Is it the playwright's own contemporary society, the social mores of the past, or our own ethical problems? Is *Julius Caesar* a play about power and succession in Rome, in Elizabethan times, or today? Is *Hamlet* a play about Elizabethan society, feudal Denmark, or about present day political problems? Is it a true mirror, one in which I shall find myself reflected, whether virtuous or scornful? That would certainly make the play highly subjective and very much reader- or spectator-oriented. Furthermore, it would mean that the play should be seen as an elastic and flexible structure, which is impressed by every age into a different form. Thus, the mirror image, although it appears at first to tow the concepts of *mimesis* and imitation, turns out to be a rather startling, novel conception.

The idea of the play as a collective memory of the past seems to contradict the idea of the play as a mirror of present day society, but in fact these are complementary notions, which help us understand ourselves and understand the past by relating the two to each other, by seeing the one in terms of the other. Such is the basic assumption underlying Shakespeare's histories.

By its very nature then, the Shakespearean play-as-mirror is eminently transferrable from culture to culture, reflecting the particular features of each audience. At the same time, it suggests a comparison of these features with those of the audience for which the play was originally written, as well as with those of the protagonists of the narrative Shakespeare adapted or 'imitated' in his play. The mirror is in fact a two- or even three-way mirror, reflecting its source, Elizabethan society and the actual audience, representing each in terms of the others. Modern-dress productions exploit this aspect of Shakespearean drama, sometimes overdoing their modernization and destroying the delicate game of mirrors.

The concept of the play as mirror is directly related to the idea of the world as a stage. While these two notions complement each other, they clash with the old Platonic ontological hierarchy which attributes truth only to firm reality, slighting art as a mere illusion, a poor imitation of an imitation. But if 'all the world's a stage', then the primacy of nature over its mirror image becomes questionable. In the game of reflections it is no longer clear which is the 'true' image and which its reflection.

Antonin Artaud took this aesthetical assertiveness one step further when he called his collection of essays *The Theatre and its Double*.[10] There have been various speculations about the referent of the 'Double'. In one of his articles, 'On the Balinese Theatre', Artaud seems to be referring to the metaphysical essence of man.

Artaud puts theatre first, making reality into 'its Double'. He does not mean everyday trivialized reality, but the climactic and catastrophic powers of nature, the uncontrollable passions, the eruptions of the irrational, the existential revelations of danger, all those elemental forces which, in his opinion, should be the domain of theatre. For him, the theatre is not an imitation of life, but, on the contrary, reality is the Double of theatre, a grasp of which is possible only through the unleashing of the irrational and metaphysical in the theatre. Aristotle approached drama from the philosopher's rational standpoint, trying to hedge and curb all revelations of the metaphysical in Greek theatre. Artaud is the poet of the irrational, attempting to liberate the Dionysiac powers circumscribed in the *Bacchae*.

In order to escape from classical limitations, Artaud turned to other cultures, not dominated by Western rationalism. He found his non-classical model in the exoticism of the Balinese theatre. In it, he found a liberation from the psychological and verbal European theatre, a pure theatre, expressive of hallucination and terror, a metaphysical rather than a realistic theatre. Artaud called for hieroglyphic signs instead of words, magic instead of logic, for the creation of 'a concrete concept of the abstract'.[11] His battle-cry 'No more master-pieces' is an outcry against subjugation to the rational spirit of classicism, an expression of his craving for mystery and danger, for theatre as a volcanic eruption, for the taking of risks.

Artaud created a platform for alternative theatre, anti-rational and anti-classical. Directors and playwrights have struggled with his visionary ideas, attempting to translate them into new theatrical forms. But, with a few exceptions, classical plays and classical ideas still seem to exercise their control on us, offering rational interpretations of human behaviour, sweeping the dangerous irrational off-stage, pretending that our culture belongs to the classical mainstream, that we are still busily engaged in bringing back the ore from Grecian coasts.

Sophisticated modern attempts to free the theatre from its classical moorings have remained partial and sectarian. Brecht recognized that his anti-Aristotelian rebellion still left him, ironically, within the conceptual framework of Aristotelian poetics, that he had in fact only reorganized the same elements into a 'Thaëter' rather than a 'Theater'.[12] Playwrights like Beckett and Ionesco have also rebelled against classical tenets, but although they have broadened our scope, their success has not invalidated the classical pieces which continue to be performed with them. Boldly following his theoretical thinking to its necessary conclusions, Peter Handke swept the stage clear of all vestiges of theatrical and dramatic convention and artifice in *Offending the Audience*. But after this energetic spring-cleaning, the stage seems to have been refilled with its old and familiar paraphernalia. Occasionally, the old masters are even reinterpreted in the light of the iconoclastic innovations.

The very persistence of avant-garde theatre is a living proof that it in no way comes close to replacing the tradition. These novelties create a long trail of small fireworks which illuminate the cultural scene without exploding it. After performances of Tadeusz Kantor's *Dead Class* and Jozef Szeina's *Replika*, we still come back to Lorca's *Yerma* and to Euripides' *Medea*.

Avant-garde theatre has turned the classical concept of *mimesis* on its head. For both Plato and Aristotle, art was an imitation of reality, although each understood reality differently. But already Horace took the object of literary *imitatio* to be not reality itself but its literary expression in the Greek models. With Shakespeare, the theatre is still a representation of reality, but now it is only in its theatrical expression that reality becomes meaningful. Finally, the absolute primacy of theatre over reality is asserted by Artaud: theatre is the truth, reality its mere imitation.

Today, these different approaches continue to exist side by side, in a state of unresolved tension. The alternative, avant-garde view, has challenged the classical theatre, but has not succeeded in invalidating or replacing it.

Notes

1 Horace, 'On the Art of Poetry', in *Classical Literary Criticism*, trans. T. S. Dorsch (Harmondsworth: Penguin Books, 1965), p. 88.

2 Horace, p. 80.

3 Horace, p. 83. For a discussion of this tendency in Roman writings, see J. D. Boyd, *The Function of Mimesis and its Decline* (New York, 1980), pp. 37–8.

4 Roger Ascham, 'The Scholemaster' (1570), in *Elizabethan Critical Essays*, ed. G. Gregory Smith (London, 1904), p. 7.

5 In J. E. Spingarn, *A History of Literary Criticism in the Renaissance* (New York, 1899, 2nd edn 1908).

6 *Poetics* 6. 1450a 17–19, trans. S. H. Butcher.

7 *Republic* X 597 ff.

8 Cf. note to passage in the Arden edition, ed. T. S. Dorsch (London, 1955).

9 Cf. Ben Jonson, *Every Man Out of His Humour*, III.6. 206–7. Cf. also *Hamlet*, 1877 Variorum edition, p. 228, where Hamlet's words are compared with the definition of comedy provided in *Don Quixote*.

10 Antonin Artaud, *The Theatre and its Double*, in *Collected Works*, vol. 4, trans. Victor Corti (London, 1974).
11 Artaud, p. 47.
12 Cf. Bertolt Brecht, 'Der Messingkauf', Die erste Nacht, p. 508, and 'Kleines Organon für des Theater', Vorrede, p. 662, in *Gesammelte Werke*, vol. 16 (Frankfurt am Main, 1967).

Greek drama in Rome: some aspects of cultural transposition

DWORA GILULA

Although Athens was not the only Greek *polis* to cultivate theatrical productions, its magnificent dramatic festivals eclipsed theatrical events which took place elsewhere, and from the fifth century on attracted creative playwrights from other parts of the Greek world who flocked to Athens to achieve renown. It was not, however, a one-way road. Already at a very early stage Athens exported its drama and its theatre productions. Colonists transported the institution from the mainland to the colonies where an eager welcome awaited those who had won renown in Athens. Tragic poets from Athens made large sums of money in other Greek cities (Plato, *Laches* 183a). The Sicilian tyrant Hieron I entertained at his court, among other famous poets of his age, Aeschylus, who, at the tyrant's request, revived the *Persae* at Syracuse, not long after its original presentation in Athens in the year 472 BC. The Macedonian king Archelaus, who established dramatic contests in honour of Zeus and the Muses, invited Euripides and Agathon to his court in an attempt to 'civilize' the Macedonians.

In the fourth century, poets, actors and other performers travelled even more, but it was particularly the Hellenistic period which witnessed the fastest spread of dramatic activities: Athenian comedy, no longer locally political and topical, was easily understood all over the Greek world no less than the universally appealing tragedy. Theatre buildings became an indispensable feature of Hellenistic cities. According to Pausanias, one cannot give the name of a city to places 'which possess no government offices, no gymnasium, no theatre, no market-place, no water descending to a fountain, etc.' (x,4,1, W. H. S. Jones's translation in the Loeb series). It is not the buildings themselves, however, but rather their social function which make a city.[1] Theatre buildings provided the needed spaces for dramatic performances which became the most popular kind of entertainment. Guilds of actors travelled to all parts of the Greek and Hellenistic world performing Athenian drama, thus making it into international theatre.[2]

The evidence of international acting, and of the quick spread of Attic

99

innovations throughout the Greek world, points to uniformity of acting conditions shaped by the strong influence of the Athenian practice. Drama and theatrical productions at Athens underwent continuous changes. Uniformity of acting conditions was not a result of stagnation and arrest of development, but rather of a rapid passing on of changes. Nonetheless, a production of, for example, an Aeschilean tragedy in Sicily or a Menandrean comedy in Egypt, even if contemporaneous with the original presentation in the theatre of Dionysus, must have differed from it and required some adjustments, however limited – an adjustment to a different space of performance or a different number of spectators, for example. However, the difference was not essential, for the plays were performed in the original Greek language in which they were written, by Greek actors before Greek speaking audiences, in places where drama and dramatic performances were not unknown. It was, therefore, an institution exported rather than transplanted, its impact in some respect akin to the presentation of Stoppard's *The Real Thing* on Broadway, or Williams's *Sweet Bird of Youth* in London's West End.

Although Greek was known almost everywhere, Latin was confined to its own boundaries. Because of the language barrier, the most popular entertainment of the Hellenistic world could not be enjoyed by the Romans. The storming of this last theatre-less bastion was only a question of time. Thus, in the history of the Western theatre, it is the performances before Roman audiences of translated and adapted Greek tragedies and comedies which afford the first instance of a sustained effort to transfer a considerable body of drama from one language to another, and of a transplantation of the institution of theatre from one cultural milieu to another.

Of the main aspects of this phenomenon which are worthy of attention I have chosen to comment on two: the difference in the cultural and social context of the theatre, and the difference of the performance's impact on the audience.

In Rome, the theatre, as an institution of foreign origin, never achieved the central and honourable place of its Greek counterpart. The pioneers of the Roman theatre were, necessarily, bilingual, with an extensive knowledge of Greek literature and theatre and an excellent command of Latin, their target language. Suetonius calls Livius Andronicus and Ennius *semigraeci (De gram.* 1), i.e., able to use both Latin and Greek (*utraque lingua*). They came to Rome not from Greece but from Greek and Hellenized areas of south Italy where Greek culture and arts flourished.[3] Whether slaves liberated later or free men, they were non-Romans of inferior social status with no citizen rights, a state of affairs which no doubt contributed to the low esteem of the theatrical professions no less than their classification as mercenary occupations. In contrast to Greece, writing for the stage in Rome did not bring glory, nor was it considered a civic service, while acting on the stage, not an achievement worthy of a liberal man, entailed disdain and ignominy. There is no doubt that many actors were rightly admired, but admiration did not change their status. The exemption of professional actors from military service (Liv. 7,2,12) was a disgrace and a disadvantage, for without it one could not pursue a political career.[4] The Romans themselves commented on the difference: 'no such thing was a disgrace among the Greeks' (Liv. 24,24,4). Comparing the traditions of the Greeks and Romans, Cornelius Nepos says that the Greeks did not consider it a dishonour to appear on stage and become a spectacle to the public (Praef. 5), and Tacitus comments that 'in Greece . . . it is honourable to practice even the arts of the stage' (*Dial.* 10,5).

Roman magistrates could punish actors anywhere and everywhere, until Augustus deprived them of this power 'restricting it to the time of games and to the theatre' (Suet., *Aug.* 45,3, trans. J. Gavorse). There is a serious residue in the seemingly flippant remark of Plautus that after the performance is over and the costumes taken off 'the actor that has made mistakes will get a thrashing, the one that has not, a drink' (*Cist.* 784–5, and cf. *Amph.* 26–31). After all, some of the actors were the property of their troupe-managers. Thus, whatever glory there was went to the aspiring politicians who financed the games and bought the services of writers and performers, thus gaining for themselves popularity and advancing their political careers.[5]

According to tradition (Liv. 7,2), scenic games (*ludi scaenici*) in Rome were introduced to propitiate the gods and were attached to existing programmes of various public festivals (*ludi*), of which none was connected with Dionysus.[6] Before a permanent theatre was built in Rome (55 BC), scenic performances were held on temporary wooden structures erected for the occasion in various secular places where the festivals were held, the circus, the forum, and later also before temples of gods, such as that of Magna Mater on the Palatine. Other entertainments took place in the same performing space, for unlike their almost exclusive centrality in Athens, scenic performances in Rome were part of a variety programme which included other more popular features such as rope-walking, wrestling, boxing, chariot-racing, wild-beast hunts, and gladiatorial combats, whose popularity by far exceeded all other events.[7]

Moreover, unlike in Athens, public games were not the only occasion for presenting scenic productions, these could also form a part of private festivals, such as funeral games, or of semiprivate ones vowed by individuals while in public office – the magnificent *ludi votivi* funded by spoils, which dazzled Rome and brought glory to the victorious generals.[8] Thus, the *Hecyra* and the *Adelphoe* of Terence were performed at the funeral games of L. Paullus in 160 BC given by Q. Fabius Maximus and P. Cornelius Scipio Africanus the younger, two major politicians of the time. Tragedies by Accius and Naevius were performed at votive games, as were plays with Roman plots, the *fabulae praetextae*. All these poets were paid for their plays and did not compete with each other as in the Athenian festivals. When a triumphant general paid for the games it was 'his own *res gestae* that were being celebrated' and what is more, 'such games could be put on at any time, by anyone who could afford them'.[9] The mood of such events necessarily differed from the spirit of the Athenian dramatic festivals.

P. Grimal describes the Roman comedy as resembling the god Janus: one face turned towards Athens the other towards Rome.[10] From the point of view of theatre-transplantation, it is the impact on the Roman audience of the Athens-turned face which is of interest.

The Greek playwrights shared with their public a certain common knowledge on which they could rely and to which they could allude. Explicit explanations were given only where particular information was necessary for the understanding of the plot. The Greek spectators saw on stage a creative reflection of their world artistically represented within the bounds of theatre conventions. Translated and adapted for the stage in Rome, the same plays could not create a similar rapport with the Roman audience. The very fact that Latin speaking actors impersonated Greeks, and not the spectators watching them, underlined the make-believe element of the theatrical experience. Even before uttering a word, the actors, whether performing a tragedy set in the world of myth or a comedy depicting the modern Greek world, signalled to the Roman audience dressed in their national dress, the toga (see Pl. *Amph.* 65–8),[11] by means of their characteristic Greek costumes, that what they were about to see was not a reflection of their society. The 'here' of the actors on stage was not identical with the 'here' of the audience.

All the extant Roman comedies are of Greek origin (*palliata*) and have a Greek setting. In their expositions it is made clear that the characters clad in the Greek mantle, the *pallium* (see Pl. *Curc.* 288 'these cloaked Greeks' *isti Graeci palliati*), live in a Greek city, usually in Athens. In the *Menaechmi*'s prologue Plautus says: 'Now writers of comedy have this habit: they always allege that the scene of action is Athens, their object being to give the play a more Grecian air.'[12] Evidently, Roman writers of *palliata* sensed that the Roman audience considered Athens to be more

Greek than other locations, and accordingly, in their adaptations used to change the place of the action to Athens. Plautus, however, does not always subscribe to the principle that Greek setting need necessarily be exclusively Attic, but, without shunning Athens altogether he does not hesitate, contrary to the usage of Terence, to locate his plots elsewhere, be it in Thebes (*Amphitruo*), Ephesus (*Miles Gloriosus*), Cyrene (*Rudens*), Caledon (*Poenulus*), Sicyon (*Cistellaria*), Epidaurus (*Curculio*), or an unnamed city in Aetolia (*Captivi*).[13]

To accentuate the Greek setting, typical Greek elements are emphasized and strengthened. In addition to the tendency to change the location to Athens, the names of the characters, which seemed less Greek than necessary, are replaced by others: Syros in the *Dis Exapaton* of Menander is changed to the colourful Chrysalus, in Plautus's *Bacchides* 'the plain Moschos to the quadrisyllabic compound Pistoclerus'.[14] These Greek *personae* with their fancy Greek names live in Greek houses,[15] consume Greek food,[16] and use Greek money.[17] Sometimes the fictional Greek world is brought to the attention of the Roman spectators by an occasional explicit reference to its Greekness. Thus, the Greek characters sometimes refer to their fellow men as Greek: the running slave in Plautus's *Curculio* (288) refers to persons in his town as 'these cloaked Greeks' and Menaechmus II asks the wife of his brother: 'Don't you know, woman, why the Greeks called Hecuba a bitch?' (lines 714–15).

The Greekness has a special effect when the reference amounts to a stereotypic view of the Greeks held by the Romans. Since deceit was one of the principal characteristics which the Romans attributed to the Greeks, to refer to 'Greek reliability' (*Graeca fide*, Pl. *Asin.* 198–201) would have on the Roman audience an effect of an ethnic joke, a stereotypic vice attributed to an ethnic foreign group.[18] The reference to the dissolute behaviour of the Greeks had a similar effect. The festive indulgences, such as wining, dining, and love-making, were sufficiently distinctive from Roman customs and typical to such a degree of the Greeks, that Plautus could refer to them by using the term 'to act like a Greek' (*congraecari*, *pergraecari*), although in most instances the verb is used as a summing up, or as a gloss on the above mentioned activities.[19]

When the audience is foreign and has a limited share in the assumptions of the play's world, when a distinct and pronounced gap exists between the spectators and the stage, allusive references to customs or social norms are not understood by the audience and may produce a sense of puzzlement or disbelief. In such cases the reference must be either elaborated by an explicit explanation or eliminated.

In the prologue of Plautus's *Casina*, after relating briefly that the argument of the play centres on the arranging of a slave's marriage, permitted in Greece but not found in Rome,[20] the *prologus* says to the audience: 'There are some here, who, I suppose, are now saying to each other "What is all this, for the love of heaven? A slave wedding? Slaves to take wives or propose marriage? Something new this – something that happens nowhere on earth!" But I say it does happen in Greece and at Carthage, and here in our country in Apulia; it is the regular thing there to make more of slaves' weddings than even of citizens' (67–74, trans. P. Nixon). An explanation of a similar nature, namely that in Athens slaves are allowed to have fun, is inserted in Plautus's *Stichus*. In this case the direct address to the audience breaks the play's illusion in the middle of the performance (*id ne vos miremini*, etc.): 'Yes, and you people needn't be surprised that we slavelings have our liquor and love affairs and dinner engagements: all that is permitted us in Athens' (446–8, trans. P. Nixon).

The peculiar impact of a perfect illusion of a Greek world on the Roman audience is best illustrated by the paradoxical use of the term *barbarus* and of its likes. Greeks divided the human race into two unequal groups, Greeks and barbarians, a scheme not affected by the appearance of the Romans, who did not speak Greek and were, therefore, barbarians by definition.[21] Adaptation of the Greek vision of the world by a Roman playwright necessitated an application of the term *barbarus* to the Romans themselves. As seen from the Greek standpoint, a Roman poet is a foreign poet, and therefore called *poeta barbarus* (Pl. *Miles Gloriosus*),[22] Roman customs are foreign customs (*mores barbaros*, Pl. *Stichus* 193), and Italian cities *barbaricae urbes* (Pl. *Captivi* 884). For the Roman spectators to realize the full essence of such an application, a brief dissociation from the dramatic illusion must have taken place to allow an intellectual appraisal of the audience's position versus the illusory dramatic representation. The spectators, who are at home and are watching actors presenting foreigners moving around and acting out their affairs in a foreign country, suddenly find out that they themselves are the foreigners, and the place in which they actually sit is envisioned as being in a barbarian, foreign country (*in barbaria*, Pl. *Poen.* 598). This passage of Plautus addresses the audience directly: 'This is certainly money, spectators, stage money. In a foreign country they soak this money and use it to fatten oxen' (598–9). Direct address of the audience is a conventional part of the necessary dramatic mechanism in this type of comedy. In the Greek original, it was directed at a Greek audience. In the Roman adaptation, however, if the passage is kept as it is, the dramatic illusion is extended beyond the boundaries of the stage and made to embrace the auditorium as well: the Roman spectators are transferred into Greek spectators, and Italy, their home, is referred to as a faraway foreign country.

If *barbarus* just means 'non-Greek', Roman or Italian,[23] the Roman audience is reminded, by the actors' reference to them as foreigners, that they are not a part of the illusory world they are watching, and the sense of identification with it, if not that of involvement, is momentarily broken. If, in addition, the connotation 'uncultured', 'uncivilized', a sense already found in Plautus,[24] is simultaneously activated, a tension is created between the audience's self-esteem (or self-appraisal), and the sense of cultural inferiority conveyed by the term. This tension might have been resolved in laughter, i.e., the use of the term might have been perceived as a joke,[25] if the Romans actually sensed themselves culturally superior to the Greeks, which most probably was the case, for otherwise it would have resulted in an arousal of indignation, a feeling hostile to the festive mood needed for the proper reception of comedy.

This Greek point of view is carried by Plautus out of the world of illusion and transferred into passages which are outside the drama proper. In several prologues Plautus specifies the name of the Greek play which he adapted, mentions its author and announces the title which he has given to his Latin adaptation. For example: *haec vocatur / Graece Emporos Philemonis / eadem Latine Mercator Macci Titi* ('The Greek name of this play is the *Emporos* of Philemon, in Latin we call it the *Mercator* of Maccius Titus', lines 9–10, trans. P. Nixon).[26] In the *Asinaria*, however, and in the *Trinummus*, Plautus substitutes for *Latine* (in Latin) the term *barbare* (in barbarian, or foreign language): *Demophilus scripsit, Maccus vortit barbare* ('Demophilus wrote it, Maccus translated it into a foreign (or barbarian) language', line 11); *huic Graece nomen est Thensauro fabulae: / Philemo scripsit, Plautus vortit barbare* ('The Greek name of this play is *Thensaurus*: Philemon wrote it, Plautus translated it into a foreign (or barbarian) language', *Trin.* lines 18–19). In such a context, in which factual information is imparted and no illusory world compels Plautus to maintain the Greek point of view, it is paradoxical to call Latin a foreign language unless one wishes to crack a joke.

The question, however, must be asked, whether such passages are clearly conceived as actually having an 'outside the drama proper' status. For example: the postponed prologue of the *Miles Gloriosus* is delivered by the main character of the play, the slave Palaestrio, speaking simultaneously *in persona* and *ex persona*. Palaestrio is dressed in the conventional costume of a slave, but the general information he relates has nothing to do with the part he plays in the comedy. It is *ex persona* that he faces the audience and addresses it directly: 'I will tell you the argument and the name. This comedy is called in Greek *Alazon* and we call it in Latin *Gloriosus*' (lines 86–7); but, in the same breath, he continues immediately with an *in persona* explanation: 'This town is Ephesus, that soldier is my owner' (line 88). In the *Mercator* (cited above) we encounter the same *in persona–ex persona* situation, where the young man Charinus tells the audience his miseries, which form the argument of the play, and also its Greek and Latin name and its authors (lines 9 ff.)

The vagueness of dramatic illusion may be demonstrated further by yet another fascinating example. According to the unrealistic convention common to the ancient and modern theatre, foreigners on stage speak the language understood by the audience. Thus, the Greek characters on the Roman stage speak Latin which is sprinkled sometimes with Greek words and expressions so as to create and maintain an illusion of Greek.[27] But sometimes the illusion is undermined in a peculiar way. The playwright Pacuvius makes one of his characters (Chryses) say: 'What I mention we Romans call heaven, but the Greeks call it "aether".' In a later period, Cicero, who quotes the line, already grasps the peculiar vagueness of its dramatic illusion and is able to comment on the nature of the convention, advancing at this early period the argument known today as 'suspension of disbelief': 'Just as though the man who says this were not a Greek! "Well, he is talking Latin", you may say. Just so, if we won't suppose we are hearing him talk Greek.' And later Cicero quotes another passage of Pacuvius in which a woman is made to say in Latin: '[I am] a Grecian born: my speech discloses that' (*De Natura Deorum* II,91, trans. H. Rackham in the Loeb series).[28]

All the examples above illustrate the nature of a creative transplantation of drama and theatre from one milieu to another. However, when an attempt is made to transfer a theatrical performance to another culture, with no artists to act as mediators, a transformation takes place nevertheless, prompted by the organizers or by the audience itself. Luckily, we have a description by the Greek historian Polybius of a victorious Roman general who assumed the role of a stage director.[29]

In 167 BC Lucius Anicius celebrated his victory over the Illirians with spectacular games. He hired for the occasion the most illustrious professional Greek artists, musicians, dancers, and actors. Since he was not pleased with their routine performance and neither was the audience, and since he was the one who paid their fees, he felt entitled to issue directing orders aimed at transforming the performance into one which would satisfy his tastes and expectations as well as the audience's. He ordered the performers to engage in a mock fight, and when the stunned artists obliged and pretended to attack each other, they earned boundless applause from the delighted spectators. It is a pity that Polybius declined to describe in detail the manner in which a tragedy was subsequently presented, on the grounds that people would think that he was jesting. It is clear, nevertheless, that the Roman crowds (and their leader) did not enjoy pure Greek theatre products, and when presented with them, by exerting pressure on the performers, forced them to alter their original highly sophisticated cultural performance into an inartistic substitute. For the shocked Greek historian this transformation seemed of course barbarous, tasteless, and ridiculous.

It is good to be reminded that a transplantation of theatre from one culture to another may achieve popular acclaim and even financial success, but is bound to fail artistically unless it is conceived and executed by artists of theatre, who do not mechanically transfer and transplant, but by virtue of their creativity generate a new and original production.

Notes

1 See R. Martin, *L'Urbanisme dans la Grèce antique* (Paris, 1974), pp. 30–1; see also T. P. Wiseman, 'Who was Crassicius Pansa?' *TAPA* (1985), p. 189.
2 See A. Pickard-Cambridge, *The Dramatic Festivals of Athens* (revised by J. Gould and D. M. Lewis, Oxford, 1968), pp. 279ff.; G. M. Sifakis, *Studies in the History of Hellenistic Drama* (London, 1967), pp. 1ff.; T. B. L. Webster, *Studies in Later Greek Comedy* (Manchester, 1970), pp. 99–100; T. B. L. Webster, *Hellenistic Poetry and Art* (London, 1964), pp. 15, 20–1; P. Ghiron-Bistagne, *Recherches sur les acteurs dans la Grèce antique* (Paris, 1976), pp. 154ff.; B. Gentili, *Theatrical Performances in the Ancient World* (Amsterdam/Uithoorn, 1979).
3 Livius Andronicus came from Tarentum, Naevius from Capua, Pacuvius from Brundisium, Ennius from Rudiae, not far from Tarentum, Plautus from Sarsina, Terence from Carthago. On the Roman writers in general, see W. J. Watts, 'The Birthplaces of Latin Writers', *Greece and Rome*, 18 (1971), pp. 91–101.
4 See F. M. de Robertis, *Lavoro e lavoratori nel mondo Romano* (Bari, 1963), pp. 65–71; H. G. Marek, 'Die sociale Stellung des Schauspielers im alten Rom', *Das Altertum*, 5 (1959), pp. 101–11; but cf. E. J. Jory, 'Association of Actors in Rome', *Hermes*, 98 (1976), pp. 230ff., who argues that the exemption from military service was a privilege comparable to that afforded to the Greek *technitai* of Dionysus.
5 On political success on account of the *ludi*, see H. H. Scullard, *Roman Politics* (Oxford 1951), pp. 24–5; F. Della Corte, *Da Sarsina a Roma* (Firenze, 1967), pp. 36–7; W. K. Quinn-Schofield, 'Observations upon the *Ludi Plebeii*', *Latomus*, 26 (1967), pp. 677–87.

Dwora Gilula

6 But see J. A. Hanson, *Roman Theatre-Temples* (Princeton, 1959), p. 11 and n. 17, who claims a certain connection for Roman dramatic festivals with Liber Pater; on the various festivals, see also L. R. Taylor, 'The Opportunities for Dramatic Performances in the Time of Plautus and Terence', *TAPA*, 68 (1937), pp. 284–304; A. S. Gratwick, 'The Early Republic', in *Cambridge History of Classical Literature* (Cambridge, 1982), 2, pp. 80–3.

7 See Terence, *Hec.* 4–5, 33–4; Cicero, *Mur.* 38–40; *Fam.* 11,8,1; *Sest.* 114–27; D. Gilula, 'Where Did the Audience Go?', *SCI*, 4 (1978), pp. 45–9; J.-P. Thuillier, 'Le programme athlétique des *ludi circenses* dans la Rome républicaine', *REL*, 60 (1982), pp. 105–22.

8 See E. S. Gruen, 'Material Rewards and the Drive for Empire', in *The Imperialism of Mid-Republican Rome* (Papers and Monographs, vol. 20, American Academy in Rome 1984), pp. 60–1, and 72–3 nn. 6–10.

9 T. P. Weiseman, *Catullus and His World* (Cambridge, 1985), p. 33. Wiseman calls the privately funded festivals *nobilium ludi* 'the games of the nobles', after a late-Republican funerary inscription of a mime-actress in which the term appears, see pp. 26ff.

10 P. Grimal, 'Sur les *Adelphes* de Térence', *Académie des Inscriptions et Belles-lettres* (1982), p. 39. Since only fragments remained from Roman adaptations of Greek tragedies, it is necessary to rely mainly on the evidence of the comedies.

11 See Valerius Maximus, 11,22, for the symbolizing of Romans by the toga and of Greeks by their *pallium*.

12 Trans. P. Nixon in the Loeb series. Although the plot of *Menaechmi* is of Greek origin, it is Sicilian rather than Attic (*Men.* 11–12).

13 See also D. J. Blackman, 'Plautus and Greek Topography', *TAPA*, 100 (1969), pp. 11–22.

14 E. W. Handley, 'Plautus and his Public: Some Thoughts on New Comedy in Latin', *Dioniso*, 76 (1975), pp. 123–4.

15 For a discussion of the passage of Plautus, *Most.* 754–6, which according to Grimal contains a description of a Greek house, see P. Grimal, 'La maison de Simon et celle de Théopropides dans la *Mostelaria*', in *Mélanges offerts à Jacques Heurgon* (Rome, 1976), pp. 371–86.

16 Two scenes with a cook in a central part (Pl. *Aul.* 389 ff.; *Pseud.* 790 ff.) are firmly based in the Attic kitchen, whereas in *Persa* 87–111 a meal is prepared with a purely Attic menu; see E. Fraenkel, *Elementi Plautini in Plauto* (Firenze, 1960), pp. 409ff; a cook hired in the market for the preparation of a special festive meal is by itself a Greek institution; for details of Greek wines see Pl. *Poen.* 699; *Curc.* 70; *Rudens* 588.

17 The *drachma* (e.g., Pl. *Trin.* 425; Ter. *Ht.* 601); the *mina* (e.g., Pl. *Asin.* 395; Ter. *Eun.* 169); *talentum magnum* (e.g., Pl. *Most.* 644; *Truc.* 912; *Cist.* 561); *Philippum* (e.g., Pl. *Bacch.* 868).

18 Cicero calls the Greeks *fallaces* (*ad Quint. fr.* 1,1,16; see also *Pro Flacco* 23); see N. Petrochilos, *Roman Attitudes to the Greeks* (Athens, 1974), pp. 31–53.

19 See Pl. *Bacch.* 743 (*congraecari*); *Bacch.* 813, *Most.* 20,64,960, *Poen.* 603, *Truc.* 88 (*pergraecari*); see H. D. Jocelyn, 'Anti-Greek Elements in Plautus' *Menaechmi*',

in *Papers of the Liverpool Latin Seminar*, 4 (1983), pp. 1–25; A. E. Astin, *Cato the Censor* (Oxford, 1978), p. 173; *graecari* is found later in Horace, *Sat.* 2,2,9–11.

20 See U. E. Paoli, *Comici Latini e diritto Attico* (Milano, 1962), p. 14 n. 1; Plautus, *Casina*, ed. W. T. MacCary and W. W. Willcock (Cambridge, 1976), pp. 107–8.

21 See M. Debuisson, 'Remarques sur le vocabulaire grec de l'acculturation', *RBPhH*, 60 (1982), pp. 5–32.

22 See E. Fraenkel, *Elementi Plautini in Plauto*, p. 107.

23 See e.g., *OLD*: '*barbarus* used facet. of Romans and Italians by Plautus, as if from a Greek standpoint'. Romans are mentioned by Plautus once in *Poen.* 1314: *Romani remiges* (Roman rowmen full of garlic and leek).

24 Pace Paoli, *Comici Latini e diritto Attico*, p. 14; cf. Pl. *Bacch.* 121: *O Lyde es barbarus* etc.; cf. W. M. Lindsay, *The Captivi of Plautus* (Cambridge, 1900), p. 884.

25 See G. A. Sheets, 'Plautus and Early Roman Tragedy', *ICS*, 8 (1983), p. 195.

26 See also *Casina* 31–5; *Miles* 86–7; *Poen.* 53–4, where a lacuna is postulated after 53 to account for the missing *Graece*.

27 See G. P. Shipp, 'Greek in Plautus', *WS*, 66 (1953), pp. 105–12; see also Pl. *Casina* 728–30, and MacCary and Willcock, pp. 107–8.

28 See also *Remains of Old Latin*, ed. E. H. Warmington (Loeb series 1936, repr. 1967), II, 202–3.

29 Polybius 30,22, quoted by Athenaeus 14,615b–d; cf. Thuillier (note 7, above), pp. 110-11.

Shakespeare and theatre politics in the Third Reich

WERNER HABICHT

I

Political and ideological pressures in a totalitarian State are likely to affect a public forum such as the theatre. The art of the theatre, on the other hand, has the potential to react to, to expose, or at least to undercut, such pressures. The resulting conflicts between the staging of power and the power of the stage may prove more complex and intricate than is visible on the surface. The treatment of Shakespeare in Germany under the Nazi regime is a revealing case in point.

The long-standing history of Shakespeare's reception in Germany had of course begun with the enthusiastic discovery of his plays by the intellectual avant-garde of the eighteenth century. Subsequently, Shakespeare had never ceased to be a source of theatrical inspiration and a subject of intellectual debate. That this remained true in the 1930s may appear surprising, considering the lack of obvious affinities between Shakespearean drama and the ideological tenets and cultural politics of the new rulers, which also called for a new kind of dramatic art.

Goebbels told a convention of theatre directors three months after Hitler had come to power that the German theatre of the future was to be 'heroic', 'steely-romantic', 'unsentimentally direct' and 'national with grand pathos', or else it would not be at all.[1] In countless pamphlets Goebbels's programmatic catchwords were immediately expanded into elaborate theories. Besides, the Ministry of Propaganda and its theatrical division (soon to be master-minded by Reichsdramaturg Rainer Schlösser) assumed organizational control of the well-established system of public playhouses. What was involved was political indoctrination, racial purification, more or less camouflaged censorship, restrictions imposed upon the performance of plays by non-German authors, and the emphatic rejection of earlier dramatic styles associated with naturalism, individualism or intellectualism (terms treated as dirty words).

Ultimately, the theatre of the future was envisaged as taking the shape of the *Thingspiel*, an open-air ritual theatre for the masses, which was to provide the national–socialist *Weltanschauung* with a secular liturgy. And although the *Thing* play movement practically collapsed as early as 1937, the theatrical instincts which it had been expected to release were by then channelled into the pompous staging of party rallies.[2]

None of this would seem to have been naturally conducive to the survival of Shakespeare. And yet between 1933 and 1936 the number of professional Shakespeare productions increased steadily; nearly all of the thirty-seven plays were staged somewhere in Germany between 1933 and 1944. Many theatre directors active at that time have retrospectively explained their cultivation of classics such as Shakespeare as a stratagem that enabled them to maintain their artistic integrity and to avoid putting on propagandist Nazi plays of dubious quality. But their political reticence, too, fitted in with the political scenario.

Goebbels recommended the classics for an interim period, for as long as the new national steely romanticism had not yet taken on a satisfactory dramatic shape. He also knew that the encouragement of conventionally edifying performances of classic plays was a useful method of pacifying the cultured middle class. But whereas the national classics were dogmatically subjected to revaluations, which led to the proposal of a new hierarchy of authors (with Grabbe and Kleist at the top of the list), the status of Shakespeare remained controversial – not only between Nazi supporters and their opponents (the latter could be silenced), but also within the Nazi context itself. Polemical arguing was indeed unavoidable when it came to proving the compatibility of Shakespeare with the Nazi ideology of the *Volk*, the national and racial community, as the binding force to which the individual person was to be rigorously subordinated.

II

The least of the problems to deal with – even from a nationalist point of view – was that of Shakespeare's British origin. All that was needed was recapitulations of the glorious history of Shakespeare's German reception. In a sense, Shakespeare had a special kinship with German culture and the Germanic spirit had always captivated his German admirers. In the nineteenth century this admiration had produced the myth of Shakespeare's function as a catalyst that helped to generate a truly national literature in Germany – a myth which Friedrich Gundolf's influential book *Shakespeare und der deutsche Geist* (1911)[3] had then raised to the level of an intellectual dogma. Shakespeare's supporters in the 1930s quoted

Gundolf extensively – not even Gundolf's Jewishness could prevent them; or if it did, they used Gundolf's material while denouncing Gundolf's allegedly perverse intellectualism, or else fell back into the jingoistic Shakespeare idolatry which had been current before Gundolf's work superseded it. As early as 1865, a German professor of English had had good reason to affirm that the only unsolved question concerning Germany's affinity with Shakespeare was whether it should be ascribed to Shakespeare's own Germanic background or to the industry of his German explicators.[4]

After 1933, the Nazi press cheerfully maintained both alternatives, albeit with changes of emphasis according to the state of foreign affairs. Comments on Shakespeare seldom failed to stress that as an Englishman he was at least Germanic, if not in fact Nordic. Proof was offered from various quarters. Amateur mythographers attested the Nordic origin of the myths behind Shakespeare's tragedies or fairy worlds.[5] A journal for aristocrats praised the Nordic nobility of his kings;[6] a less aristocratic organ commended the characteristically Germanic closeness to the soil of his rural origin.[7] Even the chief proponent of the new racial science, Professor Günther of Jena, stepped forward to contribute his diagnosis under the title 'Shakespeares Mädchen und Frauen', a title infamously stolen from Heine but equipped with new matter: with an appraisal of the Nordic instincts of most women in Shakespeare's plays in choosing efficient lovers and valuable husbands, by which we can learn (said Günther) how the breeding of a healthy generation, which is also advocated in the procreation sonnets, ought to be achieved.[8] It is true that the insipidity of his point did not go unnoticed. Hence a more thorough book-length racial analysis followed at once, executed by G. Plessow, who on the basis of both the portraits and the plays concluded that the Nordic element of Shakespeare's physique and soul, though predominant, was by no means free from alien admixtures of the Mediterranean and Middle Eastern types.[9]

Qualifications were a useful thing to make. And anyway the other way of explaining Shakespeare's German appropriation – in terms of national self-glorification – eventually proved more effective for purposes of political propaganda. In 1940, a bookseller's journal summarized the view which was by then the official one:

Shakespeare has become a poet of the Germans, not because of the racial kinship of his nation with ours ... but because the German spirit, German scholarship, German thoroughness and the German capability of recognizing and supporting great geniuses of other nations have conquered Shakespeare not only for us, but for the world.[10]

Similar – and even identical – statements had already been current in the 1870s[11] and, in 1914, had served to justify German Shakespeare performances during World War I, when one of the spokesmen was the dramatist Gerhart Hauptmann, who assured his compatriots that 'although Shakespeare was born and buried in England, Germany is the country where he truly lives'.[12] At the beginning of World War II these convictions were revived propagandistically. In September 1939, when enemy dramatists were banned from German theatres, the Ministry of Propaganda made an explicit exception for Shakespeare; he was to be treated as a German author.[13] At the same time it was possible to exploit him the other way round; in 1940 Baldur von Schirach devoted an entire issue of his journal *Wille und Macht* to the importance of playing the war enemy's classic, so that the world could see how open-minded, quality-conscious and fair the new German culture was.[14]

III

If, then, Shakespeare the author was comfortably placed in the nationalist context, temporary unrest did arise from matters concerning the translation of his works. There was of course the excellent romantic translation by Schlegel and Tieck, which for a century had withstood all attempts to supersede it. Hence the stage success of a more modern rendering begun by Hans Rothe in the 1920s raised an issue in the 1930s. At first this seemed to be one of those traditional controversies between progressive theatre professionals and purist literary scholars. The former welcomed the actability of Rothe's modern versions; the latter condemned his misguided use of scholarship in justifying the liberties he took with the texts. But since the debate was conducted in the public press, and also because Rothe's personal belligerence poured oil on the flames, the matter took on a political dimension. Rothe claimed opportunistically that if Shakespeare was to be integrated into the community-oriented culture of the Third Reich, this required the modern and popular translation he was providing.[15] His opponents adduced the very same reason to maintain that Shakespeare needed the authoritative dignity of the Schlegel/Tieck versions that had made him a German classic.

At last the controversy was stopped by Goebbels in 1936 with the dictatorial verdict that henceforth only the Schlegel/Tieck version was to be admitted on German stages. The conservativism of his decision was not without its stern logic. If Shakespeare's status as a nationalized classic was to be maintained, the standardized German text must not be tampered with. Hence, after Goebbels had spoken, Rothe was pilloried. Unpolitical scholars pilloried him out of philological conviction,[16] and some equally unpolitical theatre directors denounced him on aesthetic grounds, while the cultural and general press condemned him politically as a product of the corrupt liberalism of the twenties.[17]

But even so, a good deal of effort had to be invested in devising ideologically acceptable principles of interpretation. The party press pointed out what ammunition was available, and contributors to educational journals took especial pains to fire it off, their aim being to establish the importance of the teaching of Shakespeare in forming a militant young generation. To this end Shakespearean drama was shown to be both political and heroic.

Gustav Steinbömer's remotely Hegelian dramatic theory, published in 1932 as *Staat und Drama*,[18] was a convenient starting point; it had explained the nature of drama as being determined by historically changing relations between private and public values, and had singled out Shakespeare's plays as supreme examples of political drama in that the private values, experiences and sufferings contained in them are rigorously subordinated to the public ones – to the State in the histories and tragedies, to social structures in the comedies. These public values, identified as an imperative principle of order, only had to be replaced by the Nazi concept of the *Volk*, the binding national and racial community, and it became possible to repudiate the charge of individualism Shakespeare's plays were liable to if too much attention was absorbed by character problems.

As early as 1933 Gymnasium teachers of English were instructed by one of their militant colleagues (Wilhelm Bolle) that Shakespearean drama offered a perfect pattern of the subordination of the individual person to the State and the *Volk*, with which the Nazi movement claimed to have overcome the individualist democracy that had failed. Such insights, Bolle insisted, could hardly be expected from purely literary studies; they must be felt intuitively.[19]

Indeed Nazi propagandists and educators employed a considerable amount of intuition, especially when it came to sensing the plays' heroic qualities. For the *Volk* needed the compelling heroism of a leader. And did not Shakespeare's tragedies and histories celebrate the Germanic ideal of leadership and allegiance? Some of the leaders were easy to identify, provided one's mind was not encumbered by intellectual problematizing.[20] Henry V, for example, with his Germanic self-assurance set off against French corruption, was a clear case in point.[21] So was Julius Caesar, whose heroic greatness was defended against all criticism of his weaknesses and tyrannical inclinations; of Brutus, on the other hand, it was maintained that he fails deservedly because of his adherence to dead ideas of liberal individualism comparable to the ones that had been current in the Weimar republic.[22] Heroic upgrading of this kind was also awarded to such protagonists as Coriolanus or Macbeth,[23] and also to Hamlet, even though this meant rejecting Goethe's influential view of him as a tender soul overwhelmed by the enormity of his task.[24] And Alfred Rosenberg, the Nazi ideologist, offered heroical haloes even to Iago and Richard III by attributing the fascination of evil elicited by them to their tragically inverted Nordic potential.[25]

It is true that streamlined interpretations of this kind were at times cautiously challenged by academic experts, who did remain aware of the complexities of Shakespeare's dramatic art. L. L. Schücking, for instance, in stressing Hamlet's melancholy,[26] implicitly contradicted the heroic view of that character, and H. H. Glunz, in a book on the State in Shakespeare,[27] offered a sound historical analysis of the political substance of the plays and thus subverted Steinbömer's sweeping assertions on that subject. (Schücking was later dismissed from his university chair by the Nazis; Glunz was killed in the war.) Most professorial Shakespeare scholars, however, preferred to deal with, and to direct their students' attention to, politically neutral matters such as sources, influences, style and imagery,[28] or they devoted their research energies to discussing baroque elements in Shakespearean drama.[29]

A sophisticated public controversy, however, arose from the efforts of active dramatists to create the expected new kind of heroic tragedy exploring the destiny of the *Volk*. The adequacy of the Shakespearean model for that purpose was questioned by some, most notably by Curt Langenbeck, who in his manifesto *Wiedergeburt des Dramas aus dem Geist der Zeit*,[30] glancing at Nietzsche, emphatically rejected Shakespeare's open form, ironic mode and individualist stance, and recommended Greek tragedy as a more appropriate point of orientation. This attitude too, had a German tradition, immediately deriving from the neo-classicism of Paul Ernst and ultimately rooted in Weimar classicism; but so had the Teutonic reactions in Shakespeare's defence which Langenbeck's iconoclasm amply provoked. It was contradicted by J. M. Wehner in a series of newspaper articles,[31] and as a consequence Langenbeck offered a partial retraction. Another Shakespeare defender in 1940 was Hans Pfitzner (the composer), who, while enjoying Nazi favour, used some dangerously sensible arguments in praise of Shakespeare's power of characterization.[32] But at that time the debate on the right model for the new heroic drama was not yet settled – as indeed it never was to be.

IV

On the stage itself Shakespeare's plays remained relatively safe. Attractive performances were usually the result of dedicated practical theatre work rather than of ideological conviction, a fact which accounts for the enormous impact of major productions such as those by Heinz Hilpert or Jürgen Fehling in Berlin, by Otto Falckenberg in Munich or by Saladin Schmidt in Bochum. Political pressure was at work when it came to exploiting the impact, and also when undesirable responses were to be prevented. The official assumption apparently was that as long as performances were faithful to the text (which in fact meant employing the conservative declamatory acting style deriving from nineteenth-century practice, particularly for tragedies), they would more or less automatically generate the heroic message in the minds of the audiences, especially when these were no longer destabilized by critical reviews, which were banned by Goebbels's order in 1936. Extra guidance was sometimes offered in programme notes or accompanying lectures by party dignitaries.

When, in 1935, Lothar Müthel's Berlin production of *Hamlet*, in which Gustaf Gründgens played the title role in a blond wig, elicited controversial reactions, these were covered up on the intervention of Göring (who controlled the Berlin Staatstheater) by ideologically acceptable public appraisals, which in turn called forth a spate of articles from which *Hamlet*'s heroic image emerged. Only for Klaus Mann in exile was it possible to describe Gründgens's Hamlet as a neurotic Prussian lieutenant.[33]

At the same time some very traditional elements were eliminated, and the variety of possible responses was narrowed down. For instance, Mendelssohn's music for *A Midsummer Night's Dream* had to go for racial reasons; its replacement was declared a national task for pure-blooded German composers.[34] Experimental productions which had galvanized the theatre of the twenties, such as Leopold Jessner's modern-dress production of *Hamlet*, were now condemned as examples of degenerate art. And if the fifty or so productions of *The Merchant of Venice* recorded in Germany between 1933 and 1944 invariably exhibited anti-semitic and racist interpretations of Shylock, there was a tradition behind these. The difference was that competing traditions were now incriminated and suppressed[35] – comic Shylocks, martyrized Shylocks, Shylocks from the Jewish point of view as assessed in Hermann Sinsheimer's book written in Germany but published in exile,[36] not to mention the heroic Shylock as presented by Jessner, after his emigration, in Jerusalem in 1936.[37] Textual changes, which in the case of *The Merchant* were suggested, did not affect the part of Shylock so much, but were meant to prevent the interracial marriage between Jessica and Lorenzo from being part of the happy ending.[38] Hence even Werner Krauss's impersonation of the Jew in Müthel's notorious Viennese production of 1943 did not differ substantially from the one he himself had played under Max Reinhardt in the twenties. But it did now create a macabre effect deriving from the context of organized anti-semitism and the holocaust, and also from the fact that by then Krauss had abused his talent by appearing as the star of the Nazi propaganda film *Jud Süss*.

On the other hand, the official insistence on conservative true-to-score performance of the classics, on the principle of *Werktreue*, also gave the theatres an artistic opportunity unintended by the politicians. In fact theatre professionals in their turn increasingly adopted the credo of *Werktreue*, of staging Shakespeare 'from within the text'; for they knew that it could be used as a shield for protecting original explorations and even oppositional touches – as when, for instance, in Fehling's Berlin production of *Richard III* the cruel soldiers' black costumes were designed so as to resemble SS uniforms.[39] Some critics, whose activities had been reduced to appreciative reporting, concurred; K. H. Ruppel, for instance, openly praised productions such as these for their independence from the pressures of cultural ideologists.[40]

Perhaps it was partly because of this self-protective attitude of the theatre that, as the war went on, Nazi interest in Shakespeare subsided, and that several of his plays – and some by the German classics as well – were at last branded as undesirable: the Histories, for instance (which were suppressed by Goebbels's order in 1941), or *Troilus and Cressida* (which was too unheroic), or *Antony and Cleopatra* (too perverse and effeminate), or *Othello* (racially unacceptable).[41] And yet one of the very last plays to be performed in Berlin before the theatres went dark in 1944 was Shakespeare's *The Winter's Tale*.

In short, despite the dictatorial efforts at ideological appropriation, the image of Shakespeare in the Third Reich was far from being uniform. Shakespeare was vindicated, Shakespeare caused irritation, and the resulting inconsistencies may reflect the pragmatic ambivalences of Nazi theatre politics as well as the contradictions inherent in the German Shakespeare tradition. But perhaps they also reflect the ambiguities of Shakespearean drama itself, as well as its power to take care of its own defence.

Werner Habicht

Notes

1 'Rede des Reichspropagandaministers Dr. Josef Goebbels vor den deutschen Theaterleitern am 8. Mai 1933', in *Das deutsche Drama*, 5 (1933), p. 36. (Translations from German sources are the present author's.)

2 For recent general accounts of Nazi theatre politics see B. Drewinak, *Das Theater im NS-Staat* (Düsseldorf, 1983), and, from a Marxist point of view, J. Wardetzky, *Theaterpolitik im faschistischen Deutschland* (Berlin, 1983). See also H. Brenner, *Die Kunstpolitik des Nationalsozialismus* (Reinbeck, 1963); G. Rühle's introduction to his anthology *Zeit und Theater 1933–1945*, vol. 5 (Frankfurt, 1974), pp. 9–74; and the documentary volume by J. Wulf, *Theater und Film in Dritten Reich* (Frankfurt, 1966, repr. 1983).

3 10th edn (Godesberg, 1947).

4 B. Tschischwitz, *Nachklänge germanischer Mythe in den Werken Shakespeares* (Halle, 1865), p. 1.

5 For example, H. Dietz, 'Nordischer Mythus in der englischen Literatur', *Neuphilologische Monatsschrift*, 10 (1939), pp. 307–10; K. Schümmer, 'Shakespeare: Nordischer Mythus und christliche Metaphysik', *Hochland*, 36 (1939), pp. 191–205.

6 H. Ch. Mettin, 'Die Bedeutung des Adels bei Shakespeare', *Deutsches Adelsblatt*, 55 (1937), pp. 994–6.

7 G. Ringeling, 'Shakespeare und der Landmensch', *Zeitwende*, 14 (1937–8), pp. 739–46.

8 *Shakespeare Jahrbuch*, 73 (1937), pp. 85–108.

9 G. Plessow, *Um Shakespeares Nordentum* (Aachen, 1937).

10 H. Sauter, 'Shakespeare heute?', *Der Buchhändler im Neuen Reich*, 5 (1940), p. 55.

11 For an almost identical precedent, see K. Fulda, *William Shakespeare: Eine neuere Studie über sein Leben und Dichten (. . .)* (Marburg, 1875), p. 125.

12 'Deutschland und Shakespeare', *Shakespeare Jahrbuch*, 51 (1915), vii–xii.

13 Cultural Press Conferences of the Reichspropagandaministerium of 20 September 1939 and 16 July 1940.

14 *Wille und Macht*, 8 (1940), no. 3.

15 H. Rothe, *Der Kampf um Shakespeare* (Leipzig, 1935), p. 45.

16 Even the verdict of such thoughtfully balanced contributions as those by L. L. Schücking (*Kölnische Zeitung*, 1936, no. 146, p. 9 and no. 153, p. 9) and H. H. Glunz (*Kölnische Zeitung*, 1936, no. 124/25, p. 17) was, in the last analysis, unambiguously anti-Rothe.

17 Besides countless newspaper articles, entire issues of cultural periodicals such as *Bausteine zum deutschen Nationaltheater*, February 1936, and *Wille und Macht*, 4 (1936), no. 7, were devoted to this case.

18 G. Steinbömer, *Staat und Drama* (Berlin, 1932).

19 W. Bolle, 'Shakespeare im Rahmen der Bildungsarbeit an der Höheren Schule', *Neuphilologische Monatsschrift*, 4 (1933), pp. 362–74. For a discussion of further pedagogical approaches see R. Küpper, *Shakespeare im Unterricht*

(Würzburg, 1982), pp. 125–37, 186–8, and R. Lehberger, *Englischunterricht im Nationalsozialismus* (Tübingen, 1986), pp. 112ff.

20 The existence of problems with regard to Shakespeare was flatly denied by the dramatist Thilo von Trotta: 'Shakespeare did not know the alleged problems, that nineteenth-century invention' ('Shakespeare und wir', *Nationalsozialistische Monatshefte*, 5 (1934), p. 1147).

21 K. Schrey, 'Der englische Lektüreunterricht in der Oberstufe', *Die neueren Sprachen*, 45 (1937), p. 305.

22 W. Spiegelberg, 'Shakespeares Caesarbild', *Neuphilologische Monatsschrift*, 10 (1939), pp. 177–89. The theatre critic R. Bierdrzynski, when discussing Bernhard Minetti's impersonation of Brutus, came to a similar conclusion (*Schauspieler, Regisseure, Intendanten* (Heidelberg, 1944), p. 18).

23 L. Eckhoff, 'Heroismus und politisches Führertum bei Shakespeare', *Zeitschrift für neusprachlichen Unterricht*, 37 (1938), pp. 97–112; E. Meyn-v.Westenholz, 'Die Spannung der Weltanschauungen in Shakespeares *Macbeth*', *Deutsche Lehrerinnen-Zeitung*, 50 (1933), p. 256.

24 For example, H. Rochocz, 'Hamlet für die deutsche Jugend', *Die Neueren Sprachen*, 41 (1933), pp. 211–20; O. Stumpfe, 'Der Protagonist der Gegenwart', *Die Literatur*, 40 (1937/8), pp. 328–30; R. Huch, 'Hamlet und wir', *Monatsschrift für das deutsche Geistesleben* (1939, i), pp. 100–3.

25 Alfred Rosenberg, *Der Mythus des 20. Jahrhunderts*, 5th edn. (Munich, 1933), p. 306. The point was often taken up and elaborated; for instance by A. Krüper, *Die nationalpolitische Bedeutung des englischen Unterrichts* (Frankfurt am Main, 1935), p. 86; R. Schlösser, 'Der deutsche Shakespeare', *Shakespeare Jahrbuch*, 74 (1938), p. 24; H. Klitscher, 'Des Menschen Wille und sein Schicksal', in *Englische Kultur in sprachwissenschaftlicher Deutung: Festschrift für Max Deutschbein* (Leipzig, 1936), pp. 85–100.

26 L. L. Schücking, *Der Sinn des Hamlet* (Leipzig, 1936).

27 H. H. Glunz, *Shakespeares Staat* (Frankfurt, 1940).

28 It is worth noting that among the fifty or so doctoral dissertations on Shakespearean subjects accepted by German universities between 1933 and 1945 at least the one by W. Clemen was to make a lasting international impression; it recently went into a new English edition as *The Development of Shakespeare's Imagery* (London, 1977).

29 For a survey of this approach, and also for an attempt to relate it to the Nazi ideology, see P. Meissner, *Shakespeare* (Berlin, 1940). It was, however, relatively easy for M. Lehnert to remove the symptoms of Nazi conformism from his post-war re-edition of the book. A more thoroughly ideological book-length contribution such as E. Eckhardt, *Shakespeares Anschauungen über Religion und Sittlichkeit, Staat und Volk* (Weimar, 1940) was, however, an exception rather than the rule.

30 In fact C. Langenbeck's *Wiedergeburt des Dramas aus dem Geist der Zeit* (Munich, 1940) only continued the anti-Shakespeareanism uttered by some Nazi dramatists and aestheticians of note, such as E. W. Möller (cf. Rühle, *Zeit und Theater*, p. 49) or K. Gerlach-Bernau, *Drama und Nation* (Breslau, 1934),

Werner Habicht

p. 81. For an assessment of the literary context see U.-K. Ketelsen, *Heroisches Theater* (Bonn, 1968).
31 Reprinted in J. M. Wehner, *Vom Glanz und Leben deutscher Bühne* (Hamburg, 1944), pp. 20–38.
32 H. Pfitzner, 'Shakespeare-Dämmerung?' *Shakespeare Jahrbuch*, 77 (1941), pp. 74–92.
33 Klaus Mann, *Mephisto* (re-ed. Reinbeck, 1980), p. 333.
34 See the extensive documentation in F. K. Prieberg, *Musik im NS-Staat* (Frankfurt, 1982), pp. 144–64.
35 The incrimination was elaborately justified by E. Frenzel, *Judengestalten auf der deutschen Bühne* (Munich, 1940).
36 Reprinted in English as *Shylock: The History of a Character* (New York, 1963).
37 See A. Oz, 'Transformations of Authenticity: *The Merchant of Venice* in Israel 1936–1980', *Deutsche Shakespeare-Gesellschaft West, Jahrbuch* (1984), pp. 167–9.
38 See J. Wardetzky, *Theaterpolitik im faschistichen Deutschland*, p. 83.
39 See W. Quadflieg, *Wir spielen immer* (Frankfurt, 1982), p. 66.
40 K. H. Ruppel, *Berliner Schauspiel: Dramaturgische Betrachtungen 1936–1942* (Berlin, 1943), p. 22.
41 See I. Pietsch, 'Das Theater als politisch-publizistisches Führungsmittel im Dritten Reich', Dissertation (Münster University, 1955), p. 229.

The generation of *Life Is a Dream* from *Oedipus the King*

ELI ROZIK

The use of previously dramatized myths for new plays is a common procedure in the theatre. A notable example is the use of the myth of Oedipus as dramatized by Sophocles, in later plays such as *Oedipus* by Seneca, *Oedipe* by Corneille, *La machine infernale* by Jean Cocteau, etc. In this chapter my intention is to demonstrate how two plays which seem to dramatize two different myths could have been generated from one another by the application of some rules of adaptation; in particular, how *Life Is a Dream* by Calderón de la Barca[1] could have been generated from *Oedipus the King* by Sophocles.[2]

I do not intend to embark on a full comparison of the two plays, but just to make a point regarding the transference of a myth from one play to another, and especially from one culture to another. I am aware of the fact that the plays are usually compared on the thematic level since they both deal with the theological problem of fate. In this paper, however, I intend to show transformations which affect the myth itself. I am also aware of the fact that the Spanish play is usually viewed as an adaptation of the myth of Buddha[3] for a Christian audience. I anticipate that following the method applied in the subsequent analysis a much stronger connection to the Greek play will become evident. Furthermore, I expect that some of the rules which underlie possible generative relations could be established between plays which prima facie do not resemble each other on the mythical level.

It can be assumed that the reason for a far-reaching adaptation resides in the incompatibility of the source to fundamental notions of the target culture. These notions do not concern religious or moral issues only, but also poetic ones. I have attempted elsewhere to demonstrate that religious considerations may affect preference of plot-patterns,[4] and that transformations might be dictated by transition from one plot-pattern to another. My thesis in this article will be based on the plot-patterns described by Aristotle in his *Poetics*,[5] especially with regard to the two types of tragedy he suggests:

1. The change of fortune should not be from bad to good, but reversely, from good to bad. It should come about as the result not of vice, but of some great error or frailty, in a character either such as we have described, or better than worse. (p. 47: 1453a15)

2. In the second rank comes the kind of tragedy which some place first. Like the *Odyssey*, it has a double thread of plot, and also an opposite catastrophe for the good and for the bad. It is accounted the best because of the weakness of the spectators; for the poet is guided in what he writes by the wishes of his audience. The pleasure, however, thence derived is not the true tragic pleasure. It is proper rather to Comedy, where those who, in the piece, are the deadliest enemies – like Orestes and Aegisthus – quit the stage as friends at the close, and no one slays or is slain. (p. 48: 1453a35)

In the subsequent discussion I shall refer to the first type as 'hamartia plot-pattern' and to the second as 'second rank plot-pattern'. I assume that both are harmonious patterns, i.e., they suggest balance between the quality of the characters (good, bad, hamartia) and the nature of the consequences (failure, success).[6]

In its practice Spanish Golden Age drama shows clear preference for the second rank plot-pattern. Theoretically, such a tendency derives from the hedonistic principle, which is accepted as the main principle of Spanish poetics.[7] It is noteworthy, that, when he explains the predilection for the very same pattern in his own time, Aristotle too ascribes it to the taste of the audience, although he blames it. Obviously, the audience's taste in seventeenth-century Spain was fundamentally determined by Catholic faith. As elucidated below, preference for this plot-pattern mainly derives from religious considerations.

I suggest that the basic rules of adaptation in Spanish Golden Age drama originate in the need for accommodation with three basic constraints:

1 the terms of reference of the Christian contemporary audience;
2 the sensitivity of the Christian contemporary audience;
3 the features of the second rank plot-pattern.

For methodological reasons I will isolate the plot components of *Oedipus the King* from the cultural terms of reference and present them in neutral terms. In the subsequent paragraphs I shall refer to the former as 'mythical layer' and to the latter as 'interpretative layer'. This basic distinction will provide the appropriate background against which the specific religious interpretations given to the mythical layer in the Greek and Spanish versions would become isolated and thus comparable. This distinction is of crucial importance since it is my intention to show that adaptation reaches the mythical layer as well as the interpretative. The mythical layer of *Oedipus the King* can be outlined as follows:

a *Opening situation*
  1. Father – prophecy that the newborn will kill his father and marry his mother;
  2. Son   – prophecy that he himself will kill his father and marry his mother.
b *Motivation*
  1. Father – to prevent fate;
  2. Son   – to prevent fate.
c *Action*
  1. Father – orders to kill son;
  2. Son   – attempts to prevent killing his father and marrying his mother.
d *Outcome*
  1. Father – failure (fate is consummated);
  2. Son   – failure (fate is consummated).

Both characters fail with regard to their own motivation. Conversely, their failure means the success of the Gods, the antagonists, whose basic motivation is to bring about the prophecy. It is notable that, whereas the motives of the father and the son are identical – to interfere with fate – there is a fundamental difference with respect to their actions: Oedipus tries to avoid killing altogether, whereas his father actually tries to kill his own son.

On the religious level, Sophocles focuses on the decision of Oedipus to prevent an inauspicious fate. Since the prophecy reflects the will of the Gods, Oedipus's decision to abandon Corinth must be construed as an act of refusal and defiance. But the hero's attempt is also founded on sound ethical considerations, since he is trying to avoid the perpetration of two abominable crimes. The degree of morality of his decision in the eyes of a Greek audience is in direct proportion to the sense of calamity which his fate would have provoked in them. However, in the context of a fate imposed on him by divine powers, all his moral considerations look as though they contest their divine authority. In this cultural context, the fact that he sees himself as knowing better and doing better than the Gods definitely characterizes him as a case of hubris, which is a particular case of hamartia. Furthermore, his decision, which ironically epitomizes human wisdom, is presented in terms of blindness. The whole play revolves around this basic metaphor, in particular his 'quest' towards self discovery, which eventually leads to the blinding of his corporal eyes.[8] Blindness

leads him to see truly, like Tiresias, and prepares him for the world of
Oedipus at Colonus.

Oedipus's blindness is a particular case of hamartia because of his
basically positive characterization, especially his good intentions, despite
his terrible infringement on divine order. If we assume that in Sophocles
justification of divine order is presupposed and that hamartia is capable of
upsetting it, catastrophe is the means of restoring this order, and is both
proportional and fully justified. Oedipus fails on the mythical level, but on
the interpretative level his failure reconfirms the validity of the Greek faith
– the play truly befits the hamartia–catastrophe pattern, as suggested by
Aristotle, which allows balancing initial hamartia with ultimate catastrophe.

I assume that Spanish Golden age poetics could not have accepted this
kind of restoration of order and this type of final balance. In this cultural
context, Oedipus's actions could not have been understood as a case of
hamartia. In fact, even in the Greek version, neither the killing of
Oedipus's father nor the marrying of his mother is seen as his fault.[9] But in
this rendering he is blamed for preferring his ethical considerations to total
submission to the will of the gods. Such blame could not have been
accepted by the Spanish either. They would rather hold the gods
themselves morally responsible for Oedipus's predicament.[10] Apparently,
the Greek version does not preclude a contradiction between the gods'
precepts and the gods' will, and possibly, even assumes malice on their
part.

Laius could not have been accepted as a case of hamartia either.
Although he attempts to prevent the consummation of fate, he commits a
crime which is not less iniquitous than the one he is trying to prevent. He
exchanges parricide for infanticide. Laius, therefore, could not have been
accepted for the opposite reason: for a Spanish audience there was no
positive characterization that could have mitigated such an abominable sin.

Moreover, Spanish poetics could not have accepted this kind of
restoration of order because Sophoclean catastrophe does not take into
account the overwhelming positive traits of Oedipus, and especially his
good intentions, even if he fails in preserving divine order. In such a case
catastrophe cannot be accepted as the proper end for a balanced plot-
pattern. Consequently, with no hamartia and no balanced structure it is
rather difficult to see how Spanish poetics could have accepted the Greek
version as the best way to bring about the ritual reconfirmation of their
basic idea of divine order.

As mentioned above, in Christian drama of the seventeenth century
preference is given to fully balanced structures, especially of the 'second

rank' type. For hamartia plot-patterns, apparently, there are two basic ways to balance the plot: by gradually deepening the hero's weakness up to the point of sheer evil and eventual catastrophe, as in Shakespeare's *Macbeth*, or by stressing his good traits and preserving the hero from catastrophe by means of forgiveness and reconciliation, as in *Le Cid* by Corneille. In both cases such plot-patterns merge with the structure of second rank tragedy. In *Life Is a Dream*, for Basilio's plot, Calderón prefers the second way.

In this play the plot-pattern is aimed at bringing about the reconfirmation of a particular dogma in Catholic Christianity, with regard to the problem of predestination.[11] The answer to this specific theological problem is rooted in the concept of freedom of choice (*libre albedrío*). Seemingly, there is a contradiction between this principle and the omnipotence and omniscience of God. However, the relationship between them finds a harmonious solution in the play: the moral meaning of the events, although predetermined and obviously known beforehand to God, remains the choice and the responsibility of the individual. Thus, in the fictional world of *Life Is a Dream*, Basilio is indeed brought to his son's feet, as predicted by the stars, but, in contrast to his own interpretation of the prophecy, as an act of humiliation in his old age, the event is instilled by his son with Christian forgiveness and reconciliation. According to this view, the ancestral question as to whether fate could or could not be altered becomes meaningless, since the moral–religious meaning of the events remains to be determined anyway. In fact, it is the benevolent and optimistic notion of the role played by human beings in the scheme of the universe which determines the choice of reconciliation plot-patterns in Spanish comedy.

The basic choice of the reconciliation structure for the fictional world of *Life Is a Dream* dictates a series of subordinated changes which reach not only the interpretative layer of the play but also the mythical one. Therefore, the rejection of motifs which do not conform with the mentioned structure (third constraint), in addition to those which do not conform with Christian terms of reference (first constraint) and Christian sensibility (second constraint), underlies the generation of *Life Is a Dream* from *Oedipus the King*. In the following paragraphs I will attempt to explore the primary changes generated by these basic constraints.

As stated above, I assume that Calderón could not have seen any fault in Oedipus's behaviour. Therefore, for him, Oedipus could not have been the protagonist of a hamartia structure. In fact, Calderón chose to put Laius, Basilio in the Spanish version, in his stead.[12] Oedipus's father is a natural choice since, as mentioned above, Laius commits a crime, which basically resembles the one Oedipus is predestined to. In order to prevent the consummation of his son's fate, he decides to murder him. His considerations, apart from being selfish, can also be construed as criticism of the moral standards of the gods, and consequently characterized as hubris; there is no problem in shifting from the son to the father, who provides an equivalent disrupting factor as required by the hamartia structure. Furthermore, we detect a clear transference of traits from Oedipus to Basilio. The king is characterized by his court as the wisest of men (II.i.580), he is admired especially for his ability to 'read' the stars, and he acts accordingly. However, in spite of all his wisdom, when confronted with the ultimate consequences, he is presented, like Oedipus, as a self-glorifying 'blind' human being, i.e., as a tragic 'alazon'.[13] Again, if we take into consideration his basic positive characterization and his good intentions, especially toward his realm, and also toward his son, his mistaken ways become an obvious instance of hamartia.

The prophecy itself could not have been accepted by Christian sensitivity as a genuine manifestation of the will of God, since, as mentioned above, it implies malice on his part (second constraint). In addition, from a structural point of view, parricide and incest are not the kind of acts whose meaning could have been easily changed so as to conform with eventual reconciliation (third constraint). Consequently, we assume that Calderón altered the prophecy into 'He was born to trample me . . . And make of my gray hairs his very carpet' (Act I, p. 424), which is interpreted by the king as humiliation in his old age.[14] It is noteworthy that in the Spanish version the prophecy focuses on the appearances of the foreseen event, a fact that perfectly suits the intention to change the meaning previously assigned to it (third constraint). Hence, the king's contention that Segismundo will be a tyrant and conquer his father can easily be discerned as an unwise interpretation of the image seen by him in the stars.

As to the mother – actual incest is changed into a dubious interpretation of her death while giving birth to Segismundo as the first indication of his fierce nature (second constraint): 'Thus, Segismundo was born into the world, / Giving a foretaste of his character by killing his own mother', (Act I, p. 423).[15] This contention is by no means part of the prophecy and eventually proves to be mistaken (third constraint).

Laius orders his son to be left at the mercy of wild animals, which for a newborn baby actually means death. Such a decision would have revolted a Christian audience of the time, since, as mentioned above, it means the perpetration of a crime not less hideous than the one he was trying to prevent (second constraint). Furthermore, it is difficult to expect a son to alter his feelings toward a father who actually ordered his murder (third constraint). Therefore, we again assume that Calderón changed the order of the king from outright death into seclusion in a tomb-like prison, far away in the mountains. Such a decision preserves the original motivation – to prevent fate – and also has the advantage that it can be easily reversed: first, by the king himself, who wants to examine his own decision (II.i) and secondly, by the army's rebellion (III.i).

The decision to seclude the young prince entails a radical change in the way he was to be brought up. Instead of living with kings, whom he relates to as his parents, like Oedipus, Segismundo is reared almost as an animal without ever being enlightened about his fate and without ever being given the opportunity to decide for himself what to do with his own life. He is denied his basic human rights, as conceived by Christian faith, to freedom of choice and to Christian education to guide it. Thus, he becomes the victim of his father's decision. From the Christian audience's point of view, Segismundo's plot moves from innocent suffering to final redemption, thus conforming with the second rank plot-pattern.

The confinement of Segismundo is indeed reminiscent of the myth of Buddha, who was secluded by his father in his vain attempt to prevent him from becoming a monk. However, not only the reasons for his seclusion but especially the pattern of his spiritual growth are utterly different. Calderón prefers to present Segismundo's spiritual growth in the guise of the ascent from animal nature to humanity. This is done in three stages in which he successively acquires the three basic components of an accomplished human being: sheer existence, freedom of choice and understanding. These elements are represented metaphorically at the beginning of the play by his furs (animal existence), his chains (lack of freedom) and the feeble candle-light (lack of understanding) (I.ii).[16] Eventually he reaches human understanding which rules freedom of choice, and thus, in the last scenes, he becomes an embodiment of the idea of humanity. Segismundo becomes the wisest of men because of his genuine recognition of the limitations of the human condition. Paradoxically, Segismundo and Oedipus reach the same degree of wisdom by opposite ways.

The ultimate consequences of the plot definitely prove that the king misread the stars, that he did not take into account the power bestowed upon humans to impart meaning, right or wrong, to basically neutral events. Although he actually kneels at Segismundo's feet, as predicted by the stars, the meaning of the event is diametrically altered from humiliation to forgiveness and reconciliation. As it appears, Basilio's worst mistake resides in denying his son the means to cope with such an inauspicious fate, i.e., Christian education. Basilio not only disregards Christian teachings but also denies them to his nearest of kin. Undoubtedly, he has disrupted a fundamental rule in the mechanism of the universe. While a

Greek audience would have accepted a catastrophic ending, the Christian audience expects the opposite: the forgiveness and reconciliation granted by Segismundo. Undoubtedly, the plot-structure of *Life Is a Dream* demonstrates that for its particular audience only this type of final accord and harmony could act as a reconfirmation of their cultural beliefs. Eventually, after these transformations, the mythical layer of the plot for Basilio looks as follows:

opening situation:
1 Prophecy – humiliation (and submission);
2 Motive – to prevent fate;
3 Action – to seclude the prince;
4 Outcome – failure (fate is consummated).

All these changes are determined, directly or indirectly, by the new conceptual frame of reference and sensitivity and by the preference of a different plot-structure. Furthermore, they affect not only the interpretative material interwoven in the text, but also the mythical layer itself. There are other changes which do not result in different acts or characters, but rather reflect a search for equivalent motifs in terms of the culture of the new audience, as in the following examples:

1. Basilio is versed in astrology. This 'science' should be seen as an equivalent of the Greek oracle of Pytho. Both fulfil exactly the same function in the fictional world: they disclose to the human eye the knowledge of the future, which in principle is restricted to divine powers alone. However, in contrast to the latter, astrology was not regarded by Orthodox Christianity as a legitimate source of transcendent knowledge. Furthermore, the fact that Basilio relies more on astrology than on Christian dogma should be understood as his main tragic flaw.[17]

2. The characterization of a king as a person who ignores Christian teachings was unusual in Spanish Golden Age drama, not only because of the audience's loyalty to the crown, but also and foremost, because of the well-known sensitivity of the royal family to theatrical portraits of kings.[18] This might have been the reason for setting the plot in far-away Poland, probably conceived of by the Spanish as lying at the edge of the Christian world, in a cultural as well as a geographical sense. Such a removal in space could be viewed as an equivalent of the mythical reality in which the story of Oedipus was set. However, in the Christian version a shade of Paganism is attached to the king.[19]

These examples relate to elements of the fictional world which have no real impact on the structure of the plot. Nevertheless, even in the context of such equivalents, elements of deviation still occur. There are, however, changes which, since they affect features of the theatrical medium, should be seen as sheer translations into the theatrical vernacular of the target culture. I refer especially to the interchange of theatrical conventions. In the following paragraphs I will attempt to illustrate this principle by means of two sets of conventions which fulfil two basic functions in the fictional world: disclosure of inner thoughts and feelings of the characters, and interpretation of the plot in terms of the audience's culture.

Theatrical language presents a whole set of conventions capable of fulfilling a basic function in theatrical discourse: the communication to the audience of the feelings and thoughts of the main characters, while concealing them for one reason or another from other characters.[20] Soliloquy fulfils this function in the most undisguised way since it involves a character speaking directly to the audience. The entire set of conventions capable of fulfilling this function include also soliloquy to self; aside (to audience and to self); confidant; dialogue with choriphaeus; confession; reading of personal documents (diary, letter, etc.); and background music. Particular cultures show a preference for specific conventions, and the exchange of conventions on such grounds should be seen as a genuine case of translation.

Sophocles presents Oedipus's thoughts by means of pseudo-dialogue with the chorus, notably with the choriphaeus. This convention conveys additional meanings, usually attached to the chorus as representative of the community. As such, the chorus also enjoys natural authority, which is used for the sake of theatrical irony.[21]

Spanish theatre in the seventeenth century clearly prefers the confidant convention for the same purposes.[22] In fact, the introduction of this functional character reflects the attempt to avoid overt departure from the principle of similarity which underlies iconic communication. In other words, it reflects the intention to disguise soliloquy by lending it the appearance of dialogue.[23]

A typical confidant of the Spanish Golden Age is the *gracioso*, the base and witty stock type servant. His characterization as a servant justifies his master's disclosure of his innermost thoughts and motives. In addition, in order to foster the dialectic nature of this confidence, the *gracioso* is also given other traits which contradict his master's, such as cowardice and gluttony.

Similar considerations apply to the serious version of the 'servant'. Among other things, Clotaldo functions as confidant to the king (II.i, II.xiii, III.xiii). In accordance with the principle of contrasting characterization, Clotaldo, who is characterized as a perfect knight, counterpoises all the negative traits of Basilio.

In Spanish drama of the period, contrasting characterization is extended to the mood of the play: the *gracioso* is characterized as a comic figure and is also used to lend a comic dimension to the fictional world. This should be seen as part of the process of adaptation. Thus, whereas the main characters maintain a serious and lofty tone throughout the play, the servants introduce a comic one. Such a mixture was very much appreciated by Spanish audiences of the time.[24]

Clarín is the *gracioso* of *Life Is a Dream*. He serves in turn all the main characters of the play. This unusual feature saves Calderón from needing a separate confidant for each of the main characters, as in Racine's plays. In addition, it characterizes Clarín as the servant of many masters. Thus, the *gracioso* introduces a theme opposite to that of the loyalty of the archetypal knight, which plays a central role in the play.

Clarín imbues almost every scene with his comic viewpoint, sometimes even through his mere presence. Furthermore, it is my view that this admixture of moods, which in this particular culture is not viewed as an aim in itself, accentuates the archetypal moral purity of the knight. Presumably, Calderón's audiences, *Don Quijote de la Mancha*'s readership, could not have taken the idealized picture of knighthood any more, were it not for the refinement of the *gracioso*. In other words, the introduction of the *gracioso* makes the fundamental tragic mood acceptable, and consequently evokes a serious response in the audience.

The confidant convention is functionally equivalent to dialogue with choriphaeus and should be seen as a case of translation since it affects the communication system of theatrical discourse. The addition of the comic mood, which is a feature of the fictional world, does not contradict the former conclusion since confidants are functional characters who are used for other functions as well.[25]

Theatre language also presents a set of conventions capable of communicating to the audience the proper conceptual meaning of the plot, religious, philosophical or ideological, from the author's point of view. This function is absolutely necessary because of the independent nature of dramatic characters, who also display an independent point of view. The necessity is especially conspicuous where there is a gap between the categorization by the characters and the expected categorization by the audience. Originally this function was fulfilled by the chorus. The set of conventions capable of this function includes: the *raisonneur*, the honest man, the prophet, the God, the drunkard, etc. Occasionally this function is fulfilled by the main characters.

In *Oedipus the King* the conventions used for this purpose are the chorus and the prophet Tiresias. Both of them enjoy the authority needed to ensure recognition of their function by the audience. In contrast, Calderón, prefers the confidant convention. Again, Clotaldo and Clarín fulfil this function. They provide opposite interpretations of the same plot, the one correct, and the other mistaken.

Clotaldo is the honest man of the play. He is an adaptation of the shepherd of the original myth. Christianity uses the metaphor 'shepherd' for spiritual mentor. Jesus himself is viewed as the archetypal shepherd. Consequently, when the decision of Laius to leave the newborn baby in the woods by the hand of his shepherd is transformed into Segismundo's confinement, it is quite natural that a spiritual guide should be left with him in his prison. Although, in principle, according to his father's decree, the young prince should have been kept in a natural condition like an animal, with no education, there are quite explicit indications of Clotaldo's basic Christian teachings (I.vi.752). The motif of 'life is a dream' which is a central topic in Christian faith, also reflects a succinct knowledge of Christianity (II.xviii.2140–7).

In fact Clotaldo is the only character to express explicitly the ultimate moral of the play:

> . . . no es cristiana
> determinación decir
> que no hay reparo a su saña.
> Sí hay, que el prudente varón
> victoria del hado alcanza; (III.xiii.3111–15)

> . . . it is not a Christian judgement
> To say there is no refuge to his fury.
> A prudent man can conquer fate itself. (p. 476)

This attitude to fate is in contradiction to the way Basilio had approached the question; Clotaldo's view presents Basilio's attitude as an infringement of the Christian dogma and therefore as a clear case of hamartia. Clotaldo's words finally determine the hamartia-structure of the plot, with the Christian amendment – forgiveness instead of catastrophe.

A few verses earlier, Clarín too gives his interpretation of the situation:

> mirad que vais a morir
> si está de Dios que muráis! (III.xiii.3090–1)

> Although you flee from death, yet you may find it
> Quicker than you expect, if God so wills. (p. 475)

Seemingly, this view befits Clarín's own ultimate experience very well: he tries to escape death by hiding in a tree and is shot dead. Furthermore, his

Eli Rozik

conclusion is faithfully reiterated by the king himself, who actually echoes his last words:

> Mirad que vais a morir
> si está de Dios que muráis! (III.xiii.3092–3)

The message of the play seems to be implied in the reiteration of these words. However, the intention of such an unusual repetition is to the contrary. It reduces the king's viewpoint to the absurd, since he thoughtlessly accepts the view of a base, frivolous and amoral character.[26] According to Clotaldo's view, Clarín's life could well have been due to end, but it is up to him to bestow upon it the meaning of cowardice or heroism. Basilio, by echoing Clarín's last words, shows that he is still making the same mistake, since the real question is not if fate could be changed or not, but what meaning could be given to it.

This procedure of having a twofold interpretation is equivalent to the ancient one, since it is easily reduced to two basic functions: the presentation of the wrong interpretation by the tragic character, reinforced in this case by the *gracioso*, and of the right one, from the viewpoint of the author, represented by a functional character such as Clotaldo. Calderón's procedure is a clear case of translation from one functional character to another.

In conclusion, it can be seen that the main differences between *Oedipus the King* and *Life Is a Dream* can be explained by taking into account the small number of cultural constraints discussed in this paper. Other, secondary constraints could be added, such as those that regulate the addition of secondary plots,[27] the treatment of time and place, the setting of modes, etc. These cannot be dealt with within the scope of this article. However, all of them in conjunction could fully account for the vast majority of differences between the two plays.

Notes

1 Pedro Calderón de la Barca, *La vida es sueño* in *Diez comedias del Siglo de Oro*, ed. J. Martel and H. Alpern (New York, Evanston and London: Harper and Rowe, 1968). English version by Roy Campbell in *The Classic Theatre*, ed. Eric Bentley (Garden City, NY: Doubleday, 1959).
2 Sophocles, *Oedipus the King*, trans. D. Greene, in *Greek Tragedies*, vol. 1, ed. D. Greene and R. Lattimore (Chicago: University of Chicago Press, 1968).
3 Apparently, Calderón was acquainted with the myth of Buddha, which was introduced to Europe by the Arabs, through the adaptation of Lope de Vega in his play *Barlán y Josafá*. For further sources see Michael D. McGaha (ed.) *Approaches to the Theater of Calderón* (Lanham, NY and London: University Press of America, 1958).

4 Eli Rozik, 'Generic Transformation in Drama', *Assaph* C.1, 1984.

5 Aristotle, *Poetics*, in *Aristotle's Theory of Poetry and Fine Art*, trans. S. H. Butcher (New York: Dover, 1951).

6 For a discussion of the concept 'hamartia', see Gerald F. Else, *Aristotle's Poetics: The Argument* (Leiden: E. J. Brill, 1957), pp. 378–85. In my opinion both views can coexist. For the notion of balance in hamartia plot-patterns I rely on Aristotle's concept 'moral sense', p. 45:1453a2.

7 Lope de Vega, 'Arte nuevo de hacer comedias'. English version: 'The New Art of Writing Plays in this Age', in Barret H. Clark, *European Theories of the Drama* (New York: Crown, 1947).

8 Bernard Knox, 'Sophocles' *Oedipus*' in *Tragic Themes in Western Literature*, ed. Cleanth Brooks (New Haven, Yale University Press, 1960). See also Bernard Knox, *Oedipus at Thebes* (New Haven and London: Yale University Press, 1966 (1957)).

9 Sophocles, *Oedipus at Colonus*, trans. R. Fitzgerald in *Greek Tragedies*, ed. D. Greene and R. Lattimore (Chicago and London: University of Chicago Press, 1960), p. 123:270–81.

10 Cf. Oedipus's final words in *Oedipe* by Pierre Corneille, in *Théâtre Complet*, ed. M. Rat (Paris: Garnier, 1960), vol. 2e, p. 76. For the difficulty of Christianity in seeing Oedipus's deeds as sinful, see Pierre Corneille: 'Trois discours sur le Poème Dramatique' in *Corneille Critique*, ed. R. Mantero (Paris: Buchet-Chastel, 1964), p. 204.

11 The debate on predestination and freedom of choice was very vivid in Calderón's life time. There were supporters of predestination in Spain, like the Jansenists in France.

12 Laius was *basileus* and so was his son, although he viewed himself as *tyrannos*.

13 Northrop Frye, *Anatomy of Criticism* (Princeton: Princeton University Press, 1957), p. 217.

14 'había de poner en mí las plantas, y yo rendido a sus pies me había de ver . . . siendo alfombras de sus plantas las canas del rostro mío' (I.vi.720–5).

15 '. . . nació Segismundo, dando de su condición indicios, pues dió la muerte a su madre', (I.vi.702).

16 Pedro Calderón de la Barca, *La vida es sueño*, autosacramental in *Témoins de l'Espagne*, Textes bilingues, 2 (Paris: Klincksieck, 1957). See also Everett W. Hesse, *Calderón de la Barca* (New York: Twayne, 1967), pp. 144–5.

17 See Frank G. Halstead, 'The Attitude of Lope de Vega Toward Astrology and Astronomy', *Hispanic Review*, 7, 1939, pp. 205–19; and 'The Attitude of Tirso de Molina Toward Astrology', *Hispanic Review*, 9, 1941, pp. 417–39. As for Calderón's attitude to astrology, see E. W. Hesse, 'Calderón's Concept of the Perfect Prince in *La vida es sueño*', in *Critical Essays on the Theatre of Calderón*, ed. Bruce W. Wardropper (New York: New York University Press, 1965), p. 120.

18 Lope de Vega, 'El arte nuevo de hacer comedias', 'elíjase el sujeto y no se mire . . . si es de reyes, aunque por esto entiendo que el prudente Felipe, rey de España y señor nuestro, en viendo un rey en ellas se enfadaba'.

19 In addition to astrology, the names used by Estrella and Astolfo to praise the king are Tales and Euclides and not Christian ones (I.vi.579).

20 Eli Rozik, 'Theatrical Conventions', to be published in the *Proceedings of the Bochum Symposium on the Theory of Drama and Theatre, 1984.*

21 Eli Rozik, 'Theatrical Irony', in *Theatre Research International*, vol. 11, no. 2, 1986.

22 Jacques Scherer, *La Dramaturgie Classique en France* (Paris: Nizet, 1959), pp. 39–50. Cf. P. Corneille, *Théâtre Complet*, pp. 193–5.

23 J. Scherer, *ibid.*, p. 48 and P. Corneille, *ibid.*, p. 196.

24 Lope de Vega, 'lo trágico y lo comico mezclado, . . . harán grave una parte, otra ridícula / Que aquesta variedad deléita mucho.'

25 Conventions may fulfil different functions and the same function can be fulfilled by different conventions. See Eli Rozik, 'Theatrical Conventions'.

26 On Clarín as a negative character, see E. M. Wilson, 'On *La vida es sueño*', in *Critical Essays on the Theatre of Calderón*, p. 80. On Clarín as an interpreter, see E. M. Wilson, *ibid.*, and A. E. Sloman, 'The Structure of Calderón's *La vida es sueño*', in *Critical Essays on the Theatre of Calderón*, pp. 90–100.

27 There is controversy among scholars as to the justification of Rosaura's plot following the criticism of Marcelino Menéndez y Pelayo, *Calderón y su teatro* (Madrid, Revista de Archivos, 1881). Cf. E. M. Wilson, *ibid.*; A. E. Sloman, *ibid.*.

Claudel and Vitez direct Molière

YEHOUDA MORALY

Translated by Daphne Leighton

Claudel is known as the patron saint of traditional theatre; he bears the flag of the theatrical 'arrière-garde'. However, in his theoretical writing on performance and directing, Claudel develops ideas which are every bit as innovative as those of Brecht or Artaud. In 1949, at the age of eighty-one, Claudel staged *Les Fourberies de Scapin*. His production can only be compared to those of Antoine Vitez who, at the Avignon Festival, in July 1978, presented four of Molière's plays (*L'Ecole des femmes*, *Tartuffe*, *Don Juan*, *Le Misanthrope*) as if they were about the same man and the same woman, as if they were a single play, an epic on the meaning of life. Disappointed by love in *L'Ecole des femmes*, the hero turns to religion in *Tartuffe*, but does not find his way there either. Atheism also fails him, as we see in *Don Juan*, *Le Misanthrope* finally confirms the impossibility of total solitude, of deadening oneself to society.[1]

A production by Jouvet of *Les Fourberies de Scapin*, presented early in 1949, inspired Claudel's new project. The dramatist did not appreciate Jouvet's work and noted in his diary that the production was nothing more than:

the memory of the play in a young girl's dream. His Scapin in white satin and blue ribbons is like a bottle-imp who needs all his wits to keep his feet on the ground. His two old men are ridiculous, like monstrous trembling puppets caught in spiders' webs. Metro Lemarck's interference is incomprehensible! And the Mediterranean has become a gentle land, grey as turtle doves, stained with the blood of a slaughtered bird.[2]

The indefatigable old man immediately imagined an alternative staging of the play:

It should be something acted in a tavern by amateurs in an atmosphere of wine and tobacco, with the toilets not far away. Have the old men played by young people, and Scapin by a defrocked priest, Zerbinette by an old procuress. Young people, old drunks, etc. . . .

1 Antoine Vitez in rehearsal at the Studio d'Ivey, 1978.

Pantomime. People coming out of the toilets doing up their trousers. Someone brings in a basket full of wigs. Moustaches blackened with ashes. Molière's actors enjoying themselves.[3]

Claudel spoke of his ideas to Pierre-Aimé Touchard, the administrator of the Comédie-Française, who considered putting on these *Fourberies* the following February for *mardi gras*. During the summer, the production that had begun as a dream became realized in a new version of Molière's text, *Le Ravissement de Scapin*, the last of Claudel's plays.[4] Twenty years later, it was Pierre-Aimé Touchard, now the director of the Ecole du Conservatoire National, who introduced into this bastion of tradition a teacher whose new method of interpretation made a great impression on the Parisian theatrical world. This was Antoine Vitez.

Teaching in Lecoq's school, Vitez had noticed that the actor's imagination, which can operate freely with specific objects or ideas, appears to be totally stultified by classical texts. Neither the actor nor the director can approach the text neutrally; their thoughts are already conditioned by their cultural heritage. Hamlet is a tragic hero. Scapin is a comic buffoon. These preconceptions restrict personal creativity. If the actor is to act freely, to be completely immersed in the part, he must be divested of the images his culture has imposed on him. As therapist of the theatre, Vitez invented a series of strategies – le dépaysement ('defamiliarization'), montage, amnesia – which would allow the actor, and thus the spectator, to perceive the text in a new light.

Le dépaysement

Le dépaysement (defamiliarization) may be effected by placing a classical scene in a completely different setting. For example, Elvire talks to Don Juan from a car, or on a beach, or from a telephone booth. This is just the technique Claudel uses. What disturbed Claudel in Jouvet's production was the lack of a fresh view of the text. Jouvet's capricious Scapin and shaky old men are identical to all previous portrayals of Scapin and Géronte. They merely perpetuate a tradition which obscures the text itself. Claudel's objective, therefore, was an exercise in 'defamiliarization'. The play was to be set, not in Naples, but in a Paris tavern with people drinking wine:

A large room in a tavern full of tables where some men and women are sitting. The room is thick with smoke. At one of the tables people are playing dice, at another, Mora. The loser's nose is blackened with a cork and a candle. The tavern is near the Théâtre-Français and is frequented mainly by theatre people.[5]

Two young boys enter this den of iniquity carrying a large wicker hamper on their shoulders. They are offered a drink and everyone gathers around their mysterious burden. It contains the costumes for the forthcoming production of *Les Fourberies de Scapin* by the Théâtre-Français. Angry and frustrated at being left out, the out-of-work actors decide to put on the play on the spot. One of the carousers becomes their director:

> *A.*   . . . *Les Fourberies de Scapin* since we all know the play and have acted in it . . .
>
> *X.*   Hurrah!
>
> *Y.*   (*nudging another Y*) It's the scene-shifter.
>
> *A.*   I shall continue . . . and since here we are, all dressed and ready, I suggest we play ourselves . . . hic cup, hiccup . . . How do you say it?

Yehouda Moraly

Le Père Noble. Hic and nunc.[6]

The drinkers get ready, combining Racine, Corneille and Molière in a joyous literary carnival. The adaptation of the play retains only those passages which are pure theatre. The characters of Octave, Léandre and Hyacinthe disappear. We are left with the gags, Scapin's 'fourberies': the scene in which Scapin persuades Argante that Octave was forced to marry: the scenes where he extracts money from the two fathers to further the cause of their sons' love affairs; and the scene of the sack. Here, then, theatre is restored to its origins, to carnival, and Claudel remembers his very first play, *L'Endormie* (1886).

The sign and the signified

Claudel, as director, separates the theatrical sign from that which it signifies. Western realistic theatre endeavours to establish iconic identity between sign and signified, actor and character, costume and clothing, and between the stage set and the place where the action is meant to unfold. Even if realistic settings are now considered outmoded, 'good acting' is still equated with total identification with the character represented. In his *Scapin*, Claudel emphasized the separation between the sign and the signified. The theatrical sign was to be the exact opposite of the signified it interpreted. So, for example, the stage-manager proposes assigning wigs and roles by drawing lots. Le Père Noble, however, has a different suggestion:

Le Père Noble. With your permission, the old will play the young and the young will play the old. It's only at sixty that one begins to understand what youth is all about.

D. Fine! And there's nothing like youth for seeing the old as they really are. I'm the one who'll play Argante.[7]

The signified, purified of all superficial resemblance to the signified, can then be perceived more clearly. This theory is identical to the one developed that same year by Genet in *L'Enfant Criminel*. In a child's pocket a piece of wood is more dangerous than a real knife. For the piece of wood is not dangerous in itself; freed of any material equivalence, its symbolic meaning of violence and death is seen in all its clarity. In *Notre-Dame-des-fleurs*, Divine's dentures are the most royal of crowns; a real crown of diamonds or pearls would only distract from the concept of crown. The ignoble dentures point to the archetype, the very essence of 'crown'. The real Madame is the one played by her opposite. The true becomes false

138

since the apparent qualities and kindness of Madame serve to mask her real nature. It is only in the carnival scene of *Les Bonnes* that we see Madame as the cruel archetypal mistress. Here the lady, a vile tyrant, is *the* mistress whose relationship with her servants is inevitably tragic. For though she makes use of her maid's intelligence and sensitivity, the mistress negates her as a person.

Claudel too uses contraries. Who will play Scapin? Claudel had first wanted him to be played by a defrocked priest, and next by the philosopher Descartes himself, his polar opposite. Combining these two ideas, he had Scapin played by a former actor who has become a sexton at the Church of Saint-Roch, and who is the illegitimate son of Descartes, of whom he is the spitting image.

> *Le Père Noble.* Mossieu Descartes!
> *M. Ledessous.*   (*who, crouched unassumingly in a*
> *corner, has said nothing until now*) You know
> I'm not Monsieur Descartes. I'm Monsieur Ledessous.
> (*He is wearing a large felt hat like the famous*
> *philosopher Descartes in the portrait by*
> *Franz Hals. He is dressed in a shabby*
> *black costume, his collar soiled by snuff.*
> *And what is this bruise over his right eye?*
> *His flesh can be seen through the holes in*
> *his stockings. Next to him is le Camarade,*
> *also in black, but even more tattered.*)[8]

This strange sexton (he frequents taverns and steals the purse belonging to the one who plays Géronte) plays Scapin, adding passages from *Le Discours de la méthode* to the text of Molière in a way which recalls *Tartuffe*. Le Camarade, dressed in black, is Descartes' double,[9] as is Laurent, Tartuffe's servant, who is also dressed in black. In this way, Claudel embodies the character's deep meaning. The traditional way of playing Scapin with ribbons and stripes, hopping and skipping, in the style of the *commedia dell'arte*, ended by deadening Scapin's 'fourberies'. The main trickery – total hypocrisy – is protected by a mask of philosophy or religion.

Claudel disguised Scapin as Tartuffe; Vitez gives us a Tartuffe identical to Scapin. Vitez himself, just at the moment of Tartuffe's entrance, comes onto the stage dressed in black, with the demeanour associated with the character of Tartuffe since Fernand Ledoux's interpretation. But Vitez is being Laurent, Tartuffe's double.[10] Tartuffe himself makes his entrance, leaping like Nijinsky in *Le Spectre de la rose*. He is a handsome, dynamic, pleasant young man. In short, he is Scapin. In the same production,

2 *Jany Gastaldi in* Tartuffe.

Dorine the servant is played by Nada Strancar, an actress in the tragic style, with the voices and movements of a Greek princess. Jany Gastaldi, too childish even to play Agnes, acts the powerful Elmire. This 'therapy' of the part, which separates the theatrical sign from its hereditary culture image, restores Tartuffe to us. Instead of the boring classic, we now see a new play by a playwright of genius.

I would like to add one further example of theatrical interaction between the sign and the signified. Scapin–Descartes wants to make the mule claimed by the imaginary swash-buckler a concrete figure:

He makes signs that someone should send him the blind man's dog. It is passed around from hand to hand. It has wheels.[11]

The 'mule' is the dog belonging to the blind man who plays the hurdy-gurdy throughout the play. But the dog is not a real dog. It is a toy dog on wheels. Claudel's sense of humour is exercised on the aberrant form of the theatrical sign. Vitez uses the same comic method in his *Molière* (Avignon, 1978) and in *Grisélidis* (Avignon, 1977).

Montage

Claudel's approach to the play allowed him to suggest several conceptions of the same part. Two young drinkers want to play the part of Géronte. Both will interpret the role, each with one leg in the pair of trousers. After a while, the police arrest one of them. Géronte is then played by only one character. The police arrest him too. The Innkeeper agrees to play the part of Géronte, but he is not willing to be beaten, as he should be according to the text. And just as Scapin suggests the trick of the sack to Géronte, Scapin–Descartes suggests that the Innkeeper hang the sack on a hook which is used to hoist the wine casks up to the attic. The sack is to be hoisted up to the rhythm of blows. And like Géronte, the Innkeeper will be beaten, in spite of the precautions he has taken. He needs only to be robbed to identify completely with the character he is playing. Before long, this too happens. During the spoken chorus, which the audience itself performs, playing the various soldiers who threaten Géronte, Descartes' double rips open the sack and snatches the Innkeeper's purse. The Innkeeper's feigned fury soon becomes only too real:

> *The Innkeeper.* Scoundrel! Traitor! Villain!
> So this is how you murder me.
> (*He puts his hands in his pockets, realizes
> that the purse has disappeared and grabs hold of
> the culprit. His insults are now for real.*)
> You blackguard! Thief! Loafer! Villain![12]

Then, in a parody of apotheosis, Claudel, jumping audaciously to the final scene, has Scapin–Descartes carried off to the attic, whence the robber will run away. The part of Géronte is thus interpreted in totally different ways: two drinkers in the same costume, a single drinker; the Innkeeper as actor, the Innkeeper no longer acting but shouting in earnest because he has been robbed.

Suddenly Claudel violates even this crazy logic. Where is Géronte? Someone, in this seventeenth-century setting, yells that he is on the telephone. Realistic justifications matter little. Claudel, using the technique of superimposing one theatrical image on another, makes the characters into a composite 'photo-montage'.

Vitez also used the principle of 'non-mémoire' – amnesia. In his productions, the actors' performance is divided into different interpretations, each one forgotten as soon as it has been presented. Sganarelle loves Don Juan. Sganarelle hates Don Juan. The acting is a collage of feeling with no attempt made to create a consistent, homogeneous character. Such a character could only exist in the theatre.

From the character to the group, from performance to ritual

X, Y, Z: there are no characters in the staging proposed by Claudel. A group of actors does everything, is everything: actor, wardrobe-mistress, stage-director, author. 'There is no more author. We are the author. We're the ones who so need what follows that we make it happen.'[13]

The distinction between stage and auditorium disappears. If a prop is missing, the spectators give it to the actor. In one scene Scapin grabs a hat and then goes and puts the hat back on the person to whom it belongs. The audience is wardrobe-mistress and make-up artist: '*Sylvestre is fitted out by drawing him a moustache.*'[14] And according to this model of dramatic festivity, audience and actors interact constantly. The actor takes the audience to task. Scapin, reporting the horrors of a lawsuit, supports his arguments by bringing in members of the audience: '*With every other word, he grabs one of those present, not caring if it's a man or a woman, and brings that person into the action.*'[15] Géronte's famous line: 'What did he want to go in that galley for!' is repeated in turn by all present. It becomes a game; Géronte gives a signal and the audience responds. This signal becomes that of the conductor.

> Géronte.　I *makes a sign to the chorus with both arms.*
> Chorus.　(*a single pathetic voice from a corner*)
> 　　　　What did he want to go in that galley for!
> 　　　　What did he want to go in that galley for!
> 　　　　What did he want to go in that galley for!
> 　　　　(*Deep voice from the depths of the toilets*)
> 　　　　What did he want to go in that galley for![16]

In the same way, the famous sack scene is interpreted by the entire audience, who plays all the characters dreamt up by Scapin to torment Géronte. '*The scene which follows must be organized like a choral chant, with the various people present taking part. Scapin is to conduct with his cudgel.*'[17] Finally, the audience is the prompter. A mere detail, one might say; the actors forget their lines. But the audience which prompts is metaphoric. For Claudel, the writer speaks for the people:

The writer speaks instead of the people, with the tacit assent given him by the audience as soon as the actor opens his mouth. On the stage or elsewhere, he unburdens the multitude of the inexpressible sigh which it carries, confused, in its bosom.[18]

The mode of performance proposed by Claudel does away with the notion of character. From 1886 to 1954, apart from in his great symbolist plays, Claudel uses the chorus to play all the parts. The protagonist only emerged from the choral mass to demonstrate the universality of his cry. Today, this phenomenon of theatre without characters is not at all uncommon. In many great productions of the seventies, such as *Frankenstein*, *Akropolis*, *Orlando Furioso*, *1789*, the individual character is replaced by a group who play the different 'roles' in the manner described in *Le Ravissement de Scapin*. The actors of Savary and Ronconi 'play at' being different characters, who are presented only to be immediately transformed. As in *1789*, it is the group that we notice, rather than any particular theatrical figure. The abolition of individual characters changes the nature of the theatrical event. Performance becomes a ritual. The fictional events serve as a pretext for a real Dionysiac revelry, a state of wild abandon. What happens, whether mass or carnival, refers back to no other reality than that of the theatrical event itself.

Questioning the theatre

Through his staging of *Les Fourberies de Scapin*, Claudel suggests a theory of the origins of theatre. From this drunken, dishevelled group of people drinking in this tavern, theatre will burst forth as a free, chaotic carnival. The same overflowing *joie de vivre* characterizes Claudel's plays from *L'Endormie* (1886) to the *Ravissement de Scapin* (1949). Vitez's Molière cycle is also a carnival.

Vitez chose to have the four Molière plays performed in front of a backdrop with a palace '*en trompe l'œil*'. This palace was an exact replica of the auditorium of the theatre of the Conservatoire (the national school of dramatic art) where students tremble in fear as they wait their turn to take part in the final competition, in which they must interpret, according to the ancient traditions of the Conservatoire, these same images of French classical theatre (valet, servant, Célimène) which Vitez violates, inverts, tramples, pulverizes, with all the enthusiastic wild abandon of a *mardi-gras* carnival. The production is, in effect, a black mass. In the very place of the cult of Scapin and Célimène, the teachings of the Conservatoire are flouted.

For Claudel carnival and chaos are only a transitionary stage. All his 'experiments in drama' have the same structure. Confusion and chaos culminate in a heavenly choir. In the production under discussion, from the opening scene of drunkenness to the Latin chant at the end, the progression toward harmony is audible in the music. Claudel saw the theatre in the image of Creation. In a few hours, or in two million years, the primaeval chaos of Genesis becomes the celestial choir of the world to come.

143

This movement is the opposite of that of Vitez's productions, in which the primaeval chaos becomes more and more intense. At the end of his plays, the death toll rises: Arnolphe commits suicide, Tartuffe is executed. Vitez wanted *Le Misanthrope* to be followed by *Le Malade imaginaire* (where 'even death becomes impossible'). Theatre is chaos.

But what is most important for Claudel, as for Vitez, is the question theatre asks itself. Claudel does not use the theatre, as Pirandello does, to bear witness to the theatricality of human relationships. Like Genet, Claudel is concerned with the processes of theatre. The three women in *Les Bonnes* are Genet split up, watching himself act, in order to know what art is. The real innovation in *Les Bonnes* is that there are no characters. Claire is Solange and Solange is Madame. These three lunatics are three aspects of Genet questioning himself about the origin of theatre. The dishevelled drunkards in the tavern also reflect upon theatre. Art is self-reflexive. And if we compare Planchon's *Tartuffe* with that of Vitez, it is clear that Vitez has rid his work of all psychological and political issues. His Molière cycle is concerned, above all, with theatre.[19] This desire to make theatre self-reflexive, characteristic of the last plays of Claudel, seems to be central to the times. Art speaks only of itself. What is art? Where is it going? What is its meaning in relation to reality? No longer interested in the outside world, theatre questions itself about its origins and function.

Unfortunately, of course, Claudel was not really a director. He was only dreaming. In that same year (1949), he thought about three texts: *Le Partage de midi* which he had written in 1905, *Les Fourberies de Scapin* and *Tête d'Or*. In this third adaptation, which was partially published under the title of *Tête d'Or 49*, he simply applied all the techniques used in *Le Ravissement*. *Tête d'Or* is set in a concentration camp. The hero, who has long blond hair, is played by a consumptive with the Jewish name of Simon Bar Yona. The symbolic tree is the stove-pipe in the prisoners' dormitory. There are two Cébès, just as there were two Gérontes, and the princess is a Jewish waiter whose face is seen only through a hole cut in sackcloth. Cébès and Tête d'Or die in the course of the rehearsals.

But Jean-Louis Barrault was not able to realize these three fantasy productions. Claudel was too innovative. Even today, who would dream of giving the part of Tête d'Or to a consumptive foundling, or of casting Descartes in the part of Scapin? Who else would have the Church represented by a Jewish waiter, and Géronte by two drunkards with one leg each in the same pair of trousers? He would meet violent objection, be accused of being a vandal, an iconoclast, and a traitor. In 1949, Claudel was ahead of his time. He had adapted these three plays, written in another context, not according to the theatrical conventions of his time, but according to those of tomorrow.

Notes

1 'We have performed the four plays at the same time as if they were one tetralogy ... We have brought out the parallels between the characters and the situation in the four plays. *Le Tartuffe* could be played as an avatar of *Don Juan*. And the role of Don Juan is like that of Alceste: the same passion inflames them both' (Antoine Vitez, *Programme notes for the Avignon Festival*, July 1978).

2 Paul Claudel, *Journal*, vol. 2 (Paris: Gallimard, 1969), pp. 674–5. All translations are those of the translator of this article.

3 *Ibid.*

4 In 1951 it seemed as though Claudel's *Fourberies* would be presented together with Jean-Louis Barrault's production of *L'Echange*. The Société des Auteurs obliged Claudel to choose a new title for this adaptation. In 1952 the play was published under the title *Le Ravissement de Scapin* in the magazine *Opéra*.

5 Paul Claudel, *Le Ravissement de Scapin*, in *Théâtre II* (Paris: Gallimard, 1965), p. 1340. Could this be the Le Ruc, an elegant café near the Comédie-Française with its crimson and velvet plush surroundings? A present day equivalent would be a suburban dive frequented by extras from a nearby film studio. The extras use the soda siphon and the juke-box to evoke those captivating films in which they would be only the props.

6 *Ibid.*, pp. 1342–3.

7 *Ibid.*, p. 1343.

8 *Ibid.*, p. 1344.

9 In *Sous le rempart d'Athènes*, an experiment by Claudel in 1927, each character was played by two actors. One spoke the text, while the other performed the actions. This shadow of Descartes makes only one movement instead of M. Ledessous (Descartes), only one but the main one. He snatches the Innkeeper's purse.

10 Remark overheard in the auditorium by Vitez's assistant, Eva Lewinson: ' – It's Tartuffe!
   – No, it's Vitez!'

11 Paul Claudel, *ibid.*, p. 1357.

12 *Ibid.*, p. 1373.

13 *Ibid.*, p. 1337.

14 *Ibid.*, p. 1360.

15 *Ibid.*, p. 1358.

16 *Ibid.*, pp. 1367–8.

17 *Ibid.*, p. 1373.

18 Paul Claudel, *Mes Idées sur le théâtre* (Paris: Gallimard, 1966), p. 24.

19 This is not the only possible reading, but it seems to me the best.

The role of the target-system in theatrical adaptation: Jalāl's Egyptian–Arabic adaptation of Tartuffe

CAROL BARDENSTEIN

Literature is one major realm of cultural activity in which intercultural influence takes place, and perhaps nowhere else as explicitly as in literary translations and adaptations from one linguistic and cultural system to another. Despite the undeniable relations existing between the original or 'source'-texts, and the translated or adapted 'target'-texts, translation and adaptation are essentially goal-oriented, or teleological activities, conditioned to a great extent by the goal they are serving. These goals are determined primarily by the recipient or target-system, for it is in this system and this system alone that the translated or adapted text will ultimately function as a textual-linguistic product.[1]

Gideon Toury describes translation as a 'socially-oriented' type of activity. Translation is not, as it is sometimes made out to be, an isolated meeting between the translator and a text to be translated, with the translator free to define translational problems in his own terms, and to 'unleash', as it were, totally new, personal solutions onto the target-system. Rather, the translator and the process of translation are subject to various types and degrees of constraints imposed from within the recipient system.[2] These constraints or influencing factors are the various sets of literary and translational norms existing within the target literary system, which shape the produced text from the outset of the translation process. They influence the very selection of the text to be translated, the formulation of the translated or adapted text, as well as the status of that text within the recipient literary system. This is perhaps most conspicuous in literary adaptations, in which the adapter explicitly emphasizes the text's acceptability within the target cultural system.

I emphasize this target-text and system orientation in the study of literary adaptations, because this aspect has not been adequately or systematically examined in studies of the play I propose to discuss here. *al-Shaykh Matlūf* is an adaptation of Molière's *Le Tartuffe*, undertaken in the late nineteenth century by Muhammad 'Uthmān Jalāl.[3] Existing studies of this play tend to make comparisons between small sections of the source-text, Molière's *Le Tartuffe*, and the target-text, Jalāl's *al-Shaykh Matlūf*, concluding largely on an intuitive basis that a particular section of Jalāl's text is or is not 'equivalent' to the source-text, or does or does not fit some social norm of nineteenth-century Egyptian life. This is done without systematic elucidation of a concept of equivalence, and without a distinction between the different types and levels of equivalence (formal, functional, linguistic, literary-textual). Nor do these studies consider the position of the target-text with respect to existing norms within the Egyptian literary system. Instead of any systematic approach to these issues, the existing literature manifests an almost *ad hoc* approach, reflecting the individual preferences, prejudices and idiosyncrasies of the researchers.[4]

In several studies, critical judgement is passed on sections of Jalāl's text for not corresponding sufficiently to actual social or behavioural norms of Egyptians living at that time – that is, on the basis of lack of verisimilitude in these sections (e.g., would a *shaykh*, or Muslim pious man, actually drink wine, or put his hand on the thigh of the married woman of a household). They do not question, however, whether it was 'likely' for Molière's Orgon, the head of the household (or Jalāl's Ghalbūn) to be hiding under the table and to go unnoticed by Tartuffe/Matlūf during the mock seduction scene. The degree of verisimilitude in literary pieces is a norm-regulated phenomenon. This means that it may vary from text to text in terms of its acceptability in the recipient literary system, and it cannot be presumed automatically that a particularly high degree of verisimilitude is a necessary requirement for acceptability. In *Qaragoz* or puppet theatre, for example, or other popular farces, the repeated and violent excessive beating of one character by another certainly did not represent actual social norms of people of that time, but it did conform to contemporary norms of dramatic performance, with clear dramatic functions. The degree of verisimilitude was not an essential criterion for acceptability within the literary system. Such distinctions must be made for statements about the effect of the degree of verisimilitude on target-system acceptability to have any degree of validity.

Before being able to undertake the larger task of giving a full description of norms of equivalence in *al-Shaykh Matlūf*, comparing them with the norms in other adaptations by Jalāl or by other adapters of the period, a first step is necessary. This first step is to examine closely the adapted text,

Matlūf, and its relations to its target-system: i.e., to examine its relation to some of the existing norms in the nineteenth-century Egyptian literary system (linguistic, literary-textual, dramatic, etc.) in terms of the selection and formulation of the text itself, and its status within the target-system. It is this first step that I will attempt in the present discussion. In so doing, I am in no sense denying or reducing the role of the source-text, *Le Tartuffe*, in the production and status of the adapted text, and indeed will refer to its role in some of the examples discussed below. I am merely attempting to highlight the target-system's role and to establish it as a priority *before* attempts to establish specific source/target-text relations and norms of equivalence.[5]

The status of the body of translated or adapted literature within a given literary system may vary, depending upon the particular system into which it is being integrated, the particular historical period, etc. The status of a body of translated literature may be 'secondary' (in the sense defined by Even-Zohar) in which case the indigenous literature provides the system's major literary models and norms, while the body of translated literature is only peripherally, if at all, participating in shaping these norms. Translated literature may also, at certain times and under particular conditions, assume a 'primary' position within a given literary system, in which case it actively participates in the formation of the literature's central models and constitutes an integral part of that literature's innovative forces.[6]

The second half of the nineteenth century has come to be referred to as the beginning of a literary (as well as overall cultural) Renaissance in Egypt, largely because this period witnessed the appearance and spread of new kinds of writing, of new and different genres of literature that had not previously appeared in these forms in the Egyptian–Arabic literary system. At this early stage the majority of these new writings were translations or adaptations from foreign literatures. In fact, during this period of flux, translated and adapted literature seems to have assumed a primary position in shaping the major literary models of the Egyptian literary system, introducing many features that did not exist there before, and that would have been unlikely to arise through the indigenous system's own means. This role was bound to be particularly pronounced in cases of those adaptations or translations from foreign genres that had practically no existing counterpart, or that had only rudimentary or loosely related counterparts in the Egyptian literary system – the novel, for example, or the Western form of 'official' theatre.

During this period of transition in Egypt's literary system, no set norms existed either for the adaptation of theatrical texts, or for the composition of texts for precisely this form of theatre, for an adapter such as Jalāl to conform to or to deviate from. Jalāl did have some immediate predecessors and contemporaries who were engaged in adapting plays, or in other ways bringing this Western form of theatre to Egypt,[7] but their attempts had not yet established clearly identifiable norms within the overall literary system. What does an adapter do when faced with what is, in many senses, nearly a vacuum of norms in his own literary system, in undertaking to adapt a text such as Molière's *Tartuffe*? The two-pronged solution that presents itself, and which Jalāl seems to have employed, was: (1) to draw upon those other areas that *do* exist within the linguistic–literary system, and which *do* have their own sets of norms, using them in his adaptation in ways which may either conform to or deviate from their traditional usage in the literary system, and (2) to introduce what appear to be essentially new literary forms and elements in his adaptation, that are not part of the target-system convention (most likely finding their source or inspiration in the source-text, although not necessarily). Jalāl himself described what he did in his adaptations as 'removing from them their French garb, and dressing them in Arab garb',[8] although being more precise, he was dressing them in specifically Egyptian garb, with the Egyptian colloquial dialect, characters, and customs, in what has come to be referred to as the 'Egyptianization' or *tamṣīr* of plays.

The target cultural system begins to exert its influence starting with the very selection of the works to be adapted. Why, at this period in Egypt's literary history, would a French classic theatre-piece such as *Tartuffe* be selected for adaptation? What does this choice reflect in the nineteenth-century Egyptian literary context?

First, in understanding the choice of a text from French literature as opposed to other world literatures, the special status that French culture held among certain select sectors of Egyptian society at the time must be cited, as part of a broader identification of these sectors with French culture. Furthermore, several viceroys, among them most notably Ismāʿīl, and other members of the ruling class, most of whom had had a French education, and some of whom had developed a penchant for French classical drama, were at times, though not consistently, in the position of patronizing theatre troupes and directly or indirectly encouraging the translation and adaptation of texts for the theatre. Also, French theatre in particular seemed to enjoy a special status in Egypt, among those limited segments of Egyptian society that did attend the performances of foreign theatrical troupes. French, Italian, Greek, Armenian and other foreign troupes performed in Egypt at this time. But Haggagi notes in his work on the subject that the general opinion of the Egyptian spectators of these performances was that those of the other troupes were 'second rate' and clearly inferior to those of the French companies.[9] Thus based on performances by foreign theatre troupes witnessed by Egyptians in Egypt, limited as this exposure may have been, French theatre became respected as an ideal to emulate.

The educational missions begun by Muḥammad 'Alī earlier in the century had first been sent to Italy and elsewhere, but subsequently came to be increasingly and then almost exclusively sent to France. These missions played an important role in giving rise to a new sector of Egyptian society educated in French, some of whom had extensive contact with the French literary system. For those who were not members of the educational missions to Europe, like Jalāl, the School of Languages in Cairo provided another point of contact with French literature, as part of the diverse and extensive curriculum there. Many literary translations and adaptations from French were the products of students of this school, and of those working in the Bureau of Translation attached to the school, Jalāl among them.

The wave of largely Christian Syrian and Lebanese immigration to Egypt in the second half of the nineteenth century must be mentioned in this regard as well. Their pioneering and influential role in the new literary developments of this period is well-known, and as Christians, many of them had had French schooling in the well-developed network of French missionary schools in their countries.

And why the selection of a classical French play, part of the canon of 'high' literature as it were? This choice occurs in the background of other choices at the time, when others were adapting and translating non-classic, non-canonical forms, such as farces, comedy sketches and revues, etc.,[10] as well as classics from world literature. Jalāl's selection of *Tartuffe* (and his other adaptations of Molière, Corneille and Racine) manifests a conspicuous desire, in line with certain trends of reform at the time, to educate the Egyptians, to make classical world literature a part of the average Egyptian's cultural education, and specifically to make this 'high' literature accessible to segments of Egyptian society which had previously had no access to it. Jalāl had very explicit views about the didactic and 'civilizing' role of theatre, and clearly felt that this play, as others he adapted, had something of value to teach to the Egyptian public. But in his not merely translating, but 'Egyptianizing' these plays, Jalāl implicitly supported borrowing from the West, but selectively; learning what was deemed valuable from the West, but appropriating it into Egyptian culture, expressing it in Egyptian terms and Egyptian cultural symbols. It is also probable that in choosing *Tartuffe*, Jalāl sensed that comedy was a mode very likely to meet with a favourable reception by the 'people of the joke',[11] as the Egyptians are popularly referred to, in what would constitute some of their first exposure to Western forms of theatre.

Thus we find that numerous circumstances and conditions in nineteenth-century Egypt and its literary system actively influenced the selection of such a text for adaptation. Once having selected the text to adapt, Jalāl had to make the basic and essential choice of which language variety to use in his adaptations, in light of the phenomenon of diglossia, or actually multi-glossia in the Egyptian–Arabic linguistic–literary system.

This phenomenon is the usage of different varieties of Arabic: the classical or formal literary variety (*Fuṣḥa*), the vernacular or colloquial dialect (*'Aamiyah*), and the numerous shades between these two poles. In brief, the conflict of diglossia in Arabic literature is between possible demands for verisimilitude, and the notion that a privileged language form, or one with an elevated status, should be used in literature, and specifically in canonical 'high' literature. The latter notion finds its roots of authority in Islam, or in the Koran specifically, considered to have come down in a 'perfect' form of Arabic. By extension, in subsequent literary developments, it was deemed necessary to emulate this language form in any belletristic undertaking, even if its content was of a secular nature. The problem with verisimilitude in literature (particularly acute in theatrical texts, being composed entirely of dialogue) is, quite simply, that no one actually speaks this formal literary form of Arabic (*Fuṣḥa*) in natural spoken contexts.

It would be too much of a digression to detail here all the complexities of the diglossia controversy in Arabic literature. Suffice it to say that Jalāl used the Egyptian colloquial dialect in his adaptations, and a form that accurately reflected the natural spoken idiom of his time.[12] As a generalization, and inevitably an over-simplification, it may be said that before this influx of translations and adaptations into Egyptian literature, the language usage conventions of indigenous literary production were as follows: formal literary Arabic was used in canonical literature, which included the classical style of poetry, religious texts, etc., and the colloquial idiom was used in non-canonical literary forms, which included various forms of popular poetry,[13] anecdotal collections, etc. The colloquial dialect was also used in a number of dramatic forms, such as the popular farces, the Qaragoz puppet plays, and performances by improvisational troupes.[14]

But for the new form of European theatre and texts, adapters such as Jalāl (as well as those attempting original compositions) had no clear set of norms to follow or deviate from in terms of choice of language variety. One might have expected comedies to be adapted or translated into the colloquial, in view of the fact that indigenous comic dramatic forms were in the colloquial for the most part, and in view of the subsequent development of the prevalent norm of the colloquial being used in comedy. But the majority of translated and adapted plays of the period, including comedies, were in formal literary Arabic, often in rhyming prose. It seems that being drawn from classic world theatrical literature, these plays had a special, somewhat elevated status within the Egyptian literary system. Various attempts were also made at conventionalizing language variety distribution, for example, having educated characters speak formal literary Arabic, and uneducated characters speak the colloquial; or city-dwelling characters speak the literary variety, and villagers and peasants speak the colloquial. There was also a general movement towards the use of the colloquial in theatre at the time, overlapping to a great extent with a trend of Egyptian nationalism, represented by people such as Yaʿqūb Ṣanūʿ, who wrote his plays in colloquial prose, and ʿAbdallah al-Nadīm, who used the colloquial as well in his nationalistic plays.

Thus Jalāl's choice to use the colloquial was not a totally unique one in his context and literary system, but the specific choice of using colloquial rhymed and metred verse (*zajal*) in the adaptation of a French classic comedy was a unique one. His choice reflected that period's growing awareness of a distinct Egyptian identity and Egyptian patriotism, as well as the 'corrective' or reforming spirit of the time, in seeking to 'remedy' the average Egyptian's ignorance of international cultural trends, and to cultivate in him a taste for Western theatre. Jalāl's aim was to make these plays accessible to a broad Egyptian public, and in choosing to adapt French classics into the colloquial, he was attempting to break the barrier of the relative linguistic exclusivity existing between canonical and non-canonical forms of art, and of theatrical art specifically, within the Egyptian literary system.

Jalāl made the more specific choice of using colloquial verse throughout *al-Shaykh Matlūf*, and the manner in which he used it illustrates one of the solutions Jalāl used in his adaptation technique. In the absence, within the Egyptian literary system, of set norms of prosody in the particular genre he was adapting, he drew upon existing prosodic norms in other areas of the literary system (colloquial and formal literary poetry) and modified them somewhat in both form and function, by taking them out of the context in which they were traditionally used.

Clearly in choosing this particular prosodic form,[15] Jalāl was trying to achieve at least formal equivalence with the Alexandrine verse used in Molière's *Tartuffe*. Each line of an Alexandrine couplet has twelve syllables, and of course, the lines are rhymed in couplets (aa, bb, cc, etc.). Despite the vast differences between French and Arabic prosody, the form

Jalāl used also yields twelve syllables, and a similar rhyme scheme. This particular metre (*rajaz*) was an established one in the Egyptian literary system, but its traditional usage was in various forms of poetry, organized into discrete segments as poems or stanzas of poems. Removed from their traditional context, and placed in this new context, the *rajaz* rhyme and metre in the colloquial were used in alternating utterances of characters' dialogue, and were sustained throughout a five-act play.

Jalāl's use of this type of versification in a theatrical piece as dialogue resulted in the breaking of a prosodic convention that had existed in its traditional use in poetry within the Egyptian literary system, namely, the preservation of the single verse as a discrete indivisible unit. Breaking of the verse unit occurs approximately 100 times in the play (corresponding in most instances to Molière's division of verses) in various forms. In some instances, a character has one hemistich of dialogue, and the next character speaking completes the verse with the second hemistich. In other instances, a single first hemistich or single second hemistich may be divided into the utterances of as many as four different characters. Some of the verse divisions are examples of stichomythia, dialogue in alternate parts of lines used in sharp disputation, characterized by rhetorical repetition, or taking up of the opponent's words.[16]

Jalāl was not the first to break the unity of the verse in theatrical dialogue,[17] but his were some of the earliest examples of this. Thus Jalāl's use of this colloquial prosodic form is indeed an instance of employing norms existing in the target literary system in his adaptation. But the fact that he used them in a literary context different from their traditional one, the different function accorded to them in this new context, and the alteration of some of these norms, all contributed to the introduction of new literary forms and usages into the Egyptian literary system.

It is important not only to point out Jalāl's use of colloquial poetry in relation to existing norms in the Egyptian literary system, but also to examine how the use of versification itself acted as a constraint, or an active factor, in the formation of the text *al-Shaykh Matlūf.* For although the *rajaz* is considered one of the simplest of the Arabic poetic forms, both in terms of its metre and rhyme scheme, the requirement of sustaining a particular sequence of long and short syllables and rhyme, coupled with the dictates of attempting to adhere closely to the semantic component of an already composed source text, *Tartuffe,* none the less combined to produce a very considerable set of constraints on the adapter. Clearly these constraints exist throughout the text, but their weight is most apparent when 'irregularities' arise, apparently due to these constraints. 'Irregularities' here refers to phenomena that appear to be contrary to the norms posited by Jalāl himself in adapting the text. One such phenomenon in the play is Jalāl's insertion of words in formal literary Arabic with irregular distribution, which are distinct from the language variety he chose to use, the Cairene Egyptian colloquial dialect. There are some literary Arabic insertions that are not 'irregular', for example those that fit within the context of a Koran citation or other religious references. But the 'irregular' instances referred to here are those which seem to have arisen in order to meet the constraints imposed by the metrical requirements (i.e., the colloquial dialect word, which would not have met the metrical requirements, is substituted by a formal literary equivalent word, which does). These instances yield distinctly awkward formulations that appear to have no other compensating function. They illustrate a lack of consistency with regard to a particular norm set up by Jalāl within the adapted text – the use of the colloquial – as a result of the interference of, or constraints imposed by another norm posited by Jalāl – the use of rhymed and metred poetry. It is also probable that this 'interference' made the text somewhat less acceptable in the Egyptian linguistic–literary system.[18]

Jalāl's choice of using colloquial rhymed and metred verse in his adaptations was one of several options within the range of possible colloquial literary forms. Another possibility was colloquial prose, which was used by both Yaʻqūb Ṣanūʻ and ʻAbdallah al-Nadīm in their theatrical compositions, and which later became an established convention in most of Egyptian theatrical comedy. Colloquial rhymed prose was an option as well. Despite the fact that Jalāl stands out as one of the early pioneers in using the colloquial in a canonical genre, Jalāl's specific choice of using rhymed metred colloquial verse sustained throughout a play did not develop into a norm within the Egyptian literary system, either in the adaptation or in original composition of theatrical texts. Nor was it, according to my knowledge, attempted again by any other adapter at all. It is possible that in adapting this play into verse, besides clearly imitating Molière's source text, Jalāl hoped to elevate the style and status of the text, to compensate for the 'risk' taken in using the 'non-canonical' colloquial for adapting a canonical classic. There seems to be some indication that it was perceived as such, but ascertaining this would require further research.[19]

It should be noted that Jalāl stands apart from most of his contemporary adapters in having been concerned primarily with the publication of his adaptations as texts, and in not having been directly involved in acting, directing or producing the plays. While this had various consequences, it acted in the service of establishing a written tradition of theatrical texts, to be read as well as performed, and in the colloquial dialect. For many theatrical texts from that period were never published, having been adapted, translated or composed by people directly involved in the plays' production, whose primary concern was seeing that these plays were performed. These plays never became available to the public as written texts to be read. Many have been lost, or in the best of cases, preserved in manuscript form in public or private archives.

Jalāl's adaptations themselves did not, in fact, become part of a corpus of widely read theatrical texts, and are primarily of interest to students and scholars of that period in Egypt's literary history. However, the development of a tradition of written theatrical texts to be read, besides their existence as performed texts, *has* gained a strong foothold in the Egyptian literary system.

A close look at what might appear to be a minor feature of the play *Matlūf*, namely Jalāl's adaptations of the names of characters, is surprisingly revealing in terms of illustrating other aspects of the relations between this adapted text, and the recipient Egyptian literary system. It illustrates the interplay between considerations of the source-text and the target literary system in the process of adaptation. These considerations are manifest as (1) a strong tendency to make the characters' names possible Egyptian Arabic names (i.e., the consideration of verisimilitude with respect to the target-culture); (2) granting a literary function to some of the names in terms of the character's role in the play; and (3) in some of the names, seeking formal equivalence (e.g., phonetic similarity) with the names of Molière's characters.

Thus, for example, the names of some characters respond only to the requirement of being possible Egyptian names, without having any additional literary-textual function within the play, and do not phonetically resemble the corresponding names of Molière's characters, such as the character 'Salmān' for Molière's 'Cléante', or 'Aḥmad Nabīh' for 'Valère'. Then there are names that have an enhanced literary function, with the verisimilitude consideration played down for comic effect, such as the name 'Ghalbūn' for Molière's 'Orgon'. In this instance, the names sound somewhat similar, with a close to rhyming ending. 'Ghalbūn' is certainly not a 'likely' Egyptian name, but its meaning gives it a literary function relating it to the character and role of 'Ghalbūn' throughout the play. The name comes from a root with the generalized meaning of 'poor, miserable', which fits the character of Ghalbūn not only in his state of weakened authority in his household, but in terms of being duped by the deceitful Matlūf. In this instance, Jalāl considered the source-text item in terms of phonetic similarity, but his prime consideration was that the name have a clear literary and comic function in the Egyptian target-system.

With the name 'al-Shaykh Matlūf', corresponding to Molière's 'Tartuffe', Jalāl has also considered the source-text in using a rhyming sound to draw a formal similarity. But in this case too he put a special emphasis on the character's name having a literary function within the play and recipient literary system. For the generalized meaning of the root of the name 'Matlūf' is 'ruin, destruction', with the particular grammatical form of his name meaning 'ruined' or 'the ruined one', perhaps alluding not only to the ruin and corruption he tries to instigate in the family household, or to himself as a 'morally' ruined man, but also to the downfall that is his outcome at the end of the play. Neither of the names 'Matlūf' or 'Ghalbūn' are 'realistic' names in terms of verisimilitude considerations of the Egyptian context, but they certainly do conform to norms of acceptable names within a literary piece for a caricaturing or otherwise comical effect.

It becomes apparent from even such a limited sample, that the particular balance struck between source-text considerations and target-text and system considerations differs greatly from item to item of the adapted text. Since each item of the adapted text is a semiotic entity which can have a meaning and function on numerous levels, it also becomes apparent that each of these items can have different degrees of what can be called 'richness'. The choice of the name 'Matlūf' has a high degree of acceptability in the Egyptian target-system on a linguistic level, as well as having a literary-textual function within the adapted text. This is in addition to corresponding to the source text item 'Tartuffe' on the formal phonetic level, as well as to the role of the character 'Tartuffe' in the source-text – i.e., to a literary-textual function in the source text. This stands in conspicuous contrast, in terms of relative 'richness', to the choice of the name 'Salmān' in the adapted text for Molière's 'Cléante'.

The preceding discussion might appear to be an over-reading of significance into the apparently peripheral sample of the choice of characters' names in an adaptation. Besides serving to simplify the task of trying to discuss in English Egyptian dialect adaptation solutions to French adaptation problems, this small sample illustrates, in a simplified fashion, many of the fundamental issues involved in the adaptation of theatrical texts from one language and literary-cultural system to another. That is to say, it manifests the extent to which the original or source-text influences the target-text, and perhaps more notably in these examples, the extent to which target linguistic and literary systems and their norms determine, or at least set some guidelines for, the range of possible items chosen in the adapted text. This sample also demonstrates a few different ways in which, and degrees to which, items in the adapted text may conform to or deviate from those norms, with implications for acceptance within the target Egyptian literary system.

Many features of Jalāl's adaptation clearly find their most immediate source, or at least most conspicuous influence, in the source-text *Tartuffe*. Some of these features overlap substantially with norms already established in related dramatic forms in the Egyptian literary system, and some overlap only very minimally. The dominant influence, for example, in the formation of Jalāl's character the 'Shaykh Matlūf' was Molière's character 'Tartuffe'. But the shaykh, or Muslim man of religion, as a familiar character in certain other indigenous dramatic forms in the Egyptian literary system has a considerable history, overlapping in some aspects with Jalāl's 'Shaykh Matlūf', and differing in others. The presence or absence of certain literary norms or features within the recipient literary system, and the resonance or lack of apparently newly introduced features with those norms, can have significant implications for the reception and integration of a particular feature into the target literary system.

Badawi cites the 'distinguished ancestry' of the mock-preacher in Arabic literature of humour, from the works of al-Jāḥiẓ to the 'maqāmāt'.[20] In Ibn Dāniyāl's medieval shadow play *'Ajīb wa-Gharīb*, one of the first of the parade of characters to appear is the Muslim preacher, who makes a 'mock-sermon', in which he basically describes in 'religious' language, twisting certain religious references and symbols, his methods of deceiving people to obtain money from them, praising the drinking of wine, and advising his listeners to follow in his path.[21] The conspicuous characteristics of such a mock-preacher are being a swindler, using a religious identity as a cloak for his deception of people, and being avaricious.

The presence of a later version of the 'turbanned shaykh' or pious Koran reciter is cited as a recurring character in the Qaragoz puppet plays, which were performed in Jalāl's time. The character in these plays also tries to exploit people, usually Qaragoz himself, in the name of religion. But the character has taken on a number of other aspects. He is an object of mockery to a much greater extent than the previous shaykh character described, and is not presented as a terribly serious threat. He is a would-be exploiter and swindler who, like almost any character sharing the stage with Qaragoz, eventually gets clobbered with his ever-active beating stick. An additional feature is that the shaykh tries to use formal literary Arabic (*Fuṣḥa*) in talking to other characters, as a way of pretentiously trying to put himself in a position superior to those he is addressing, speaking in a manner deliberately designed to make others feel inferior and ignorant for not being able to understand. His very use of this kind of speech, however, simultaneously makes him an object of mockery and ridicule. This is partly because it meets with utter lack of comprehension on the part of the characters he intended to intimidate, which can be a rather formidable weapon itself at times. He is also ridiculed because he cannot actually 'pull off' speaking formal literary Arabic, and often ends up speaking what is actually the colloquial dialect with certain changes in pronunciation, many of them incorrect, to make it sound as if he is speaking the formal variety.

The 'Matlūf' character introduced by Jalāl certainly embodied some of the traits of other past 'corrupt shaykh' characters. He was a hypocrite and an imposter, essentially in the business of swindling others for his own material gain, and assuming a religious veneer to cloak his true aims. He was to marry Maryam, Ghalbūn's daughter, but lusted after Anīsa, Ghalbūn's wife, as well. He gorged on food and indulged in wine-drinking. He succeeded in duping Ghalbūn into signing over his house and property to him under false pretences. He did, however, constitute a serious threat, and although other members of the household spoke of him disparagingly, he was not a clear object of mockery throughout the play like some of the other shaykh characters in the Egyptian dramatic-literary system. The characteristic of trying to speak formal literary Arabic (*Fuṣḥa*) as a means of lording it over those he is trying to exploit, or as the butt of mockery, is notably absent in Jalāl's depiction of his shaykh character. It appears that this was a relevant and available feature existing in the literary system that Jalāl did not choose to draw upon, despite the fact that it is easy to imagine how this might have enriched his depiction of the shaykh character, and despite the fact that the hypocritical '*Fuṣḥa*-speaking' shaykh went on to become established more firmly as a normative character in the Egyptian literary stock.[22]

Despite the absence of the latter particular feature, it is clear that the 'Shaykh Matlūf' character as depicted by Jalāl, in resonating with certain existing norms of the 'shaykh imposter' character in Egyptian drama and literature, had an enhanced potential for being accepted and integrated into the Egyptian literary system. Nearly every scholar discussing this character has claimed that the fact that Matlūf indulged in wine-drinking presents a problem in his characterization, because of being so out of tune with social mores of the time. I would be more inclined to say that a shaykh in nineteenth-century Egypt trying to convince people of his piety, was indeed not likely to gulp down wine in front of those very people, but that this did not necessarily present a problem in terms of his depiction as a character in a play, i.e., as a literary or dramatic convention.

I would approach in a similar fashion the numerous very explicit sexual references Jalāl's characters make, almost none of which are found in the source-text, *Tartuffe*. In *Tartuffe*, for instance, we find the maid Dorine saying that if the neighbours are complaining about the excessive social activity at Orgon's house, it is only to divert attention from their own intrigues, without specification of those intrigues. In Jalāl's text, these intrigues are made far more explicit: 'People are always coming in and out of there / And there's a flood of water outside the bathroom door', the second hemistich being a very explicit allusion in the Egyptian dialect to sexual intercourse having taken place.[23]

Dorine describes another complaining neighbour in general terms as someone who has aged and whose beauty is fading. Jalāl's parallel character 'Bihāna' describes this ageing as 'when her hair turned white, and her breasts began to sag'.[24] Similarly, during the mock-seduction scene, when Elmire is trying to tell Tartuffe to slow things down a bit, the most explicit she becomes is referring to 'les choses qu'on demande', whereas in Jalāl's text, Anīsa tells Matlūf that they have plenty of time, at least three or four hours, until she will go to 'put on some see-through clothes / And prepare the bed and arrange every-thing'.[25]

Numerous such examples exist in the play, some of which have been cited by scholars as flaws or problematic deviations from Molière's text similarly on the basis that these expressions would have been offensive to public taste at the time. These bawdy and explicitly sexual elements, however, resonated with features of other existing popular dramatic forms of entertainment in the Egyptian literary system, such as the Qaragoz puppet play and popular farces. The fact that these features did overlap with those in existing popular dramatic forms, and lent the play a more 'popular' flavour, could clearly prove effective in the service of Jalāl's desire to make this play accessible to an Egyptian audience that was more broadly based in terms of class.

The above discussion has been an attempt to outline the relation of Jalāl's adaptation, or a limited selection of certain aspects of it, to the Egyptian literary system, in terms of the formation of the text *Matlūf* in relation to the norms existing in that system, as well as its acceptability as a product within that system. Many other features of *Matlūf* interact with norms in dramatic and other literary forms that existed in the Egyptian literary system in ways similar to and different from those described above. Much remains to be said about, for example, the norm of the prologue, the contrived happy ending brought about through the intervention of a powerful entity, the presence or absence of music, etc. These and other features of Jalāl's adaptation deserve separate detailed studies.

Carol Bardenstein

Notes

1 Gideon Toury: 'Toward Description Translation Studies: Goals, Procedures and Some Basic Notions', in *In Search of a Theory of Translation* (Tel Aviv: Porter Institute for Poetics and Semiotics, 1980), p. 82.
2 Toury: 'German Children's Literature in Hebrew Translation', in *In Search of a Theory*, p. 141.
3 *al-Shaykh Matlūf* in the collection of comedies by Muḥammad 'Uthmān Jalāl, *al-Arba'Riwāyāt min Nakhb al-Tiyātrāt*, in *al-Masraḥ al-'Arabī: Dirāsāt wa-Nuṣūṣ*, vol. 4, ed. Muḥammad Yūsuf Najm (Beirut, 1964). First published separately in 1873 (Cairo).
4 A recent study of *al-Shaykh Matlūf* by S. Ballas is an exception to this, in raising the question of the position of Jalāl's method of adaptation with respect to contemporaneous norms of translation and adaptation. See Shimon Ballas, 'Itālah 'ala manhaj Muḥammad 'Uthmān Jalāl fi al-tarjamah', *al-Karmil: Abḥāth fi al-Lughah wal-Adab*, vol. 6 (Haifa, 1985), pp. 7–36.
5 A theatrical adaptation, like any theatrical text, and in contrast to the short story or novel, is in the unique and complex position, as Elam has pointed out, of functioning as a semiotic entity simultaneously in two distinct but related semiotic realms; see Keir Elam, *The Semiotics of Theatre and Drama*, New Accent Series (London: Methuen, 1980), pp. 2–3. It functions as a 'performance text' in the performer–audience transaction on the one hand, and functions as a text that is a written mode of dramatic fiction, designed for stage performance, which may also be consumed as 'read' literature, on the other. The norms and conventions in these two realms may overlap, but by and large they are distinct. Without digressing here into the complexities of this factor, it is important to at least acknowledge this distinction, and in the ensuing discussion, I have attempted to maintain this distinction, and to indicate it explicitly when relevant.
6 Itamar Even-Zohar, 'The Position of Translated Literature Within the Literary Polysystem', in *Literature and Translation: New Perspectives In Literary Studies*, ed. James S. Holmes, Jose Lambert and Raymond Van den Broeck (Leuven: Acco, 1978), pp. 117–20.
7 Such as Mārūn al-Naqqāsh, Ya'qūb Ṣanū', 'Abdallah al-Nadīm, etc.
8 Jalāl's Introduction to collection of comedies, *al-Arba'Riwāyāt*, ed. Najm, p. 4.
9 Haggagi, 'European Theatrical Companies and the Origin of the Egyptian Theater (1870–1923)', *American Journal of Arabic Studies*, 3 (1975), pp. 83, 84–5.
10 Representative of this trend in a different literary genre is also the profusion of detective stories and mysteries adapted and translated from French and English, appearing in newspapers of that period.
11 *Ahl al-nuktah*.
12 Noted by H. Blanc, 'La Perte D'une Forme Pausale Dans Le Parler Arabe du Caire', *Mélanges de l'Université Saint Joseph*, XLVIII (Beyrouth, 1973–4), p. 384. This obviously must allow for the distinction between 'natural' spoken

language and the literariness of literary language. The language in Jalāl's adaptations generally reflected natural spoken idiom on certain linguistic levels (lexical items, morphology, etc.) but of course it would not be 'natural' for a native speaker of the time to invert word order, or to speak in rhyming metred poetry, as do the characters in Jalāl's texts.

13 Such as *zajal*, the *mawwāl*, etc.

14 These dramatic forms, by and large, had no written texts, or at most, had minimal written blueprints or outlines.

15 Dimeter, *rajaz zajal*.

16 For example, in the argumentative scene between the maid, Bihāna, and the head of the household, Ghalbūn, in which he is furious with her for speaking ill of the Shaykh Matlūf, the word 'blasphemed' (*kafart*) is picked up in Ghalbūn's retort. Bihāna says: 'You mean I'm blaspheming if I tell you the truth?!' and Ghalbūn retorts: 'Yes, you've blasphemed both the Prophet Muḥammad and Christ!' (p. 30, *Matlūf*, Najm edition).

17 'Amer has pointed out that Marūn al-Naqqāsh did this as well in the play *al-Bakhīl* (*The Miser*); 'Aṭṭia 'Amer, *Lughat al-Masraḥ al-'Arabī*, (Stockholm, 1967) pp. 46–7.

18 The question of to what extent insertion of formal literary Arabic (*Fuṣḥa*) items in predominantly colloquial literary texts was acceptable, or a norm within the Egyptian literary system (and the possible variety of functions of such insertions) is currently under study by the author. It is also conceivable that these 'irregular' insertions call attention to a distinction between *Matlūf* as a written text and as a performance text. In this sense, the orthography in the written text would indicate the form that fulfils the metre requirement at the expense of language variety consistency, whereas in actual performance, 'correction' might have been made in favour of language variety consistency at the expense of conforming to metrical norms, for it would be less likely for the average spectator to notice the latter non-conformity.

19 It is interesting to note in this regard that in an article appearing in *al-Ahrām* newspaper in 1915, in which a vaudeville theatre troupe in Cairo is criticized on the basis of its 'low' content and language style, the writer closes by recommending that this troupe use, in its adaptation of plays 'a language similar to that of Muḥammad 'Uthmān Jalāl in his Arabization of Molière's plays' (*al-Ahrām*, 8 June 1915, p. 4). This would seem to imply that in its context, Jalāl's language style had some slightly elevated status in comparison with that of other forms of comedy adapted into the colloquial dialect. Whether or not this attitude is attributable specifically to his use of colloquial verse, or whether it actually reflects disapproval of the content of vaudeville plays, is something that could only be established through further study. It is difficult to assess other reactions and attitudes at the time to Jalāl's use of colloquial verse, because criticism or comments about the language of the plays often actually represent stances with respect to other more general issues, such as being against the use of colloquial as opposed to literary Arabic in written literature, or being critical of plays of foreign origin.

Carol Bardenstein

20 M. M. Badawi, 'Medieval Arabic Drama: Ibn Dāniyāl', *Journal of Arabic Literature*, 13 (1982), p. 103.

21 Ibrāhīm Ḥamāda, *Khayāl al-Ẓill wa-Tamthīliyāt Ibn Dāniyāl* (Cairo, 1963), pp. 196–8.

22 Ya'qūb Ṣanū' ridicules the pretentious language of the shaykhs in a play from that period. Also, a slightly later manuscript exists of a satirical play by S'adīq Fahmī Ḥusayn called *al-Ustādh*, from 1919, apparently influenced by *Tartuffe*, and which incorporates the pretentious and comic use of formal literary Arabic (*Fuṣḥa*) into the depiction of the lewd and corrupt turbanned shaykh. We find this aspect later in a secondary character of a play by Najīb al-Rīḥānī (1928), who is a shaykh speaking in *Fuṣḥa* constantly telling jokes and anecdotes that no one understands. A very popular manifestation of this character appeared in the well-known song by Sayyid Darwīsh/Badī'Khayrī entitled 'al-Shaykh Qufā'a', a shaykh who tries to make his very popular colloquial expressions sound like formal literary Arabic, to a very comic effect. He hyper-corrects, by pronouncing the 'qaf' where it does not belong, adding formal literary word endings to English words ('finish' becoming 'finishun'), etc.

23 Jalāl, *al-Shaykh Matlūf* in *al-Arba'Riwāyāt*, p. 13, line 13.

24 Jalāl, *al-Shaykh Matlūf*, p. 13, line 25.

25 Jalāl, *al-Shaykh Matlūf*, p. 71, line 21.

Chekhov in limbo: British productions of the plays of Chekhov

VERA GOTTLIEB

Naturalism – or 'Ibsenite symbolism'? The 'subjectively painful' – or the 'objectively comic'? The sleepy reveries of trivial people (as parodied by Peter Ustinov in *The Love of Four Colonels*) – or a rigorous exploration of the need for perspectives on life? A collection of charming eccentrics and neurotics – or a careful patterning of social and class groups?

This either/or approach has characterized British Chekhov productions from the first one in 1908 – George Calderon's production of *The Seagull* at the Glasgow Repertory Theatre – up to the present time with the recent productions of *The Seagull*, directed by Charles Sturridge, and *The Cherry Orchard*, directed by Mike Alfreds. But it is exactly this approach which has rendered much of British Chekhov inadequate: the very essence of a Chekhov play lies in its balance. As Irving Wardle suggested in 1973:

> It seems to me that British Chekhov generally suffers from the same complaint as British farce. We cannot hold a balance between sympathetic involvement and comic detachment.[1]

The challenge of the play in production is in how exactly such a balance – or analogous balances – is to be achieved. Sometimes that challenge has been met: for example by Anthony Page's production of *Uncle Vanya* at the Royal Court Theatre in 1970;[2] by Richard Eyre's production of *The Cherry Orchard* in 1977 in a version by Trevor Griffiths, and by another version, this time of *The Seagull* by Thomas Kilroy at the Royal Court Theatre in 1981, in which the action of the play was transferred to turn-of-the-century Ireland. It is not accidental that out of these three memorable productions, two of them were versions of the plays in which the emphasis was clearly on communicating the *ideas* of the plays to a British audience, rather than on a 'portrait gallery'.

Some of the difficulties of Chekhov production in Britain are common to those of many plays transplanted from one culture to another, but other problems arise from a wanton disregard of the social and historical context

163

Vera Gottlieb

in which a play was written – from an apparently 'apolitical' stance (conscious or otherwise) on the part of the director. This *apparently* apolitical approach is, in fact, political – from the earliest British productions until Richard Eyre's 1977 *The Cherry Orchard*, an unquestioning political assumption governed the interpretation of the plays in performance. Chekhov's was the 'voice of twilight Russia'; he was 'the poet and the apologist of ineffectualness', and he deals with 'the tragedy of dispossession'. This interpretation increasingly coincided with the prevalent British view of the Russian Revolutions of 1905 and 1917, and was further strengthened by the mood of disillusionment and dejection which partly characterized the inter-war years. The plays were performed as tragedies in which it was assumed that the voices or forces of change in the plays were potential agents of destruction; in which it was assumed that the other characters were charming and blameless victims of circumstances beyond their control, and in which it was assumed that Chekhov's tone and intention was a sorrowing evocation of a valuable way of life gone for ever. It is only in the last ten or fifteen years that Chekhov's use of irony has really been explored in productions. These political assumptions were also reinforced by the translation, in the inter-war years, of Chekhov's stories, of Dostoyevsky and of Gogol in which English views of the 'Slav soul', of the 'typically Russian' and of 'Russian philosophizing' seemed to be confirmed and were overlaid on Chekhov's dramatic characters.

The emphasis, then, was on 'tragic character' to the virtual exclusion of 'social comedy' – an emphasis reinforced, in turn, by the influence of Stanislavsky on the English theatre: character exploration rather than the exploration of ideas in a play. Over the eighty years of Chekhov production in Britain a strange anomaly has arisen: the plays are *always* staged within a period setting or, at least, with period costuming; but, with very few exceptions, the period itself or social context of the plays has been ignored. We are given 'the period' in appearance, but almost never in substance. The characters wear late-nineteenth-century dress, but the plays do not 'voice' the economic, social, philosophical, and political preoccupations of Chekhov's Russia. Character is isolated from milieu and from context in a way which is peculiarly British – and historically un-Russian. In the uncritical assumptions of so many British productions of Chekhov, much more is revealed about Britain than about Chekhov. As Kenneth Tynan wrote:

We have remade Chekhov's last play in our image just as drastically as the Germans have remade *Hamlet* in theirs. Our *Cherry Orchard* is a pathetic symphony, to be played in a mood of elegy. We invest it with a nostalgia for the past which, though it runs right through our culture, is alien to Chekhov's. His people are country gentry: we make them into decadent aristocrats.

Next, we romanticize them. Their silliness becomes pitiable grotesquerie; and at this point our hearts warm to them. They are not Russians at all: they belong in the great line of English eccentrics. The upstart Lopakhin, who buys up their heritage, cannot be other than a barbarous bounder. Having foisted on Chekhov a collection of patrician mental cases, we then congratulate him on having achieved honorary English citizenship.[3]

This, I would suggest, is a major stumbling block to Chekhov in the English theatre – a self-imposed narrowing of understanding and vision which compounds the normal difficulties of translating or transposing a play. These common difficulties must be mentioned, however briefly, in order to put the argument into a perspective. First, and most obviously, there are linguistic difficulties: the nuance of Russian does not translate well into English and there are almost insuperable problems in translating both idiom and irony; terms of endearment or disapproval, achieved in Russian through subtle variations in address, have no real counterpart in English. Equally problematical is the fact that the volubility of Russian in moving rapidly from 'laughter' to 'tears' often comes across as over-emotional or neurotic when translated into English; and the Russian language does not carry class distinctions: like French and Italian, but unlike English, it is not possible to gauge the background of a character from the mode of speech. In the English theatre the class of a character is immediately apparent in the use of accent or dialect, but in Chekhov's Russian the servants are only distinguishable by the form of address to their masters or occasionally (as with Firs) by the use of *kartavet*.[4] The gentry, on the other hand, are only ever differentiated by their occasional use of French, and thus Yasha's use of French in *The Cherry Orchard* reveals his class aspirations. English productions of Russian plays, however, have almost invariably imposed the British class system on the characters' mode of speech: servants are played with 'working-class' accents while Lopakhin, for instance, is frequently played as a Northerner – as a kind of bluff Yorkshire businessman.

Geographical differences also create misunderstandings in production: the Russian countryside and the *nature* of Russian provincialism are organic to both the structure and the settings of Chekhov's plays – as indeed is the *size* of Russia. The distance from Moscow of the provincial setting of *Three Sisters*, for example, is crucial to an understanding of the whole play: distance creates a provincial milieu in which 'colours fade, thoughts become debased, energy gets smothered in a dressing-gown, ardour is stifled by a house-coat, talent dries up like a plant without water'.[5] But isolation in Chekhov's plays is almost always interpreted in British productions as a purely philosophical concept, and not as a geographical reality. The isolation of Sorin and Konstantin in *The Seagull*, of Vanya and Sonya at the end of *Uncle Vanya*, or of the three sisters, is partly *literal*. The absence of a real English equivalent prompted Thomas Kilroy's version of *The Seagull* in which the action was set in turn-of-the-century Ireland, a social equation which was more readily understood by English audiences and which brought the characters immediately into focus. In the majority of productions, though, the sense of isolation seems to emanate only from character, and not as a result of a real understanding of the setting and milieu. In much the same way, the theme of ecology – the forests in *Uncle Vanya*, or the full significance of the setting in Act 2 of *The Cherry Orchard* – is often missed or, again, put down to character idiosyncrasies.

A further problem of translating a play, however, lies in the cultural and philosophical differences between the country from which a play originates, and the country in which it is performed. For the sake of brevity, two examples relevant to British Chekhov will have to suffice: humour and the area of 'positive affirmations'. There *are* similarities between the Russian and the English use of irony and understatement, but there is a significant difference in, for example, the interpretations and usages of farce, and hence of the farce elements in Chekhov's plays. In the Russian theatre from the eighteenth century to the present day, whether in Gogol or in Chekhov, farce is partly philosophical; in the English theatre, farce more often than not is physical. This was clearly evident in one of the moments in Charles Sturridge's *The Seagull* in which Arkadina (played by Vanessa Redgrave) 'grabs Jonathan Pryce (Trigorin) by the knees, throws him to the ground and crawls between his out-spread legs while fondling his bottom and declaring him to be a great writer'.[6] In the words of Francis King in the *Sunday Telegraph* (11 December 1965), Redgrave's Arkadina was 'vulgar'. Redgrave is one of the least vulgar of actresses but here the use of English farce vulgarized both the character and the play at that moment.

The question of 'positive affirmations' is, perhaps, a more contentious one: there is a peculiarly English embarrassment at people or characters who 'spout' positively about life or who talk idealistically or hopefully about the future – even though he sugared the pill, Shaw has still not really been forgiven for using the stage in this way; hence, perhaps, the difficulty English actors, directors and audiences have had with characters like Vershinin or Tusenbach or Trofimov. In England it is quite difficult to avoid a laugh at Anya's 'Good-bye, house. Good-bye, old life', and Trofimov's 'And welcome, new life' *unless* Trofimov as a character has been established as a serious contributor to the ideas of the play, even if a somewhat ridiculous figure. In Mike Alfreds's production, courageous and innovative though it was, Trofimov was one of the great weaknesses.

Last but not least in this short-list of 'transposing' factors, there is the difference in interpretations of realism in the two cultures: Soviet Russian productions of Chekhov are not only post-Stanislavsky, but are also post-Vakhtangov, post-Meyerhold, and post-Tairov. Russian realism, from the nineteenth century to the present day, encompasses many kinds or sub-divisions of realism, ranging from grotesque realism (Gogol) to satirical realism (Saltykov-Shchedrin), and Chekhov's realism refined, as Nemirovich-Danchenko put it, 'to the point where it became symbolic'.[7] But all forms of realism are associated in Russia with social realism, with the very purpose of art and literature, and the obligation of the artist to society (this is, indeed, part of the debate in *The Seagull*). The function is social, educative and, in the broadest sense, political. British productions of Chekhov are, however, post-Stanislavsky in their assumption of naturalism and, until Richard Eyre's 1977 *The Cherry Orchard*, followed by Peter Gill's production of the same play at the Riverside Studios, London, and Trevor Nunn's *Three Sisters* in 1979, and now Alfreds's production, have largely remained so. This has meant not only the assumption of naturalism but also a kind of *carte blanche* for the actors to 'be' the character often to the detriment of the ideas contained in the plays. Debate, which sits uneasily on the English stage, is treated as something which emanates from Chekhov's charming idiosyncratic characters, not from the whole social fabric of the plays.

All these problems of 'transposition' were very evident in one or the other of the latest British Chekhov productions – Sturridge's *The Seagull* and Alfreds's *The Cherry Orchard*, the first of which seemed to contain all the problems mentioned and with few redeeming features, while the second has made a valuable contribution to British staging of Chekhov, albeit with some crucial weaknesses. Both productions received good reviews, *The Cherry Orchard* more so – and deservedly so. But as so often in the history of productions of Chekhov in Britain, the major critical attention was focused on the portrayal of the characters by 'star' performers. To denigrate the crucial importance of actors in a production would be as foolish as to denigrate the contribution of character to a play, but the point is that almost none of the critics analysed what the directors were actually trying to communicate of the play's meaning as a whole. Is it because the meaning or point of these plays is so familiar to us? If that were so, then surely there would be no argument about the constant reinterpretation of Shakespeare's plays in performance? Is it because we all share the same view of what Chekhov's plays are saying? If so, then Richard Eyre's controversial production would not have been a landmark in the history of British Chekhov – or, if that is so, then that would suggest a dangerous over-simplification and misreading of a rather simple and boring drama-tist. Or is it because few are actually concerned with what the plays are 'about' – that, it would seem, is not the emphasis of British Chekhov, and it is not what makes Chekhov the most frequently revived European dramatist in the British theatre. Russian productions of Chekhov, on the other hand, have in recent years created a considerable demand for tickets on the black market, have 'taken on' Moscow Art Theatre Chekhov with vigour, have placed Lyubimov's theatre, the Taganka, under attack, have caused open arguments amongst audiences – have been varied and *alive*. It was Sir John Gielgud who made the point with reference to Shakespeare that 'each generation rediscovers Shakespeare in terms of its own time'. Few attempts have been made to rediscover Chekhov in nearly eighty years of productions.

The critical emphasis on the actors, however, matches the actor's own love of playing a Chekhov character, and for the actor the 'Stanislavsky' potential is vast. Sometimes, as in the case of Ian McKellen's Lopakhin, this can result in a complete, vivid and absolutely intelligent reading of the character, but that is more often the actor's intelligence at work than the director's overall concept of the play's meaning and a character's contri-bution to that meaning. Thus McKellen's portrayal of Lopakhin gave a meaning to the play which was not matched or balanced by the other performances. Even where part of Alfreds's strength and achievement was in directing an ensemble, the production was marred by a lack of cohesion. Again, what was it *saying* to us? This lack of cohesion was partly a result of isolating some of the characters from their social and historical context. Alfreds's Ranevskaya (played by Sheila Hancock) seemed a far cry from the actual landed gentry of Chekhov's Russia, and of all of the critics only Milton Shulman in the *London Standard* (11 December 1985) makes any reference to this weakness: 'There was for me only a certain lack of instinctive authoritative breeding.' Sheila Hancock's Ranevskaya was much more English middle-class than Russian gentry; she lacked poise (though not pathos) and the finesse of a Russian woman of her class at that time – educated, travelled, and socially both gracious and sophisticated.

Vanessa Redgrave's Arkadina went even further against the credible behaviour of the character's fame, class and social background: Redgrave's Arkadina slapped Shamrayev hard in the face in the middle of the argument about the horses in Act 2, with the resounding cry: 'every summer they insult me'. As Michael Billington pointed out in *The Guardian* (5 August 1985): 'this is a woman who (according to the text) once took medicine to a wounded washerwoman and bathed her children in a tub. You'd never guess it from Ms Redgrave's focus on Arkadina's egotistic triviality.' Redgrave's performance, taken purely as an acting performance, was stunning – but had little to do with the character as indicated in the text. It is the most recent example of the actor seizing on a Chekhov character to the detriment of the complexity and the ideas of the play. As Michael Billington put it in an earlier review: 'The flaw in Mr Sturridge's approach is that he minimises the play's intellectual content.'[8] Redgrave/Arkadina's little dance in Act 2 à la Joyce Grenfell brought the house down, but cheapened Chekhov's complex characterization – we do not seem to have absorbed Chekhov's own criticism of Stanislavsky's moments of exhibitionism in the portrayal of his characters.

It is odd that British productions of Chekhov's plays provide 'class stratification' for the characters in their mode of speech, but not always in their mode of action or behaviour. There is still a failure (except in the Page production of *Uncle Vanya*, in the Eyre and Gill productions of *The Cherry Orchard*, the Kilroy *The Seagull*, and Michael Frayn's version of *Platonov*, *Wild Honey*) to explore the behaviour socially appropriate to a particular character and that, as previously suggested, is due to a failure to recognize the class position and class assumptions of a character. As Trevor Griffiths aptly observed in the preface to his version of *The Cherry Orchard*:

For half a century now, in England as elsewhere, Chekhov has been the almost exclusive property of theatrical class sectaries for whom the plays have been plangent and sorrowing evocations of an 'ordered' past no longer with 'us', its passing greatly to be mourned. For theatregoers . . . Chekhov's tough, bright-eyed complexity was dulced into swallowable sacs of sentimental morality . . . Translation followed translation, *that* idiom became 'our' idiom, that class 'our' class, until the play's specific historicity and precise sociological imagination had been bleached of all meanings beyond those required to convey the necessary 'natural' sense that the fine will always be undermined by the crude and that the 'human condition' can for all essential purposes be equated with 'the plight of the middle classes'.[9]

Ranevskaya's blindness to realities is not a peculiarity of her character – it is a *class* blindness. Her 'political' and 'economic' assumptions are no more idiosyncratic than those of Lady Hunstanton in Wilde's *A Woman of No Importance* – the comedy lies partly in the disparity between Ranevskaya's view of the world, and the world as it is. For her, selling the estate for summer *dachas* is 'vulgar'. Equally, it is because she is so cushioned and blinkered by her class that she is unable to see that times have changed – and therein lies the individual tragedy but, as both

Lopakhin and Trofimov in their different ways try to point out, it is an *avoidable* tragedy.

None of this, however, will be clear to British audiences until it is generally accepted that characters in Chekhov's plays are partly defined by their social milieu. By the same token, the British theatre has yet to come to terms with the character of Trofimov in *The Cherry Orchard*. Only in Eyre's production was Trofimov treated seriously and given the weight of *ideas* that the character contributes. In Mike Alfreds's production the portrayal of Trofimov seriously weakened the whole fabric of the play: instead of 'balancing' Lopakhin, Trofimov here was: 'no true idealist – the voice of the people who will soon create a new social order – but a cold-hearted, self-regarding humbug, certain to ruin Ranevskaya's ardent daughter Anya'.[10] Few of the critics even mentioned Laurence Rudik's Trofimov, but the omission is serious and revealing: playing Trofimov as a 'self-regarding humbug' is, intentionally or not, a political statement on the part of the actor and the director – and a reactionary one. Trofimov as Chekhov creates him serves as an idealist in juxtaposition with Lopakhin the realist/materialist. He is the only character who actually suggests that change may be positive, and that Ranevskaya and Gaev are not simply innocent victims of an inexplicable tragic destiny, but that they are 'living on credit'. The crucial line 'All of Russia is our orchard', with all its resonance of expansion from the particular to the general, was completely lost in this production. Trofimov is an inadequate, shabby and ludicrous individual, often comic, but what he says contributes significantly to the meaning of the play as a whole.

Perhaps at this stage I must make it clear that I am not seeking a reduction of the play on simplistic ideological grounds, but a *contextual* understanding. For too long and with only the few exceptions already mentioned, British Chekhov has been composed out of what Tynan called 'the great line of English eccentrics'. But all Chekhov's plays are rooted in social observation – what we find is a complex and subtle reflection of his contemporary society. All the major plays are concerned with money – or the lack of it; economic change is a constant theme, as indeed is encroaching industrialization. In *Uncle Vanya*, *Three Sisters* and *The Cherry Orchard* the philosophy of change, of faith in the future and in human potential are constant and crucial leitmotifs; no easy answers and, in fact, no answers at all are suggested, but the questions *are* posed by Chekhov. The method is oblique, partly because that was Chekhov's method, but partly also because these were plays written under the strictest censorship. As Chekhov put it: 'It's like writing with a bone stuck in your throat.'[11]

This obliqueness offers the British theatre an alibi to present the characters in a kind of social limbo. Again and again the reviews of Alfreds's *The Cherry Orchard* praised the isolation of the characters (an isolation reinforced by the setting[12]), but the point is not that the characters are figures in an abstract landscape à la Beckett, but characters who isolate themselves in a clear social milieu. The stronger the social definition, the more isolated they seem one from the other. Their inability to receive, to listen or to see, is at one and the same time creating a social disease, and symptomatic of it. They carry, it would seem, some measure of responsibility for their own lives, and it is partly this which in Russian terms makes the plays *comedies*. In recent years, more and more British productions have concentrated on the comedy in the plays, but the concentration, again, has been on the form, not the content. The situation is not dissimilar to British Brecht; Brechtian form but an artificial separation from substance and meaning.

In his review of Alfreds's *The Cherry Orchard* in the *London Standard* (11 December 1985), Milton Shulman unintentionally crystallizes a major inadequacy in British productions of Chekhov:

I think that this portrait of inept people making ludicrous and futile efforts to cope with the vagaries of existence has got the emphasis right. They are an endearing and bumbling lot.

But Chekhov is *not* Beckett. Shulman's assumption is that we poor human beings do not and cannot control our own destinies. Behind Shulman's comment is a political assumption, and it is one which is very prevalent in Britain today. But it is not a view shared by everyone any more than it is shared by all Chekhov's characters. It is Lopakhin who says in Act 2 of *The Cherry Orchard*:

The Lord gave us these huge forests, these boundless plains, these vast horizons, and we who live among them ought to be real giants.

In this way, Chekhov poses the questions. Our need to debate the issues is as pressing as it was for Chekhov's contemporaries.

Finally, the point must be made that the staging of a social milieu need not presuppose absolute realism or Moscow Art Theatre naturalism in the depiction of that milieu. One of Alfreds's achievements lay in his innovatory stylization of *The Cherry Orchard*. A production may be stylized, like Meyerhold's *The Government Inspector*, or symbolist, like Tairov's *The Seagull*, but English Chekhov for an English audience which understands little or nothing of the background of Chekhov's characters, must take the society into serious account – as would be the case with the production of Wilde's plays or, indeed, any Restoration play. It is one of the ways of

Vera Gottlieb

ensuring that the issues are debated. But there is a real problem for the director and the designer: somehow the connection with social and historical reality must be established in a new way. Today we do not assume realism in setting, and Stanislavsky naturalism came and did overload the plays with distracting details and trivia. The question remains: how does one communicate a reality which is socially and historically unfamiliar to an audience?

Notes

1 Irving Wardle, *The Times*, 1973.
2 Starring Paul Scofield as Vanya, Colin Blakeley as Astrov, and Anna Calder-Marshall as Sonia, in an adaptation by Christopher Hampton.
3 Kenneth Tynan, *Tynan on Theatre* (Harmondsworth: Penguin, 1958), p. 273.
4 A particular way of speaking Russian which was either obsequious or posing.
5 V. A. Simov, the designer of all Stanislavsky's productions of Chekhov's plays at the Moscow Art Theatre, quoted in E. Braun, *The Director and the Stage* (London, 1982), p. 70.
6 Victoria Radin, *The New Statesman*, 9 August 1915.
7 Quoted in M. N. Stroeva, 'The Three Sisters in the Production of the Moscow Art Theatre', in *Chekhov – A Collection of Critical Essays*, ed. R. L. Jackson (NJ, 1966), p. 121.
8 *The Guardian*, 29 April 1985.
9 Trevor Griffiths, in *The Cherry Orchard: A New English Version* (Pluto Press, 1978), p. v.
10 Francis King, *The Sunday Telegraph*, 15 December 1985.
11 Chekhov Archives, Yalta.
12 'Paul Dart sets the play in a translucent abstract box lined with white gauze curtains and a canopied ceiling which tense, snap free and shiver to the ground at the very end . . . only a few props – chalk-grey rocking horse, playpen, table and chairs within an outer skin of blue sky and rosy-white clouds the full height of the Cottesloe . . .' Michael Ratcliffe, *The Observer*, 15 December 1985.

Intercultural aspects in post-modern theatre: a Japanese version of Chekhov's *Three Sisters*

ERIKA FISCHER-LICHTE

Theatre between cultures

Transferring plays from one culture to another has a fairly long tradition on European stages. Omitting the Roman adaptations of Greek drama, we can date it back to the late sixteenth or early seventeenth century, when English, Dutch and Italian groups of actors were moving from one country to another all over the continent. They introduced plays of their own tradition to the theatres of their host countries and initiated a process of cross-pollination among different European cultures. The process of consciously intended mediation between the cultures grew into a theatrical programme when Goethe proclaimed the era of *Weltliteratur*: 'A national literature has little left to say, the age of world literature has dawned and each of us must contribute to hastening its arrival.'[1]

On his small provincial stage in Weimar, Goethe established a repertoire that comprised the most important dramas of the Western world including, for instance, Sophocles' *Antigone*, Shakespeare's *Hamlet, Henry IV, Macbeth, Julius Caesar* and *Othello*, Corneille's *Cid*, Racine's *Phèdre*, Molière's *The Miser*, Calderón's *The Magnanimous Prince* and *Life Is a Dream*, and comedies by Gozzi and Goldoni, all these in addition to plays by Lessing, Schiller and himself. Since Goethe was convinced that the audience would neither understand nor appreciate the dramas of foreign cultures if he staged them without any alterations, he did not shrink from shortening and even – sometimes – changing them considerably. Any given production of a foreign play proved to be a mixture of elements taken from two cultures: the one in which the play originated, and the one in which it was staged. It was the aim and function of these mixtures to promote intercultural understanding.

Although Goethe's Weimar theatre may be considered an important step towards the proclaimed goal of a world theatre, yet it was limited to

European drama: taking a play out of its original context was carried out within the confines of European culture as a whole.

Interest in foreign theatrical traditions went beyond the boundaries of Europe for the first time with the avant-gardists. Meyerhold, for example, used elements of the Japanese theatre,[2] Brecht borrowed from the Chinese,[3] Tairov from the Indian theatre[4] and Artaud took the Balinese as his model for a new theatre.[5] Of course, they did not intend to employ theatre as a means of mediating between their own culture and those of the theatrical forms they were adopting and adapting: rather, they were in search of a new theatre. Each wanted to exploit some of the theatrical forms in these Oriental cultures in order to accomplish their particular purposes. They simply borrowed those principles, texts and styles of staging which they considered to be useful in achieving an avant-garde theatre style. Thus, the mixing of elements from at least two different theatrical traditions aimed at and resulted in the development of a new theatre. Nevertheless, by proceeding in this manner, they did introduce aspects of some Oriental cultures into Europe.

The Japanese audience became acquainted with the European theatre tradition for the first time some decades earlier. As early as 1885 an adaptation of *The Merchant of Venice* was performed in Kabuki style. However, a consciously intended mediation of European theatrical culture did not begin until the new century had started, that is in 1901, when the first faithfully translated text of a Western play was staged in Tokyo: Shakespeare's *Julius Caesar*. Ten years later, this performance was followed by a completely westernized production of *Hamlet* staged by a company called 'Bungei Kyokai' (the Literary Society).

That company and the 'Tsukiji Little Theatre' (established in 1924 by Kaoru Osanai) were the very first to initiate and systematically develop a special Western-oriented theatre usually known as 'Shin-geki' (New Drama). This was a theatre which totally cut itself off from traditional Japanese forms such as Kabuki and Noh, devoutly subscribing to Western models. Its repertoire consisted exclusively of Western – usually contemporary – plays, the favourites being those of Ibsen and Chekhov. The acting style strove for a realistic, even naturalistic, reflection of reality as developed by Stanislavski, the admired master. Shin-geki did not intend to form a mixture between Japanese and European theatrical traditions, but rather to present a purely European Theatre.[6]

At the same time that avant-garde theatre directors in Europe abandoned the illusionistic theatre as antiquated and unable to produce a stimulating and really artistic performance, and discovered the innovating possibilities inherent in the highly stylized theatre of the Far East, literary societies in Japan were praising the innovative potential of Western drama, because they were bored with the rather uniform texts of Kabuki and Noh, and were no longer able to appreciate the theatrical values of these old traditional theatre forms. For them, modern theatre had to be Western theatre. Like the European avant-gardists, the Shin-geki hoped for a renewal of the theatre by referring to a totally different, and therefore exotic, theatre tradition.

After World War II, Shin-geki flourished again in the wake of the progressive westernization in all phases of Japanese culture and society. This period lasted until the late sixties. The 'modernization' brought about in the theatre by Shin-geki companies was in fact westernization. The genuinely Japanese theatre tradition was not only neglected but expressly negated for the sake of an illusionistic, life-like and realistic theatre. The Shin-geki claimed to be the only modern – that is, legitimate – theatre in Japan.

It was against this status quo of Shin-geki that the 'little theatre movements' burst out violently in the late sixties. They strove neither for an exclusive return to Japanese theatre traditions nor for a complete denial of Western drama. Instead they protested against an elitist theatre which was nothing but a copy of an antiquated Western model and not in the least related to contemporary Japanese society and its problems. They demanded a theatre that would be able to respond to the current social situation in Japan and also to address a non-elitist audience.

One of the most prominent and influential representatives of the 'little theatre movements' is the Suzuki Company of Toga (SCOT), led by Tadashi Suzuki. Suzuki's productions often proceed from Western plays, mainly from Greek tragedies (such as Euripides' *The Trojan Women* and *The Bacchae*), but also from a favourite of Shin-geki, Chekhov's *Three Sisters*. However, this company has developed a special style of acting which can be considered a particular offspring of the traditional Japanese acting schools. 'Suzuki ... sucked much of his nourishment from the traditional and popular theatre forms of Japan. No other director has learnt and stolen so much from Noh and Kabuki, and certainly none has utilized so effectively the popular folksongs which have entered the unconscious mechanism of the psyche of Japanese non-elitist populace' (Yasunari Takahashi).[7] Thus, Suzuki's productions form particular 'mixtures' of elements from Western (foreign) and Japanese (indigenous) theatrical traditions, as did Goethe's stagings and those of the European avant-gardist stage directors.

Suzuki's work raises some interesting questions. In which ways and to what purpose does Suzuki employ dramatic texts stemming from the

Western tradition; and what is the function and aim of these particular 'mixtures'? I shall attempt to answer these questions using Suzuki's production of Chekhov's *Three Sisters* as my text.[8]

Suzuki's production of Chekhov's *Three Sisters*

Suzuki's production of *Three Sisters* did not take more than one hour to perform, which is the usual length of his productions. Chekhov's text had therefore to be drastically curtailed: more than half the dialogue was cut. The four acts were revised into ten scenes. There was nothing left of Solyony, Fedotik, Rhode and Ferapont and only one line of Kulygin's text remained. With the exception of Andrei, Suzuki merged together all the male characters, i.e. the military people, and distributed their speeches between two characters called 'Man 1' and 'Man 2'. In the main, they were given the philosophizing passages of Tuzenbach and Vershinin and also Tuzenbach's expression of his faith in the coming of a new era (Act 1), Vershinin's reflections about a better future (Act 1, Act 2) and the confessions of love to Masha (Vershinin) and Irina (Tuzenbach). The other texts of Man 1 and Man 2 were taken from Vershinin's complaint about his personal situation (Act 2) as well as Chebutykin's refusal to work (Act 1) and his announcement that he was going to leave (Act 4). Although most of Vershinin's text was given to Man 1 and what was left of Tuzenbach's to Man 2, this principle was not consistently observed. Sometimes Man 1 spoke Tuzenbach's or Chebutykin's lines and Man 2 Vershinin's or Chebutykin's. On the other hand, some speeches were given to both of them at once such as Vershinin's departing phrases to Olga (Act 4), Irina's desiring words 'Moscow! Moscow! To Moscow!' (Act 2) and Olga's last long passage at the end of the play. The text was certainly not distributed between Man 1 and Man 2 according to any individualizing principle.

On the other hand, the text of the three sisters was shortened without limiting its effectiveness in moulding their separate individualities. Olga's constant complaints about her work at school and the headache it causes her, as well as her warnings and admonishments to her siblings, survived in Suzuki's version ('Don't whistle, Masha', Act 1; 'Stop that, I can't bear it', Act 3; 'Let it rest Andryusha', Act 3; 'Calm yourself, Masha', Act 4). Masha's text concentrated on the topics of her unhappy marriage and her love for Vershinin (Act 2). Irina was characterized by her desire for work in the beginning (Act 1), her refusal to allow Tuzenbach to talk to her of love (Act 1), her complaint about her work at the telegraph station (Act 2) and her desperate outburst about the misery and failure of her life (Act 3). The shortened text suffices to shape clearly the individuality of each character as well as to delineate the traits all three of them have in common: their memories and their dreams of Moscow as the symbol and guarantee of a better life.

Apart from the three sisters and Man 1 and Man 2 the characters of Andrei, Natasha and Anfisa also remained intact. The love-scene between Andrei and Natasha from the end of Act 1 formed here Scene 4: it presented both of them full of hope and happiness. Andrei had his second and last appearance in Scene 8, first asking his sisters to respect his wife Natasha and confessing to them his debts (Act 3), but then complaining to Man 1 and Man 2 that his wife was a 'small, blind sort of thick-skinned animal. In any case, she's not a human being' (Act 4).

Natasha appeared again in Scene 7: '*carrying a candle; she enters from the door on the right and crosses the stage without speaking*' (Act 3). She appears for the last time at the end of Scene 9, where, satisfied that all were going to leave the house, she shouts to the maid: 'What's a fork doing here, I'd like to know? Hold your tongue!' (Act 4). Only so much of Andrei's and Natasha's speeches were left as to show their initial circumstances and what had become of them.

Anfisa, the old nurse from the country, was presented as a friendly woman caring for the three sisters, providing them with food and tea. The text originally spoken by Olga: 'If we only knew, if we only knew!' was here given to Anfisa as the last lines of the play. The division of characters into three groups (the three sisters, Man 1 and 2 and the others) as suggested by Suzuki's adaptation of Chekhov's text, was further emphasized by certain scenic components and arrangements. Whereas the three sisters and Man 1 and 2 stayed on stage all the time, or, in the latter case, almost until the end, Andrei, Natasha and Anfisa appeared and left alternately. While the three sisters and Man 1 and 2 wore European clothes almost exclusively, Andrei, Natasha and Anfisa were dressed in traditional Japanese garments. By way of the sign-systems: 'appearance / exit' and 'costume', an opposition was formed between the three sisters and Man 1 and 2 on the one hand and Andrei, Natasha and Anfisa on the other.

Within these larger groups another opposition was constituted through the sign-system of movement. Whereas Andrei and Natasha walked erect, Anfisa crossed the stage in a squatting position. While the three sisters moved on or between three European armchairs set up side by side backstage and three Japanese straw mats lying side by side frontstage, Man 1 and 2 during the first nine scenes were 'imprisoned' in two huge wicker baskets backstage (reminding the spectator of the dustbins in Beckett's *Endgame*), just able to raise their heads over the edge, and in the last scene left the baskets, moved all over the stage and, finally, departed.

Among these different oppositions the one between the three sisters and Man 1 and 2 seemed to be the most important. According to the de-individualizing tendencies of Suzuki's text version, Man 1 and 2 were dressed totally alike, wearing black suits and shoes, huge sunglasses and umbrellas which they put up when leaving the baskets. As long as they were kept in the baskets, they went on philosophizing. It was made very clear that philosophy is nothing but a compensation to them. After Scene 9 all the stanzas of the Horst-Wessel-Song were sung in German and suddenly Man 1 and 2 seemed to revive. They jumped out of the baskets and rushed over the stage, making their departure for real life, the war. These men were without any individuality – theorizing about a better life as long as they were kept immobile, and hurrying eagerly 'to arms' and violence, when war and destruction are about to burst out.

The three sisters, on the other hand, were presented as three individuals who, none the less, had some features and properties in common. Each was dressed differently: Olga had a Japanese hairstyle and her clothes were a mixture of European and Japanese elements. Masha's head was covered with a topi and she wore a long European dress with a knitted multi-coloured shawl around her shoulders. A large red ribbon was tied in Irina's hair; she wore glasses, a long skirt, a blouse and a jacket. None of the three had shoes – their feet were incased in white woollen socks. Each carried a handbag: Olga, a patterned paper bag; Masha, a wicker bag with long handles and Irina a dark leather bag. Each held in her hand an open umbrella – all the time. Olga's, in fact, was quite ruined.

The significance of these umbrellas derives from the fact that middle-class women in Japan during the thirties used to carry open umbrellas when shopping. As Suzuki explained in an interview, even their pet dogs were fitted out with smaller versions. The umbrella was understood as a sign of the 'modern', that is westernized, attitude of its possessor.

In the production, the umbrellas functioned as a symbol of the dreams which the sisters constantly clung to, dreams of 'Moscow' or of a Western way of life. As they are all alike in this respect, the gestures they performed with the umbrellas, both at the beginning and end of the play, were precisely synchronized. At other times, their gestures were used to characterize their different individualities: Olga's rather resigned attitude towards life; Masha's briskness and desire for both love and escape as well as her sense of humour (in the meal scene) and Irina's growing desperation because of the failures in her life.

The space within which the three sisters moved was marked by the

3 The meal scene (Scene 6, the beginning of Act 2).

European armchairs backstage and the Japanese mats frontstage. In the beginning they sat or squatted on the armchairs and in the end they stood on them, clutching their umbrellas as if hoping to 'levitate'. At the end of Scene 3 the three sisters left the chairs and went forward to the mats, where they sat down in the Japanese manner and had the meal which Anfisa brought them on three small tables.

This world between the armchairs and the strawmats in which the three sisters live was also characterized by music. Movements, gestures and words were accompanied by instrumental music, partly of European–romantic origin (with the violin and piano dominating), partly as though taken from the soundtrack of a Hollywood film. The music pointed to the dreams and desires, hopes and illusions which determine and ruin the life of the sisters.

Since the stage-architecture was basically Japanese, it can be assumed that what was happening on stage could be understood as going on within the context of Japanese culture. In this respect, Suzuki's production of Chekhov's *Three Sisters* can be seen as a harsh critique of westernization as it has taken place in Japan after World War II. The process is shown to entail a de-humanization of life; to men it has brought a philosophy of a better life in the future, which, none the less, has been unable to keep them from aggression and violence. To the women, on the other hand,

4 The final scene (Scene 10).

westernization introduced dreams and hopes of happiness (in love) and self-fulfilment (in work), which cannot be realized in the current situation.

Whereas Shin-geki companies used to present Chekhov's plays as images and models of the most desirable Western life, which were to be copied and taken as a guide even if they had nothing to do with the actual Japanese situation, Suzuki adopted the opposite points of view and staged Chekhov in order to demonstrate critically what happens when this model is actually followed unconditionally. That does not mean that he is preaching a return to traditional Japanese culture. By presenting Andrei and Natasha as undoubtedly Japanese, Suzuki rendered such a conclusion impossible. Besides, he did not deal with the question of the traditional Japanese ways of life in this production, but rather with the problems brought about by unquestioning and excessive westernization. Quite paradoxically – at least from the point of view of Shin-geki – Suzuki succeeded in responding to the current situation in Japan by staging a European play.

Rise of a 'world theatre'?

Above all, the enormous impact of Suzuki's productions was brought about by specific techniques of body movement. Suzuki has even elaborated a special kind of physical training to help actors acquire the necessary abilities. Essentially, the training consists of stamping the ground without letting the upper half of the body sway. Suzuki explains his method as follows:

Of course, emphasizing the fact that the construction of the human body and the balance of forces which support it are centred on the pelvic region is not thinking unique to my method; but almost all the performing arts invariably use such thinking. Only, I believe it is specific to my training that first of all the actors are made to feel conscious of this by stamping and beating the ground with their feet. In our daily life, we tend to disregard the importance of the feet. It is necessary for us to be aware of the fact that the human body makes contact with the ground through the feet, that the ground and the human body are inseparable, as the latter is, in fact, part of the former, meaning that when we die we return to the earth – to make the body, which usually functions unconscious of its relationship aware of this fact by creating a strong sense of impact through the beating of the ground with the feet.[9]

Suzuki's method and its theoretical foundation are deeply rooted in Japanese culture. In traditional forms such as Noh and Kabuki actors very often convey the feeling that the feet are planted firmly on the ground. This is symbolized in such movements as 'sliding steps' (*Suniashi*) or stamping (*Ashi-byoshi*) which are meant to express the affinity with the earth. Suzuki's actors perform many of those movements which were developed in Noh and Kabuki and originally stem from ancient rituals.

In all Japanese performing arts the performers stamp from time to time, which signifies the treading down of evil spirits as the late anthropologist Shinobu Origuchi explained. Such a gesture might also mean an arousal of energy activating human life. This interpretation is represented in the Opening Ritual of the Heavenly Stone Wall in the Japanese Creation Myth, where a goddess named Ameno-Uzumeno-Mikoto dances on a wooden tub. Origuchi describes her dance as follows: 'Perhaps the tub symbolized the earth. The goddess stomped on it and struck it with a stick while making loud noises; actions supposed to wake up and bring out the soul or spirit that was believed to be under the tub, whether sleeping or hiding, in order to send it to the unseen sacred body of the god near by.'[10]

In this context it becomes understandable why ancient Japanese stages were built on 'places closely bound up with the sense of danger we feel whenever we are confronted by a sense of our own destruction: for example, in a cemetery, at the frontier between two villages, at the line of demarcation between two kinds of space . . . In these places local spirits (*genii loci*) are said to reside.'[11] By stamping on the stage floor Noh and Kabuki actors conjure up such spirits in order to acquire their energy.

Even though Suzuki is deeply aware of the Japanese origins of the acting technique he has developed, he claims that it is founded on a condition basic to all human beings: 'Perhaps it is not the upper half but the lower half of the body through which the physical sensibility common to all races is consciously expressed; to be more specific, the feet. The feet are the last remaining part of the human body which has kept, literally, in touch with the earth, the very supporting base of all human activities.'[12]

This means that the special way in which Suzuki's actors use their body is meant to be performed and understood in all cultures without any regard to their differences and peculiarities. This technique, together with Suzuki's insistence on combining European dramatic texts with an acting style derived from the Japanese theatre, form the basis for the realization of a 'world theatre'. This world theatre is supposed to be received and understood in all cultures because it is based on universals of human expression. These universals are, in Suzuki's opinion, language and the human body. Since language is developed to the highest degree of expressivity in European drama, and the human body as a means of expression is similarly exploited in the traditional Japanese theatre, Suzuki aims at their combination in order to create and establish an intercultural form of theatre, a theatre which would have a strong effect on audiences all over the world.

In this respect, Suzuki's endeavours meet with those of other leading stage directors in Europe and in the United States. For years, Peter Brook has argued for the realization of what he calls 'cosmopolitan theatre', for the elaboration of a 'theatrical language' understandable in all cultures.[13] For this purpose he has looked for elements that could be used in different theatrical traditions: European, African, Asian, American. The most convincing results of this procedure have been the productions of *Orghast*, performed in the ruins of Persepolis in 1971; a little later *The Ik*, a story of an African tribe about to die out; in 1977 *The Conference of the Birds*, an adapted version of a medieval play written by the Persian mystic Attar, and most recently the *Mahabharata*, performed in a deserted quarry near Avignon.[14]

Another striking example is Robert Wilson's gigantic project of *the CIVIL warS* which consists of different parts being produced in Cologne (Germany); Rotterdam (The Netherlands); Marseille, Lyon and Nice (France); Rome (Italy); Tokyo (Japan) and Milwaukee (USA). It was originally planned to bring these parts together on the occasion of the Olympic Games in Los Angeles (1984) in one enormous performance that would take about 24 hours. It is a characteristic feature of at least those parts I am acquainted with (the knee-plays, Milwaukee, and the German part, Act 1, Scene A; Act 4, Scene A and Epilogue), that elements of different cultures are used simultaneously, as for example, images from German and American history (Frederick the Great and Lincoln) or physical movements from the Japanese Noh and those imitating human gestures outside any gravitational field. It is not the point here to discuss whether Wilson's undertaking involves an exploitation of cultures, rendering their essentials into insignificant elements which only serve to present something 'new' or 'exotic'.[15] In the context of this paper I merely wish to emphasize the fact that the project was planned, produced and performed not only as an international but also as an intercultural enterprise.

Ariane Mnouchkine's stagings of Shakespearean plays (*Richard II, Henry IV*, and *Twelfth Night*) might also be considered as attempts to realize similar tendencies. In these productions she combined a European text with elements taken from Oriental theatres, mainly from the Japanese Noh and Kabuki, elements such as costumes, music, gestures and movements. By proceeding in this manner, Mnouchkine wanted to 'estrange' the Shakespearean text, which proves ultimately to be no less strange than the Japanese theatrical elements, and thus, achieved a 'hyper-realistic' mode of representation. The point she was trying to make was that European dramatic texts stemming from past periods may seem just as strange to us as any material taken from a foreign culture. We have no immediate access to either a foreign culture or the past of our own culture. It was the aim of Mnouchkine's 'hyper-realism' to make the spectator aware of the 'fact' that our own past culture is as strange to us as the tradition of a foreign culture. It may well be, as some critics argued, that the employment of Japanese elements served only a decorative purpose (mainly in *Richard II*) and that the proclaimed hyper-realism was not actually achieved.[16] None the less, it should be stressed that Ariane Mnouchkine's intention was founded on an intercultural perspective.

There are still a number of other examples (as, for instance, the Odin Theatret of Eugenio Barba), but those mentioned above will suffice to emphasize that intercultural awareness forms an essential part of post-modern theatre.[17] It seems that many leading stage directors would support the demand for 'world theatre' – not a world theatre in the Goethean sense, promoting intercultural understanding by the way of mediating between cultures, but rather a world theatre conceived as an 'intercultural' mode of theatrical expression and representation and thus accessible to human beings all over the world. Goethe was convinced that the products of a foreign culture can be made understandable to the members of our own culture only by way of a conscious mediation: by translation or adaptation. The above mentioned stage directors of today, on the other hand, are striving for a theatre that will be enjoyed and understood by members of different cultures, because it uses an 'intercultural' – i.e., a universal – theatrical language.

While I have certain doubts as to the theoretical plausibility of such a world theatre, this is quite another matter, equally worthy of reflection and investigation. Here I endeavoured to show that post-modern theatre seems to be characterized and dominated by intercultural tendencies in a way that is unknown in the history of Western as well as of Japanese theatre. It may well be that this type of interculturality reflects a general development in the culture of post-industrial societies (and even in some societies in the Third World): one can observe a certain tendency of different cultures to merge into one world-culture. Whether such a world-culture will in fact arise and what it will look like is, for the time being, impossible to predict. Perhaps the search for a universal theatrical language in post-modern theatre indicates that the theatre has already passed into this new era.

Notes

1 'Nationalliteratur will jetzt nicht viel sagen, die Epoche der Weltliteratur ist an der Zeit, und jeder muß jetzt dazu wirken, diese Epoche zu beschleunigen.' *Conversations with Eckermann*, 31 January 1827.
2 See *Meyerhold on Theatre*, trans. and ed. Edward Braun (London: Methuen & Co., 1969).
3 See *Brecht on Theatre*, trans. John Willett (New York: Hill & Wang, 1964).
4 See Alexander Tairow, *Das entfesselte Theater* (Köln: Kiepenheuer & Witsch, 1964).
5 See Antonin Artaud, *Collected Works* (New York: International Publications Services, 1968–74).
6 See Peter Arnott, *The Theatres of Japan* (London/New York: Macmillan, 1969).
7 In *SCOT: Suzuki Company of Toga*, ed. the Suzuki Company of Toga (Tokyo, 1985), p. 21.
8 I had the opportunity to see a performance of this production at the Frankfurt Theatre Festival in September 1985. I have used the English translation of Suzuki's version of the text, and the minutes of an interview with Suzuki at the Festival.
9 *SCOT*, pp. 6ff.
10 *Ibid.*
11 Masao Yamaguchi, 'The Provocative and Privileged Space and People in

Japan' a paper read at the ISISSS Conference 1985 in Bloomington, Indiana, p. 4.
12 *SCOT*, p. 6.
13 Peter Brook, *The Empty Space* (London: MacGibben & Kee, 1968).
14 See A. C. Smith, *Peter Brook's 'Orghast' in Persepolis* (London: Eyre Methuen, 1974); Peter von Becker, 'Der Sommernachtstraum des *Mahabharata* – Peter Brook dramatisiert das größte Epos der Welt. Neun Stunden Theatergeschichte beim Festival in Avignon', *Theater heute*, 9 (1985), pp. 6–11.
15 See Erika Fischer-Lichte, 'Jenseits der Interpretation. Anmerkungen zu Robert Wilsons/Heiner Müllers Text von *the CIVIL warS*' in *Kontroversen alte und neue*, ed. Albrecht Schöne, vol. 11, ed. W. Voßkamp and E. Lämmert (Tübingen: Niemeyer, 1986); Erika Fischer-Lichte, 'Postmoderne Performance: Rückkehr zum rituellen Theater?' *Arcadia*, 22:1 (1987).
16 See Peter von Becker, 'Die Sonnenkönigin des Theaters: Ariane Mnouchkine und ihr Théâtre du Soleil', *Theater 1984*, Jahrbuch der Zeitschrift *Theater heute*, pp. 12–19; Peter von Becker, 'So schön, um wahr zu sein – über Ariane Mnouchkines Shakespearezyklus und *Heinrich IV* im Théâtre du Soleil', *Theater heute*, 4 (1984), pp. 15–17.
17 Cf. Michel Benamou, Charles Caramelle (eds.), *Performance in Postmodern culture* (Madison, Wisconsin, Coda Press. Inc., 1977); Richard Schechner, *The End of Humanism* (New York; Performing Art Journal Publications, 1982); Richard Schechner, *Between Theatre and Anthropology* (Philadelphia, University of Pennsylvania Press, 1985).

Mr Godot will not come today

SHOSHANA WEITZ

Introduction

In May 1985 the Haifa Municipal Theatre celebrated the opening of a new auditorium in Wadi Salib, the centre of the Arab section of the city, by presenting a bilingual Arab–Israeli version of *Waiting for Godot*.

Haifa is a bi-national city with a large Arab population. The local university has many Arab students, and the Haifa theatre recently took on several Arab actors and technicians as part of its regular company. These Arab company members also constitute the core of the new Arab theatre, the first and only professional Arabic theatre in Israel.

The Haifa company is socio-politically oriented. Its repertoire comprises plays which are meant to deal, directly or indirectly, with the problems of current Israeli society and with the ideological issues of Jewish Israeli existence, such as the relations between Judaism and Zionism (as in its production of Sobol's *Soul of a Jew*), the moral and psychological consequences of the Holocaust, and the Jewish–Arab conflict, which is a constant, acute issue in Israel.

The bilingual production of *Waiting for Godot* is in keeping with the *raison d'être* of the Haifa theatre. It relates directly and explicitly to Israel's socio-political circumstances. The interpretation of the play by director Ilan Ronen is meant to present Beckett's universal parable in an Israeli context. In Ronen's production

> Vladimir and Estragon appear to be two Arab construction workers of the group who come daily from the occupied territories and wait at the 'slave markets' on the outskirts of Israeli cities for somebody to hire them for a one-day job. When Master Pozzo passes their way . . . he speaks Hebrew, the masters' language.[1]

The production was given an Israeli context by altering Beckett's stage directions and making manipulative use of two languages: Hebrew and Arabic. The dialogue and the *mise en scène* followed the author's script (though some cuts were made), but the set, the costumes and the stage props were drastically changed. The *Jerusalem Post* review by U. Rapp described it as follows:

The stage floor is covered with sand and gravel. The tree was replaced by a scaffold. The bowler hats have been replaced by unmistakably Middle-East caps. The tramps speak Arabic and the master Hebrew; the play has become a parable about the ambiguous bonds which hold Jews and Arabs together.[2]

Vladimir and Estragon were portrayed by Mackram Hoori and Yusuf Abu-Varda, well-known Arab members of the Haifa company. Pozzo and Lucky were acted by Ilan Toren and Doron Tavori respectively, both Jewish. There were two versions of the play, Arabic and Hebrew. In the Arabic version, presented to Arab audiences, Vladimir and Estragon speak Arabic, Pozzo speaks Hebrew to Vladimir and Estragon, and distorted limited-vocabulary Arabic when he commands Lucky. Lucky delivers his only monologue in an Arabic with an accent different from that of the others. The Hebrew version, intended for Jewish audiences, differed from the Arabic in one respect only: instead of speaking Arabic, Vladimir and Estragon spoke Hebrew with a marked Arabic accent.

The production evoked a public uproar. On the one hand, right-wing commentators and politicians accused the theatre of using public budgets to conduct propaganda for the Palestine Liberation Organization (PLO); several members of the Haifa City Council suggested cutting the theatre's subsidy. On the other hand, however, most of the theatre reviewers praised the artistic merits of the production (the acting in particular), though some of them questioned the artistic legitimacy of the interpretation and condemned the director for distorting and particularizing Beckett's universal message.

The debate over the legitimacy of the interpretation is an interesting subject in its own right, but lies beyond the scope of this paper. The interpretative intent of the Haifa production was clear. The Haifa *Waiting for Godot* was meant to be actualized within a local Israeli field of reference. The director's intention to 'close' Beckett's 'open' text within a defined and bounded Israeli political context was publicly stated and is implied by the linguistic choices described above and the non-verbal elements such as the set, the costumes, and the properties.

The study methodology

A study was undertaken to examine the reactions of both Arab and Jewish spectators of the production in relation to the director's stated and implied intentions.

Specifically the following two questions were examined:

To what extent has the performance succeeded in creating a local political possible world?[3]

Can the local world coexist with the abstract universe suggested by the play?

The study also dealt with the influence of socio-political circumstances on the response of audience members, and examined audience competence in knowing how to relate to stage conventions and stage metaphors, etc. and audience 'openness' towards the interpretation of the play. The study was based on an empirical field survey which examined the reactions of three separate groups of viewers: Israeli Jews, Israeli Arabs, and Palestinian Arabs. These spectators saw the play in various locations in Israel during the first six months of its run.

The research team interviewed nearly 300 spectators (about 150 Jewish Israelis and about 80 Israeli Arabs and 70 Palestinian (East Jerusalem) Arabs) using open and closed questionnaires.[4] Data were gathered in Tel Aviv, Haifa, East Jerusalem, and West Jerusalem, in two kibbutzim (communal Israeli agricultural settlements), and in four Arab villages in Israel. Because of the bilingual nature of the production, the group of interviewees (the sample) was not representative of the population of regular Israeli theatre-goers. It was, however, a valid sample of the actual spectators of both versions of *Waiting for Godot*, thus providing valid data on their perceptions and interpretations. It also sheds light on the ideological standpoint and the socio-political status of the three groups.

The sample population

The sample included a variety of personalities, national origins, ideological views and cultural norms, which undoubtedly influenced the responders' perceptions. In political terms the Jewish group represents the dominant majority national group in Israel. The two Arab groups represent two different segments of the Arab population of Israel: the Israeli Arabs and the Palestinians of East Jerusalem. While the two Arab groups share the same nationality, language, and culture, they differ in political status and socio-historical circumstances. The Israeli Arabs are a minority population segment in Israel. The Palestinians of East Jerusalem have been living under Israeli occupation for the last twenty years. Because of these differences we studied these two Arab groups separately.

The cultural differences between Jews and Arabs are too broad a topic to be discussed here. Nevertheless, it is necessary to point out some aspects which relate to theatre and its place in these two cultures.

The Jewish Israeli culture is Western; the majority of the Jewish theatre-goers are of European origin, and the Hebrew theatre forms part of the world-wide theatre. In Tel Aviv one may see the same plays and musicals that may be seen in London or New York. Theatre is the most popular performing art form among Jews in Israel. Jewish Israelis are devoted theatre-goers, and thus have much more theatre experience than do their Arab counterparts.[5] The Jewish spectators are, in general, familiar with Western drama; in the questionnaire, 70 per cent of the Jewish responders asserted that they had read or seen *Waiting for Godot* before attending the Haifa production. The play had been mounted five or six times from 1954 on by various theatres in Israel.

The dramatic genre most popular with Jewish Israeli audiences is the realistic play which focuses on social and national issues. One may say that the Jewish Israeli spectator likes to see himself represented on stage, and likes to focus on his contemporary problems.[6] This characteristic should be borne in mind when examining the analysis of the results of the survey.

The Arab culture has a rich tradition of story-telling, which includes folk legends and fables. Input from Western theatre has been gradually influencing Arab culture, and recently Arab theatre groups have assimilated Western elements into their traditional presentations.

There are few Arab theatre troupes in Israel, most of them non-professional. Those that do exist combine Western dramatic techniques with traditional Arab story-telling. This style is very well exemplified by the work of the El-Hakhavati Theatre (the name means The Story-teller), an East Jerusalem troupe which has gained an excellent reputation for its colourful productions that turn Arabic folklore into nationalistic political allegories.

Both Hebrew and Arabic theatre productions in Israel tend to be politically oriented; yet their preferred forms are different. The Jews enjoy realistic fare while the Arab audiences are more at home with representational forms like allegories and fables.

The nature of the responses

To establish the possible world of the Haifa Theatre's *Waiting for Godot*, a sample of spectators was asked to describe the characters and to state where the events in the play took place.

The character descriptions

The descriptions of the characters yielded a wide range of attributes from extreme political allegory ('Godot is Arafat', or 'Godot represents our brothers in the Arab countries who promise to help but never do'), to highly bizarre and probably personal images ('Godot is a drug-pusher', or 'Lucky is the outcast handicapped person'). Most of the answers, however, could be grouped into three main categories: existential/universal, national/political, and class-oriented. Many answers fit more than one category, or hover on the borders between two or all three.

The different attributes within each of the three categories are rarely synonyms. Even within the same paradigm the differences between the attributes proved to be very substantial. For instance: 'anyone' and 'waiting for that which will never come' both fit into the existential/universal category. Yet, while the attribute 'anyone' (in regard to a character) is general, abstract, and neutral, the expression 'waiting for that which will never come' represents an interpretative attitude toward the plot, and expresses an 'existential mood' which proves to be a characteristic feature of the Israeli Arab sample.

There is a notable difference between the traits attributed to the two leading characters and those related to Pozzo and Lucky. Vladimir and Estragon tended to be described either in relation to their defined action within the plot (such as waiting) or by defined proper or common nouns (such as 'Israeli' or 'a worker'). Pozzo and Lucky, on the other hand, tended to be described by open abstract terms (such as 'colonialist' or 'wretched').

It appears that the difference in the way the two pairs of characters are perceived is the result of the different semiotic organization of each of the pairs. This difference is an immanent structural principle of the dramatic script. It was emphasized in the Haifa production, and was evidently perceived by the spectators.

With respect to Vladimir and Estragon, the most conspicuous aspect of the analysis of answers has to do with the differences in the answers of Arab and Jewish viewers in two areas: (1) the Jews clearly and unequivocally prefer the existential/universal possibility over all the others, whereas among the Arabs there is a broader distribution of responses with no uniform preference. (2) The Jews tended to ignore the distinction between Vladimir and Estragon, relating both of them to the same category, whereas the Arab responders tended to perceive considerable differences between them.

To begin with, the Arabs tended to see Vladimir in the existential/

universal context while Estragon tended to be seen in the class-oriented frame of reference. The Jewish sample paid little attention to social issues which ranked quite high in both the Arab samples. (44 per cent of the Arabs perceived Estragon as being poor and hungry, or as being a worker, v. 19 per cent of the Jews.) Though many of the responders perceived Vladimir and Estragon within the existential/universal field of reference, there is a significant difference between the samples with regard to the specific items selected. The two Arab samples gave priority to the perception of Vladimir as 'waiting for that which will never come' (34 per cent in Israel and 40 per cent in East Jerusalem), while the Jewish sample gave priority to the attribute 'anyone' (27 per cent).

The Arab spectators who chose to perceive the dramatic characters within the national/political frame tended to see them as reflections of their own national group. Throughout the questionnaire, the Palestinian Arabs were more likely to perceive Vladimir and Estragon as Palestinians than as Israeli Arabs, while the Israeli Arabs inverted the proportions.

With respect to Pozzo, as was true for Vladimir and Estragon, there was a significant difference between the responses of the two Arab samples and those of the Jewish group. The Jewish sample gave priority to the existential/universal context describing the character as 'anyone' or as 'user and oppressor' and placing the national/political option at the bottom of the scale. The Arabs' answers are again more widely distributed, and the two Arab groups again differ from one another. The Israeli Arabs exhibit a stronger tendency towards class orientation (25 per cent of this group saw Pozzo as 'bourgeois'), while the Palestinian Arab responses were divided evenly among the three possible contexts.

With regard to Pozzo the variations within each paradigm were more notable than they were with respect to Vladimir and Estragon. The majority of respondents described Pozzo using the nouns 'exploiter' and 'oppressor'. These are, on the one hand, abstract and general and, on the other, applicable to the socio-national reality.

A significant fraction of the Jews (22 per cent), however, chose to describe Pozzo by the open neutral attribute 'anyone', while the majority of the Arabs rejected this possibility, as evidenced by the fact that only 2 per cent of the Israeli Arabs and 5 per cent of the Palestinians chose this option. The audience response towards Pozzo sheds light on the differences between the two Arab populations. Among the Palestinians Pozzo was perceived primarily as 'exploiter and oppressor' (24 per cent), 'colonialist' (22 per cent), and 'conqueror' (15 per cent), whereas in the Israeli Arab sample he was seen mainly in terms of social class relations: he was seen as 'bourgeois' by 25 per cent, and 17 per cent perceived him as an 'Israeli Jew' whom many described as a 'rich contractor'.

Lucky, like Pozzo, tended to be described with open, abstract nouns which fit two or more categories; the national/political option ranks relatively low. The reaction to Lucky emphasized the tendency of the Arab samples to give priority to open but not-neutral attributes. One evidence of this is that the attribute 'exploited' which may be related to both social and political context ranked highest in both Arab samples. In contrast, the Jewish sample gave priority to 'oppressed', which in Hebrew bears connotations of both oppression and depression and may reflect neutrality, or even detachment, on the part of the responders.

Again, only a minority of the responders related Lucky to the national frame of reference. The majority of those who did so, however, perceived Lucky as a Palestinian.

As was mentioned regarding Vladimir and Estragon, those who chose to place these characters within the local context tended to relate them primarily to their own national group. The case of Lucky is different; this shows, I believe, that the responders acknowledge the low status of the Palestinian Arabs in the local political hierarchy.

The tendency of the Arab spectators to relate the underdog to their own national group was clear. Of the Israeli Arabs, 9 per cent described Lucky as 'Palestinian' and 8 per cent said that he was an Israeli Arab like themselves. Among the Palestinians, 15 per cent placed Lucky in their frame of reference, while only 3 per cent saw him as an Israeli Arab.

Godot's case is unique. There is an ontological difference between the concept of Godot and that of the other characters. Since Godot never appears on stage the spectator's concept of the 'character' depends not only on the interpretation of the dramatic events, but on his imagination as well, and, apparently, on his personal temperament and his socio-national state of mind.

In spite of the undefined nature of Godot, audience reactions to him reveal the same pattern seen for the other characters. Most of the answers in the Jewish sample tended to describe Godot in abstract, neutral terms such as 'hope' or 'the meaning of life'. The Arab samples differ from one another; the differences appeared to reflect a specific socio-national mood which resulted from the ideological standpoint of the viewer as well as from his or her socio-political circumstances.

For all three samples the attribute 'hope' ranked highest, but for the Palestinian sample 'change' ranked as high as 'hope', while in the Israeli Arab sample it was matched by 'the salvation which will never come'. The difference between the two Arab samples can be seen clearly in their ranking of 'change' and 'the salvation which will never come'. 'Change', which ranked highest among the Palestinians, was fifth for the sample of Israeli Arabs, and fourth in the Jewish group. 'The salvation which will never come' ranked as high as 'hope' in the Israeli Arab sample, but only fourth in the Palestinian sample.

There is a clear connection between the wish for change and the rejection of the notion that salvation will never come. By the same token, it is no wonder that a group whose majority feels that salvation will never come has very little faith in the possibility of 'change'.

Apparently, the members of all three samples perceived Godot through a self-reflective mirror.

The perceptions of locale

The answers to the question of where the action of the play takes place follow the pattern indicated with respect to the personality attributes. The existential possible world was chosen by the majority of the responders in all three samples.

Here too, the differences in each category were revealing. It is clear that the Arabs in both samples gave priority to abstract but not-neutral attributes such as 'everywhere under occupation' (23 per cent v. 13 per cent for the Jewish sample), while the Jewish responders preferred abstract neutral images such as 'a lonely place somewhere' (34 per cent v. 10 per cent for both Arab samples).

The tendency for viewers to project their own circumstances onto the stage production was also quite evident. A majority of those Israeli Arabs and Jews who chose a concrete field of reference described the location as Israel. The Palestinians who chose this category gave priority to 'the occupied territories'. It should be noted that in all three samples only a small minority described the place as being 'a construction site' (10–11 per cent among the Palestinians and in the Jewish sample, and 3 per cent in the Israeli Arab group). As mentioned before, the director and the stage-designer, the senders, took great care to shape the stage within this context. The discrepancy between their intentions and the perception of 90 per cent of the responders is revealing and merits further study.

The possible worlds for the Haifa production

The analysis of the audience reactions sheds light on the relations between what the senders intended (as made manifest by their use of set, costumes, and linguistic choices) and what the spectators in fact perceived. The analysis also casts light on the effect of the viewers' ideological parameters, and socio-political conditions, on their perception and interpretation of the play.

It is immediately apparent that there is a wide gap between the sender's intentions and what spectators of the Haifa production of *Waiting for Godot* received. The majority of the responders did not 'see' what the senders meant them to see, and did not respond to the rhetorical devices (such as the stage design, the props, and the use of two languages) meant to guide them towards a local political interpretation of the play.

All three groups gave low ranking to the explicit local political possible world. It is evident that this production was perceived primarily within an existential/universal perspective, secondarily within a class-oriented context and only last as related directly to the Israeli–Arab conflict.

Although the direct local political message of the production was not perceived, or not accepted, by the majority of the responders, most of the responders did relate the theatrical world to their own socio-national situation, at least indirectly.

Throughout the study it was evident that the Arab responders tended to perceive Vladimir, Estragon, and Lucky as reflections of their own national group, and they tended to relate the dramatic space to their social and political status. Another fact to notice is that most of the responders did not acknowledge the role of the specific rhetorical devices designed to create the local political field of reference. When responders were asked how they had arrived at the perceptions they reported, most related their information to the plot and to the dialogue, though in many cases it is quite obvious that this was not the case. Thus for example, there was no indication in the play that Estragon was a workman, yet most of those who described him as such attributed the information to the dialogue.

The collective possible worlds

The analysis of audience responses facilitates the reconstruction of an interpretative cluster (in semiotic terms, a set of signs conveying a single meaning) for each of the three samples – each cluster comprising a potential possible world.

The two Arab samples portray worlds which are substantially different, both from the Jewish world and from each other. In the Israeli Arab possible world Vladimir is 'waiting for that which will never come', Estragon is a 'worker', Pozzo is an 'exploiter and oppressor' and also a 'bourgeois', and Lucky is 'exploited'. In this dramatic universe the events take place 'everywhere under occupation' and Godot represents, equally, 'hope', and 'the salvation which will never come'.

It may be inferred that for this segment of the population the social element is of greater concern than the national one; the oppressor is described as bourgeois, and also as an Israeli Jew who, to Israeli Arabs, represents the dominant group in national terms and the employer in a socio-economic context.

The members of the Palestinian sample perceive Vladimir and Estragon as do the Israeli Arabs, but Pozzo is described as 'exploiter and oppressor' and, equally, as a 'conqueror'. As in the other Arab sample Lucky is perceived as 'exploited' and the place is identified as 'everywhere under occupation'.

For the members of the Palestinian group Godot represents 'hope' and 'change', and, to a lesser degree, 'the future of the Palestinian Arabs'. One may assume that for this group 'waiting for Godot' means waiting for a material–political change.

The Jewish Israeli possible world is clear, coherent, and considerably different from that of either Arab sample. In the Jewish Israeli possible world, Vladimir and Estragon are 'anyones'; Pozzo is 'anyone' and also an 'exploiter and oppressor'; and Lucky is 'oppressed'. The dramatic events occur 'somewhere, in a deserted place'; and Godot represents 'hope' and 'the meaning of life'.

The Jewish Israeli fictional universe is existential and universal. It is open, abstract, and general; it seems to ignore the political level, and it does not reflect national identity. In these terms one may say that the Jewish interpretation corresponds with the conventional approach to *Waiting for Godot*.

The missing paradigm

The portrayal of the collective national possible worlds clearly indicates that in the process of interpretation the spectators project an authentic emotional state of mind, revealing real, deep, uncontrolled feelings. They follow the 'guidelines' of the dramatic script and benefit from the open form which enables them to relate the dramatic characters to their own world. The analysis of the responses to the questions showed that the Arab spectators project their national identity onto the play, while identifying themselves with the underdog. The members of the Jewish sample, on the other hand, did not identify with any of the characters, but chose to locate the events within an abstract, general, and uncommitted interpretation; they neglected to compose a Jewish Israeli possible world.

Because of their own historical experience of oppression and alienation the Jewish readers and spectators tended to identify with the oppressed, the members of minority groups and the underdogs. The 'hunted refugee' is a recurrent motif in Jewish literature and drama, and the assumption of the stance of the outcast victim has been a shaping determinant of Jewish and Israeli culture.

A Jewish interpretation of the Haifa *Waiting for Godot* was suggested by some of the Jewish reviewers of the production, who interpreted it on a political basis and pointed to the analogy between the Jewish refugee and the Palestinian in the West Bank. A good example is Sarith Fuchs's critical review:

Pozzo is a Nazi. When he yells 'pig!' at Lucky, one can visualize a well-educated German shouting 'Jewish pig', and the oppressed Lucky seems the personification of the Jewish refugee . . . [But] the fascist–colonialist Pozzo is [also] a Jewish Israeli contractor. His tortured . . . slave speaks Palestinian Arabic, and the two tramps . . . are Arab workers waiting for salvation, but, meanwhile, they are chatting, playing, and looking for any excuse not to help their tortured brother. The place is . . . not the end of all roads. It is . . . a construction site . . . the stage of the Palestinian drama.[7]

Fuchs presents a Jewish world in a comparison with a Palestinian one, to demonstrate that the Haifa production 'forces' the spectators to draw an analogy between the two worlds. In her words: 'The local designers set a trap for the Jewish spectator, forcing him to see . . . that we (the Israeli Jews) have turned from tortured refugees into torturing slave-drivers.'[8]

However, unlike Fuchs, the Jewish responders in our study did not 'fall into the trap'. They did not 'see' the Jewish context and could therefore avoid the unpleasant analogy. The Jewish responders to the open questionnaire did not offer attributes which could relate Vladimir, Estragon or Lucky to the Jewish frame of reference. Ironically, the two responders who described Pozzo as a Nazi were Arabs.

The Jewish responders did not create a Jewish possible world, thus avoiding the need to draw an analogy between the Jewish refugee in Europe and the West Bank Palestinian. The logical result would have been a comparison between the Israeli conqueror in the occupied territories and the Nazi soldier in Europe – an analogy unacceptable among Jewish Israelis.

It might be argued that, because the persons sampled in the study are neither as experienced as the theatre reviewers nor as politically oriented, they did not pay as much attention to the non-verbal elements which were intended to lead to the local context. Rather, they focused on the plot and perceived the play (as Beckett probably intended) as an existential fable about the existential human condition.

This claim is only partially correct. While the Jewish spectators did overlook the non-verbal elements of the production, so did the Arabs. Nevertheless, the Arabs perceived both the explicit and the non-verbal dimensions of the production while the Jewish Israelis neglected to do so. Beckett's two lead characters differ considerably from one another. The Arab spectators sensed this distinction and expressed it by projecting each into a different frame of reference. The Jews, on the other hand, did not make this distinction. They overlooked the unique aspects of the two tramps and chose to see both of them as identical vague entities, 'anyones', who inhabit a general undefined world unrelated to their own concrete existence.

Finally, the majority of the Jewish responders had read or seen *Waiting for Godot* prior to attending the Haifa production. Evidently, they 'understood' the intentions of the production, and rejected the 'implied' message by shifting from the concrete reality of the stage to an abstract empty world. This shift enabled the Jewish sample to avoid any ideological implications in the performance, and to stay within the boundaries of a 'safe' general existential/universal context, which did not require concrete political conclusions.

Both the Arab spectators and their Jewish counterparts chose to relate to the characters and events of the play as metaphors. All of them preferred the open metaphorical existential interpretation to the closed local political one. But while the Arab viewers used the open metaphorical form of the play to project concrete anguish or hope, or both, the Jewish audience used it as an excuse not to hear, see, or understand.

Although the studied sample cannot be taken as a valid representation of the Israeli population, the possible worlds presented here do reflect, to a degree, the socio-national perspectives of the three groups of spectators considered in this study. One sees the stress, rage, and yearning for freedom of the Palestinians; the resignation and helplessness of Israeli Arabs who are a 'minority group' within the Jewish state; and the ideological conflict within the Jewish spectators, who are torn between the traditional self-image of the 'righteous victim', and the real political status of the 'conqueror'.

This analysis reveals something of the degree to which historical–political and ideological positions may affect perception and interpretation in the theatre.

Many questions have necessarily remained unanswered. Perhaps the most important deals with the relationship between the poetic and structural organization of a play and the way it is perceived. A further stage

Shoshana Weitz

of the study will examine some aspects of the perception process itself. It will deal with the numbers and types of possible worlds created by various individuals, the codes which might have been activated in the process of 'world creating', and the conditions which determine the transition from one world to another.

It may be apt to conclude by quoting Jonathan Culler's remark that an interpretation made by a community of spectators may be taken to be a 'communal delusion', and this delusion 'is a social fact in its own right . . . more interesting and significant than the supposed reality it is said to conceal'.[9]

Notes

1 B. Evron, 'Bravo!', *Yediot Aharonot* (Hebrew, translated by the author), 16 January 1985.
2 U. Rapp, 'Ambiguous Bonds', *The Jerusalem Post*, 25 January 1985.
3 The term 'possible world' is used here in the sense of a hypothetical or desirable state of affairs in which certain events are organized in a certain order within a hypothetical time and place. See U. Eco, *The Role of the Reader* (London: Hutchinson, 1979), p. 219.
4 Twenty-five Jews and twenty-five Arabs were interviewed by open questions; the answers provided the attributes later used in a closed, multiple-choice questionnaire presented to an additional 250 spectators.
5 On the theatre attendance in Israel see G. Rahav, S. Weitz and G. Zeltzer, 'The Emergence of A New Theatre Audience in Israel', Seventh International Congress of Theatre Critics, Tel Aviv, Israel, November 1981.
6 This is based on an unpublished survey of the subscribers to the Israel National Theatre Habimah, in 1986 by S. Weitz and G. Rahav.
7 S. Fuchs, 'Godot and the Palestinian Problem', *Maariv* (Hebrew, translated by the author), 30 November 1984.
8 *Ibid.*
9 J. Culler, 'Prolegomena to a Theory of Reading', in *The Reader in the Text* (Princeton: Princeton University Press, 1980), p. 53.

The adaptation and reception in Germany of Edward Bond's *Saved*

RUTH VON LEDEBUR

The first German productions of *Gerettet*: political, social, and cultural background

Edward Bond's play, *Saved*, was first performed on a German-speaking stage in Vienna on 12 May 1966, only six months after it had opened at the Royal Court Theatre in London.[1] In West Germany the 'Kammerspiele' in Munich, well known for its experimental productions, was the first theatre to include *Gerettet* in its repertoire. Soon numerous other theatres, in the big cities and the provinces alike, followed suit. In the 1967–8 season it was the highlight at no less than fifteen theatres, and by 1973 thirty-six theatres had included *Saved* in their repertoire.[2] *Saved* became the most favoured and most frequently performed of Bond's plays on the German stage, and – even twenty years later – its title comes most easily to the mind of the German playgoer, when Bond's name is mentioned.

There is no doubt that the notoriety of Bond's play added much to its popularity. As in England,[3] the German daily papers can be held responsible for the ambivalent fame that Bond gained with his first play on the German stage. Even before the opening nights, the papers commented on the scandal attached to the play.[4] 'This is a particularly vulgar and brutal play, say the augurs. How will the audience respond to this provocation?'[5] The forecasts of a scandal obviously influenced the expectations of the first-night audiences, who came to the theatre prepared for, or even expecting, a scandal.[6]

Most theatres were conscious of the fact that they were running a risk when producing Bond's play. In Dortmund, the play was 'tested' on teachers, members of the clergy and social workers in two previews before public performance. In some other cities, notices were put up in the theatres to warn the public that the play was 'unsuitable for young people'.[7] In most places, however, *Saved* met with immediate success and the actors played to full houses night after night. To some extent, this sensational success was due to the dubious publicity given in the press. On the other hand, a number of young and yet unknown directors, such as Peter Stein in Munich, rose to the challenge of the play and presented productions which were prepared with meticulous care and attention to detail.

Although many critics in the daily papers were obviously shocked after the opening nights and found neither literary nor moral 'values' in the play, in the later reviews the critics took a more favourable view and were ready to defend the play, its author and the respective production. When, in the 1967 season, the German theatre periodical *Theater heute* published lengthy critiques of the play and reviews of most productions and finally acclaimed Peter Stein's Munich production the most outstanding of that year, the original sensation ebbed away, leaving room for sounder criticism.

Saved caused Bond's rise to international fame, and he is now widely accepted as the 'single most important contemporary dramatist'.[8] *Saved* is considered a landmark of the sixties in British stage history, just as Osborne's *Look Back in Anger* was in the fifties. Bond's established literary reputation tends, however, to blur the vision of the past. In the eighties some German critics thus underestimate or simply overlook the fact that the first German productions caused much the same storm of protest and denigration as did the opening of the play in England.[9] An evaluation of past theatrical productions has, therefore, to take into account the characteristic features of that time. The following historical outline of the political and socio-cultural background concentrates on such factors as will help to establish a frame of reference for the original German reception of Bond's play.

In retrospect, the sixties in West Germany are generally termed a decade of unrest and change, as was the case in many other Western European societies. A predominant feature of the German scene was the Student Movement. Similar to the events on American campuses, it began with criticizing German academic life. The first sit-ins took place in 1966 at Berlin University, where the students demanded a reform of the curricula and the academic institutions. Soon the dissatisfaction spread to almost all sectors of society. In the same year, the 'Great Coalition' Government of Christian Democrats and Social Democrats put an end to the hopes of the German Left of a change in German society. The Student Movement joined forces with the so-called Extraparliamentary Opposition, and their joint activities became more and more radical. Public demonstrations led to confrontations with the police, particularly in university towns. In 1968, the year of student revolt in most Western countries, one of the leaders of the German Student Movement, Rudi

Dutschke, was severely injured by a right-wing radical. Violence had become a prominent feature of protest.

The general social and political issues that were at stake not only for the students but also for large numbers of intellectuals can be summed up as follows:

> A reinterpretation of Marxism, together with the teachings of the 'Frankfurt School' represented by Theodor W. Adorno, Max Horckheimer and Herbert Marcuse, formed the theoretical basis for the various political activities.
>
> The values of the 'affluent society' of the post-war era, the so-called German 'Wirtschaftswunder', were no longer taken for granted. German capitalism was regarded as a threat to German political and social welfare.
>
> For two decades American political, social and moral values and norms had served as a model for West Germany. In the sixties the USA met with increasing criticism, its focal point being the anti-Vietnam demonstrations.
>
> The Nazi past of some prominent public figures asked for a 'day of reckoning', for public debate on the crimes and atrocities of the Nazi regime and the prosecution of the Nazi criminals.

The desire for a radical change permeated all sectors of society. Besides political and social factors, it was also the growing estrangement between the younger and the older generation that influenced this development. The older generation was held responsible for all political and social problems and their historical roots. In the field of education the generation conflict resulted in a radical change of values and norms which found expression in the movement for 'anti-authoritarian education'.

Problems of adaptation

Viewing the first German productions of Bond's *Saved* in the context of the contemporary German scene helps to explain why the audience and the critics alike responded almost spontaneously to certain elements of the play such as the theme of violence or the generation conflict. If, however, it is true that a play is the expression of the 'cultural life of a nation',[10] will it retain its cultural unity once it is transferred to another 'national culture'? In the case of *Saved*, how can its cultural substance such as its South London setting and speech or the distinctive features of London's working-class youth be transferred to a German setting without being distorted?

These questions are not meant to overemphasize the differences

Ruth von Ledebur

between the two cultures, but rather to make us aware of specific difficulties in the adaptation of this play. On the other hand, we should also bear in mind that, for nearly four centuries, there has been a constant interchange between the English and the German theatre, from the time when English actors gave the first Shakespeare performances in Germany at the beginning of the seventeenth century up to the present day. German intellectual history has a long tradition of translating and adapting English drama for the German stage.

This holds true also for the influence of German drama and stagecraft on the English theatre. In our century, especially after World War II, the influence of German-language dramatists such as Büchner, Wedekind, Horvath, and Brecht has been absorbed by British dramatists. The most influential of them is Brecht, whose plays were staged by the Royal Shakespeare, the Royal Court and the National Theatre Companies in the sixties and seventies.[11] Brecht's drama and drama theory have shown British writers new techniques of staging and character presentation and of tackling public issues in their plays. Bond is among those writers 'most clearly influenced by radical German theatre'.[12] Recent criticism of Bond's plays draws our attention to many similarities between Bond's approach and Brechtian dramaturgy.[13] If, then, Bond has much in common with Brecht, there ought to be no difficulty in adapting his work for the German stage.

There were, however, only very few contemporary theatre critics aware of these similarities, which become obvious in the retrospect of literary analysis. It must also be borne in mind that the attempt to reconstruct the original German productions and to evaluate their reception relies on material from diverse and heterogeneous sources. The bulk of it comes from the theatre columns of daily and weekly papers and from theatre periodicals, the articles varying greatly not only in length and comprehensiveness but also in the critical awareness of the individual reviewer.[14] Some common characteristics can, however, be detected even in such diverse material. Apart from the sensational publicity which the first German productions received in the press, the critics were most preoccupied with the setting, the German dialogue and the central theme or 'message' of the play.

Setting and stage design in the German productions

It is common knowledge that the visual elements – setting, scenery, backdrop, stage-props, costumes, make-up, lighting, music, etc. – are prominent interpretative factors of any production and have a subtle influence on the reactions of the audience. In the case of *Saved*, the setting seems to have been a crucial point in most German productions.[15] According to the stage designs, they can be divided into four categories:

1. The production recreates a working-class milieu in the living-room scenes. The room is usually sparsely furnished: a sofa, one or two easy chairs, a dining table and chairs, a TV set. The designers aim to give an impression of squalor and poverty. In the two bedroom scenes this is underlined by ruffled and much-used bedclothes. The realism of such designs places *Saved* in the kitchen-sink tradition of the Wesker–Arden–Osborne generation. It emphasizes the 'Englishness' of the play, and a German audience tends to watch such a production with a certain aloofness. Accordingly, the milieu theory is applied to the interpretation of the play: The violence stems from this impoverished British working-class milieu. Only one sector of society is to blame for the murder of the baby; the universal human condition is reduced to miserable living conditions in England. Violence remains a 'foreign' problem that the German spectators may watch with horror but basically without any deeper concern.

2. A second type of design is less realistic than the first. Although its features are still 'working-class', they are less distinctly 'British'. In some productions this is realized by substituting emblems of an international beat culture for the working-class living-room setting. A Barbarella comic strip formed the backdrop in Dortmund, posters of Liz Taylor and Mike Todd served as scenery in Kassel; a jukebox fulfilled an emblematic function in the café scene. There are even attempts at some local colouring such as using a German pop-song ('Wenn der weiße Flieder wieder blüht') as background music. In the costumes the design aims at flashiness and gaudy colours rather than at impoverished shabbiness. Thus, *Saved* becomes essentially a play about the young generation: atrocity and violence are their problems, and their aggressiveness frightens the older members of the audience. The generation conflict, a prominent feature of the German social scene at that time, is worked into a production even in such minor details as Mary turning off the TV as news of the Vietnam War is being shown.[16]

3. Some German designers seem to have been conscious of the fact that some elements of the 'British' setting cannot be transposed onto a German background. The ringing of a bell to indicate that the park gates will soon be closing is not known in Germany. Thus the bell at the close of Scene 6 after the killing of the baby, which explains why the gang rush off in terror, would not make sense to a German audience. In the Munich production

the producer substituted the bell by the approaching steps of a policeman. The dialogue had to be changed accordingly. As the scenery indicated not a park with a pool but the banks of the river Isar in Munich, the entire scene was transported into almost authentic German surroundings. Such a production induced the audience to identify itself with what was happening on the stage.[17]

4. A fourth type of design was realized comparatively rarely in the early productions, and Zadek's ambitious Berlin production is perhaps the best example of it. Zadek aimed at anti-illusionist theatre.[18] By leaving the stage almost bare, he destroyed any illusion of the kitchen-sink atmosphere. Instead of any realistic setting, he used a metallic backdrop, an aluminium floor and extensive lighting effects. The 'London' scenes, such as the café, park and living-room, are no longer recognizable as such. For Zadek, the actor becomes the main 'medium' of the play. He has to compensate for the lack of stage props and furniture so that Harry's head, for example, functions as the TV set, his ears being 'used' as buttons by the other characters to switch it on or off. Instead of having a baby crying off-stage (Scene 4), Pam imitates the crying of the baby. In contrast to the way in which the crucial sixth scene is staged in most German productions, where during the stoning the pram is turned away from the audience so as not to reveal the baby, in Berlin the 'baby' is taken out of its pram and is, very obviously, only a doll.[19] Despite the director's intention of disillusioning the audience by creating a non-realistic atmosphere and thereby emphasizing the universality of the play's theme, the audience seemed to miss the point. According to the reviews, it was shocked by the brutality and the 'realism' of the violent action. One critic remarked that Zadek had gone against the grain of the play.[20] When analysing Bond's extensive comments on the British productions of *Saved*,[21] one realizes the truth of the critic's remark. Bond insists on the importance of all objects such as furniture and props, with a meticulous attention to detail which recalls Brecht's productions of his own plays.[22] Zadek himself countered such criticism by stating that he did not intend 'to teach his audience a lesson in social sciences'.[23]

Translation of the dialogue

When transferring a play from culture to culture, the adequacy of the translation is, of course, a crucial point. In accordance with its setting, the dialogues of the original represent a South London Cockney variety. British critics have drawn attention to the fact that although the working-class speech is true to the idiom of that region and 'feels exactly right', it is also highly formalized.[24] When questioned about the 'realism' of his play and dialogue, Bond commented as follows:

> The dialogue in *Saved* (...) isn't tape recorded, though some people seem to imagine it is. It's a very highly selected and very carefully worked and reworked form of dialogue. It has patterns of imagery and so on which reoccur throughout the play. I would have thought it was basically poetic but it is also, I hope, very true to life.[25]

How can such dialogue be adequately translated and preserve in translation the qualities of the original, which its author claims to be 'basically poetic' but also 'very virile, provocative, very terse and epigrammatical'?[26]

Christian Enzensberger, who translated most of Bond's later plays into German, comments on the problems of translating as follows: in trying to 'remember what people really say in this or that situation', he usually starts from a word-for-word translation, trying to find out 'what you really can't say in German ... It was only then that I discovered that it was easy to translate B's plays, which surely is a great compliment – a kind of proof for the universality of a text.'[27]

Klaus Reichert, the German translator of *Saved*, claims, however, that 'you simply can't translate such a play into German'. He goes on to say: 'It would be possible to adopt an equivalent German metropolitan jargon (*Großstadtjargon*); but the social discrepancy between, say, Kreuzberg (a slum district in West Berlin) and Battersea or Lambeth would be an additional difficulty.' Reichert, therefore, aims at a 'model translation', which can be used all over Germany. The translation 'attempts to render the South London speech by a "neutral" German vernacular (*allgemeine deutsche Umgangssprache*), which represents at the same time the lowest social register'.[28]

When comparing Reichert's translation with the original, one is, at first sight, struck by the accuracy of this translation. Non-standard Cockney syntax is usually rendered by its German equivalents in non-standard speech. It is, of course, on the lexical level that Bond's dialogue proves to be untranslatable. This is not due to any lack of vulgar or obscene words and phrases in the German language but rather to the difference in the extra-lingual context they refer to. 'Ich bin ja kein Geldscheißer' strikes a different note from 'I ain't made a money, y' know' of the original; the same holds true for 'Geizknochen' as a rendering of 'tight arse'.[29]

Generally speaking, on the semantic level the German dialogue is either more direct and vulgar than the original or less so. On the whole, Reichert employs comparatively few slang expressions, thereby losing much of the original 'virility' and 'provocation' of working-class speech. Reichert himself must have been aware of this deficit in his translation. In his 'Preface' he advises German actors to give their texts the 'colouring' of their local dialects and use such jargon and four-letter words as are typical of that dialect. On the other hand, he warns producers not to turn *Saved* into a 'dialect play' of any specific German region.

The advice given by Reichert was followed by most German directors of the play who based their productions on his translation.[30] It is difficult to deduce from the reviews to what degree the dialogues were 'in tune' with a local or regional dialect, and there is much controversy as to the effects of such local colouring. Some critics complain that the rendering of the dialogue according to German standards makes it sound artificial and stylized, thereby depriving the speech of its original brutality.[31] In Dortmund, they adapted Reichert's translation to the vernacular of the Ruhr mining area. As this dialect has a characteristic sing-song quality, the 'laconic unmusical quality' of Bond's original got lost. But the audience responded more easily to the play and sympathized with action and actors alike.[32]

In their attempts at a comprehensive cultural adaptation of the play, only a few productions seem to have completely translated Bond's Cockney into a German dialect.[33] The most ambitious of these was in Munich, which has already been mentioned for the local colouring of its setting and stage design. Martin Sperr, who translated the play into a Bavarian dialect variety spoken in the working-class suburbs of Munich, did not aim at a word-for-word translation.[34] Most of the jokes and the bawdiness is rendered in typically Bavarian 'slang', which as one critic complained can hardly be understood by a non-Bavarian.[35] The entire text was reworked to suit the needs of the Munich production.[36] Instead of tea, the characters have beer with their meals; Mary's teapot is turned into a coffeepot; Bond's 'yellow-niggers' as the objects of discrimination and aggression are changed to immigrant workers. When Harry, in Scene 12 tells Len about his experiences in the war, he refers to the enemy soldier whom he killed in close combat as 'some bloke'. In the Bavarian adaptation this is rendered as 'Scheiß-Ivan' (bloody Russian). By such alterations the play is almost completely transplanted from culture to culture. Peter Stein, the director, justifies the Bavarian dialect as follows:

On the one hand, the dialect is used as a means of understatement, to give the characters credibility. On the other hand, it helps the actors to establish the communicative situations in each scene. The dialect produces an effect of alienation which prevents the actors from falling back on routine speech habits and gestures. With the help of these devices we avoided intruding upon Bond's characters. Each time we rehearsed a scene, we had to find a new approach to the text.[37]

Among the critics, the Bavarian version became a controversial issue. None of them seems to have realized that with the dialect Stein aimed at Brechtian alienation. Hellmuth Karasek, a well-known theatre critic, argues that the Bavarian dialect makes light of the essential brutality of the play, as it is traditionally associated – on the German stage – with the simple-mindedness of the Bavarian farce.[38] Ivan Nagel, Stein's literary adviser, quotes members of the Munich audience responding favourably to Sperr's version. To them, the Bavarian text was 'harsher and more awe-inspiring' than both the German standard translation and the original. According to Nagel, the audience recognized that Bond's play deals not only with the decline in morals but also in language.[39] On the whole, the responses of the critics reveal that the complete transcultural adaptation of the play is certainly a 'distortion' of the original, yet its 'message' may have come across to the (local) audience even more forcibly because of the unity of its setting and speech. It may be due to this fact that the German theatre periodical *Theater heute* chose the Munich production of *Gerettet* as its 'production of the year'.

The theme of violence

In discussing the central theme of the play, violence, most critics relate it to the crucial sixth scene, the stoning of the baby, the staging of which varies greatly from production to production. In Kassel, the opening of Scene 6 when Fred showed Len how to squash a worm, prefigured the killing of the baby, who was treated like a 'toy' by the gang acting out their aggressions as in a football match. In Ulm, on a comparatively small stage, the pram with the baby was placed in the foreground so that the actors threw their stones in the direction of the audience. This terrified the spectators, who identified themselves with the victim. In Wiesbaden, as in some other German productions, the killing was acted out as a kind of ritual: the movements of the gang followed a certain rhythm and were underlined by rhythmic noises.[40] This 'choreography' placed the violence of the killing scene at a distance, yet the audience seems to have been deeply moved. For the more 'realistic' staging of this scene the critics register the immense shock caused by the 'arbitrary sadism of the teenagers',[41] whereas others are reminded of the brutal killers in the concentration camps, thus linking the play's action with the German past.

Shock and disgust at the mixture of obscenity, boredom and atrocity in this scene, and – in consequence – the refusal to accept the challenge of the play, are prominent features of the first notices in the daily papers after the respective opening nights. Bond himself knew that the audience would respond with mixed emotions to the outbreak of violence. His comment after the first performance in London in 1965 sums up these responses:

Yes, but the funny thing about Scene 6 is that everybody's reaction is different. Some people come away and say, what was all the fuss about, I thought it was very underdone; oh, it didn't affect me at all, very sort of objective, and other people came out absolutely shaking and other people can't even watch it. So it's their reaction, I mean they must ask themselves, not ask me what I think about it.[42]

Those critics who take a more positive point of view justify the violent scene by reminding their readers of even more atrocious actions on stage in Greek tragedies and Shakespeare's plays. They take Scene 6 and with it the whole play as a parable about war, and also recognize parallels to topical events, most frequently to the Vietnam War.[43] Hardly any producer or critic seems to have been aware of Bond's own intentions. In an interview he stated that '*Saved* is not an intentionally violent play – the violence happens almost like a joke'. Zadek's Berlin production certainly did not present Scene 6 'as a joke': He made the actors tear the doll to pieces, whereupon, on the first night, numerous spectators left the theatre in storms of protest, and some actors afterwards refused to take part in further performances.[44] By cutting the last scene of the play, Zadek emphasizes the violence of the action even more and destroys all hopes of a happy ending. In this, as in many other aspects, the Berlin production seems to be the most radical of all German productions. The ambiguity of the closing scene troubles most critics. Not only does the almost wordless scene lend itself to diverse realizations on stage but also to numerous misunderstandings.[45] Most German productions tended towards a pessimistic ending: the actors moved about aimlessly; the lack of communication indicating that hostility and violence may break out again at any moment.

Bond's preoccupation with violence, also in his later plays, has become a major concern for Bond's critics, who associate his plays with Antonin Artaud's 'Theatre of Cruelty'.[46] With this early play, the German critics have difficulties in establishing a link between the play's central theme and its title. As one critic states laconically: 'The title causes considerable headaches.'[47] 'The logic of the play does not convince us of the title *Saved*.'[48] To quote yet another critic: 'A chair is saved at the end, but not man.'[49]

As Len, although a 'likeable young man', is also presented as an ambivalent character in most productions, he is often criticized for his indifference to the stoning of the baby. One critic compares Len to Parsifal who means to do well but is essentially helpless.[50] None of the critics seems to have recognized in the German productions the 'desperate optimism' (Bond) of the play's chief character. This leads one to the conclusion that, contrary to the author's intentions, the German productions of the play lacked not only these signs of optimism but also the comic overtones. Bond calls his play an 'Oedipus comedy' and claims that it is 'almost irresponsibly optimistic'.[51] Most German productions focused on the central theme of the play which, according to Bond, is concerned with the 'dialectics of violence': 'As a society, we are destroying ourselves through violence.'[52] In this respect, the German stage gave a true rendering of the original.

It goes without saying that it is impossible to judge which – if any – of the numerous German productions did complete justice to the author's intentions, or whether the responses of German audiences were appropriate to the play. Apart from the different cultural context of the German adaptation, there is one general issue that points at the central ambiguity of Bond's play. As has been mentioned before, critics, producers, and audiences alike were puzzled by the discrepancy between the title of the play and its main theme. In my opinion, the violence of the central action is not counterbalanced by the 'dumb show' of the last scene, nor are Bond's comments on the inherent optimism of his play in accordance with the development of the action and the portrayal of the characters. Rather than clarifying the major issues they add to the confusion about the meaning of his play. The ambiguity of the play's title emphasizes this point.

Notes

1 For the English stage history of *Saved*, see Malcolm Hay and Philip Roberts, *Bond: A Study of his Plays* (London: Eyre Methuen, 1980), pp. 39–64.

2 See statistics in Appendix I. Malcolm Hay and Philip Roberts, in *Edward Bond: A Companion to his Plays* (London: T.Q. Publications, 1978), list all productions on the German-speaking stage except for the production at Regensburg, Stadttheater, 6 March 1970, directed by Volkmar Kamm and designed by Klaus Roth. A few dates given by Hay and Roberts differ from the dates I researched, most notably for the production at Oberhausen, which opened on 9 March 1969, not on 1 March 1968 as stated by Hay and Roberts, p. 81.

3 See reviews of the English productions in *Post-war British Theatre Criticism*, ed. John Elsom (London: Routledge and Kegan Paul, 1981), pp. 174–80, and in *Plays in Review 1956–1980*, eds. Gareth and Barbara Lloyd Evans (London: Batsford Academic and Educational, 1985), pp. 135–40.

4 In his dissertation, 'Die Rezeption der Dramen Edward Bonds im deutschen Sprachraum: eine Untersuchung deutschsprachiger Theater kritiken' (Kiel, 1983), Peter Prange reviews German theatre criticism on *Gerettet* (pp. 7–31).

Ruth von Ledebur

His overall aim is a text typology of theatre criticism, not, as in my paper, a reconstruction and evaluation of the productions. See his bibliography of reviews from daily papers and theatre periodicals, pp. 166–72.

5 Jenny Urs, 'G'schichten aus den Isarauen', in *Süddeutsche Zeitung*, 17 April 1967.

6 See Wolfgang Strauch v. Quitzow, 'Ein Kind wird gesteinigt', in *Westdeutsche Zeitung*, 22 April 1967.

7 Botho Strauß, 'Ein Stück ist ein System', *Theater heute*, 9 (1968), no. 5, pp. 36–9 (p. 36).

8 Christopher Innes, 'The Political Spectrum of Edward Bond: From Rationalism to Rhapsody', in *Modern British Dramatists*, ed. John Russell Brown (Englewood Cliffs, NJ: Prentice Hall, Inc., 1984), p. 127.

9 See Ursula Spreckelsen, *Die Konzeption des 'family life' im zeitgenössischen Englischen Drama* (Frankfurt am Main: Peter D. Lang, 1980), p. 95. Prange, in 'Rezeption Bonds', also emphasizes the positive response of the German critics.

10 Giles Gordon, 'Interview with Edward Bond', in *Behind the Scenes: Theatre and Film Interviews from the Transatlantic Review*, ed. Joseph F. McCrindle (New York: Holt, London: Pitman, 1971), pp. 125–36 (p. 134).

11 See Christian W. Thomsen, 'British Brecht', in *Das Englische Theater der Gegenwart* (Düsseldorf: August Bagel, 1980), pp. 227–44.

12 John Russell Brown in 'Introduction' to *Modern British Dramatists*, p. 5.

13 See Peter Holland, 'Brecht, Bond, Gaskill, and the Practice of Political Theatre', in *Theatre Quarterly*, 8 (1978), no. 30, pp. 24–34, and the correspondence between Bond and Holland, pp. 34–5. See also Innes, 'Political Spectrum', pp. 135–7.

14 On the diversity of theatre criticism and the methodological questions involved when using it as source material, see Gareth and Barbara Lloyd Evans's 'Introduction' to *Plays in Review*, pp. 11–47.

15 When no individual source is referred to in the notes, reviews of various productions are treated collectively. The translations from German source material into English are my own.

16 See Gerd Schulte, 'Hintertreppe oder Avantgarde', in *Hannoversche Presse*, 2 February 1968.

17 The Munich production is documented in 'Unsere Aufführung des Jahres: Edward Bond *Gerettet* inszeniert von Peter Stein im Werkraum der Münchner Kammerspiele', in *Theater heute Jahressonderheft* 1967, pp. 57–73. See also Martin Sperr, Peter Stein, and Ivan Nagel, 'Wie wir Bonds Stück inszenierten', in *Theater heute Jahressonderheft* 1967, pp. 74–6.

18 Zadek's example was followed by some productions in the seventies. For further productions in the 1981–3 seasons, see Prange, 'Rezeption Bonds', pp. 26–9.

19 See Rolf Michaelis, 'Zadeks Kontrast', in *Frankfurter Allgemeine Zeitung*, 5 July 1968, p. 12.

20 Martha Christine Körling, 'Protest um den Mord im Zeitlupentempo', in *Berliner Morgenpost*, 19 June 1968.

21 See Bond's comments quoted and analysed in Hay and Roberts, *Bond: a Study*, pp. 39–64; and in the numerous Bond interviews, see 'Bibliography' in Hay and Roberts, *Bond: a Companion*, pp. 33–4.

22 See Hay and Roberts, *Bond: a Study*, p. 57f.

23 Quoted in anon., 'Protest gegen Regisseure. Gegen Zadek', in *Theater heute*, 9 (1968), no. 8, p. 33.

24 '"Drama and the Dialectics of Violence", Edward Bond's Interview with the Editors', *Theatre Quarterly*, 2 (1972), no. 5, pp. 4–14 (p. 7). On language and style in *Saved*, see also Tony Coult, *The Plays of Edward Bond* (London: Eyre Methuen, 1977), pp. 76f.

25 Quoted in Gordon, 'Interview', pp. 128–9.

26 Some German critics are also acutely aware of the stylistic qualities of Bond's dialogue; see Thomsen, *Englische Theater*, pp. 211–27; Peter Wolfensperger, *Edward Bond. Dialektik des Weltbildes und dramatische Gestaltung* (Bern: Francke, 1976), pp. 43–5; Leo Truchlar, 'Edward Bond', in *Englische Literatur der Gegenwart in Einzeldarstellungen* (Stuttgart: Körner, 1970), pp. 476–92.

27 Quoted in Hay and Roberts, *Bond: a Companion*, p. 48.

28 Klaus Reichert, 'Vorbemerkung des Übersetzers', in Edward Bond, *Gerettet* (Frankfurt am Main: Suhrkamp, 1966), pp. 9–10.

29 For further examples, see Appendix II.

30 Hay and Roberts, in *Bond: a Companion*, do not list the translations of the German productions. Out of the thirty-six theatres which produced *Gerettet* between 1966 and 1973 twenty-nine used Reichert's translation.

31 See Volker Canaris, 'Bond, hochdeutsch', in *Theater heute*, 8 (1967), no. 12, p. 48; Ernst Wendt, 'Warten auf waswofür', *Theater heute*, 8 (1967), no. 6, pp. 8–12.

32 See Strauß, 'Ein Stück', p. 38.

33 Besides Dortmund and Munich, the following theatres used dialect adaptations: Hamburg (with touches of 'Plattdeutsch'), Basel (Swiss dialect), Vienna, Graz and Innsbruck (various Austrian dialects).

34 Appendix II also gives examples of Sperr's dialect version compared with Reichert's standard translation.

35 Wolfgang Drews, 'Der bayerische Bond', in *Frankfurter Allgemeine Zeitung*, 18 April 1967, p. 10.

36 See Sperr, Stein and Nagel, 'Wie wir Bonds Stück inszenierten', p. 74.

37 *Ibid.*, p. 75.

38 Hellmuth Karasek, 'Ins Bayerische gerettet', in *Stuttgarter Zeitung*, 17 April 1967.

39 Sperr, Stein and Nagel, 'Wie wir Bonds Stück inszenierten', p. 75.

40 See Gerhard Rühle, '*Gerettet* – ins höhere Deutsch', in *Frankfurter Allgemeine Zeitung*, 2 October 1967, p. 12.

41 Karl Robert Danler, 'Versuch einer Rettung', in *Frankfurter Rundschau*, 18 April 1967.

42 Quoted in Hay and Roberts, *Bond: a Companion*, p. 10.

43 See Drews, 'Bayerische Bond'; Rühle, '*Gerettet*'; Danler, 'Versuch'.

44 See Michaelis, 'Zadeks Kontrast'; anon., 'Protest gegen Regisseure' and anon., 'Bond ohne Milieu', *Theater heute*, 9 (1968), no. 8, p. 38.

45 See Hay's and Roberts's interesting comments on the alternative interpretations of the play's ending as pessimistic or optimistic, on the British stage (in *Bond: a Study*, pp. 55f.). Wolfensperger (in *Bond: Dialektik*) regards the dichotomy of optimism and pessimism as the central issue of Bond's plays.

46 See Wolfensperger, *Bond: Dialektik*, p. 54. The ways in which Bond's conceptions of the political and social roots of today's violence differ considerably from Artaud's and, accordingly, from the stagecraft of the latter, are beyond the scope of this paper.

47 Anon., 'Ekel, Familienkrach, noch mehr Ekel', in *Schwäbische Zeitung*, 1 March 1968.

48 Anon., 'Ein starkes Stück', in *Süddeutsche Zeitung*, 12 February 1968.

49 Anon., '*Gerettet* ist nur der Stuhl – und der Mensch?', in *Badische Neueste Nachrichten*, 1 March 1968.

50 *Ibid.*

51 'Author's Note' in Edward Bond, *Saved*. Methuen Modern Plays (London: Methuen, 1969), pp. 5–8.

52 In the *Theatre Quarterly* interview of 1972. See also Rainer Taëni, 'Ein Interview mit Edward Bond', *Akzente*, 16 (1969), pp. 564–77, which is frequently quoted in German theatre programmes.

Appendix 1

Statistics of performances of *Gerettet* (*Saved*) on the German-speaking stage, for the seasons 1965–6 to 1972–3.

Season	Number of performances	Number of theatres
1965–6	50	1
1966–7	24	1
1967–8	188	15
1968–9	110	7
1969–70	40	3
1970–1	46	5
1971–2	21	2
1972–3	29	2

Appendix II

A Examples of semantic shifts in German translation

BOND	REICHERT
I'm tired a 'im watching me all the time.	Es *stinkt mir*, daß er mich immer so *anglotzt*.
lucky	Son Schwein
I ain' touched a tart for weeks.	Ich hab seit Wochen keine mehr gehabt.
I juss got right.	Jetzt hab ich mirs grad bequem gemacht.
dinner-box	Fresspaket
Anyway, *Mum*'ll be back.	Und außerdem kommt *die Alte* wieder.
Must a' bin *bloody rotten* when yer were a kid.	Muß *scheußlich* gewesen sein, wie du klein warst.
Creep!	Du Arsch!
I done blokes in.	Ich hab schon ganz andere fertig gemacht.
I ain' a 'ippocrit.	Bin ich bescheuert?
An' 'er ol' dad'd bin bashin' it off for years.	Der ihr Alter hat sie gut angelernt.

B Reichert's translation compared with Sperr's Bavarian dialect

SPERR	REICHERT
Griagst 'Häifde vo de Guaddin.	Du bekommst die Hälfte von den Bonbons.
Wiavui Zähn hostn du scho zambackt?	Wieviel Mädchen hast du denn schon gehabt?
Hoidde ei, Deandl.	Halt dich fest, Mädchen.
Glei duschds!	Gleich kracht's!
Dadst zwoa a schaffe?	Würdest du zwei auch schaffen?
Dei hinddafotzign Karaggda mechte nod hom.	Deinen hinterhältigen Charakter möchte ich nicht haben.
Scheene Haxn host.	Schöne Beine hast du.

Whose Life is it Anyway? in London and on Broadway: a contrastive analysis of the British and American versions of Brian Clark's play

ALBERT-REINER GLAAP

Whose Life is it Anyway?, the title of a play by Brian Clark,[1] has been understood as both a real and a rhetorical question. The title implies an answer, but the answer which the play gives is that there are no final answers to the questions raised. Hence a paper on this play cannot pretend to know the answers or offer clear-cut solutions. I will, however, try to point out the central issues arising from an analysis of the most relevant alterations made by Brian Clark when asked to rewrite *Whose Life is it Anyway?* for a production on Broadway, in which a woman was going to play the role of the paralysed patient.

Whose Life is it Anyway?[2] focuses on a patient in an intensive care unit. Ken Harrison, a young sculptor, is paralysed from the neck down as the result of a road accident. It is inevitable that Ken will have to spend the rest of his life in a nursing home. He does not see any sense in living any longer: 'If I can't be a man', he says, 'I do not wish to be a medical achievement.' The play thus becomes a contest between the doctors who want to keep him alive and his own determination to remove their life support system and die with dignity. Ken's lawyer sets up a legal court in the hospital on which occasion, however, the Hippocratic Oath and the unconditional will to act freely collide with each other. The judge issues an order for Ken to be set free, but the patient decides in the end to stay in hospital under medical observation, and accepts the offer to die in the clinic.

Brian Clark's play is not about death, but about the right of the individual to make choices about his ultimate destiny. In order to drive his point home, it would have been impossible for the playwright to have had a patient who was so pitiable that most people would have wanted him to die soon. The doctors had to be believable representatives of the medical profession so that Ken's wish to die could not be interpreted as the result of bad medical treatment. Ken's decision had to be convincing and reasonable and by no means accidental. *Whose Life is it Anyway?* is a play of great appeal to anyone who has ever set foot in a hospital. But it also makes a general statement about human rights. It is directed against arbitrary authority. Its simple and powerful story works as theatre because the moral argument is left to the audience. The theatre-goer is almost forced to slip into the role of the different characters and see the problems connected with voluntary euthanasia from different points of view.

Moreover, the quintessence of the play, which is that freedom must start in the individual, is seen by the audience in the light of the specific conditions reigning in different countries. In Poland, both the doctors and the judge who decided Ken Harrison's case were unequivocally identified with the state machinery. Ken's wish for freedom was taken for an allegory of the Polish people's freedom. Elsewhere, *Whose Life is it Anyway?* has broken the reticence barrier and initiated a debate on the medical termination of life. In Zürich there was a big conference of doctors and lawyers in the theatre discussing the play. The play rang a different bell in Japan because – as Clark himself found out – the Japanese have always seen suicide as highly respectable.

In Cologne, West Germany, there were fierce protests against the performance of *Whose Life is it Anyway?* on the evening of its première: 'The right to die – that's Nazi ideology', the young Germans shouted. Obviously they did not know what the play was really about; they had merely been told that it was concerned with voluntary euthanasia, of which they take a dim view. It is understandable if people in Germany today are allergic to euthanasia as practised in the Third Reich. On the other hand they should be confronted with the problems of *voluntary* euthanasia. In an interview which I conducted with the playwright, Brian Clark had this to say:

Of course, I do understand that in Germany there is a sensitivity to the word 'euthanasia' because it was perverted by Hitler and I understand and have sympathy with people who are thereby very sensitive to the dangers of any form of killing people because they are inadequate or infirm or homosexuals or Jews or whatever – and the play quite specifically states that it is immoral to hand the responsibility of one's death to anyone else. It is also immoral to accept that responsibility, and therefore my answer is that the right and the duties remain with the individual and he must exercise it. It is the total opposite to a Nazi ideology, which deals in terms of *national* need, and the play deals in terms of *individual* need.[3]

Brian Clark originally wrote *Whose Life is it Anyway?* as a TV play for

Granada in 1969–70. It was his first play as a professional writer and he thought it was worth redoing it for the stage. But hardly anybody in England seemed to be interested in those days. Obviously people were not aware of the moral problem confronting patients in Ken Harrison's position. Seven years later *Whose Life is it Anyway?* resurfaced as a stage play; the reticence barrier had been broken. On 6 March 1978, it was first produced at the Mermaid Theatre in London with Tom Conti as Ken Harrison, and was voted best play of the year by the West End Theatre managers. A year later *Whose Life is it Anyway?* was premièred on Broadway, also with Tom Conti in the lead. Only minimal changes were made to the British text. It was virtually a British text. The setting was an English hospital. His performance won Tom Conti a Tony Award as Broadway's best actor.

When Tom Conti left the show, a number of actors 'ducked the challenge of holding an audience for nearly two hours using only their voice and facial expressions' (*Daily Mail*, 15 September 1985). Comic actress Mary Tyler Moore took what was at that time Broadway's toughest role – as the paralysed patient in Clark's play.

TV personalities as replacements in the leads of long-running plays? This is by no means a rare phenomenon in American theatres. A famous example was Dick Cavett appearing in *Otherwise Engaged*. In Clark's play, however, it was not only that. What was out of the common was that the new talking head in *Whose Life is it Anyway?* was a woman.

The playwright had made relatively few concessions to the shift of sexes. Reviews, however, were mixed. Here are a few reactions from theatre critics:

– The play has been rewritten without having shaken off its male origins. (Douglas Watt in *Daily News*, 25 February 1980)

– Apart from having suffered a sex change and a sea change (. . .) the play seems to have been trimmed considerably. The lesser characters and their dramas have all been minimized, so that everything now rests on Mary Tyler Moore's performance in the central role. (Howard Kissel in *Women's Wear Daily*, 25 February 1980)

– Samson could play Delilah, and Delilah could play Samson, but who would have the scissors? Unisex plays can only work with unisex playwrights and unisex audiences. (Clive Barnes in the *New York Post*, 25 February 1980)

Why was a *woman* asked to take over from Tom Conti? In the interview, Clark gave several reasons. First and foremost, 'a woman taking over is a modest contribution to the feminist cause . . . in which I'm a believer' Clark said and went on to demonstrate the universality of this theme:

The point about the play is that it is a play about a *person*. The gender of the person is really unimportant. That, of course, is a political statement, in terms of a world where women are often second-class citizens. So by changing it to a woman that makes that statement, saying, look, the play is exactly the same, the issues are the same.[4]

Consequently, *Whose Life is it Anyway?* was rewritten for an actress and for an American audience. Clark recounts that he had far more work in Americanizing it than he did in changing the sex. No one could imagine Mary Tyler Moore as an English woman. Thus changing the culture and the language was a much bigger job than changing the sex.

An American-English version of the script was published by The Dramatic Publishing Company in Chicago[5] in 1981. By conducting a contrastive study of this edition and the original version in British English, the most prominent alterations and the specifically American features came to light. Such an analysis can show to what extent a specific cultural and linguistic background is essential to the understanding of the play and it can thereby give an insight into the problem of transferring a play from one culture to another.

Following from what has already been said, the most important differences between the British and American version of *Whose Life is it Anyway?* can be subsumed under three headings: 'changing the sex', 'changing the culture' and 'changing the language'.

Changing the sex: a woman as the patient

The patient being a woman (*Claire* Harrison) in the American play, Clark thought he should change the sex of Claire's physician, too. He is Dr David Scott in the American script. On the other hand, the first lawyer, Claire's attorney, is a woman (*Margaret* Hill as opposed to Philip Hill in the English version). There are other slight changes due to the fact that the patient is now a woman. The flirting, the sexual banter occurs with the ward orderly and not with the young nurse. Some words and expressions have been replaced with others which are more appropriate when used by a woman. When, for instance, the nurse operates the bed to the flat position – at the very beginning of the play – Claire's comment is: 'Going down – *Orthopedics*, Gynecology, Ladies Underwear . . . ' In the English version the line reads: 'Going down – Obstetrics, Gynaecology, Lingerie, Rubber wear.' When Claire is talking to the student nurse about the sedative that she is supposed to take regularly in order to get to sleep, she says: 'It will calm me and soothe me and make me forget for a while that you can walk out here tonight and make love to your boyfriend.' Ken's words are: ' . . .

and make me forget for a while that you have a lovely body'. John, the ward orderly, can no longer plug in the razor and shave the patient. Instead, 'he dusts around room and empties wastebasket' in the American production. Ken – when talking to Dr Scott – cries out in admiration: 'You have lovely breasts', whereas Claire *asks* her doctor: 'Do you like my breasts?' And the patient's words: '. . . though I've only a piece of knotted string between my legs, I still have a man's mind' are tempered in the American version in which Claire's corresponding words are: '. . . though I've no feelings in my body, I still have a woman's mind'.

Changing the cultural context

Most of the changes in the American version of *Whose Life is it Anyway?* are, however, due to the Americanization of cultural references and of linguistic details. The most relevant alterations are due to the fact that the place of action is now an *American* hospital. The description of the set is much more detailed than in the British version. But the *List of Characters* makes the differences even more obvious. The professions and functions of those employed in the hospital are named in the American way. Dr Scott is not a 'Junior Registrar' (which would indicate that keeping records and registers is one of his duties, too), he is just called 'Claire's physician'. *Sister* Anderson is now *Nurse* Anderson, and Dr Emerson is not called a 'Consultant Physician' but a 'Medical Director'. The 'Probationer Nurse' is a 'Student Nurse' in the American play. As far as the legal aspects of Clark's play are concerned, the functions of the lawyers have been named differently in the American version from the British one. The terms 'solicitor' (for a lawyer who advises clients on legal matters and speaks on their behalf in lower courts) and 'barrister' (for a lawyer who has the right to argue as an advocate in higher law courts) reflect the elements of the legal profession in England which must be clearly distinguished. Solicitors are much more numerous. To be a barrister a man must be a member of one of the four Inns of Court. In the American version of *Whose Life is it Anyway?* the terms 'solicitor' and 'barrister' have disappeared. Both the patient's solicitor and the hospital's barrister are called attorneys – a more general term for persons with legal authority to act for others in business or law. Finally, as to the list of characters, some typically English first names and surnames have also been altered: Gillian (Boyle) is now Louise; Kay (Sadler) is Mary Jo, and the consultant psychiatrist has a Jewish name in the American script – he is Dr Jacobs (not Dr Travers).

Needless to say, Clark's play in the original bears the stamp of British life and institutions. The language used to describe the political, legal, medical and educational arrangements by which the British people manage their affairs would not be immediately understood by American audiences. The playwright had to look out for suitable American renderings or counterparts in order to achieve equivalence in difference. A careful analysis of both the British version (BV) and American version (AV) throws some light on the widespread ramifications of the playwright's attempts to Americanize his script with regard to institutional details. Some examples will suffice:

1 *Hospital*

American version (AV)	British version (BV)
she'll be transferred to a long-term institution	he'll be transferred to a long-stay hospital
ramp area	sluice room
a little hint of Lysol (Pinesol)	a little hint of Jeyes fluid (Milton)
remove the catheter	remove the drips
she takes tray of instruments	she is taking kidney dishes and instruments out of the sterilizer
cart	trolley

2 *Legal and financial matters*

AV	BV
attorney at law	solicitor
litigation partner	barrister
we can request a hearing	we can appeal to a tribunal
an autopsy	a post-mortem
Yes, your Honor (addressing the judge)	Yes, my Lord
thousands of dollars	hundreds of pounds
settle your insurance claim	get your compensation settled

3 *Education, sports and entertainment*

AV	BV
in nursing school	at PTS (= Primary Training School)
educators	educationalists
tough break (i.e. hard luck)	ping pong
a punk band	a steel band
we are going to be on the Gong Show in a month	we are auditioning for Opportunity Knocks in four weeks
jogging	football

Apart from these and many more examples which elucidate that there is much *alteration in detail*, there are other passages in the American version which show how some of the *key elements* of the play have been Americanized.

The Mental Health Act of 1959 plays an important role in the original version of *Whose Life is it Anyway?* According to this act, a patient may be admitted to a hospital, and there detained for a certain period, if he is suffering from mental disorder or if it is necessary in the interests of the patient's health or safety or for the protection of other persons (Section 26). The discussion of this section of the Mental Health Act[6] and its relevance to the consultant physician's dilemma had to be replaced with an American counterpart, if there was any. In the American production Dr Emerson is taking steps to have Claire Harrison detained in hospital under Section 972 of the *Mental Hygiene Law* as mentally unbalanced.

Habeas Corpus ('thou shalt have the body') are the initial words of an Act of Parliament (1679) which lays down a guarantee whereby nobody can be imprisoned without a fair tribunal: the particular person must be told why he has been detained, and he must be given the possibility of providing for his defence.

At the time of its enactment *Habeas Corpus* was a safeguard against dictatorship. In Clark's play the introduction of *Habeas Corpus* adds new aspects to Ken's line of argument. References to this law have been left unchanged in the American version of *Whose Life is it Anyway?* It is well-known in the United States; it is mentioned in the Constitution of the United States (Article 1, Section 9) and, in our century, was debated in connection with the mass evacuation of Japanese citizens following the Japanese attack on Pearl Harbour in 1941. Thus there was no need to change statements like: 'I would prefer to go for a Writ of *Habeas Corpus*.'

The ending of the play is another key element that has been Americanized. Ken's and Claire's final statements differ slightly but significantly.

Dr Emerson.	You might change your mind.
Claire.	I won't. But thank you. It would obviously be easier for me if I stayed (AV).
Ken.	Thanks, I won't change my mind, but I'd like to stay (BV).

Whereas Ken merely says that he would like to stay without giving reasons, Claire takes the decision because she is fully aware that staying in hospital will be easier for her – and she says so. Also the final stage directions are more revealing in the American version: '*Lights hold on Claire, as alone as anyone can ever be.*' The British version reads: '*The lights are held for a long moment and then snap out.*'

Changing the language

Not only cultural references but also linguistic details presented difficulties when rewriting the play for an American production. English words had to be replaced with American words: *truck driver* (instead of lorry driver), *light shade* (for lampshade), *ladies underwear* (for lingerie), *board meeting* (for committee meeting), *chipped* (not: minced) beef, *disabilities* as a substitute for handicaps, *a real nerd* for a real twit. Phrases and expressions had to be 'translated' into American English, e.g. catty into *bitchy*, bright and chirpy into *bright and chipper*, he can brook no denial to *he will accept no denial*. Colloquialisms, idioms and slangy expressions needed American counterparts: *screw off* (AE) as opposed to bugger off (BE), *smart cookie*: shrewd cookie, *to throw in the towel*: to cash in the chips, *to go bananas*: to go bonkers – and *pharmaceutical nightstick* for pharmaceutical truncheon (meaning: hypodermic needle). Slangy expressions and swearwords always occur among a particular group of people only. They have a special ring with these people and can hardly be used elsewhere. 'You are the bloody same people', 'bloody administration', 'to bugger off' and 'he worked his guts out' are common expressions in British English. An American audience would find them strange and un-American. Therefore Clark replaced them with: 'You are the goddamn same', 'damned administrators', 'to screw off' and 'he worked like hell'.

Finally, some examples of structural peculiarities in the two versions of *Whose Life is it Anyway?* should be given a mention. The most obvious differences can be found in connection with the use of the continuous form, prepositional phrases and plural forms.

AE	BE
but I finish next week	I'm finishing next week
I am glad you two are getting along	I'm glad you got on
the Gods are walking the earth again	the Gods are walking on earth again
about what?	what about?
for what?	what for?
of whom?	who for?
talk with	talk to
out of woods	out of the wood
on second thought	on second thoughts

The examples which I have listed and briefly commented on should give an idea of the work that awaits an author who is asked to rewrite a play for a production in a foreign country. And here it is not even a translation into a different language, but merely an adaptation of a play which is supposed to be put on in a country where just a different variety of the English language is spoken. No doubt, Americans would *understand* the original English play – in any case most of it – but they would not expect the characters to *speak* this kind of language. As Clark says, 'American and English have the same passive vocabulary but a vastly different active vocabulary.'[7]

As pointed out earlier on, in the eyes of some critics, Clark's play has suffered from both the sex change and the sea change. T. E. Kalkem, in *Time Magazine* (10 March 1980) had this to say: '. . . the switch from male to female does result in certain dissonances . . . Lines that left Conti's mouth as self-mocking witticisms seem more like sarcastic putdowns coming from Moore's . . . one expects a woman to respond differently to personal calamity than a man does.' Other critics, however, pointed out that 'the change of the lead character, from male to female, was beautifully handled' (Joel Siegel in WABC-TV, 24 February 1980), and that *Whose Life is it Anyway?* 'remains an absorbing and artfully constructed piece of work' (Douglas Watt in *Daily News*, 25 February 1980).

Transferring a play from one culture to another requires a concentration on very minute details. John, in the British version of *Whose Life is it Anyway?* creeps up behind the nurse and seizes her round the waist, and the nurse drops a dish. John tries to offer her an apology saying: 'I could not help myself, honest my Lord. There was this vision in white and blue, then I saw red in front of my eyes. It was like looking into a Union Jack.'

In the American production reference could not be made to the Union Jack. It had to be 'looking into the stars and stripes'. And Ken's question: 'What is this? Piccadilly Circus?' had to be rendered as: 'What is this? Grand Central Station?' in the American version. Transferring a play to a different culture is translating it into a different context. The 'cultural' translator is, like all other translators, a little traitor: *Traduttore – traditore!* And when preparing an American version of a British play (or the other way round) he is like the gentleman who has only just arrived from a visit to the United States. He is about to take the lift to the tenth floor of his London hotel mumbling to himself the famous words: 'Whenever I come back from America I do not know if I should lift my hat to a lady in an elevator or elevate my hat to a lady in a lift.'

Notes

1 On Brian Clark, see Albert-Reiner Glaap and Klaus Peter Müller, 'Brian Clark – Verfasser und Kritiker zeitgenossischer englisher Dramen', *Die neueren Sprachen*, 83 (1984), 697–704.
2 The following editions are available: Brian Clark, *Whose Life is it Anyway?* (London: Samuel French, 1978); Brian Clark, *Whose Life is it Anyway?* (The Slack, Ashover: Amber Press, 1979); Brian Clark, *Whose Life is it Anyway?*, ed. Albert-Reiner Glaap, Text with Annotations and Additional Texts. Separate Lehrerheft (Frankfurt: Hirschgraben, 1981).

3 *Whose Life is it Anyway?*, ed. Albert-Reiner Glaap, Lehrerheft, pp. 20–1.
4 Lehrerheft, p. 23.
5 *Whose Life is it Anyway?* A Full-Length Play, by Brian Clark (Chicago: The Dramatic Publishing Company, 1981).
6 See *Whose Life is it Anyway?*, ed. Albert-Reiner Glaap, pp. 64–6.
7 Lehrerheft, p. 23.

INDEX

Index